Lions, Tigers and Bears™

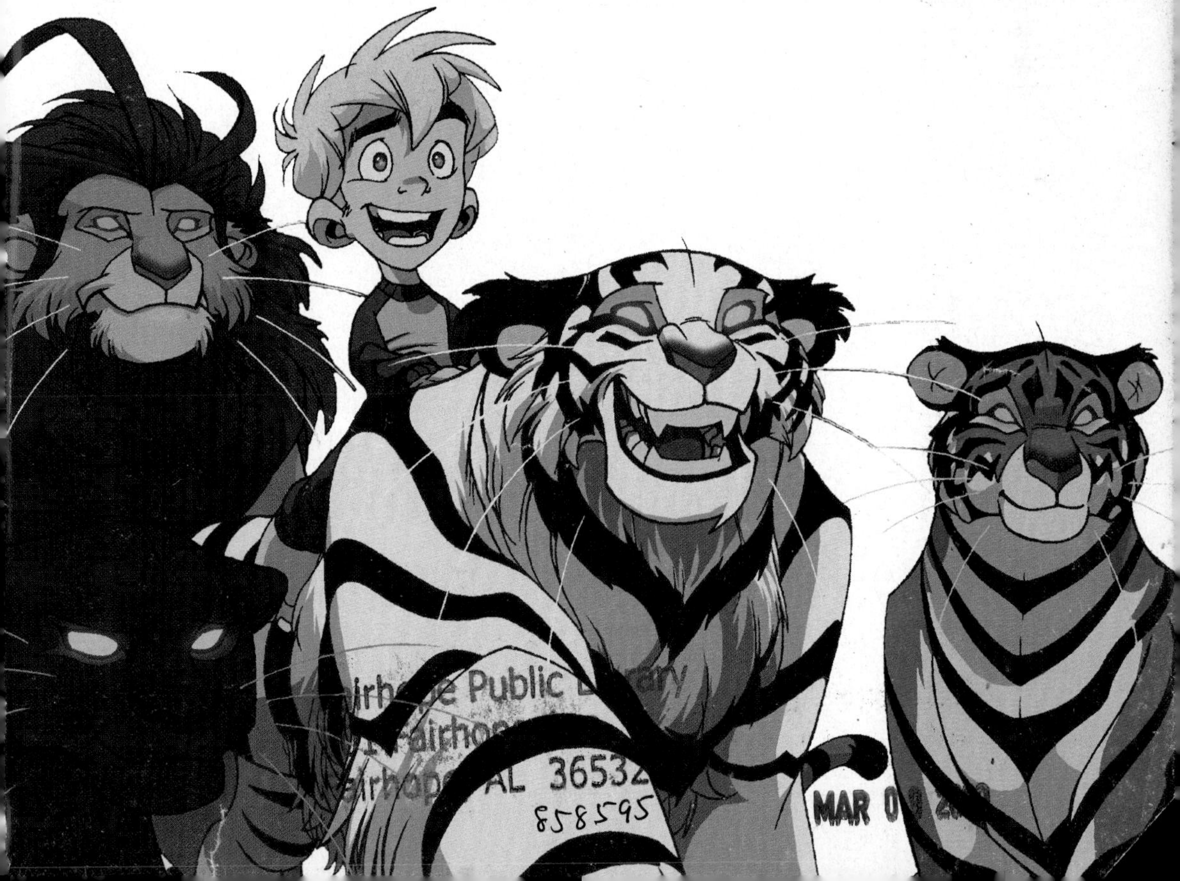

LIONS, TIGERS and BEARS ™

Created by Mike Bullock

Story	Art
Mike Bullock	Jack Lawrence

Letters by Dave Lanphear
Edited by Ron Marz

Runemaster Studios

image

IMAGE COMICS, INC.

Erik Larsen - Publisher
Todd McFarlane - President
Marc Silvestri - CEO
Jim Valentino - Vice-President

Eric Stephenson - Executive Director
Jim Demonakos - PR & Marketing Coordinator
Mia MacHatton - Accounts Manager
Traci Hui - Administrative Assistant
Joe Keatinge - Traffic Manager
Allen Hui - Production Manager
Jonathan Chan - Production Artist
Drew Gill - Production Artist

www.imagecomics.com

"Hey, I've got a really great idea for a comic..."

You know how many times I've heard that? Yeah, lots. And you know how often it turns out to be true? Considerably less than "lots." Hardly ever, in fact. So when Mike Bullock said to me, "Hey, I've got a really great idea for a comic..." I'm sure I rolled me eyes and got ready to give my stock answer. I'd explain how hard it was for relative unknowns to get a project approved ... anywhere. I'd explain the vast difference between having an idea and actually doing the work to produce a complete comic.

Then Mike told me his idea, a story about stuffed animals that come to life, and about a little boy conquering his fears. And I thought, "Gee, that is a pretty good idea." Then Mike showed me Jack Lawrence's artwork, which was bright and graceful and animated in every sense of the word. And I thought, "Wow, this could actually work." Then Mike asked me if I'd be interested in serving as editor or story consultant for this thing he called Lions, Tigers and Bears. And I thought, "Man, he suckered me right in."

So I became part of the LTB team, kind of the midwife helping the proud parents - Mike and Jack - bring their baby into the world. Hopefully my advice and cajoling did some good here and there. I remember talking Mike out of having a big toy company responsible for creating the stuffed animals (a quaint toy shop seemed so much more fitting). I badgered the guys into getting a top-notch letterer, Dave Lanphear, to put the words on the page, because nothing screams "amateur hour" like lousy lettering.

I helped Mike put together a pitch he could show around to prospective publishers, a tidy package with a story synopsis and some of Jack's finished pages. The opening day of the big comic convention in San Diego, Mike marched off to show the pitch to Image publisher Erik Larsen. He returned in fairly short order, his eyes so big I thought they'd drop out of his shiny, bald head and roll across the floor. "He said they'll publish it," Mike stammered. Nice moment, being there to see somebody's dream come to fruition.

That's been the best part for me. I've had a front row seat to watch two guys put together a book they obviously love. I've seen them become more confident in their skills with each successive issue. I might have played midwife, but Mike and Jack are the ones who did all the hard work. They're the ones who breathed life into Joey, and the Night Pride, and the Stuffed Animal Kingdom. They're the ones who made the magic you're about to discover.

To be sure, it is magic. Just ask my kids. There's no shortage of comics in my house, especially ones with dad's name listed in the credits box as "writer." But my kids don't pay too much attention to those. What they really want to know is when the next Lions, Tigers and Bears is coming out.
~ Ron Marz

Thank you for picking up this book. We really hope you enjoyed it. While this chapter of the *Lions, Tigers and Bears* saga has come to a close, rest assured that there are more stories on the way. Stay Tuned!

Mike Bullock would like to thank: God, with him anything is possible, without him, nothing would be. My beautiful wife, Angela for supporting me and my crazy dreams. My mother and father for helping my inner Joey learn to be brave. Robert, Zoe, Matilda and Jamie Salamy, you all mean more to me than words could ever express. Ken Deeg, I couldn't have imagined a better Father-in-law if I tried. Jack Lawrence, what can I say? You're simply amazing. Ron Marz, for your priceless guidance. Theo Bain, Frederik Hautain, Wil Radcliffe, Scott Kinney, Adam Lawrence, Rob Schwager and the rest of the Runemaster faithful. Dave Lanphear. Bill Papazian. Brett Burner and the rest of the Alias crew. Erik Larsen and all the wonderful people at Image Comics. All the retailers, reviewers, columnists and readers who believed in us and helped spread that belief far and wide. And most importantly, you, for sharing time with my imaginary friends.

Jack Lawrence would like to thank Theo Bain, you'll never know how you help me through every single day. I also want to thank Mike Bullock for not only pulling me into the saga of LTB, but for the trust, respect and genuine friendship that's flourished between us. My family; Mum, Dad, my little brother Bob, Sadie, Nan, my Uncle Pete and Auntie Beryl, Shane, Gary, Paula. Jan, Gregg, Asha and Nat. You all helped me more than you'll ever know at that lowest ebb right before LTB really came into all our lives. Kerry and June for continued support above and beyond. The Runemaster guys, the folks at Alias as well as Erik Larsen and everyone at Image. Thanks for having faith in us and giving us our first real shot. Lastly, I have to send out profound thanks to Adam Lawrence. From tireless enthusiasm to mucking in at a convention, to honest, unselfish friendship, you're the best mate a guy could ever hope for. I want to dedicate my part in LTB to the little guys in my life: Harrison, Hannah and my beautiful nephew, Ben. I love you, kid.

Be sure to visit us on the web!
WWW.RUNEMASTERSTUDIOS.COM

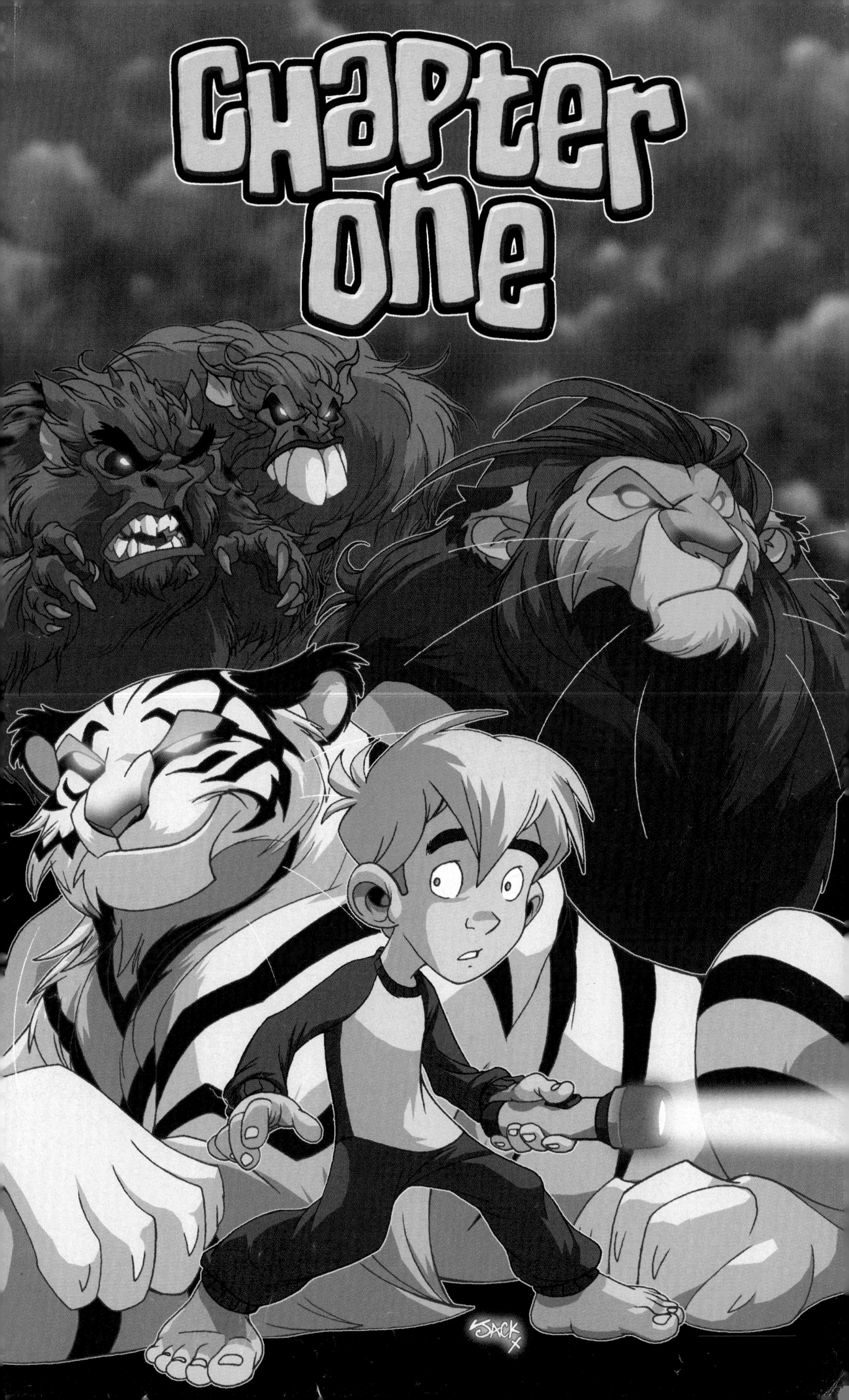
Chapter One
JACK

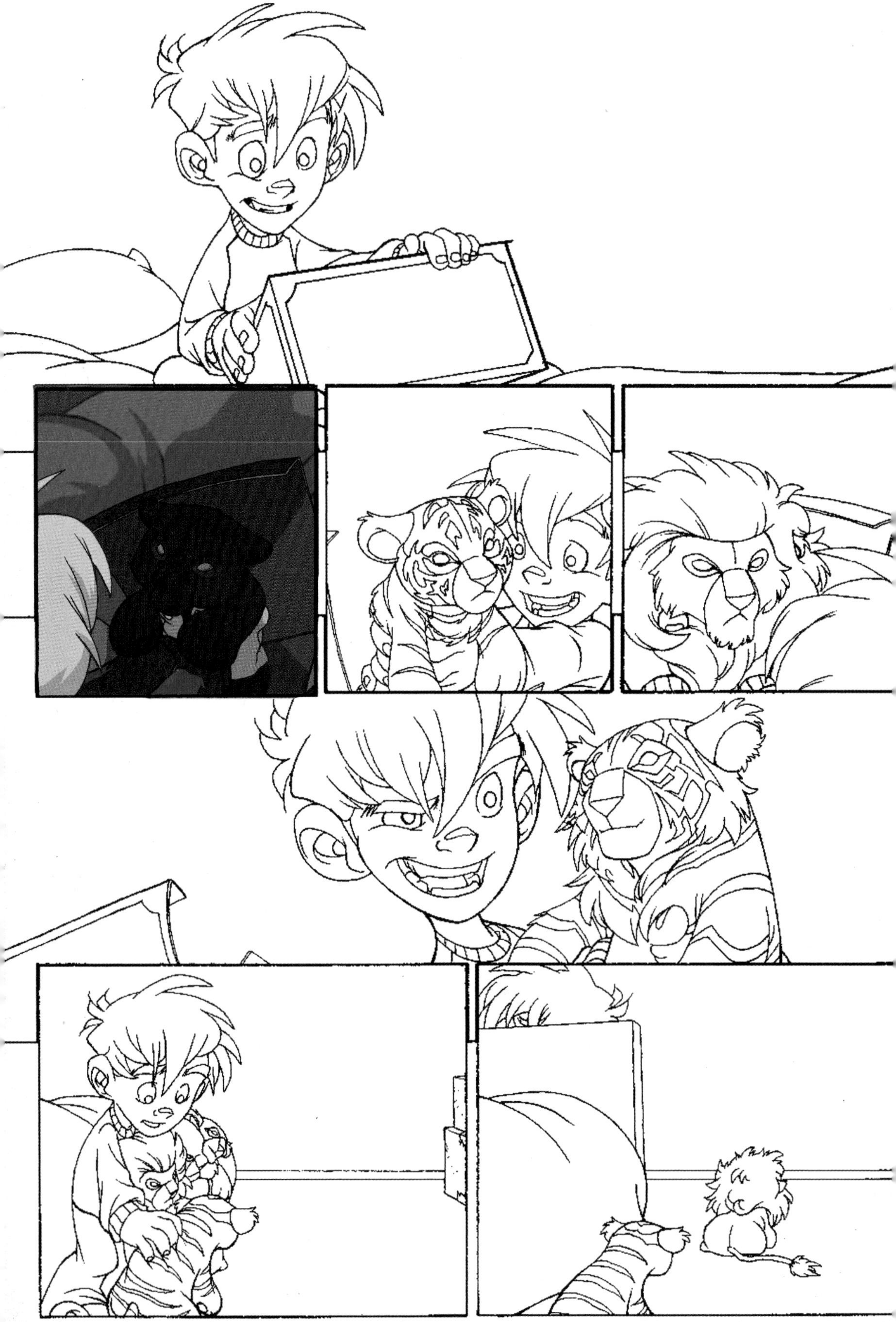

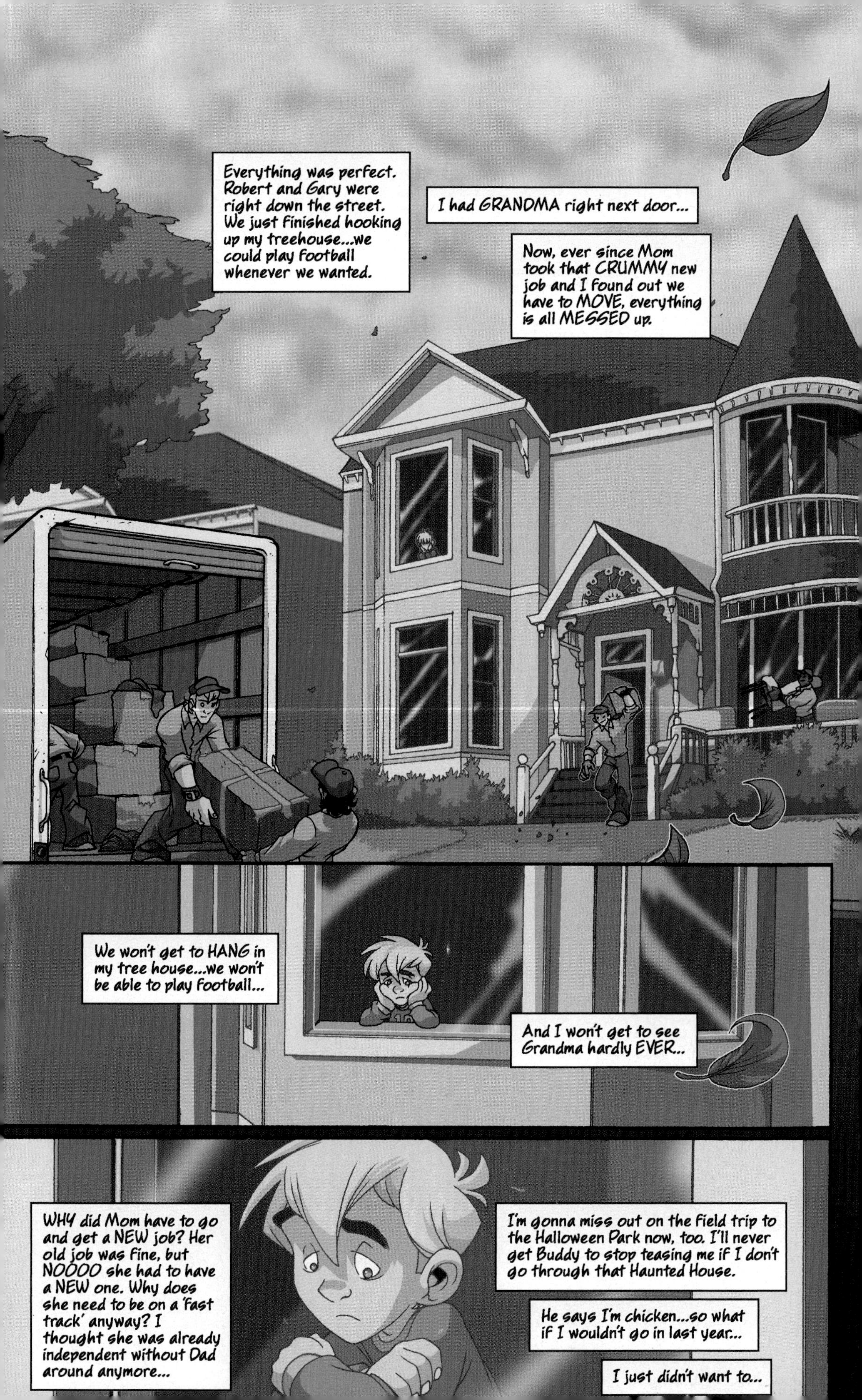

Everything was perfect. Robert and Gary were right down the street. We just finished hooking up my treehouse...we could play football whenever we wanted.
I had GRANDMA right next door...
Now, ever since Mom took that CRUMMY new job and I found out we have to MOVE, everything is all MESSED up.
We won't get to HANG in my tree house...we won't be able to play football...
And I won't get to see Grandma hardly EVER...
WHY did Mom have to go and get a NEW job? Her old job was fine, but NOOOO she had to have a NEW one. Why does she need to be on a 'fast track' anyway? I thought she was already independent without Dad around anymore...
I'm gonna miss out on the field trip to the Halloween Park now, too. I'll never get Buddy to stop teasing me if I don't go through that Haunted House.
He says I'm chicken...so what if I wouldn't go in last year...
I just didn't want to...

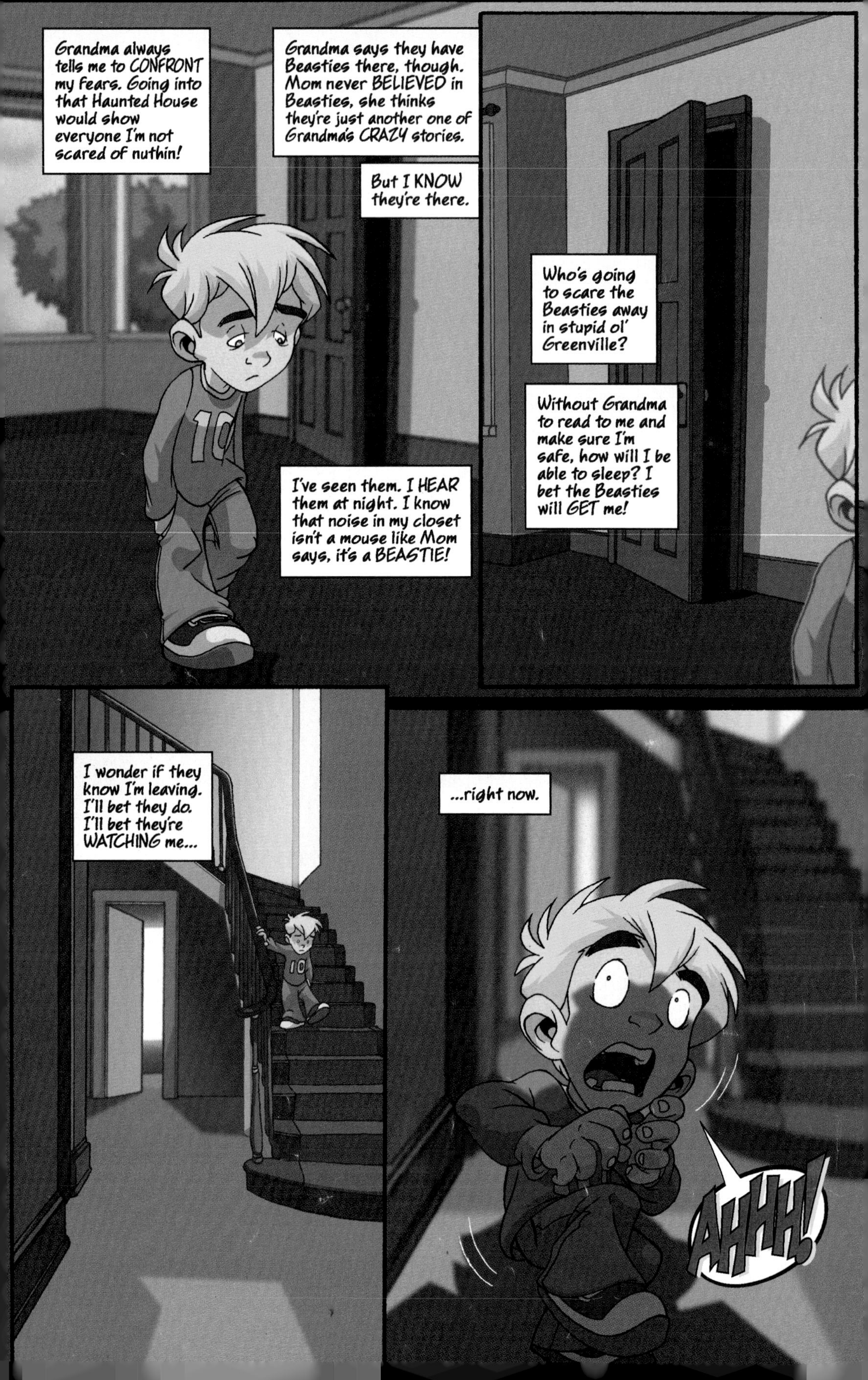
Grandma always tells me to CONFRONT my fears. Going into that Haunted House would show everyone I'm not scared of nuthin!
Grandma says they have Beasties there, though. Mom never BELIEVED in Beasties, she thinks they're just another one of Grandma's CRAZY stories.
But I KNOW they're there.
I've seen them. I HEAR them at night. I know that noise in my closet isn't a mouse like Mom says, it's a BEASTIE!
Who's going to scare the Beasties away in stupid ol' Greenville?
Without Grandma to read to me and make sure I'm safe, how will I be able to sleep? I bet the Beasties will GET me!
I wonder if they know I'm leaving. I'll bet they do. I'll bet they're WATCHING me...
...right now.
AHHH!

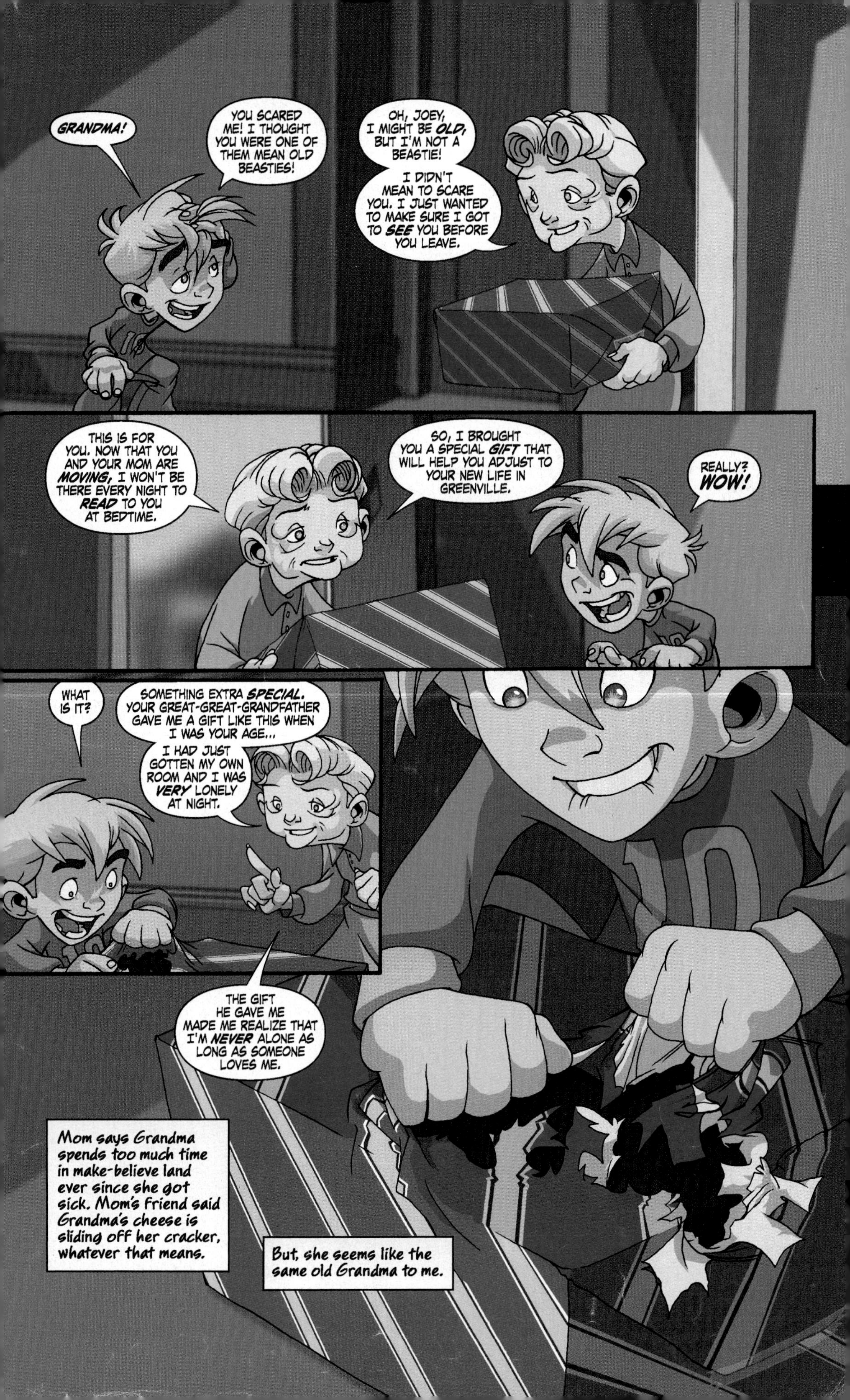
GRANDMA!
YOU SCARED ME! I THOUGHT YOU WERE ONE OF THEM MEAN OLD BEASTIES!
OH, JOEY, I MIGHT BE OLD, BUT I'M NOT A BEASTIE!
I DIDN'T MEAN TO SCARE YOU. I JUST WANTED TO MAKE SURE I GOT TO SEE YOU BEFORE YOU LEAVE.
THIS IS FOR YOU. NOW THAT YOU AND YOUR MOM ARE MOVING, I WON'T BE THERE EVERY NIGHT TO READ TO YOU AT BEDTIME.
SO, I BROUGHT YOU A SPECIAL GIFT THAT WILL HELP YOU ADJUST TO YOUR NEW LIFE IN GREENVILLE.
REALLY? WOW!
WHAT IS IT?
SOMETHING EXTRA SPECIAL. YOUR GREAT-GREAT-GRANDFATHER GAVE ME A GIFT LIKE THIS WHEN I WAS YOUR AGE...
I HAD JUST GOTTEN MY OWN ROOM AND I WAS VERY LONELY AT NIGHT.
THE GIFT HE GAVE ME MADE ME REALIZE THAT I'M NEVER ALONE AS LONG AS SOMEONE LOVES ME.
Mom says Grandma spends too much time in make-believe land ever since she got sick. Mom's friend said Grandma's cheese is sliding off her cracker, whatever that means.
But, she seems like the same old Grandma to me.

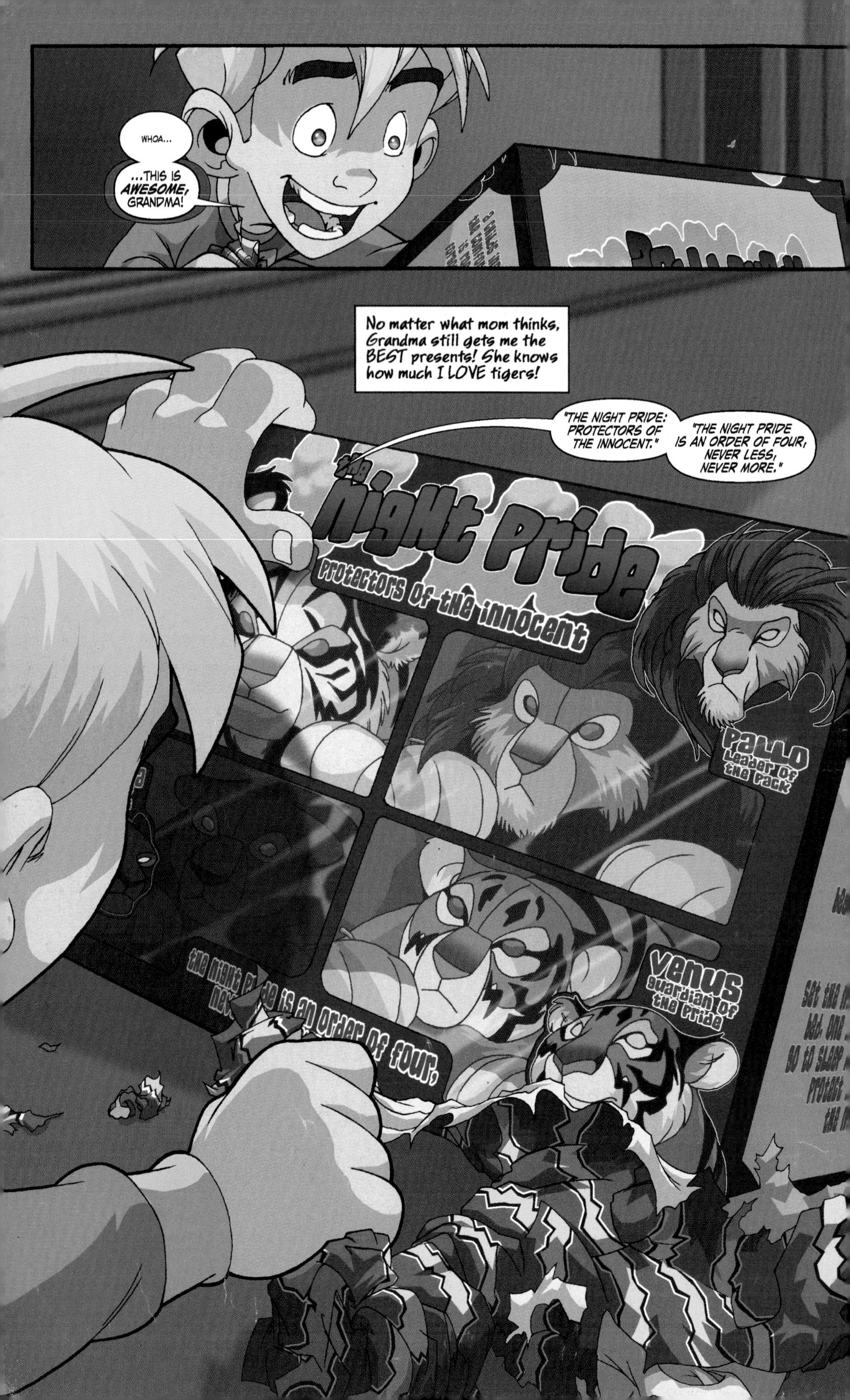
WHOA...
...THIS IS AWESOME, GRANDMA!
No matter what mom thinks, Grandma still gets me the BEST presents! She knows how much I LOVE tigers!
"THE NIGHT PRIDE: PROTECTORS OF THE INNOCENT."
"THE NIGHT PRIDE IS AN ORDER OF FOUR, NEVER LESS, NEVER MORE."
Night Pride
Protectors of the innocent
PALLO
Leader of the Pack
VENUS
Guardian of the Pride

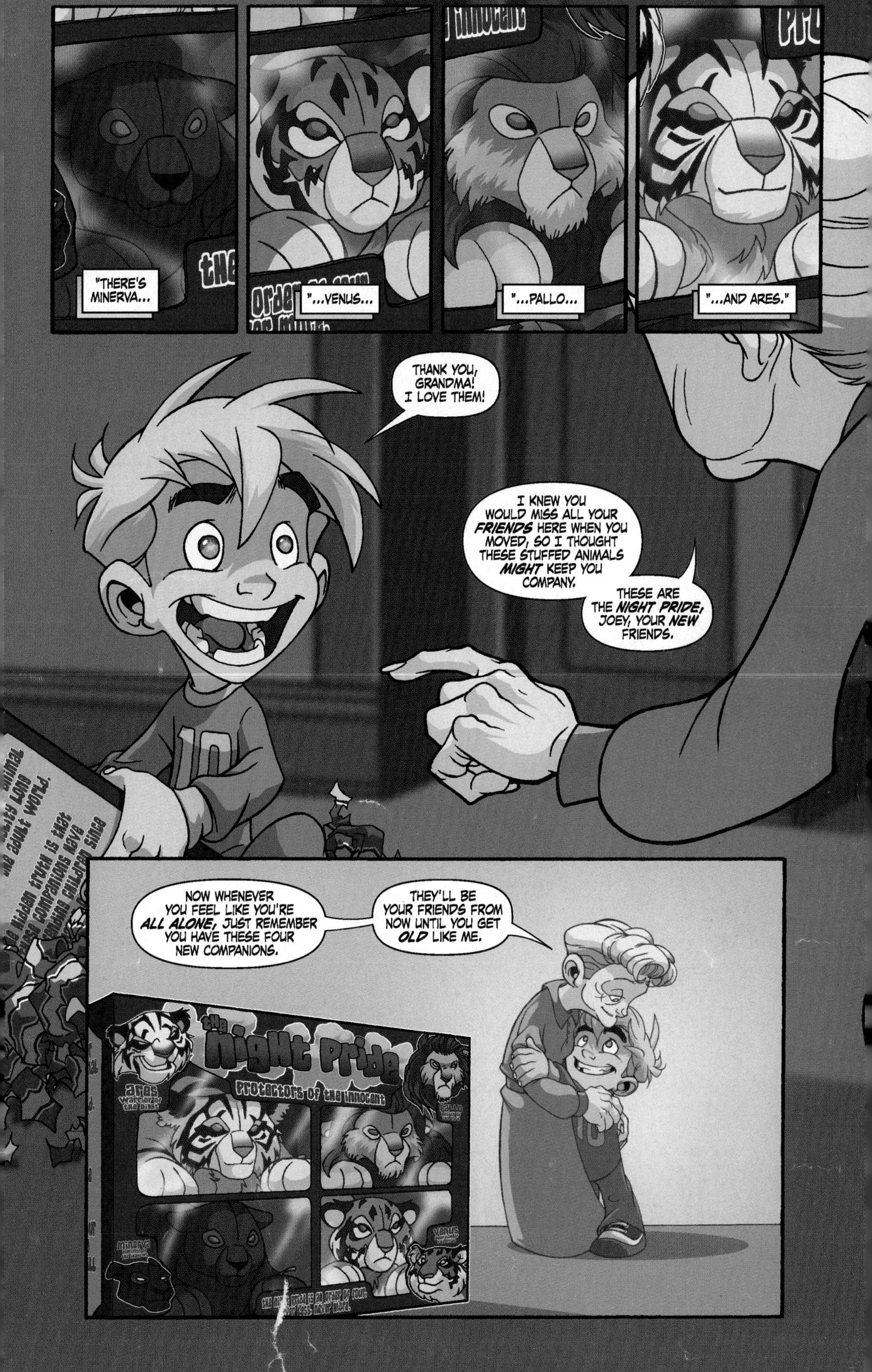
"THERE'S MINERVA...
"...VENUS...
"...PALLO...
"...AND ARES."
THANK YOU, GRANDMA! I LOVE THEM!
I KNEW YOU WOULD MISS ALL YOUR FRIENDS HERE WHEN YOU MOVED, SO I THOUGHT THESE STUFFED ANIMALS MIGHT KEEP YOU COMPANY.
THESE ARE THE NIGHT PRIDE, JOEY, YOUR NEW FRIENDS.
NOW WHENEVER YOU FEEL LIKE YOU'RE ALL ALONE, JUST REMEMBER YOU HAVE THESE FOUR NEW COMPANIONS.
THEY'LL BE YOUR FRIENDS FROM NOW UNTIL YOU GET OLD LIKE ME.
the Night Pride
protectors of the innocent
aries

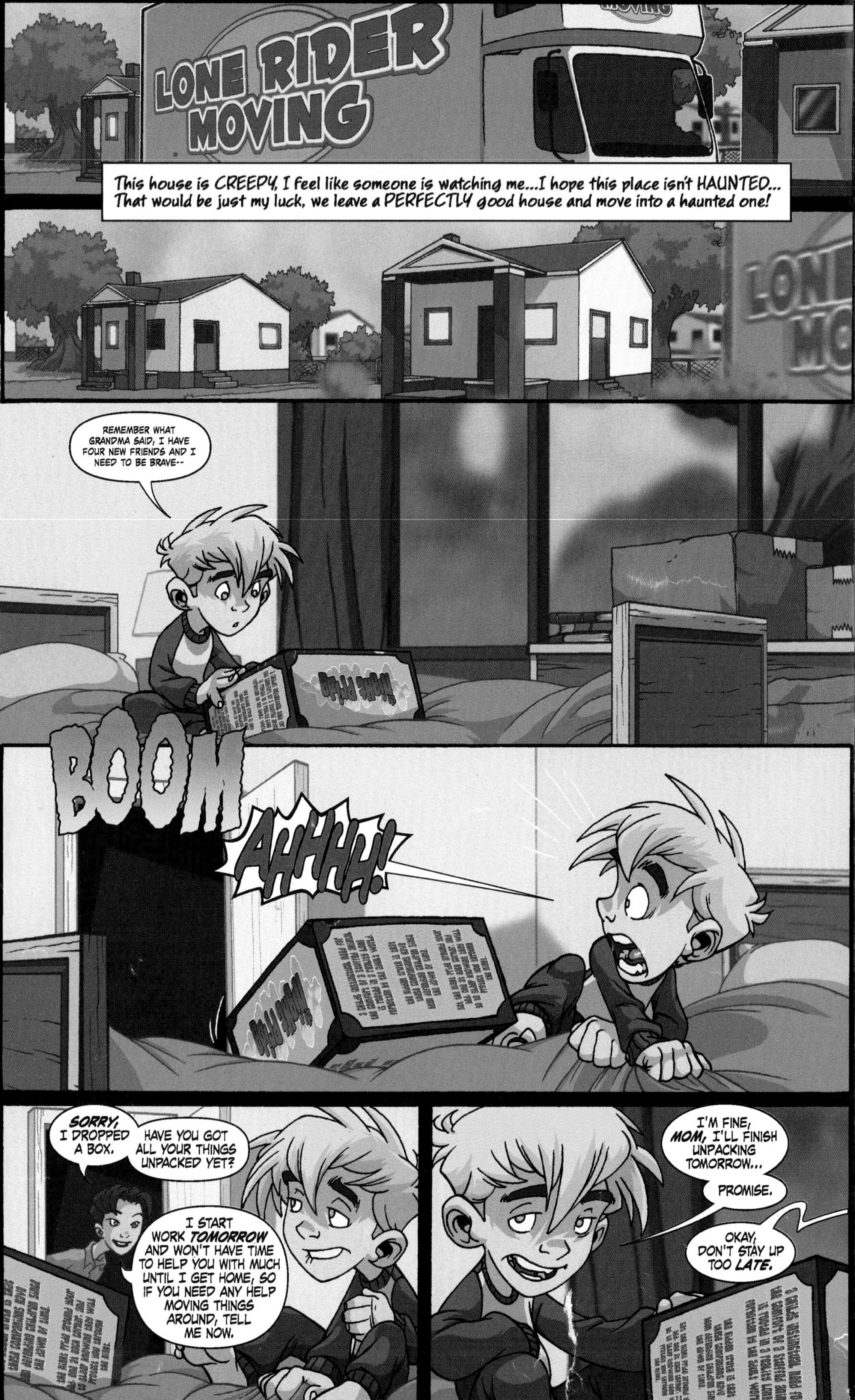
LONE RIDER MOVING
This house is CREEPY, I feel like someone is watching me...I hope this place isn't HAUNTED... That would be just my luck, we leave a PERFECTLY good house and move into a haunted one!
REMEMBER WHAT GRANDMA SAID, I HAVE FOUR NEW FRIENDS AND I NEED TO BE BRAVE--
BOOM
AHHHH!
SORRY, I DROPPED A BOX.
HAVE YOU GOT ALL YOUR THINGS UNPACKED YET?
I START WORK TOMORROW AND WON'T HAVE TIME TO HELP YOU WITH MUCH UNTIL I GET HOME, SO IF YOU NEED ANY HELP MOVING THINGS AROUND, TELL ME NOW.
I'M FINE, MOM, I'LL FINISH UNPACKING TOMORROW...
PROMISE.
OKAY, DON'T STAY UP TOO LATE.

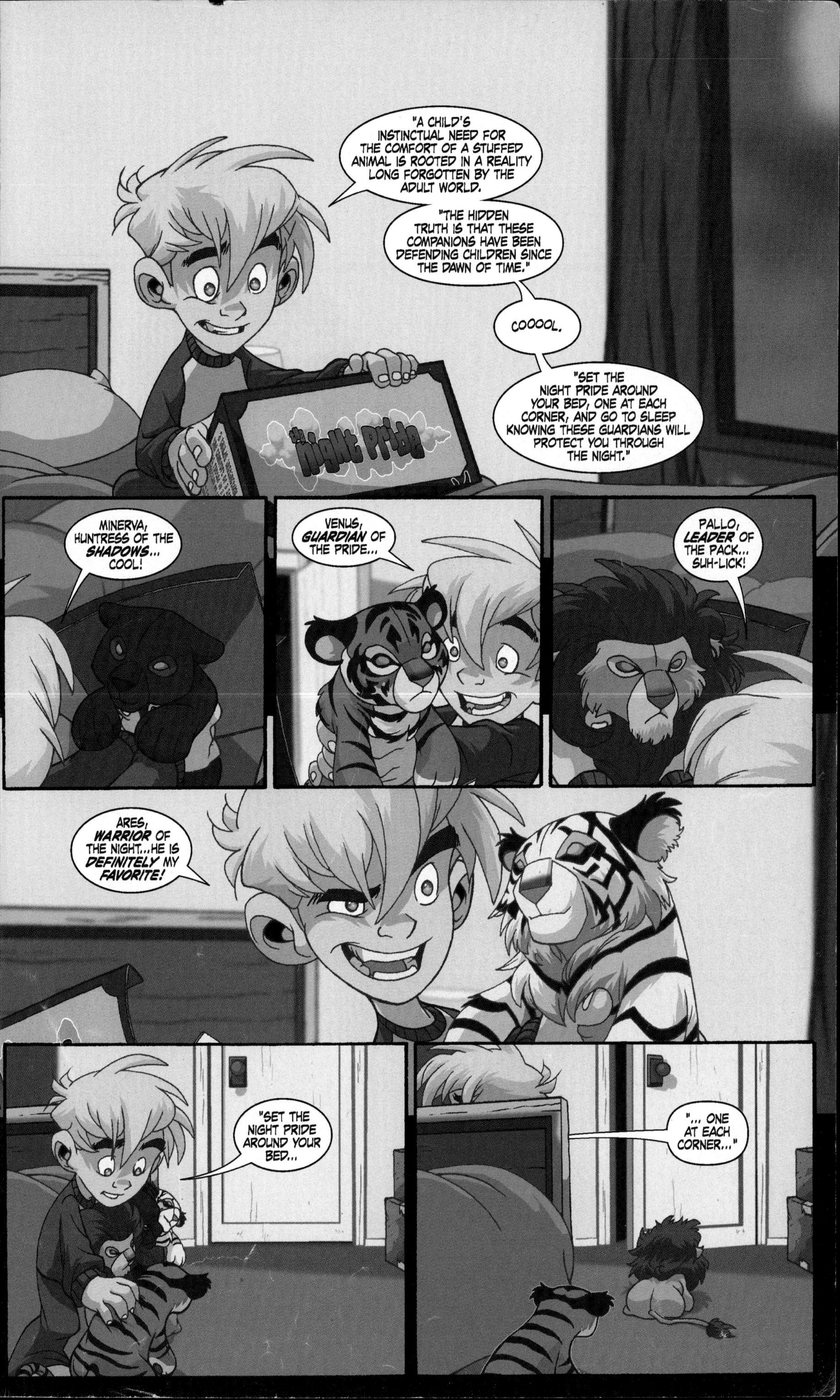
"A CHILD'S INSTINCTUAL NEED FOR THE COMFORT OF A STUFFED ANIMAL IS ROOTED IN A REALITY LONG FORGOTTEN BY THE ADULT WORLD.
"THE HIDDEN TRUTH IS THAT THESE COMPANIONS HAVE BEEN DEFENDING CHILDREN SINCE THE DAWN OF TIME."
COOOOL.
"SET THE NIGHT PRIDE AROUND YOUR BED, ONE AT EACH CORNER, AND GO TO SLEEP KNOWING THESE GUARDIANS WILL PROTECT YOU THROUGH THE NIGHT."
MINERVA, HUNTRESS OF THE SHADOWS... COOL!
VENUS, GUARDIAN OF THE PRIDE...
PALLO, LEADER OF THE PACK... SUH-LICK!
ARES, WARRIOR OF THE NIGHT...HE IS DEFINITELY MY FAVORITE!
"SET THE NIGHT PRIDE AROUND YOUR BED...
"... ONE AT EACH CORNER..."

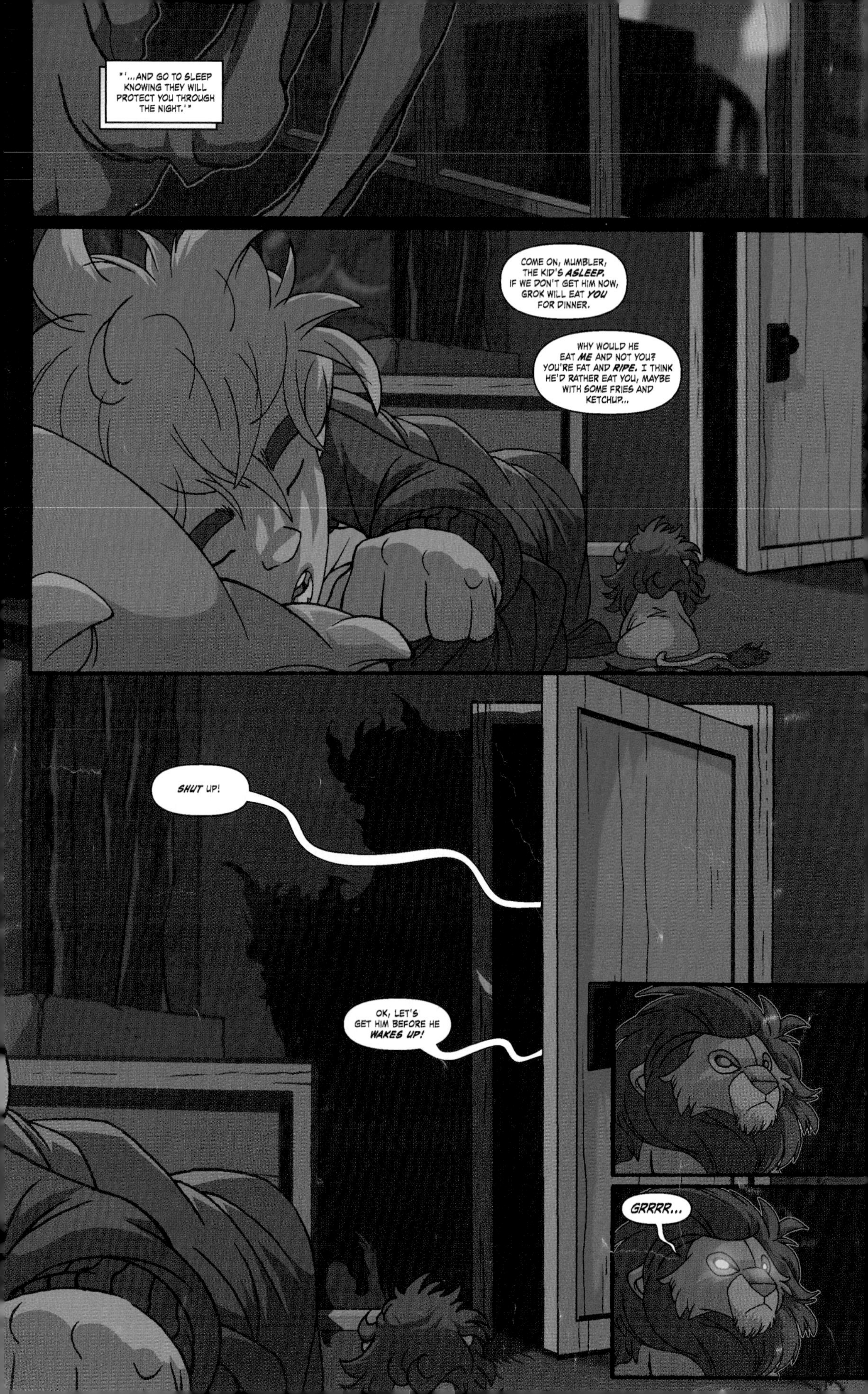
"'...AND GO TO SLEEP KNOWING THEY WILL PROTECT YOU THROUGH THE NIGHT.'"
COME ON, MUMBLER, THE KID'S ASLEEP. IF WE DON'T GET HIM NOW, GROK WILL EAT YOU FOR DINNER.
WHY WOULD HE EAT ME AND NOT YOU? YOU'RE FAT AND RIPE. I THINK HE'D RATHER EAT YOU, MAYBE WITH SOME FRIES AND KETCHUP...
SHUT UP!
OK, LET'S GET HIM BEFORE HE WAKES UP!
GRRRR...

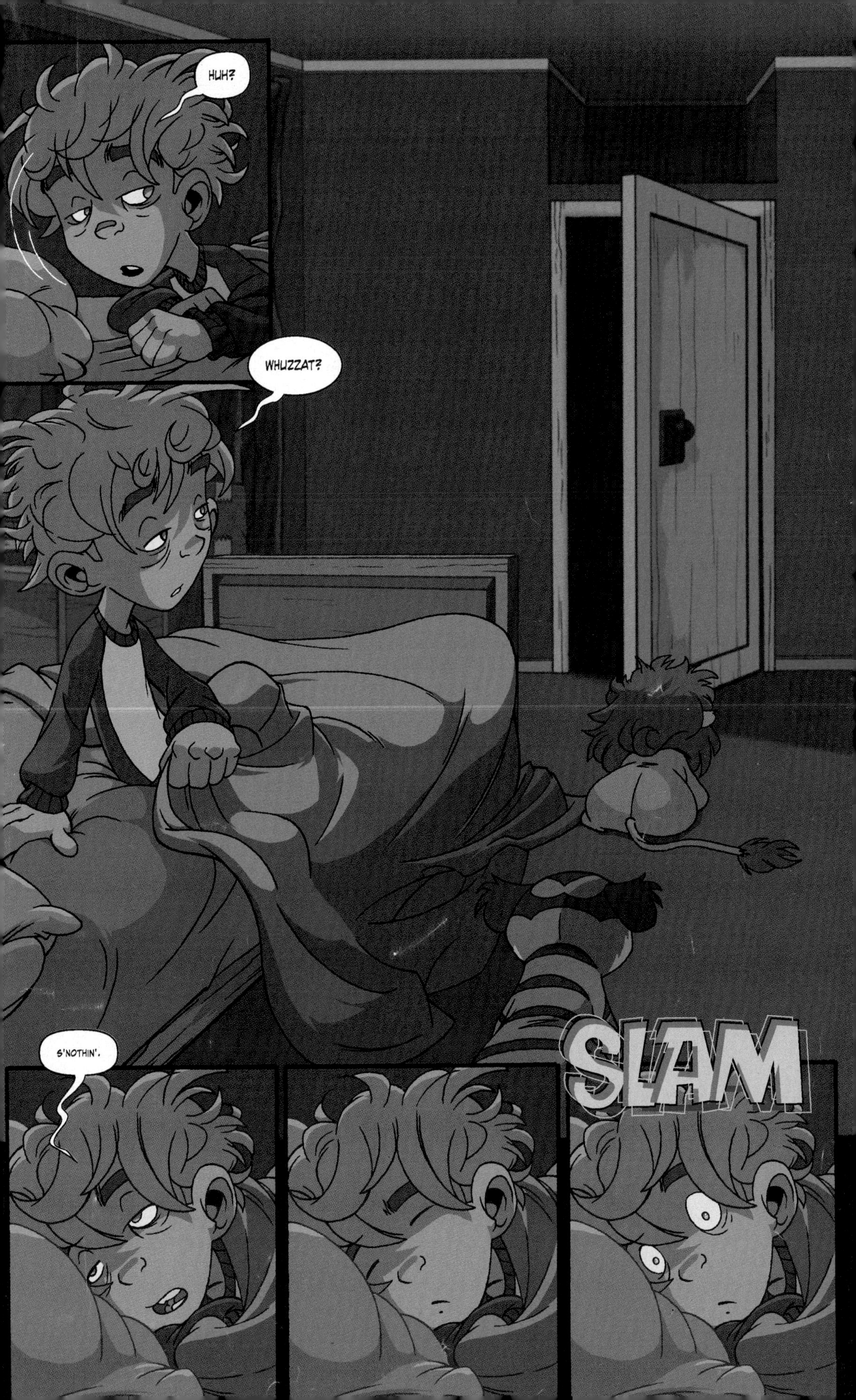
HUH?
WHUZZAT?
S'NOTHIN'.
SLAM

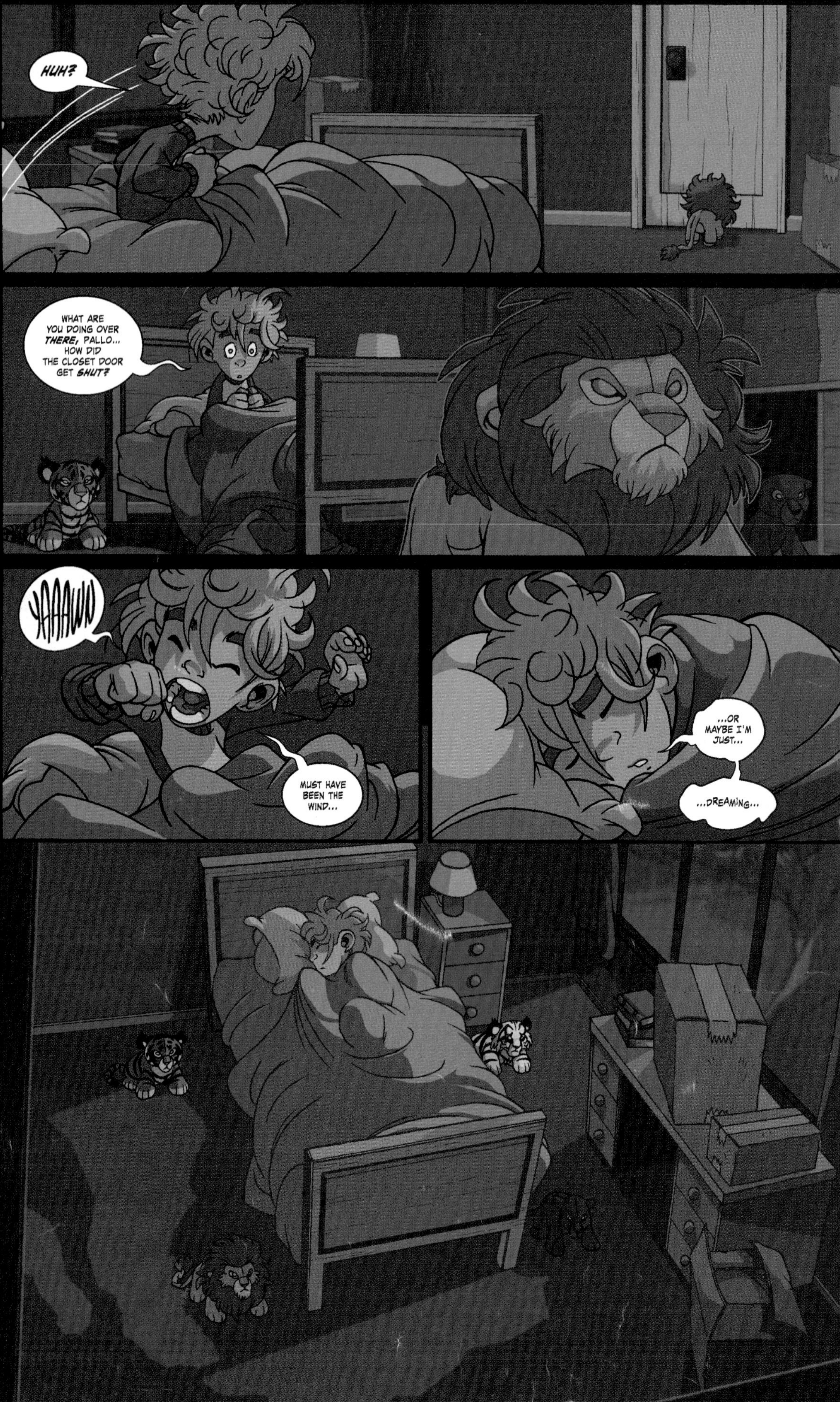
HUH?
WHAT ARE YOU DOING OVER THERE, PALLO... HOW DID THE CLOSET DOOR GET SHUT?
YAAAWN
MUST HAVE BEEN THE WIND...
...OR MAYBE I'M JUST...
...DREAMING...

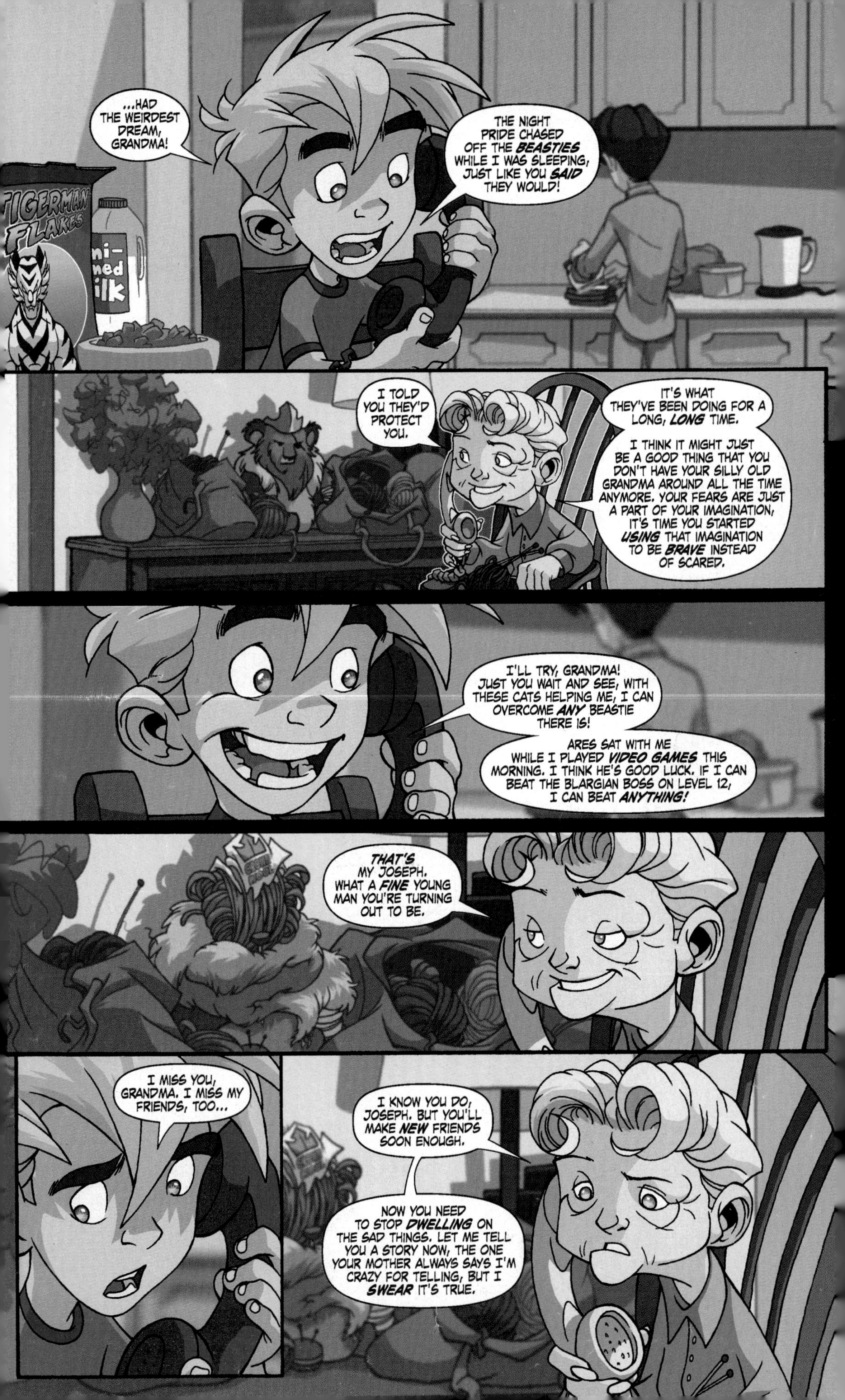
...HAD THE WEIRDEST DREAM, GRANDMA!
THE NIGHT PRIDE CHASED OFF THE BEASTIES WHILE I WAS SLEEPING, JUST LIKE YOU SAID THEY WOULD!
TIGERMAN FLAKES
I TOLD YOU THEY'D PROTECT YOU.
IT'S WHAT THEY'VE BEEN DOING FOR A LONG, LONG TIME.
I THINK IT MIGHT JUST BE A GOOD THING THAT YOU DON'T HAVE YOUR SILLY OLD GRANDMA AROUND ALL THE TIME ANYMORE. YOUR FEARS ARE JUST A PART OF YOUR IMAGINATION, IT'S TIME YOU STARTED USING THAT IMAGINATION TO BE BRAVE INSTEAD OF SCARED.
I'LL TRY, GRANDMA! JUST YOU WAIT AND SEE, WITH THESE CATS HELPING ME, I CAN OVERCOME ANY BEASTIE THERE IS!
ARES SAT WITH ME WHILE I PLAYED VIDEO GAMES THIS MORNING. I THINK HE'S GOOD LUCK. IF I CAN BEAT THE BLARGIAN BOSS ON LEVEL 12, I CAN BEAT ANYTHING!
THAT'S MY JOSEPH. WHAT A FINE YOUNG MAN YOU'RE TURNING OUT TO BE.
I MISS YOU, GRANDMA. I MISS MY FRIENDS, TOO...
I KNOW YOU DO, JOSEPH. BUT YOU'LL MAKE NEW FRIENDS SOON ENOUGH.
NOW YOU NEED TO STOP DWELLING ON THE SAD THINGS. LET ME TELL YOU A STORY NOW, THE ONE YOUR MOTHER ALWAYS SAYS I'M CRAZY FOR TELLING, BUT I SWEAR IT'S TRUE.

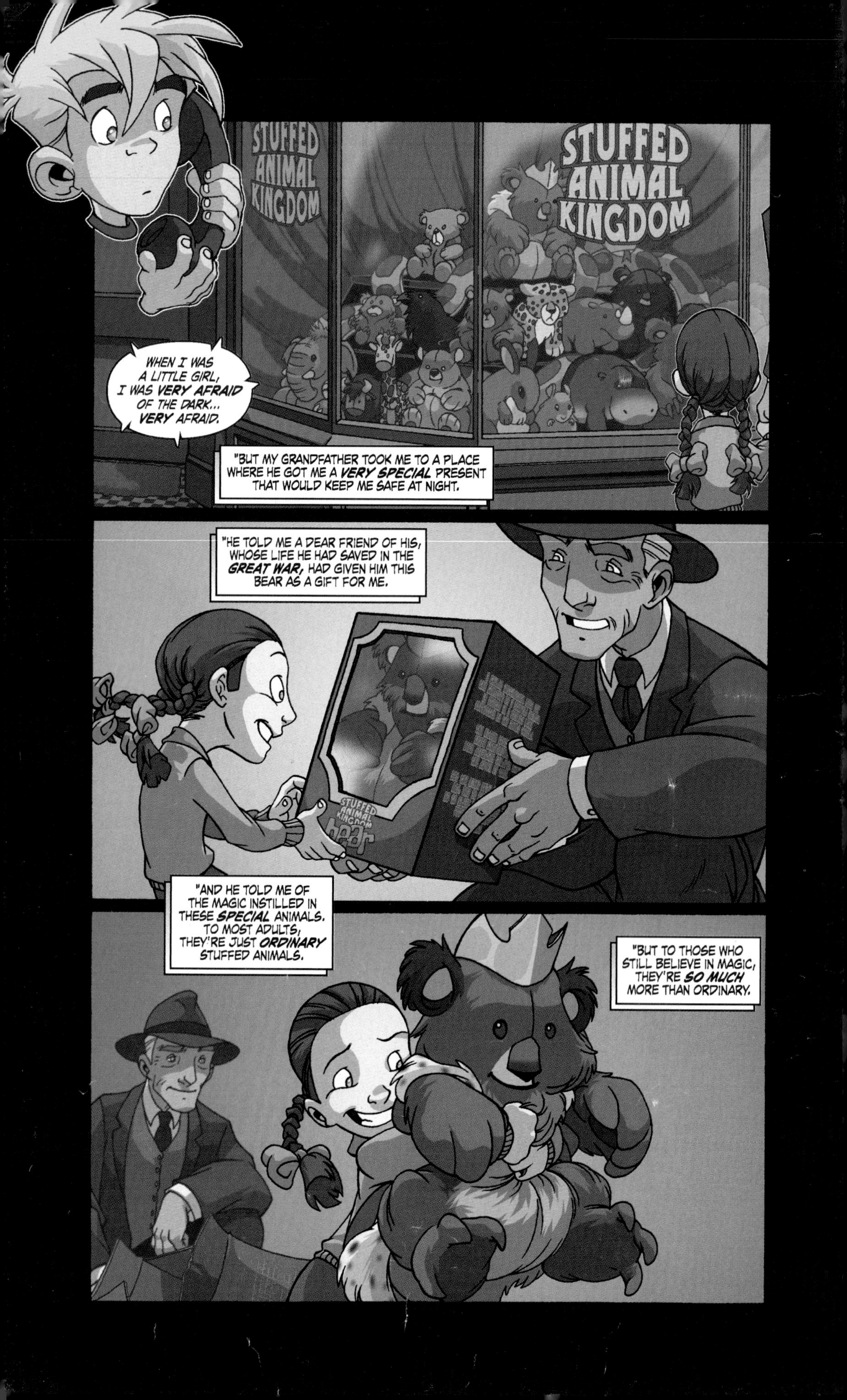
STUFFED ANIMAL KINGDOM
STUFFED ANIMAL KINGDOM
WHEN I WAS A LITTLE GIRL, I WAS VERY AFRAID OF THE DARK... VERY AFRAID.
"BUT MY GRANDFATHER TOOK ME TO A PLACE WHERE HE GOT ME A VERY SPECIAL PRESENT THAT WOULD KEEP ME SAFE AT NIGHT.
"HE TOLD ME A DEAR FRIEND OF HIS, WHOSE LIFE HE HAD SAVED IN THE GREAT WAR, HAD GIVEN HIM THIS BEAR AS A GIFT FOR ME.
STUFFED ANIMAL KINGDOM
"AND HE TOLD ME OF THE MAGIC INSTILLED IN THESE SPECIAL ANIMALS. TO MOST ADULTS, THEY'RE JUST ORDINARY STUFFED ANIMALS.
"BUT TO THOSE WHO STILL BELIEVE IN MAGIC, THEY'RE SO MUCH MORE THAN ORDINARY.

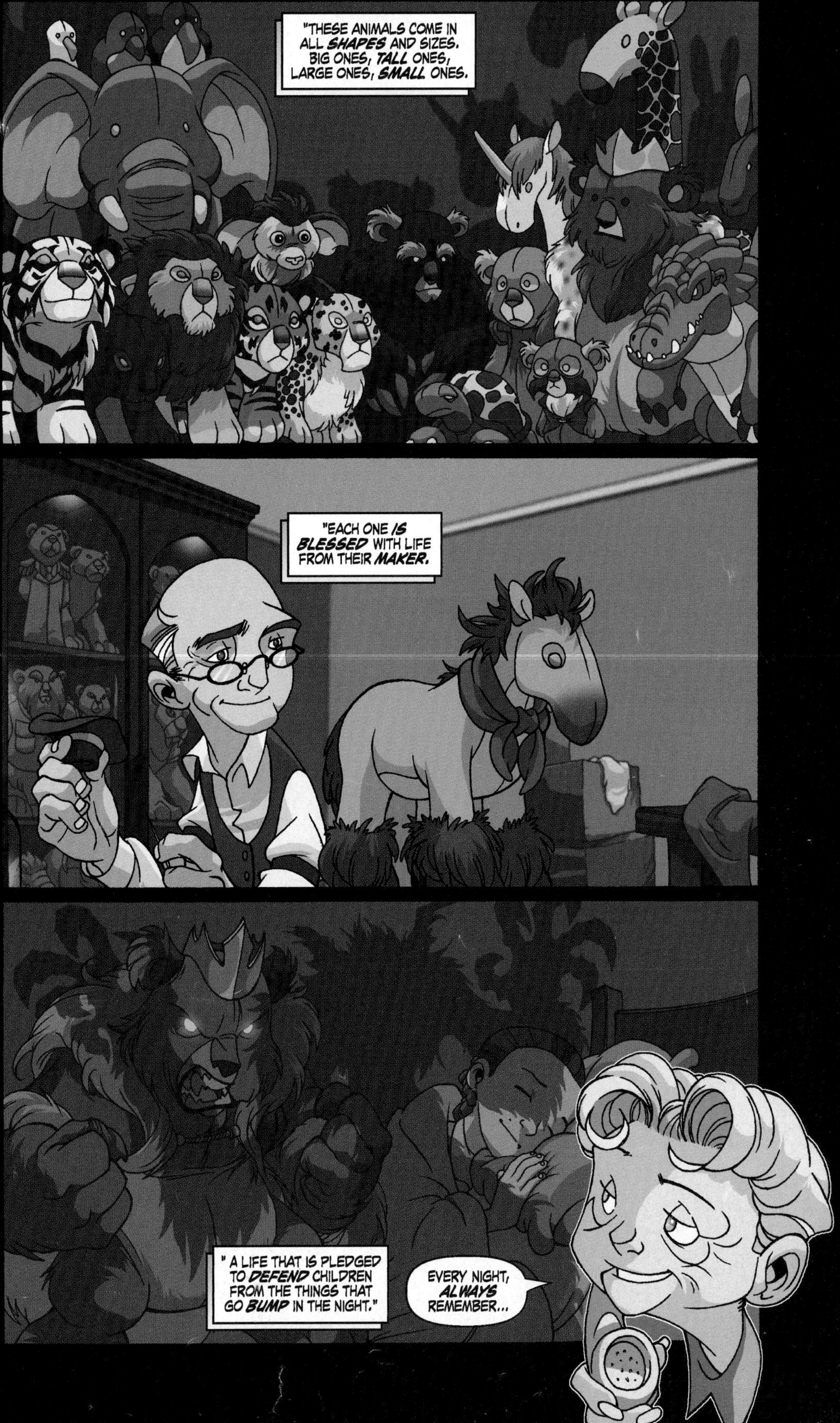
"THESE ANIMALS COME IN ALL SHAPES AND SIZES. BIG ONES, TALL ONES, LARGE ONES, SMALL ONES.
"EACH ONE IS BLESSED WITH LIFE FROM THEIR MAKER.
" A LIFE THAT IS PLEDGED TO DEFEND CHILDREN FROM THE THINGS THAT GO BUMP IN THE NIGHT."
EVERY NIGHT, ALWAYS REMEMBER...

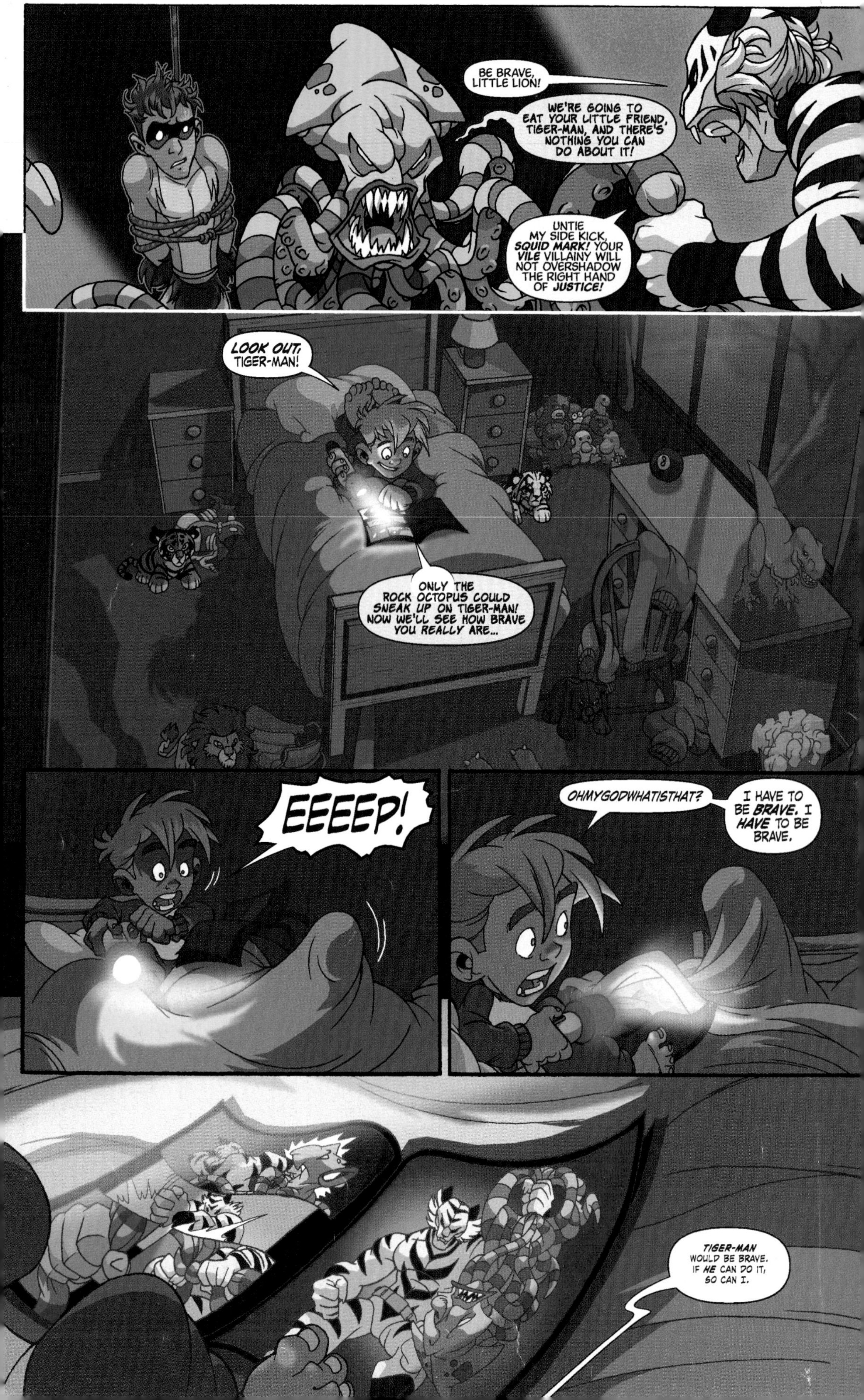
BE BRAVE, LITTLE LION!
WE'RE GOING TO EAT YOUR LITTLE FRIEND, TIGER-MAN, AND THERE'S NOTHING YOU CAN DO ABOUT IT!
UNTIE MY SIDE KICK, SQUID MARK! YOUR VILE VILLAINY WILL NOT OVERSHADOW THE RIGHT HAND OF JUSTICE!
LOOK OUT, TIGER-MAN!
ONLY THE ROCK OCTOPUS COULD SNEAK UP ON TIGER-MAN! NOW WE'LL SEE HOW BRAVE YOU REALLY ARE...
EEEEP!
OHMYGODWHATISTHAT?
I HAVE TO BE BRAVE. I HAVE TO BE BRAVE.
TIGER-MAN WOULD BE BRAVE. IF HE CAN DO IT, SO CAN I.

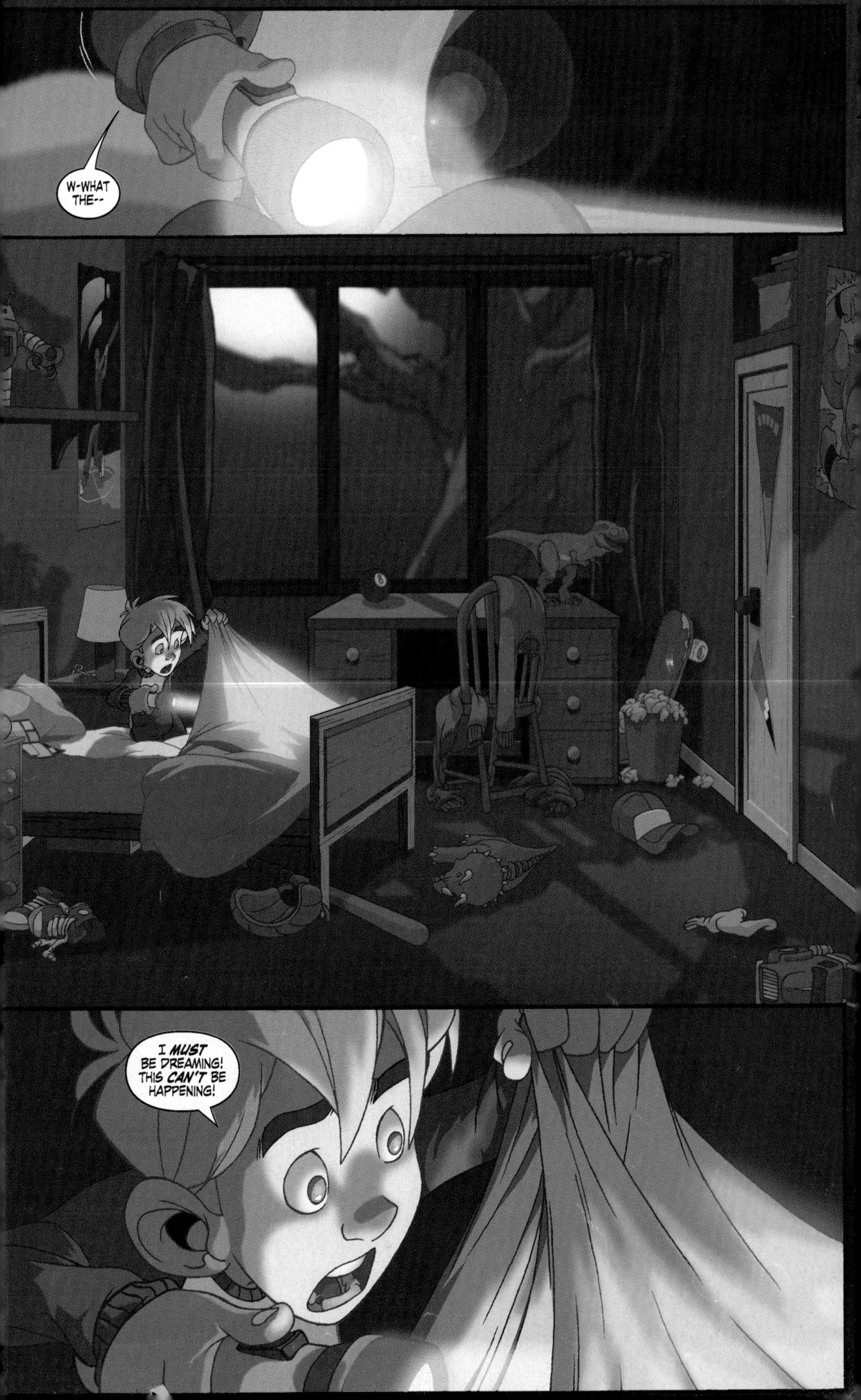
W-WHAT THE--
I MUST BE DREAMING! THIS CAN'T BE HAPPENING!

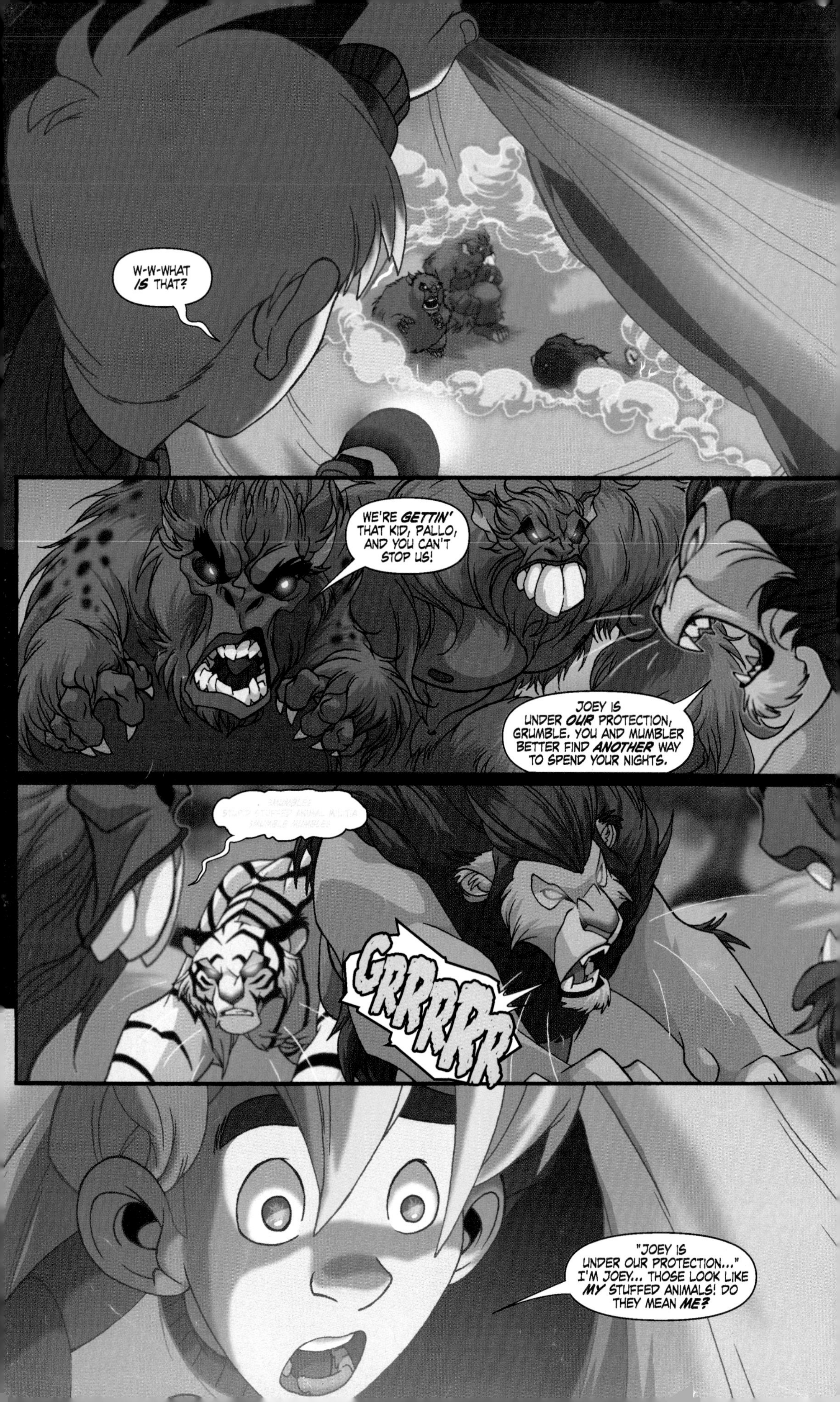

W-W-WHAT *IS* THAT?
WE'RE *GETTIN'* THAT KID, PALLO, AND YOU CAN'T STOP US!
JOEY IS UNDER *OUR* PROTECTION, GRUMBLE. YOU AND MUMBLER BETTER FIND *ANOTHER* WAY TO SPEND YOUR NIGHTS.
GRRRRR
"JOEY IS UNDER OUR PROTECTION..." I'M JOEY... THOSE LOOK LIKE *MY* STUFFED ANIMALS! DO THEY MEAN *ME?*

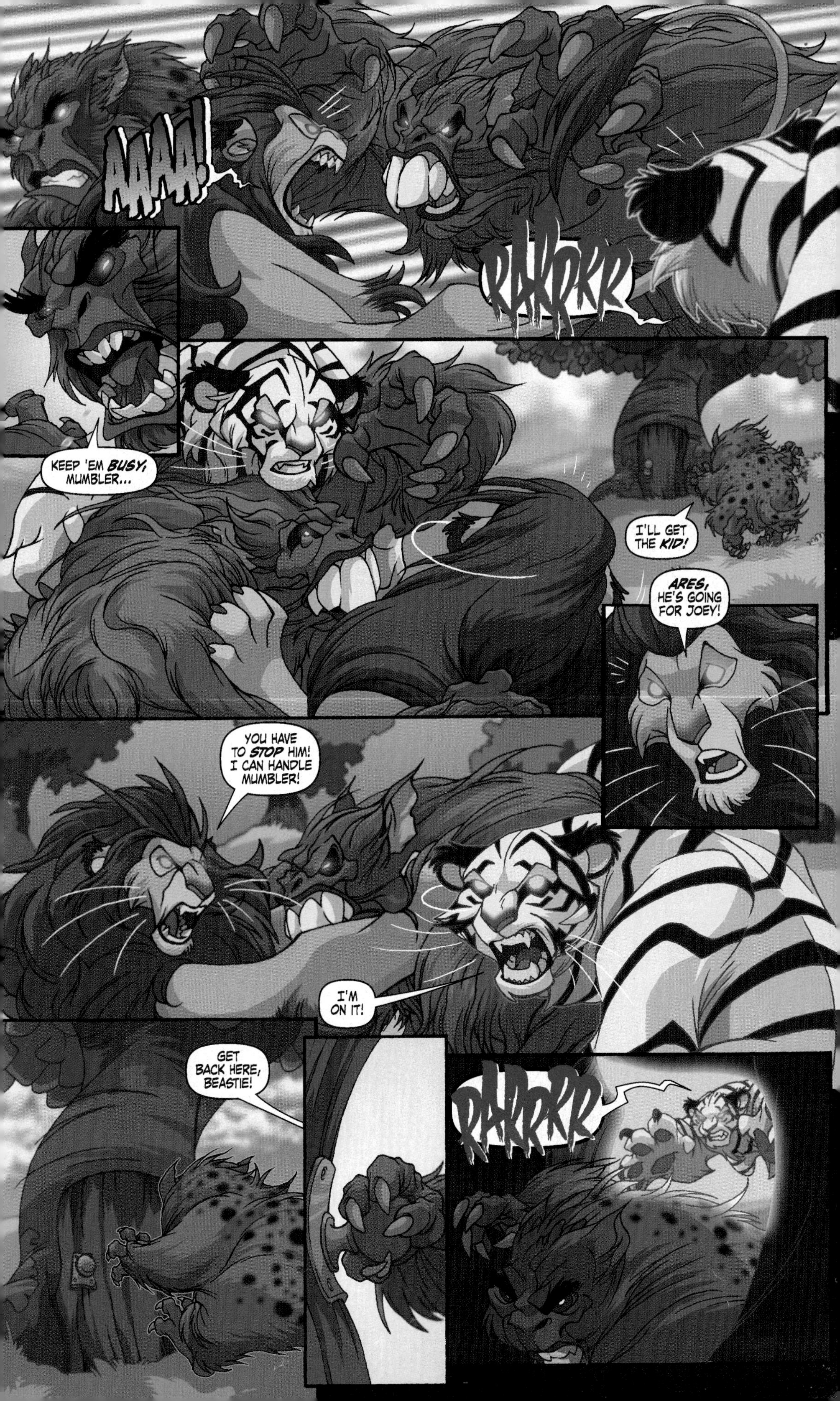
AAAA!
RAKRKR
KEEP 'EM BUSY, MUMBLER...
I'LL GET THE KID!
ARES, HE'S GOING FOR JOEY!
YOU HAVE TO STOP HIM! I CAN HANDLE MUMBLER!
I'M ON IT!
GET BACK HERE, BEASTIE!
RAKRKR

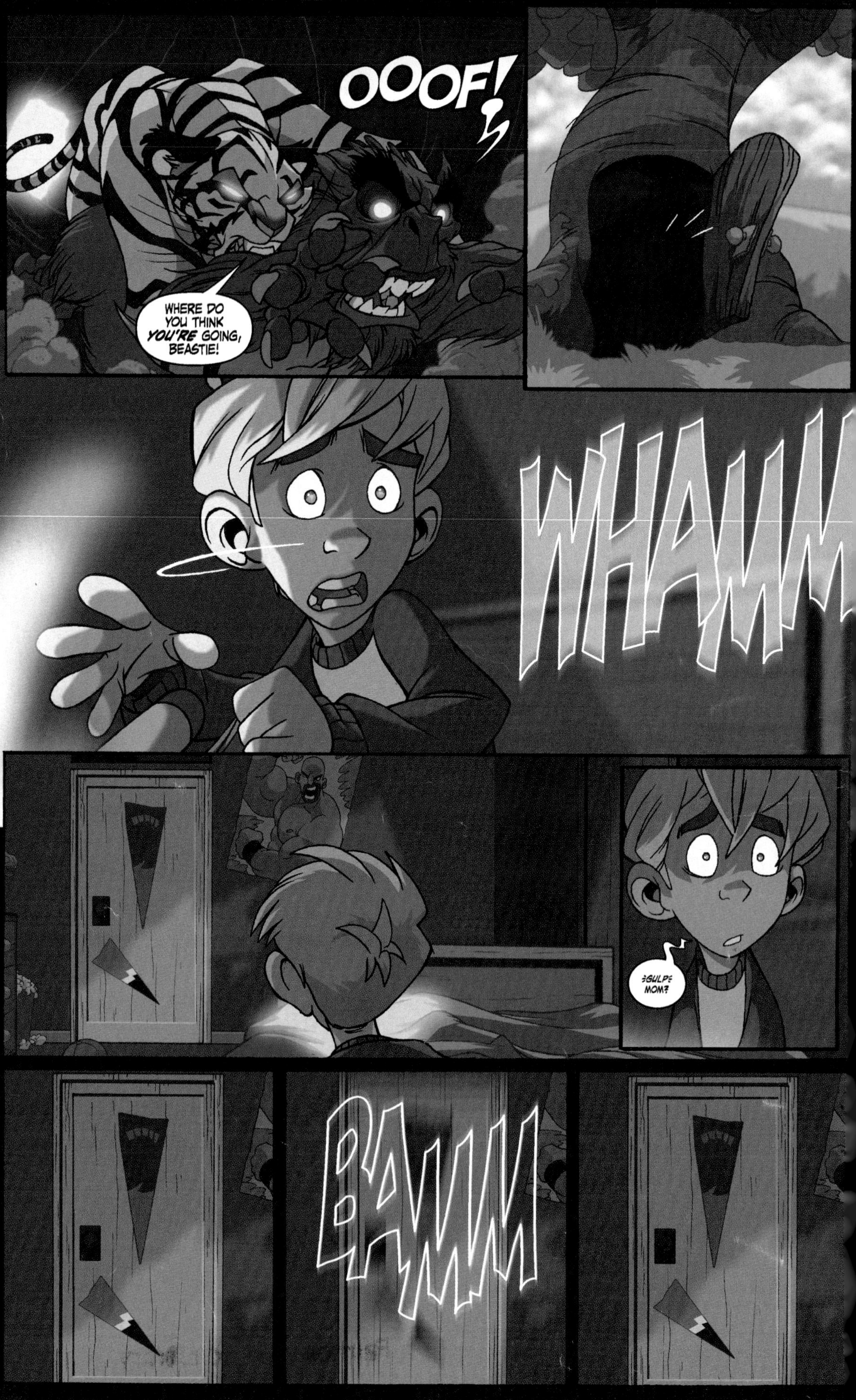
OOOF!
WHERE DO YOU THINK YOU'RE GOING, BEASTIE!
WHAMM
GULP
MOM?
BAMM

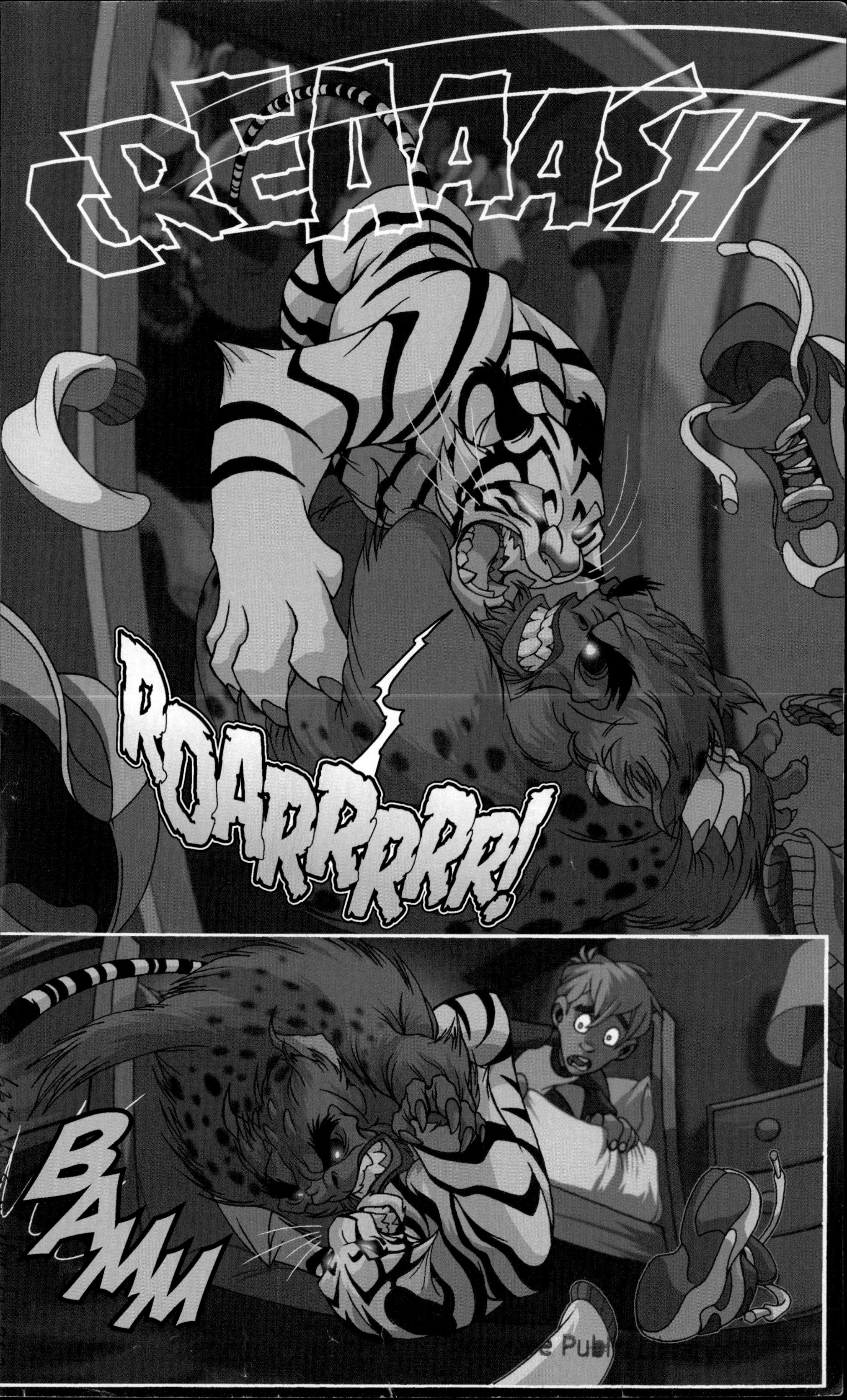
CRAAASH
ROARRRRR!
BAMM

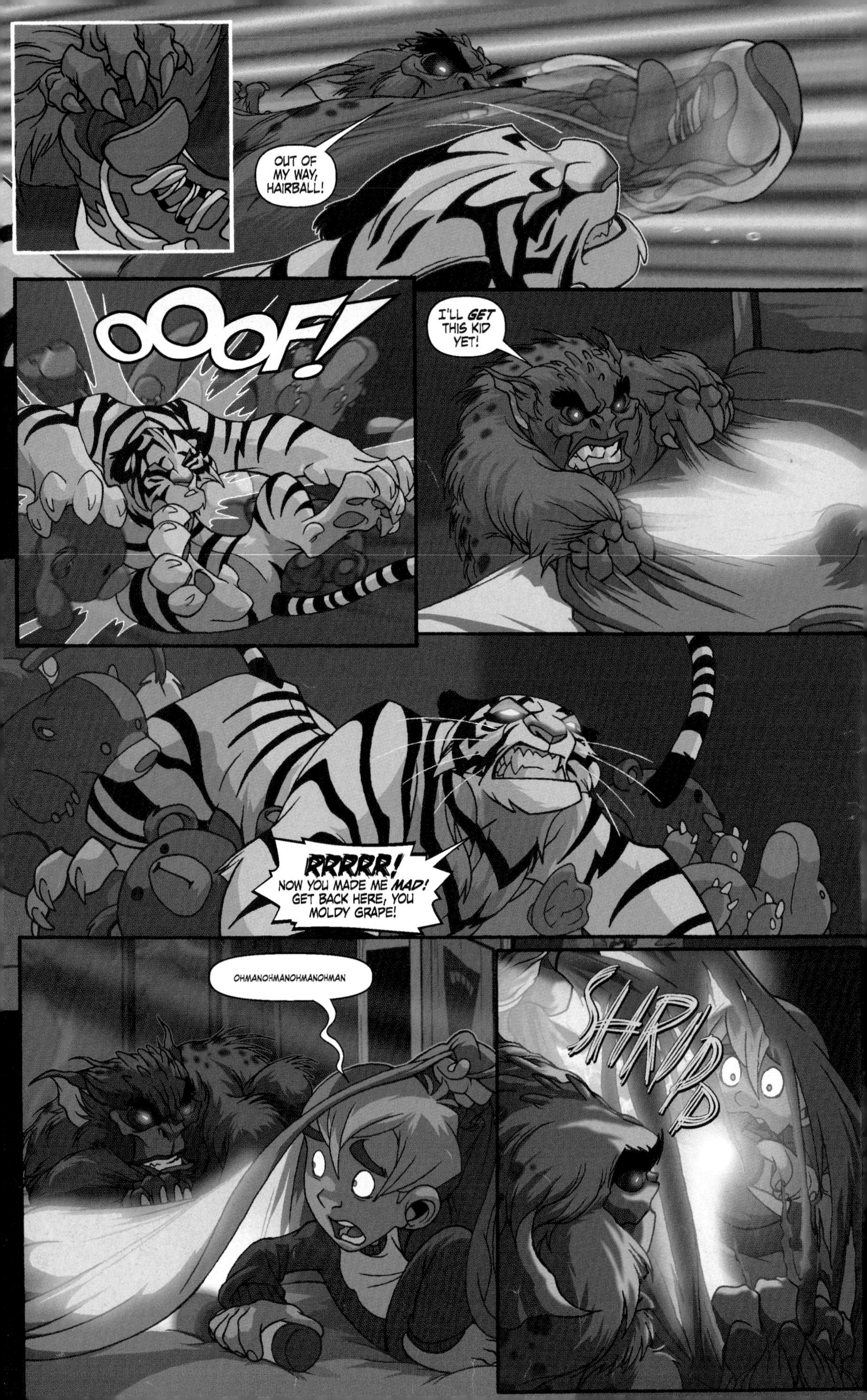
OUT OF MY WAY, HAIRBALL!
OOOF!
I'LL GET THIS KID YET!
RRRRR! NOW YOU MADE ME MAD! GET BACK HERE, YOU MOLDY GRAPE!
OHMANOHMANOHMANOHMAN
SHRIP

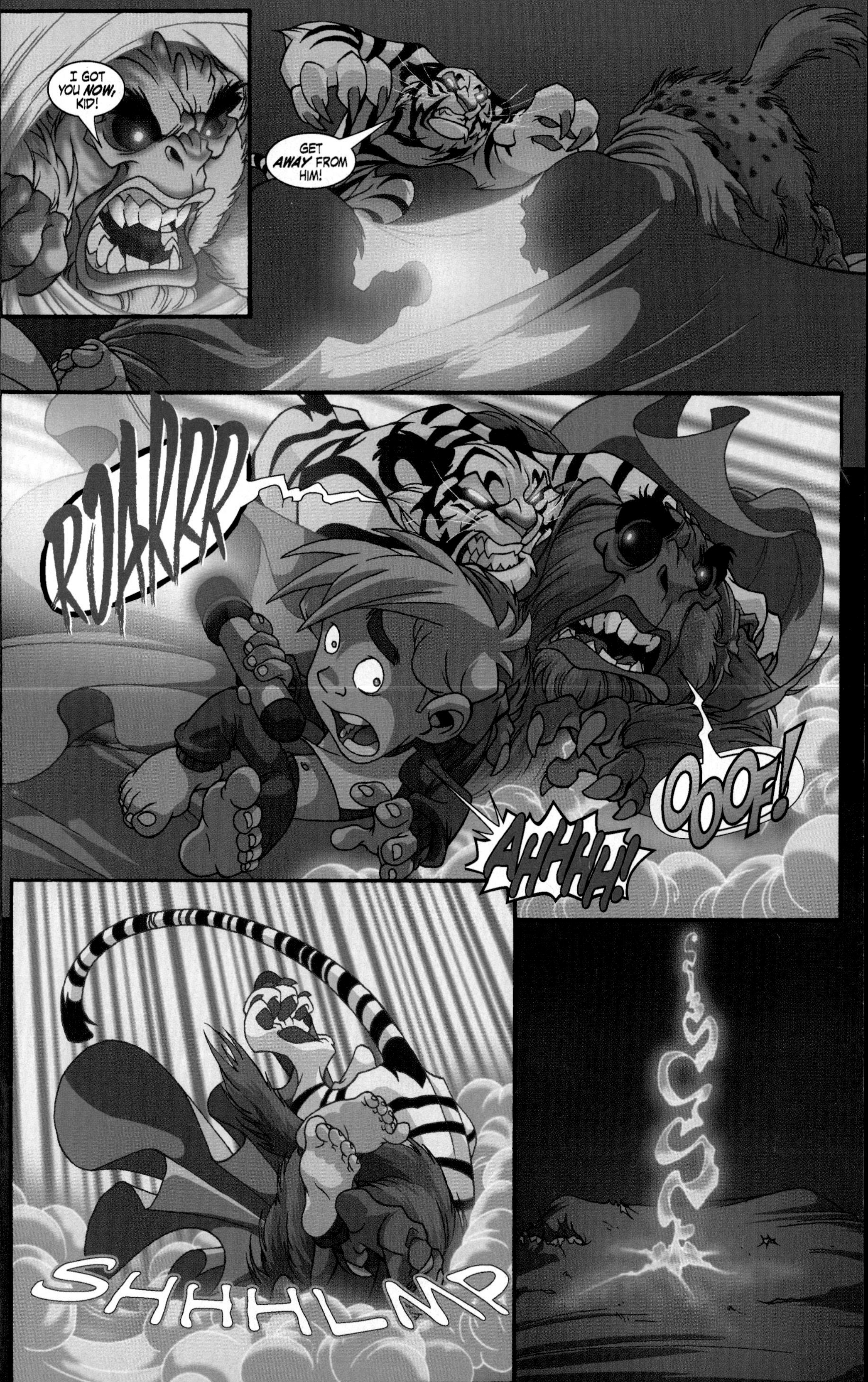
I GOT YOU NOW, KID!
GET AWAY FROM HIM!
ROARRR
OOOF!
AHHHH!
SHHHLMP

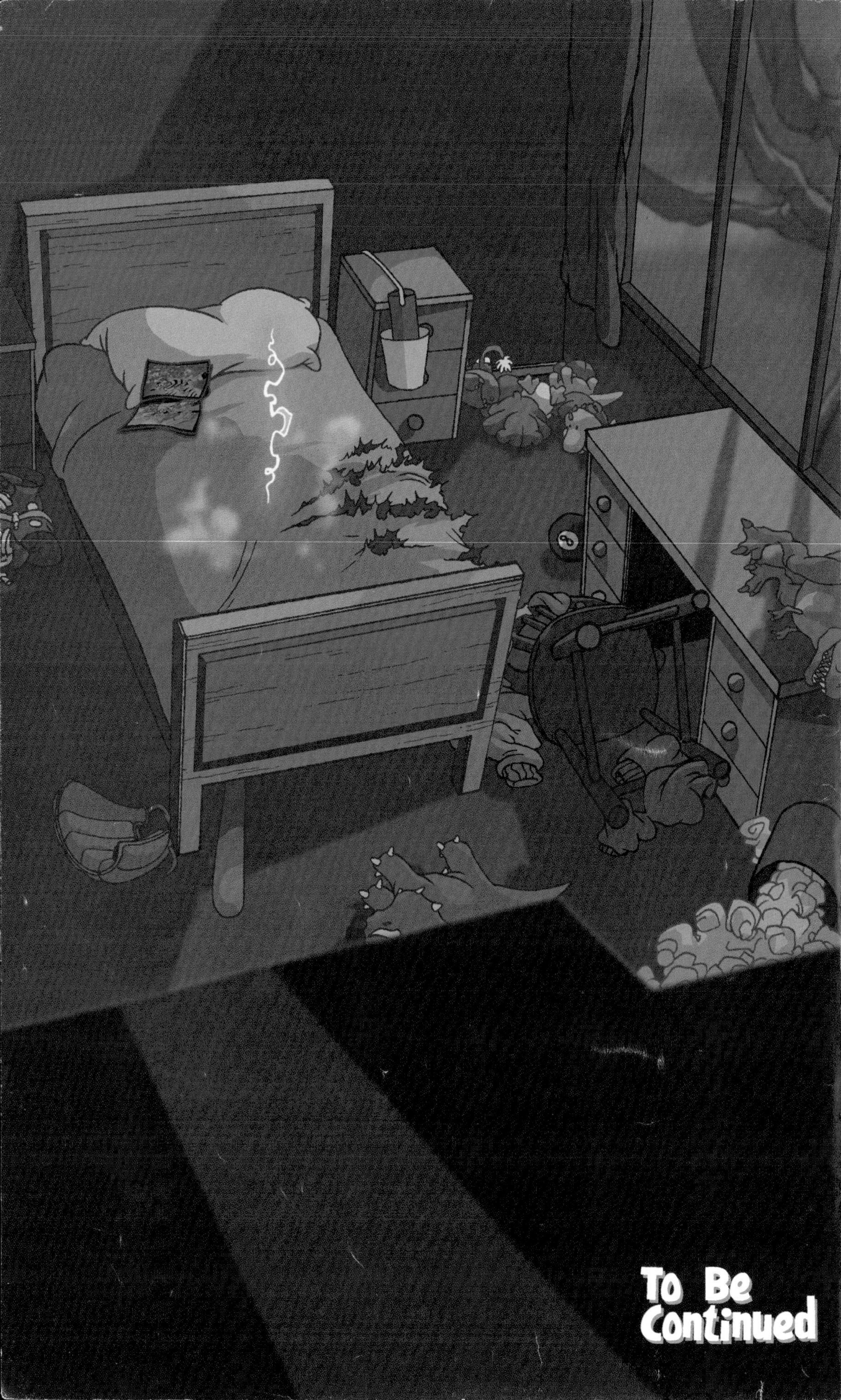
To Be
Continued

Chapter Two

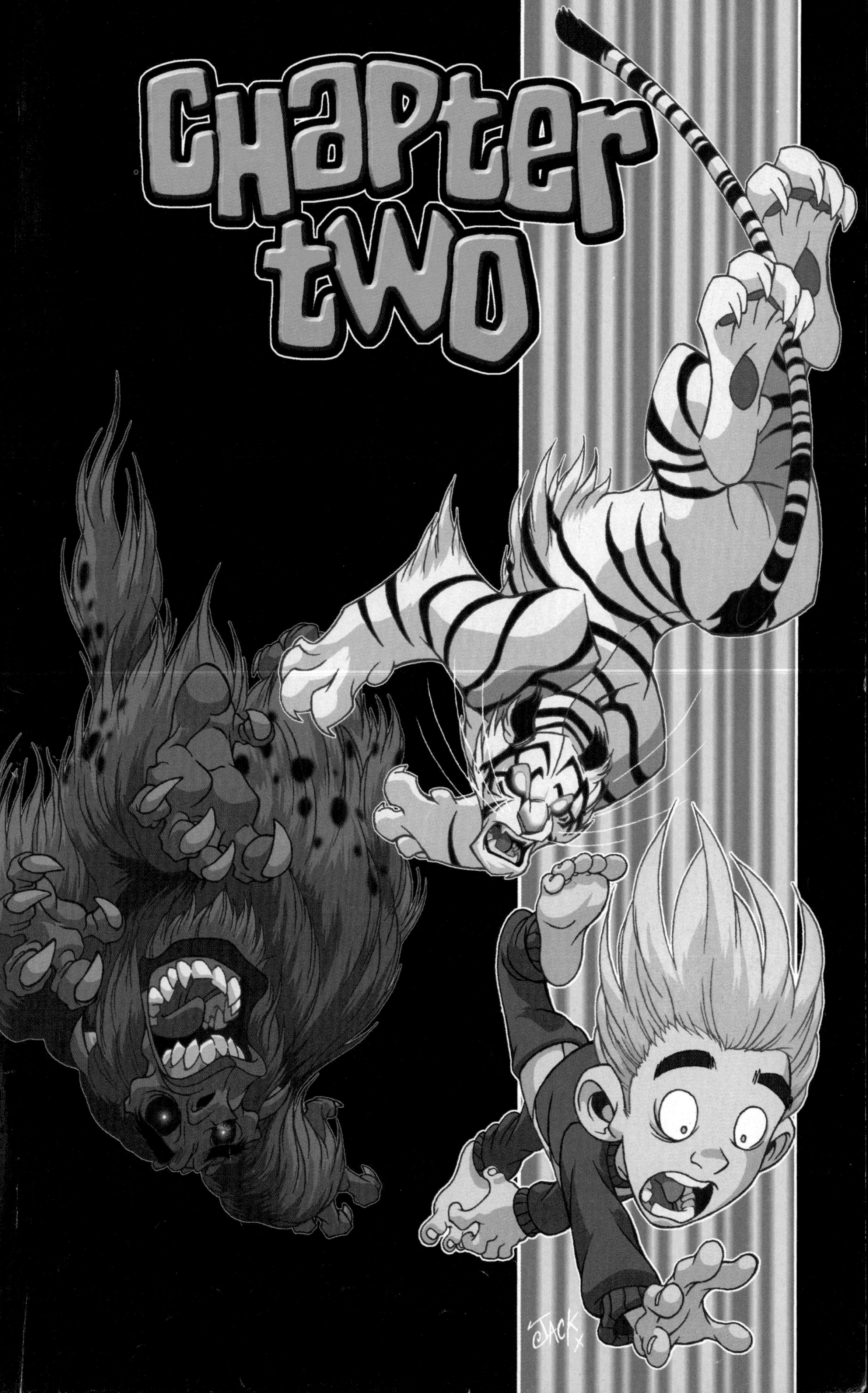
JACK

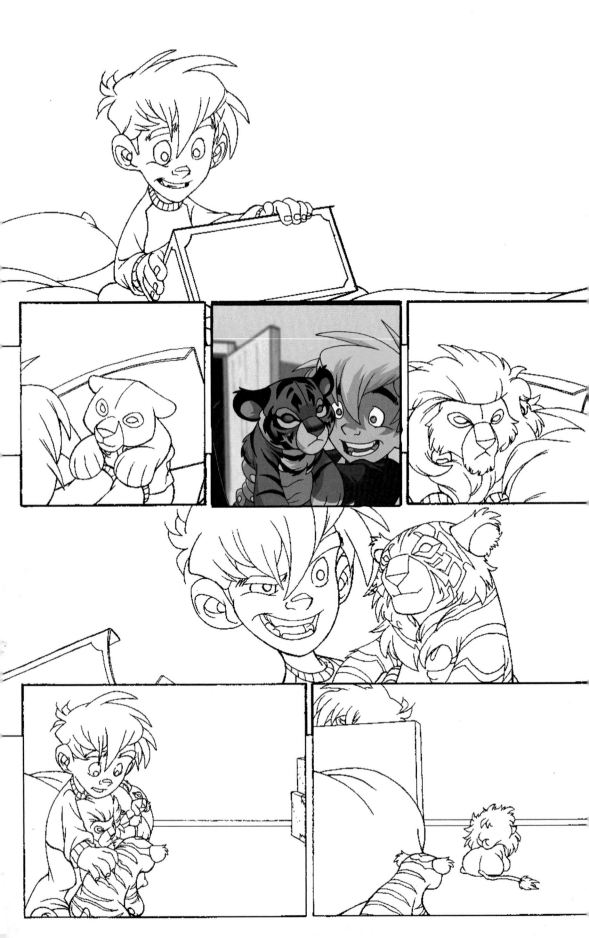

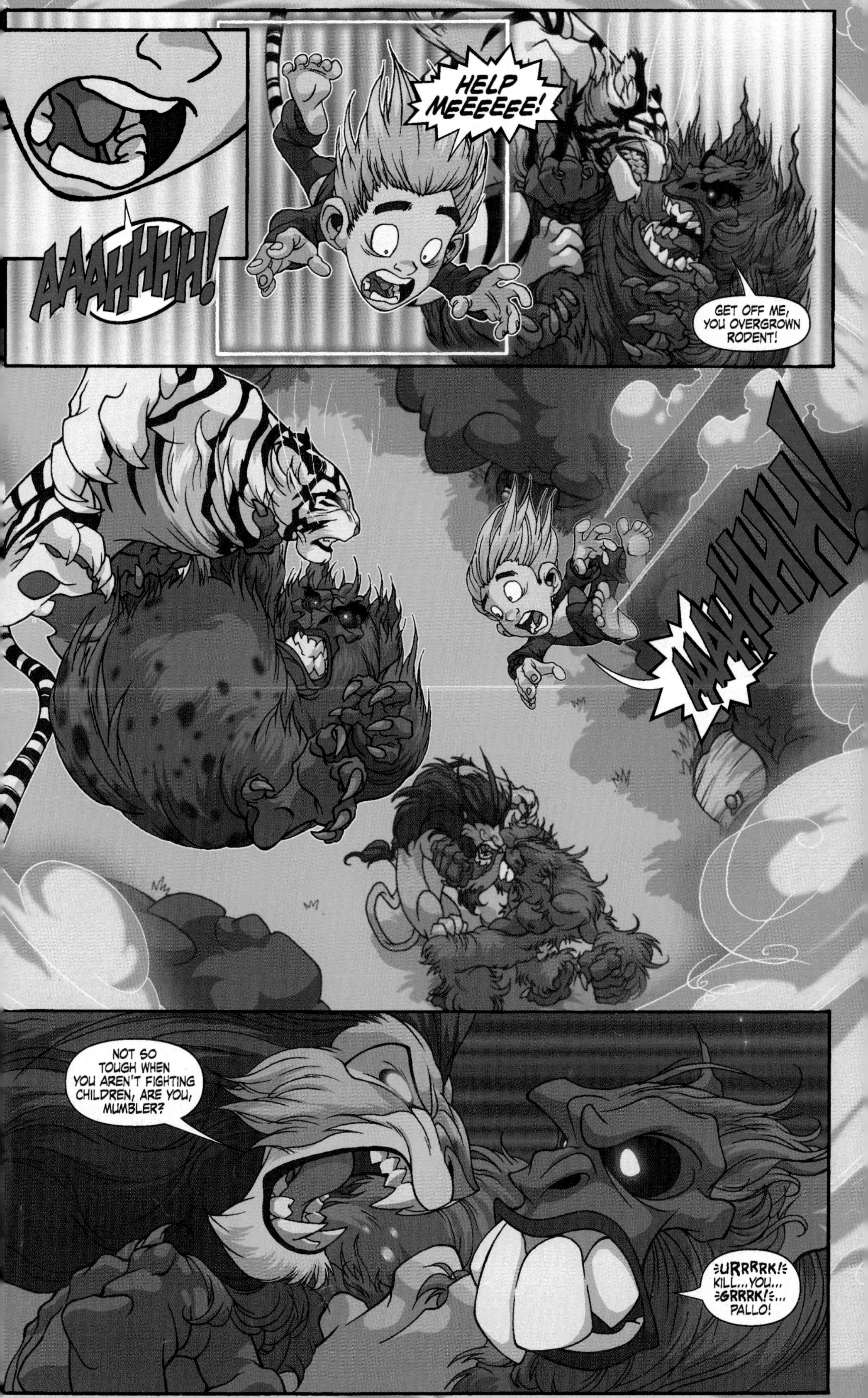
AAAHHHH!
HELP MEEEEEE!
GET OFF ME, YOU OVERGROWN RODENT!
AAAHHHH!
NOT SO TOUGH WHEN YOU AREN'T FIGHTING CHILDREN, ARE YOU, MUMBLER?
URRRRK! KILL... YOU... GRRRK!... PALLO!

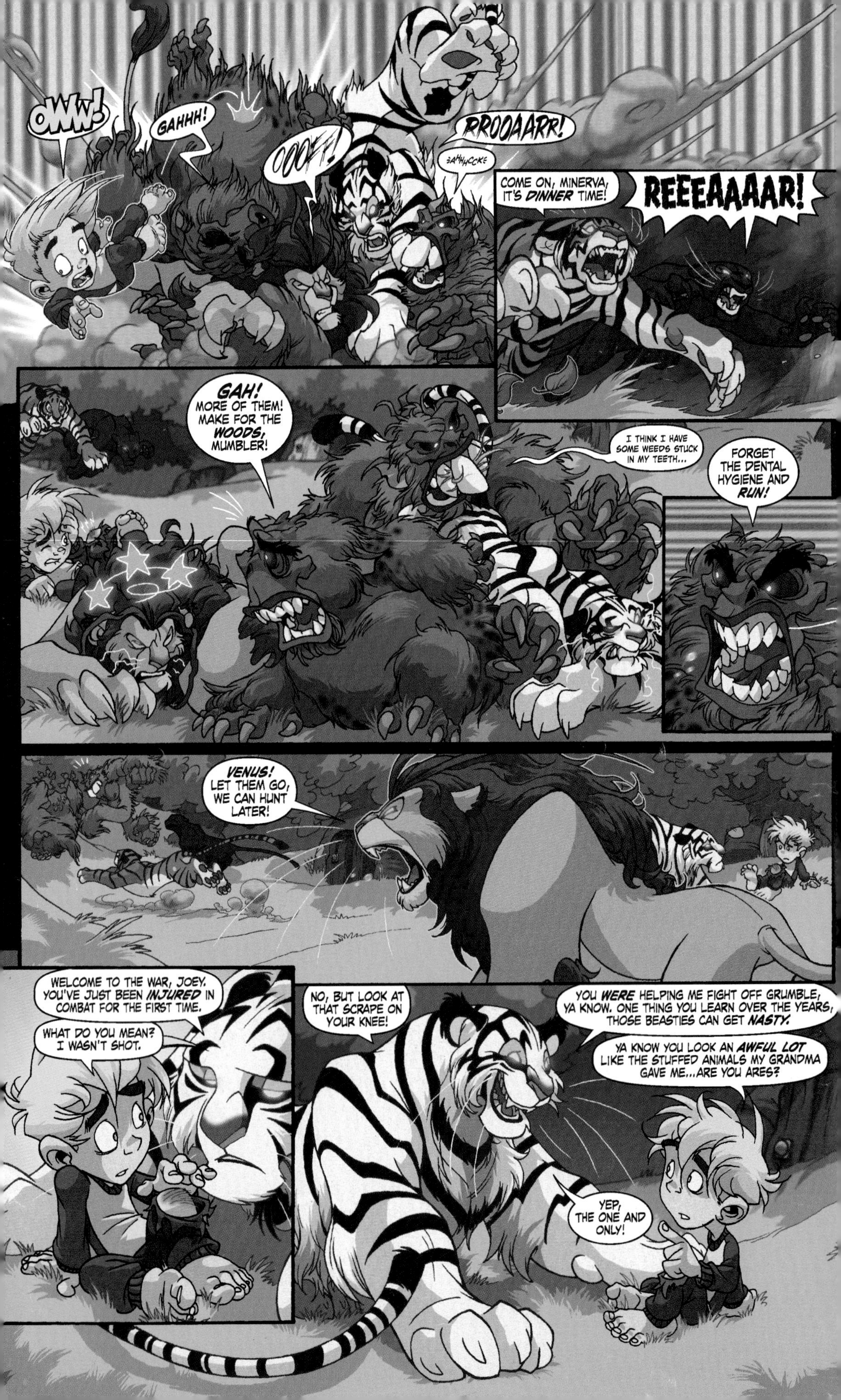
OWW!
GAHHH!
OOOFF!
RROOAARR!
AHHHCCK
COME ON, MINERVA, IT'S DINNER TIME!
REEEAAAAR!
GAH! MORE OF THEM! MAKE FOR THE WOODS, MUMBLER!
I THINK I HAVE SOME WEEDS STUCK IN MY TEETH...
FORGET THE DENTAL HYGIENE AND RUN!
VENUS! LET THEM GO, WE CAN HUNT LATER!
WELCOME TO THE WAR, JOEY. YOU'VE JUST BEEN INJURED IN COMBAT FOR THE FIRST TIME.
WHAT DO YOU MEAN? I WASN'T SHOT.
NO, BUT LOOK AT THAT SCRAPE ON YOUR KNEE!
YOU WERE HELPING ME FIGHT OFF GRUMBLE, YA KNOW. ONE THING YOU LEARN OVER THE YEARS, THOSE BEASTIES CAN GET NASTY.
YA KNOW YOU LOOK AN AWFUL LOT LIKE THE STUFFED ANIMALS MY GRANDMA GAVE ME...ARE YOU ARES?
YEP, THE ONE AND ONLY!

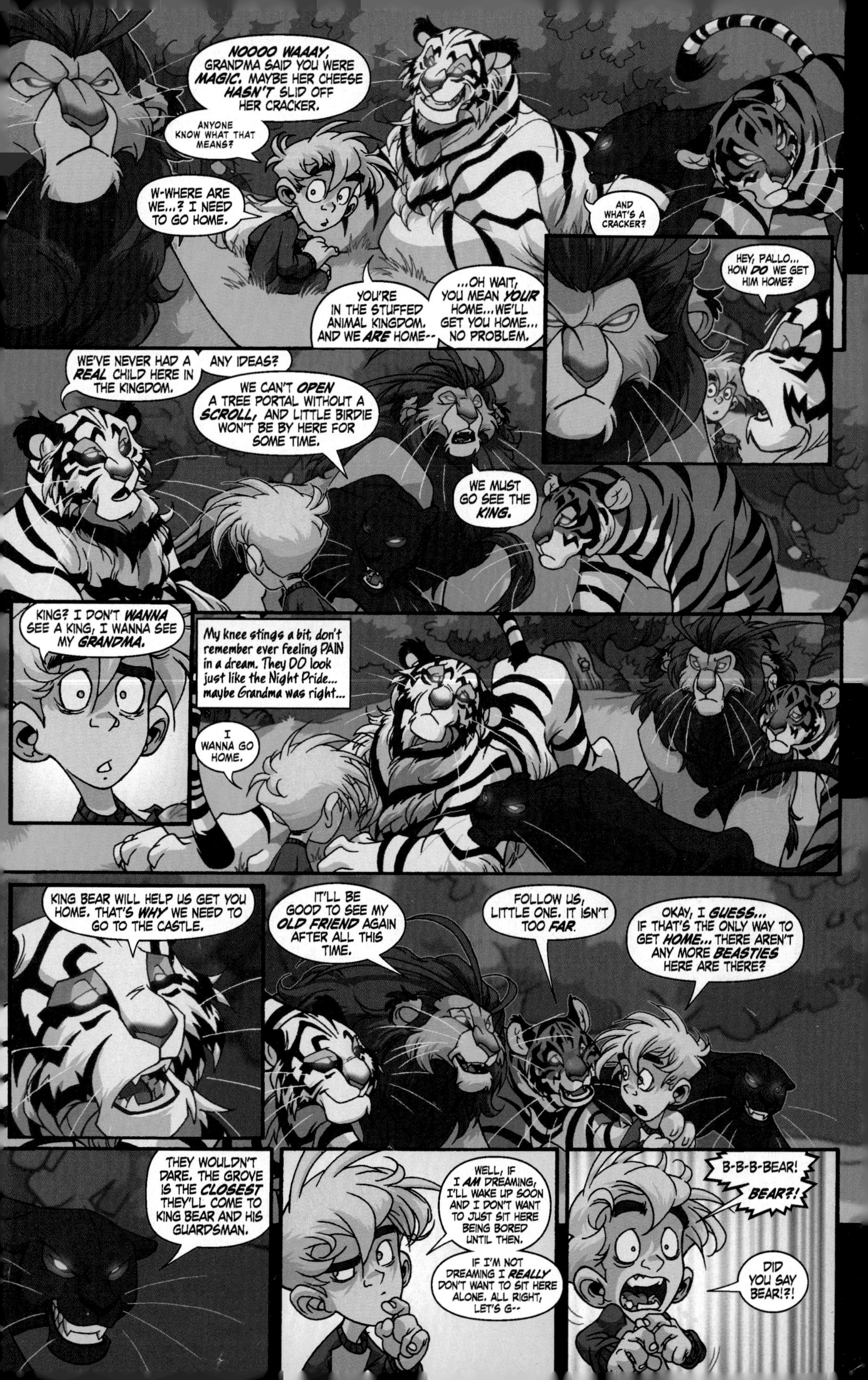
NOOOO WAAAY, GRANDMA SAID YOU WERE MAGIC. MAYBE HER CHEESE HASN'T SLID OFF HER CRACKER.
ANYONE KNOW WHAT THAT MEANS?
W-WHERE ARE WE...? I NEED TO GO HOME.
AND WHAT'S A CRACKER?
YOU'RE IN THE STUFFED ANIMAL KINGDOM. AND WE ARE HOME--
...OH WAIT, YOU MEAN YOUR HOME...WE'LL GET YOU HOME... NO PROBLEM.
HEY, PALLO... HOW DO WE GET HIM HOME?
WE'VE NEVER HAD A REAL CHILD HERE IN THE KINGDOM.
ANY IDEAS?
WE CAN'T OPEN A TREE PORTAL WITHOUT A SCROLL, AND LITTLE BIRDIE WON'T BE BY HERE FOR SOME TIME.
WE MUST GO SEE THE KING.
KING? I DON'T WANNA SEE A KING, I WANNA SEE MY GRANDMA.
My knee stings a bit, don't remember ever feeling PAIN in a dream. They DO look just like the Night Pride... maybe Grandma was right...
I WANNA GO HOME.
KING BEAR WILL HELP US GET YOU HOME. THAT'S WHY WE NEED TO GO TO THE CASTLE.
IT'LL BE GOOD TO SEE MY OLD FRIEND AGAIN AFTER ALL THIS TIME.
FOLLOW US, LITTLE ONE. IT ISN'T TOO FAR.
OKAY, I GUESS... IF THAT'S THE ONLY WAY TO GET HOME... THERE AREN'T ANY MORE BEASTIES HERE ARE THERE?
THEY WOULDN'T DARE. THE GROVE IS THE CLOSEST THEY'LL COME TO KING BEAR AND HIS GUARDSMAN.
WELL, IF I AM DREAMING, I'LL WAKE UP SOON AND I DON'T WANT TO JUST SIT HERE BEING BORED UNTIL THEN.
IF I'M NOT DREAMING I REALLY DON'T WANT TO SIT HERE ALONE. ALL RIGHT, LET'S G--
B-B-B-BEAR!
BEAR?!
DID YOU SAY BEAR!?!

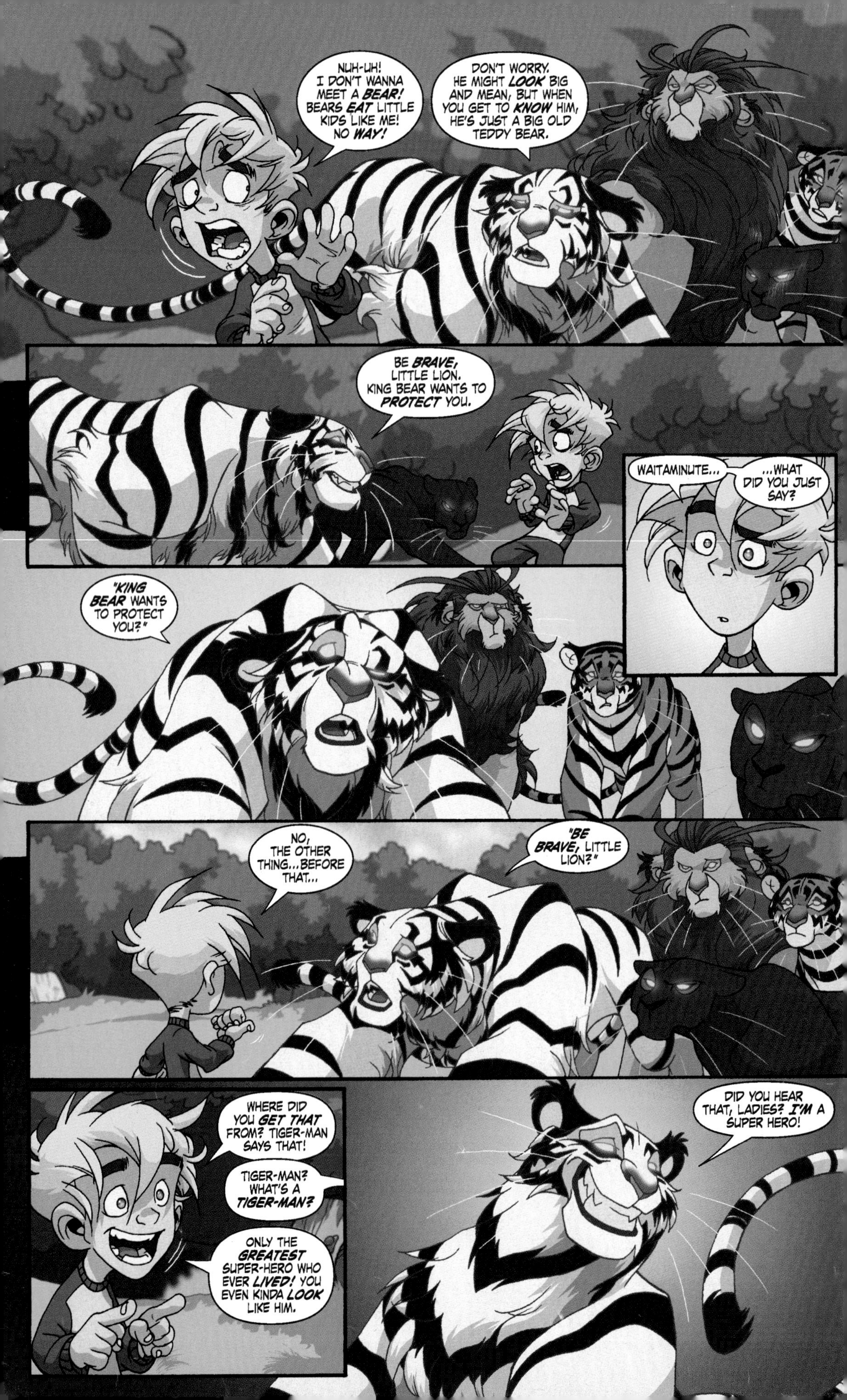
NUH-UH! I DON'T WANNA MEET A BEAR! BEARS EAT LITTLE KIDS LIKE ME! NO WAY!
DON'T WORRY. HE MIGHT LOOK BIG AND MEAN, BUT WHEN YOU GET TO KNOW HIM, HE'S JUST A BIG OLD TEDDY BEAR.
BE BRAVE, LITTLE LION. KING BEAR WANTS TO PROTECT YOU.
WAITAMINUTE...
...WHAT DID YOU JUST SAY?
"KING BEAR WANTS TO PROTECT YOU?"
NO, THE OTHER THING...BEFORE THAT...
"BE BRAVE, LITTLE LION?"
WHERE DID YOU GET THAT FROM? TIGER-MAN SAYS THAT!
TIGER-MAN? WHAT'S A TIGER-MAN?
ONLY THE GREATEST SUPER-HERO WHO EVER LIVED! YOU EVEN KINDA LOOK LIKE HIM.
DID YOU HEAR THAT, LADIES? I'M A SUPER HERO!

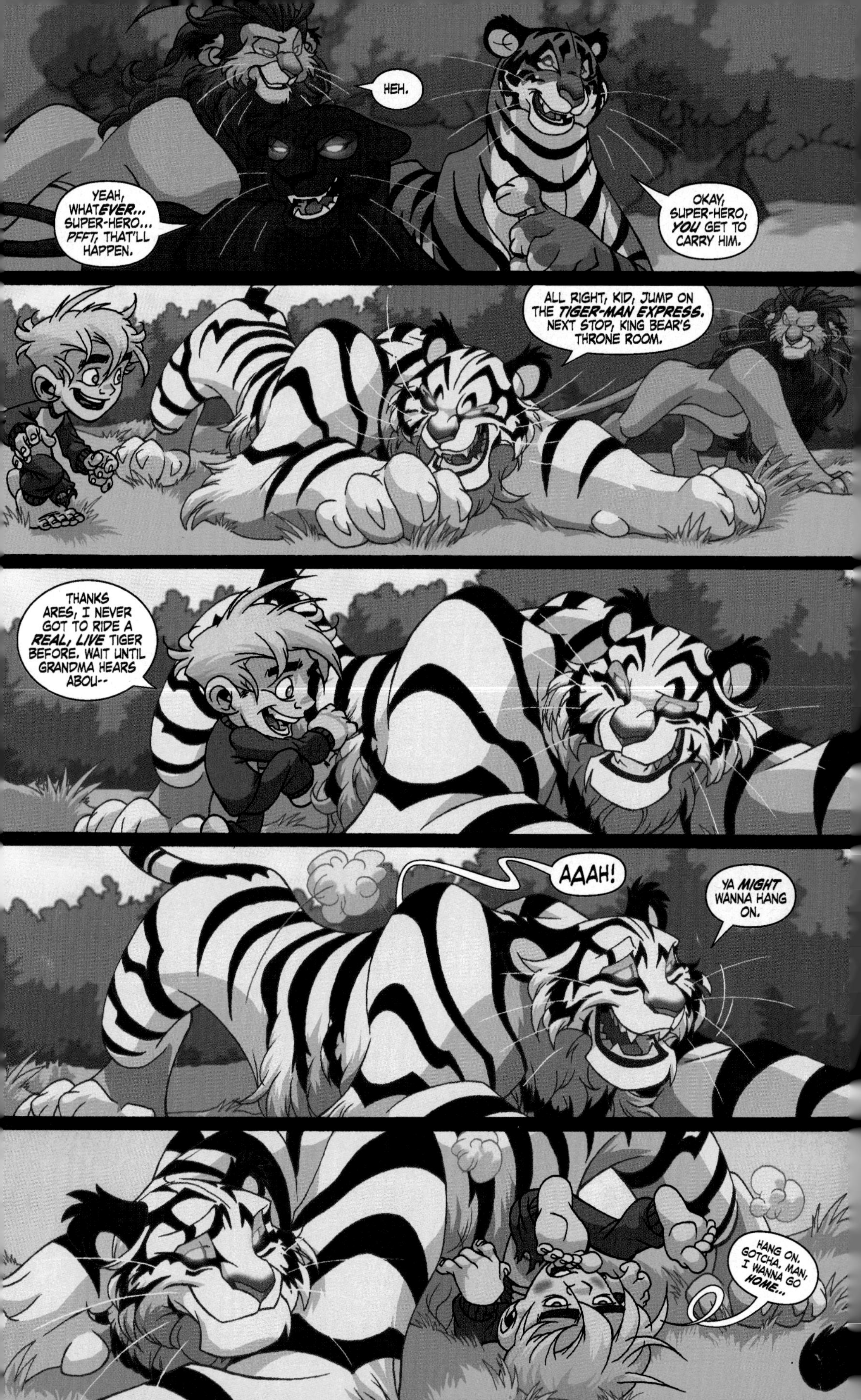
HEH.
YEAH, WHATEVER... SUPER-HERO... PFFT, THAT'LL HAPPEN.
OKAY, SUPER-HERO, YOU GET TO CARRY HIM.
ALL RIGHT, KID, JUMP ON THE TIGER-MAN EXPRESS. NEXT STOP, KING BEAR'S THRONE ROOM.
THANKS ARES, I NEVER GOT TO RIDE A REAL, LIVE TIGER BEFORE. WAIT UNTIL GRANDMA HEARS ABOU--
AAAH!
YA MIGHT WANNA HANG ON.
HANG ON. GOTCHA. MAN, I WANNA GO HOME...

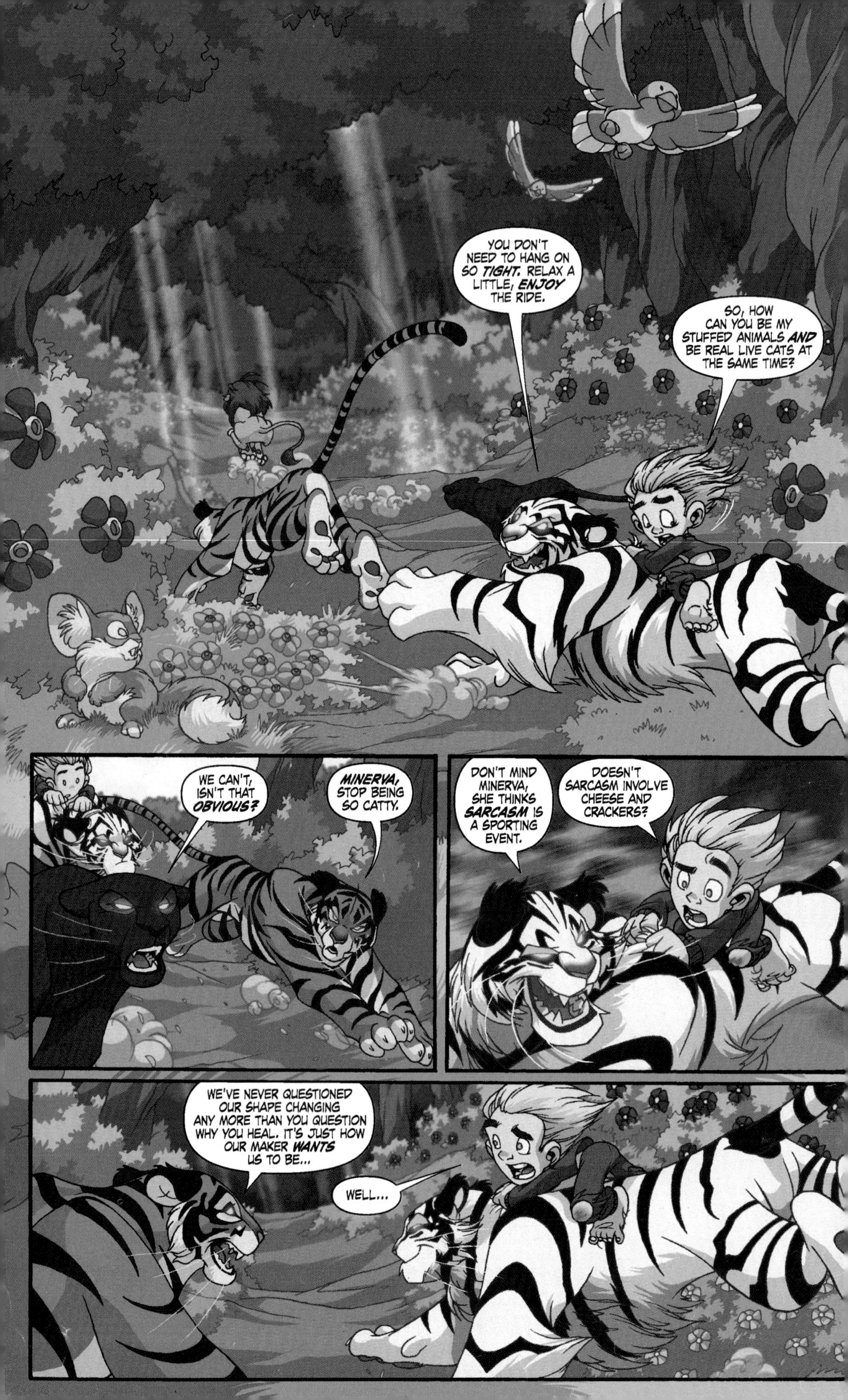
YOU DON'T NEED TO HANG ON SO TIGHT. RELAX A LITTLE, ENJOY THE RIDE.
SO, HOW CAN YOU BE MY STUFFED ANIMALS AND BE REAL LIVE CATS AT THE SAME TIME?
WE CAN'T, ISN'T THAT OBVIOUS?
MINERVA, STOP BEING SO CATTY.
DON'T MIND MINERVA, SHE THINKS SARCASM IS A SPORTING EVENT.
DOESN'T SARCASM INVOLVE CHEESE AND CRACKERS?
WE'VE NEVER QUESTIONED OUR SHAPE CHANGING ANY MORE THAN YOU QUESTION WHY YOU HEAL. IT'S JUST HOW OUR MAKER WANTS US TO BE...
WELL...

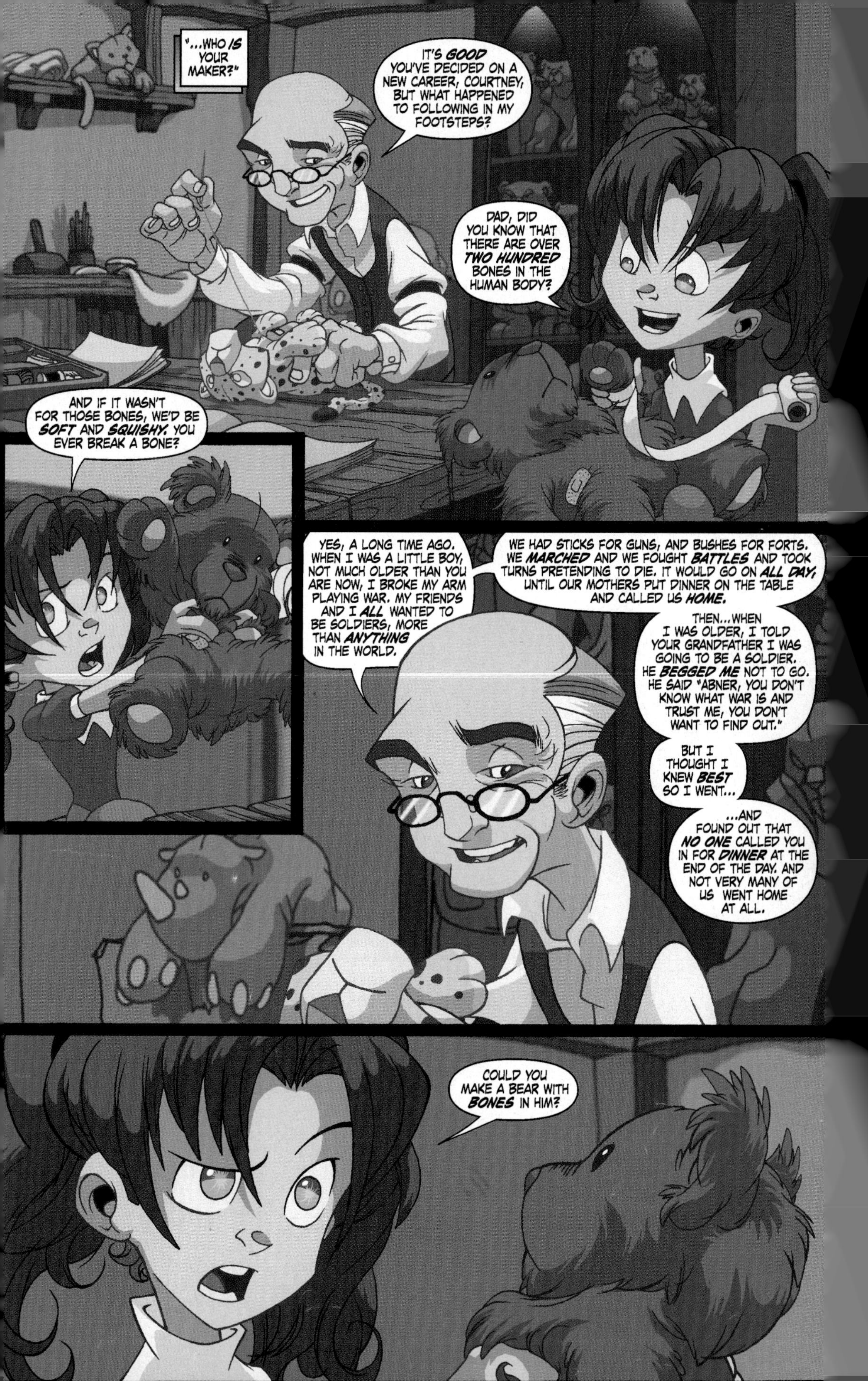
"...WHO IS YOUR MAKER?"
IT'S GOOD YOU'VE DECIDED ON A NEW CAREER, COURTNEY, BUT WHAT HAPPENED TO FOLLOWING IN MY FOOTSTEPS?
DAD, DID YOU KNOW THAT THERE ARE OVER TWO HUNDRED BONES IN THE HUMAN BODY?
AND IF IT WASN'T FOR THOSE BONES, WE'D BE SOFT AND SQUISHY. YOU EVER BREAK A BONE?
YES, A LONG TIME AGO. WHEN I WAS A LITTLE BOY, NOT MUCH OLDER THAN YOU ARE NOW, I BROKE MY ARM PLAYING WAR. MY FRIENDS AND I ALL WANTED TO BE SOLDIERS, MORE THAN ANYTHING IN THE WORLD.
WE HAD STICKS FOR GUNS, AND BUSHES FOR FORTS. WE MARCHED AND WE FOUGHT BATTLES AND TOOK TURNS PRETENDING TO DIE. IT WOULD GO ON ALL DAY, UNTIL OUR MOTHERS PUT DINNER ON THE TABLE AND CALLED US HOME.
THEN...WHEN I WAS OLDER, I TOLD YOUR GRANDFATHER I WAS GOING TO BE A SOLDIER. HE BEGGED ME NOT TO GO. HE SAID "ABNER, YOU DON'T KNOW WHAT WAR IS AND TRUST ME, YOU DON'T WANT TO FIND OUT."
BUT I THOUGHT I KNEW BEST SO I WENT...
...AND FOUND OUT THAT NO ONE CALLED YOU IN FOR DINNER AT THE END OF THE DAY. AND NOT VERY MANY OF US WENT HOME AT ALL.
COULD YOU MAKE A BEAR WITH BONES IN HIM?

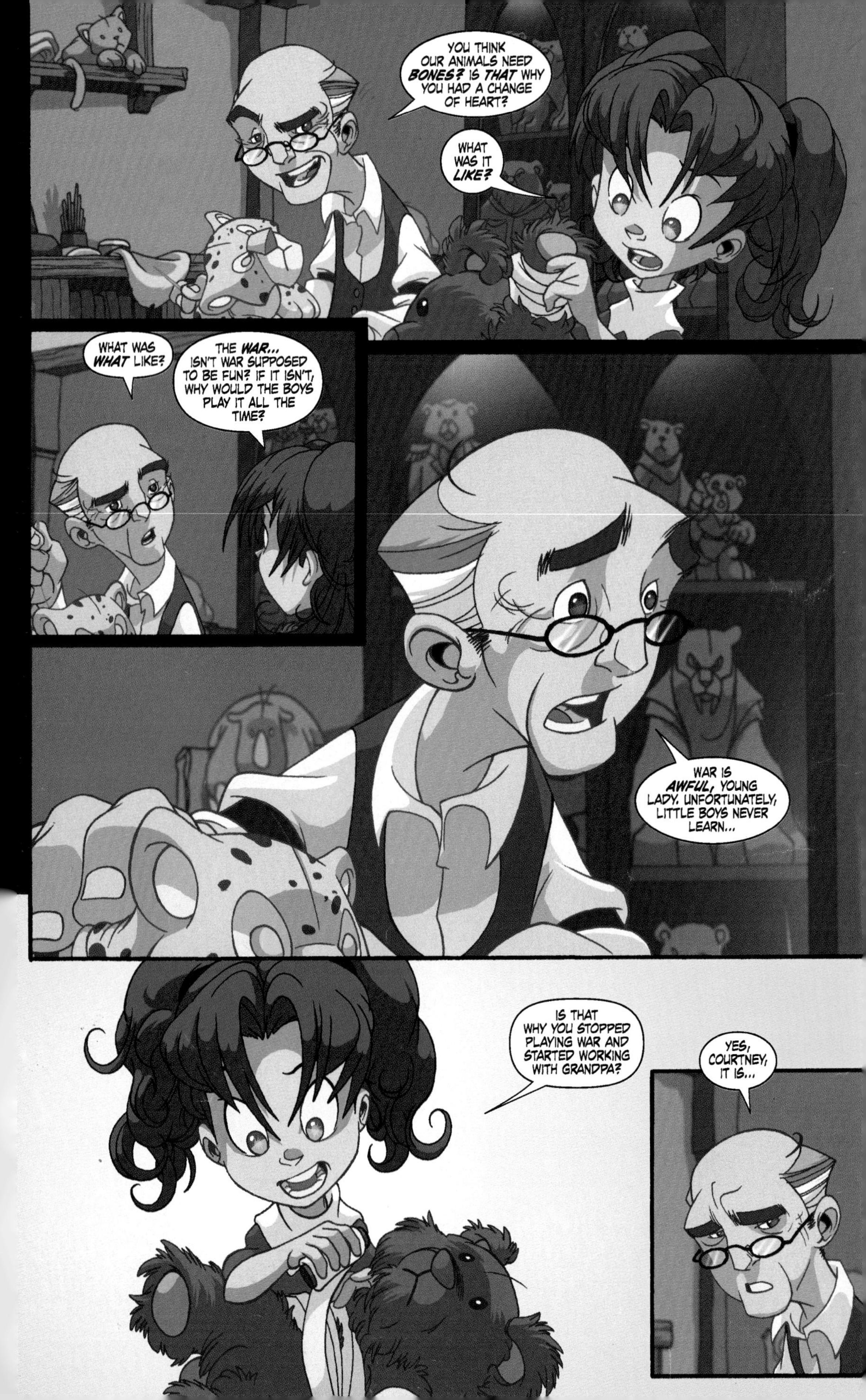
YOU THINK OUR ANIMALS NEED BONES? IS THAT WHY YOU HAD A CHANGE OF HEART?
WHAT WAS IT LIKE?
WHAT WAS WHAT LIKE?
THE WAR... ISN'T WAR SUPPOSED TO BE FUN? IF IT ISN'T, WHY WOULD THE BOYS PLAY IT ALL THE TIME?
WAR IS AWFUL, YOUNG LADY. UNFORTUNATELY, LITTLE BOYS NEVER LEARN...
IS THAT WHY YOU STOPPED PLAYING WAR AND STARTED WORKING WITH GRANDPA?
YES, COURTNEY, IT IS...

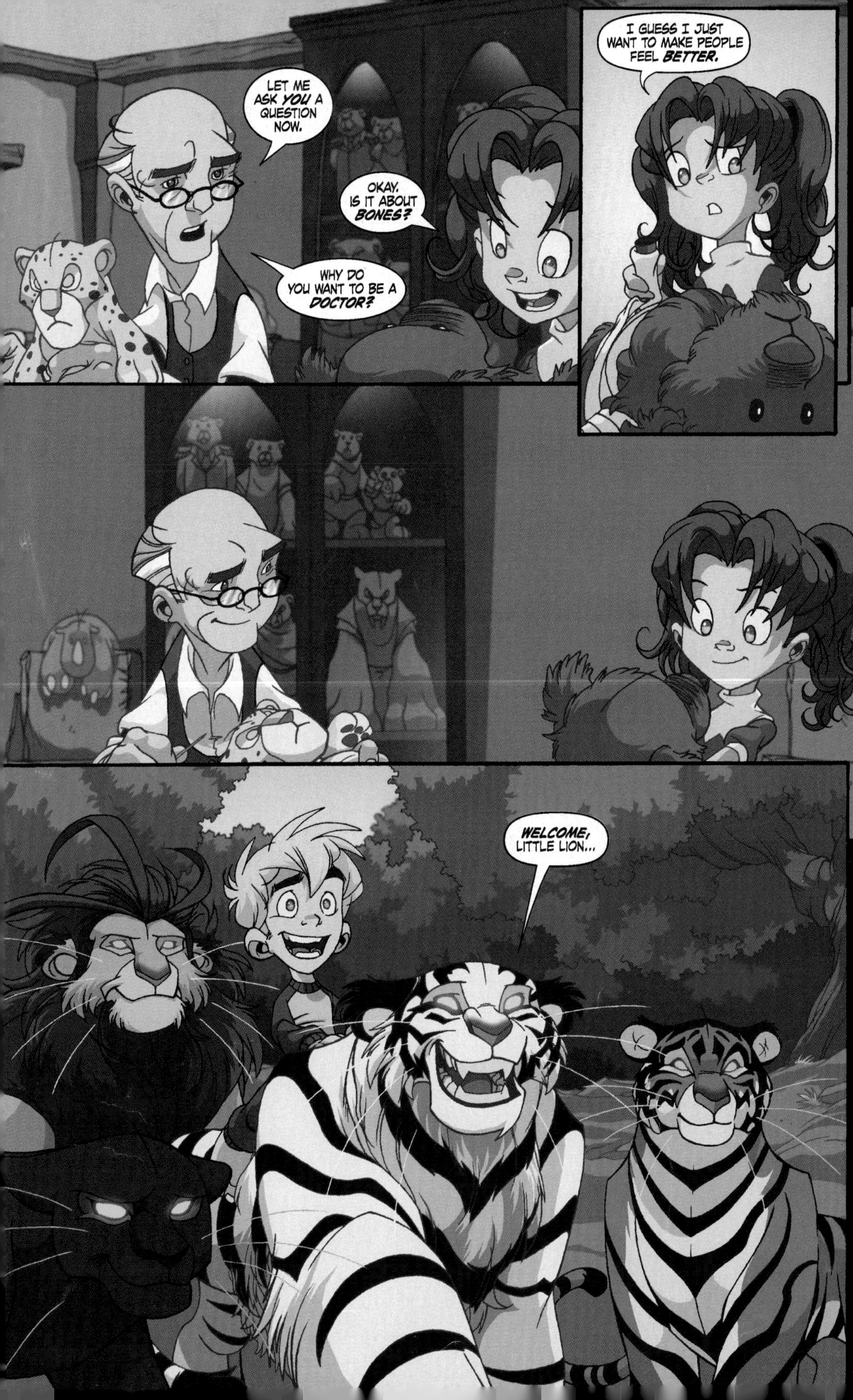
LET ME ASK *YOU* A QUESTION NOW.
OKAY. IS IT ABOUT *BONES?*
WHY DO YOU WANT TO BE A *DOCTOR?*
I GUESS I JUST WANT TO MAKE PEOPLE FEEL *BETTER.*
WELCOME, LITTLE LION...

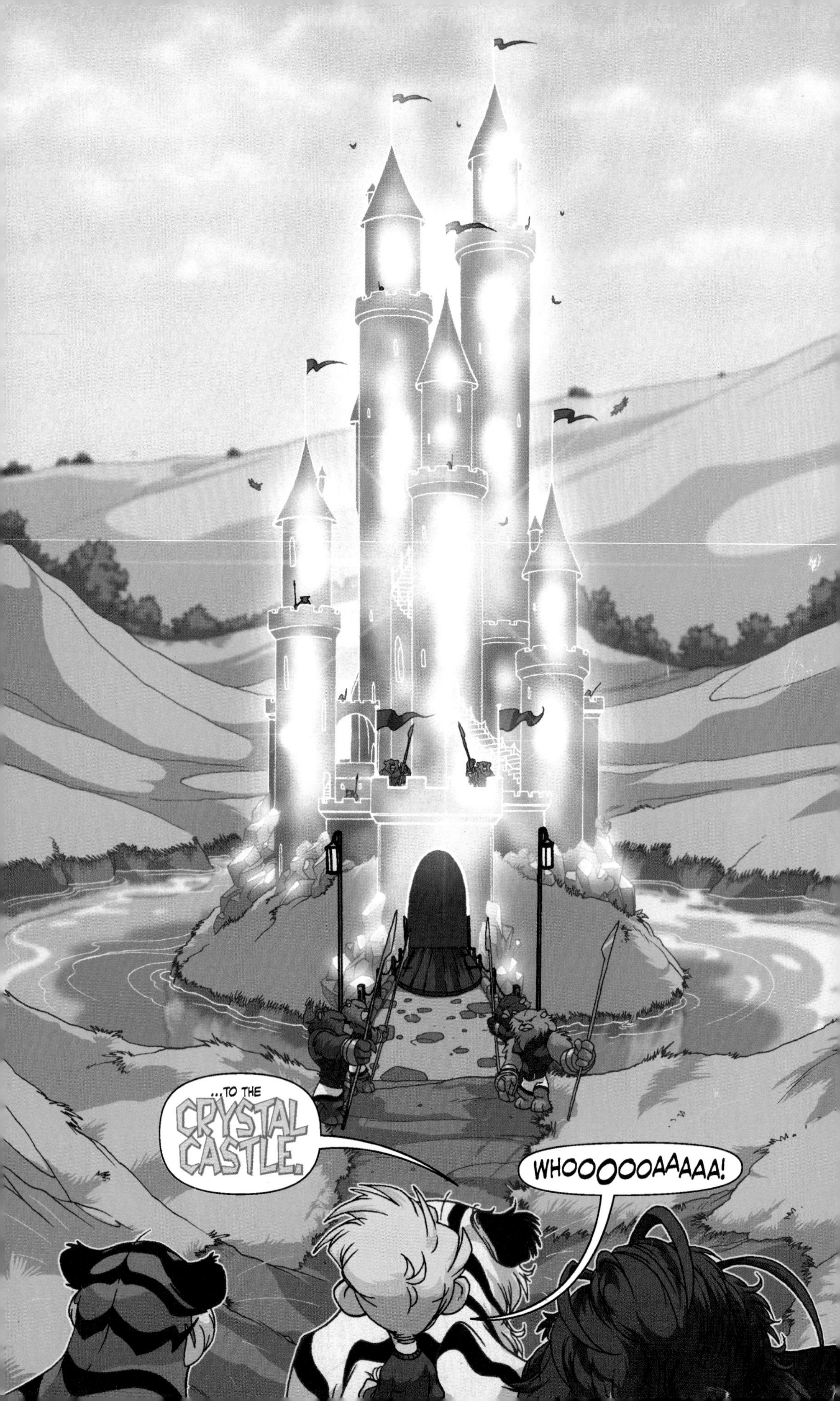
...TO THE
CRYSTAL CASTLE.
WHOOOOOAAAAA!

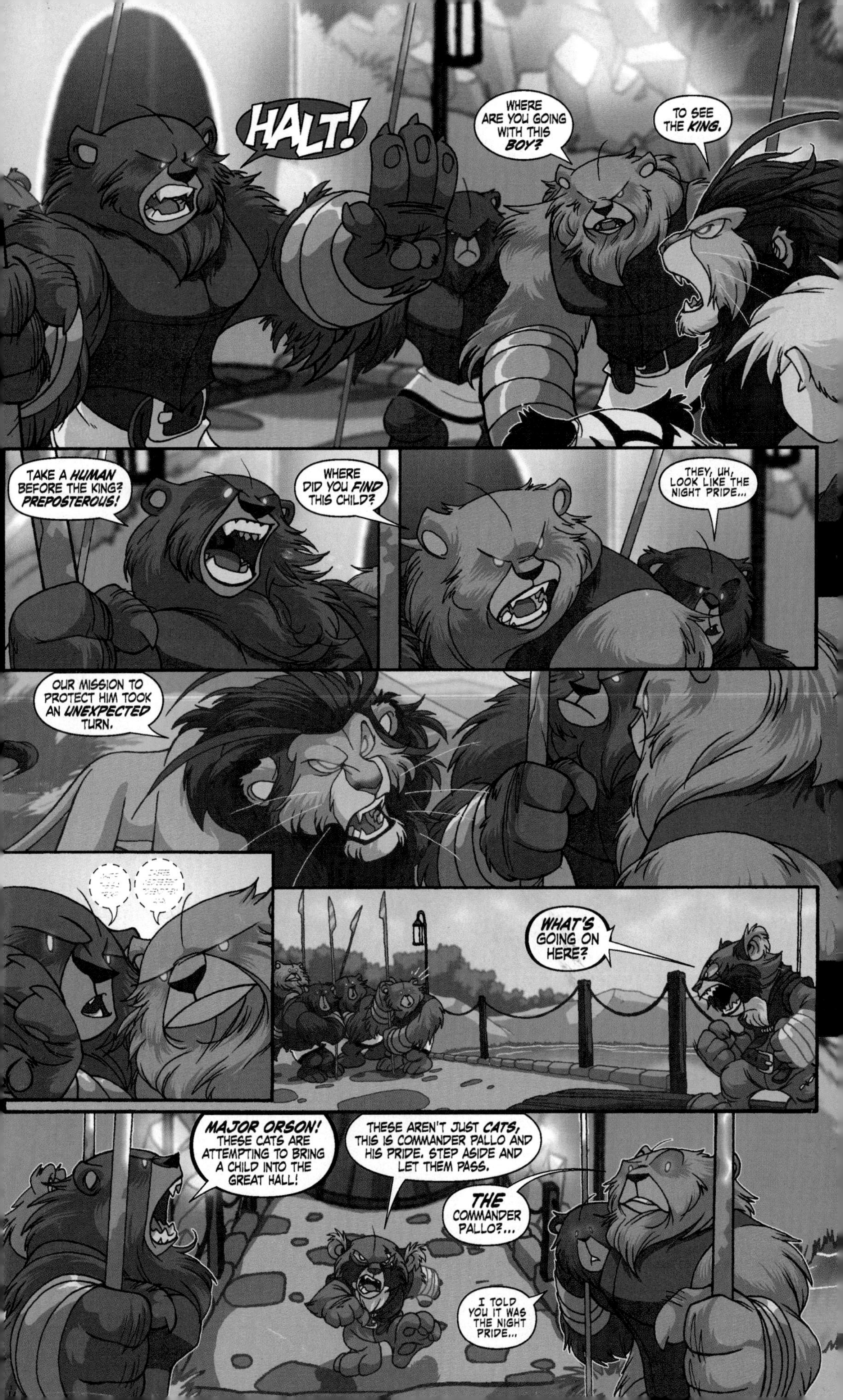
HALT!
WHERE ARE YOU GOING WITH THIS BOY?
TO SEE THE KING.
TAKE A HUMAN BEFORE THE KING? PREPOSTEROUS!
WHERE DID YOU FIND THIS CHILD?
THEY, UH, LOOK LIKE THE NIGHT PRIDE...
OUR MISSION TO PROTECT HIM TOOK AN UNEXPECTED TURN.
WHAT'S GOING ON HERE?
MAJOR ORSON! THESE CATS ARE ATTEMPTING TO BRING A CHILD INTO THE GREAT HALL!
THESE AREN'T JUST CATS, THIS IS COMMANDER PALLO AND HIS PRIDE. STEP ASIDE AND LET THEM PASS.
THE COMMANDER PALLO?...
I TOLD YOU IT WAS THE NIGHT PRIDE...

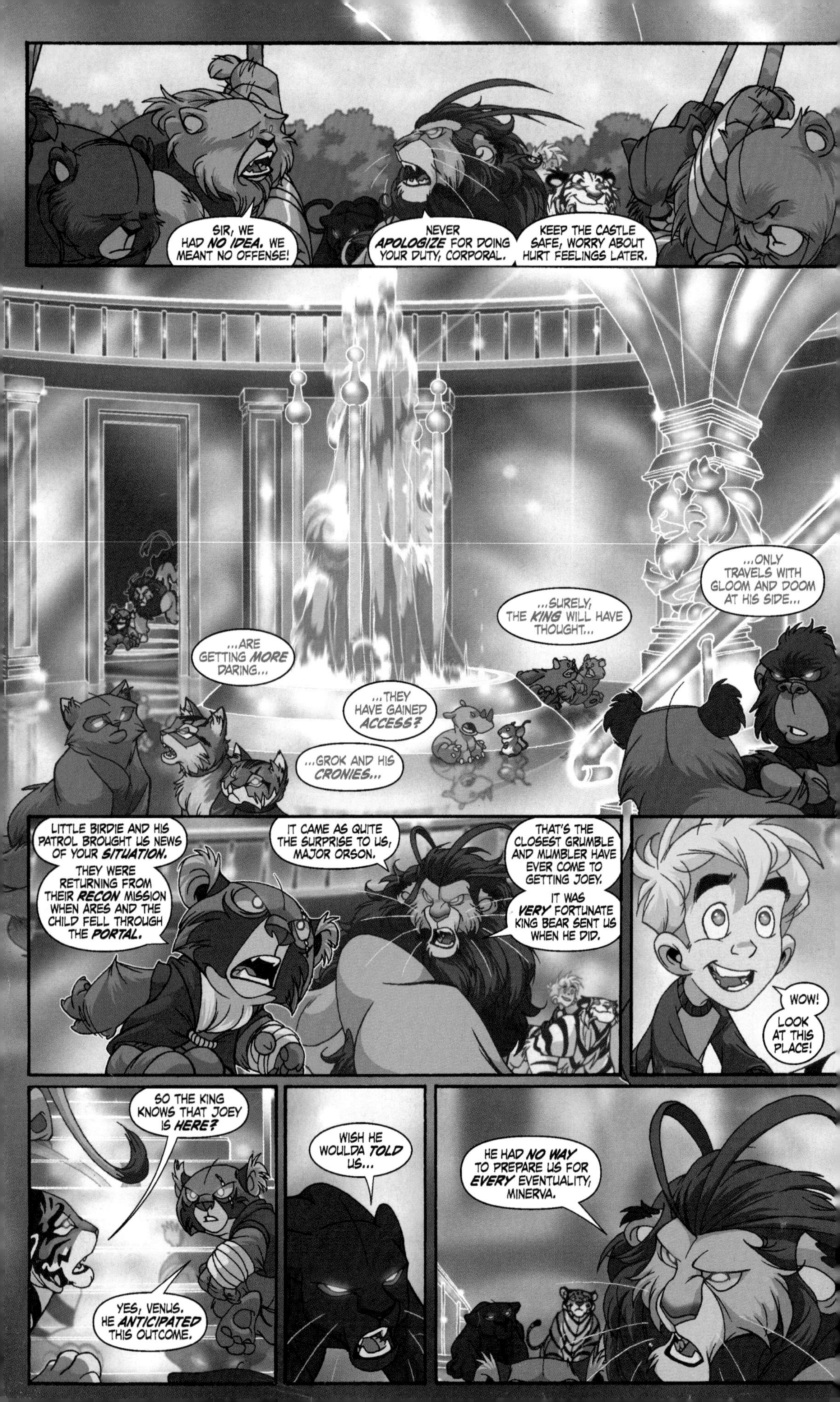
SIR, WE HAD NO IDEA. WE MEANT NO OFFENSE!
NEVER APOLOGIZE FOR DOING YOUR DUTY, CORPORAL.
KEEP THE CASTLE SAFE, WORRY ABOUT HURT FEELINGS LATER.
...ARE GETTING MORE DARING...
...THEY HAVE GAINED ACCESS?
...GROK AND HIS CRONIES...
...SURELY, THE KING WILL HAVE THOUGHT...
...ONLY TRAVELS WITH GLOOM AND DOOM AT HIS SIDE...
LITTLE BIRDIE AND HIS PATROL BROUGHT US NEWS OF YOUR SITUATION.
THEY WERE RETURNING FROM THEIR RECON MISSION WHEN ARES AND THE CHILD FELL THROUGH THE PORTAL.
IT CAME AS QUITE THE SURPRISE TO US, MAJOR ORSON.
THAT'S THE CLOSEST GRUMBLE AND MUMBLER HAVE EVER COME TO GETTING JOEY.
IT WAS VERY FORTUNATE KING BEAR SENT US WHEN HE DID.
WOW!
LOOK AT THIS PLACE!
SO THE KING KNOWS THAT JOEY IS HERE?
YES, VENUS. HE ANTICIPATED THIS OUTCOME.
WISH HE WOULDA TOLD US...
HE HAD NO WAY TO PREPARE US FOR EVERY EVENTUALITY, MINERVA.

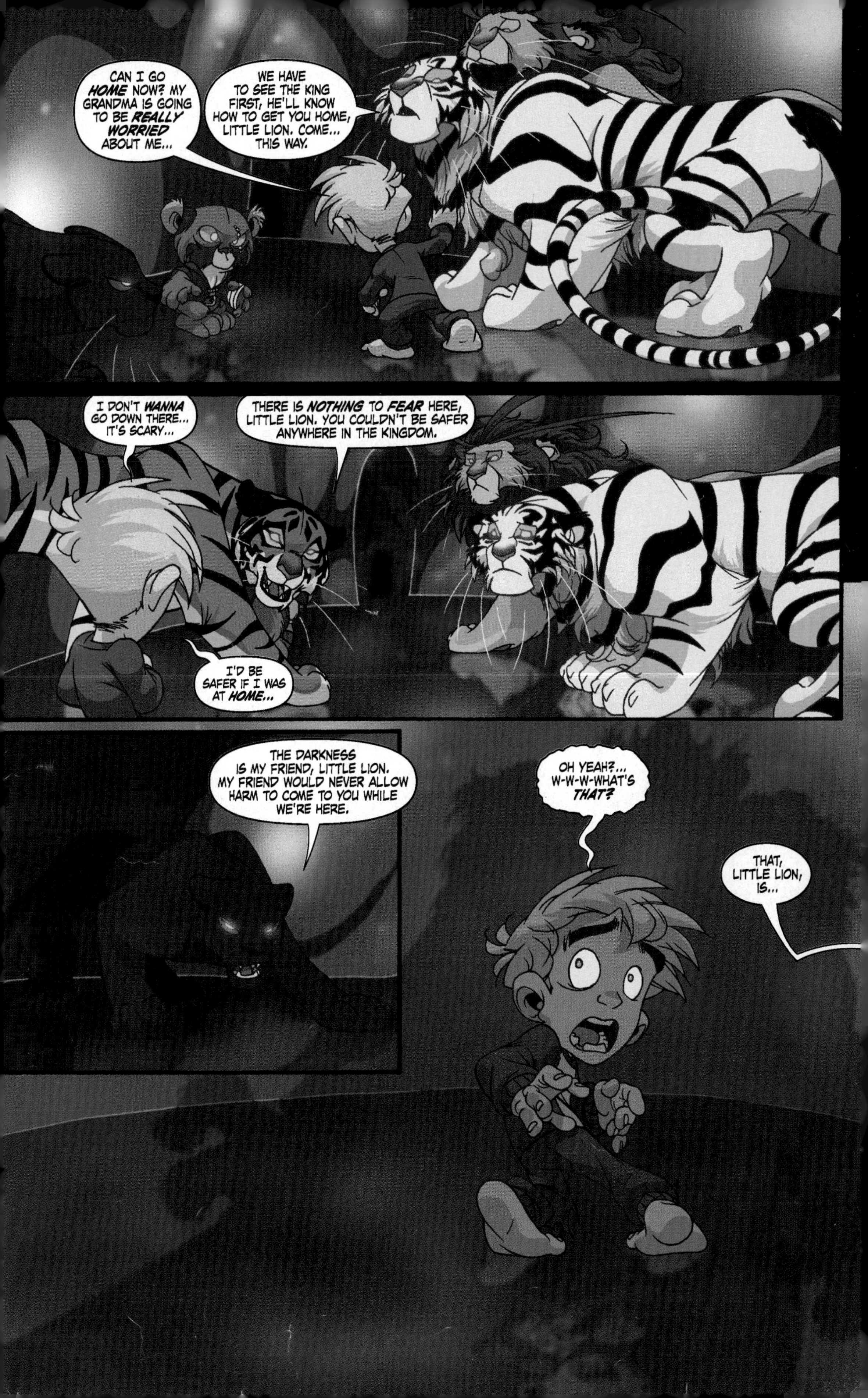
CAN I GO HOME NOW? MY GRANDMA IS GOING TO BE REALLY WORRIED ABOUT ME...
WE HAVE TO SEE THE KING FIRST, HE'LL KNOW HOW TO GET YOU HOME, LITTLE LION. COME... THIS WAY.
I DON'T WANNA GO DOWN THERE... IT'S SCARY...
THERE IS NOTHING TO FEAR HERE, LITTLE LION. YOU COULDN'T BE SAFER ANYWHERE IN THE KINGDOM.
I'D BE SAFER IF I WAS AT HOME...
THE DARKNESS IS MY FRIEND, LITTLE LION. MY FRIEND WOULD NEVER ALLOW HARM TO COME TO YOU WHILE WE'RE HERE.
OH YEAH?... W-W-W-WHAT'S THAT?
THAT, LITTLE LION, IS...

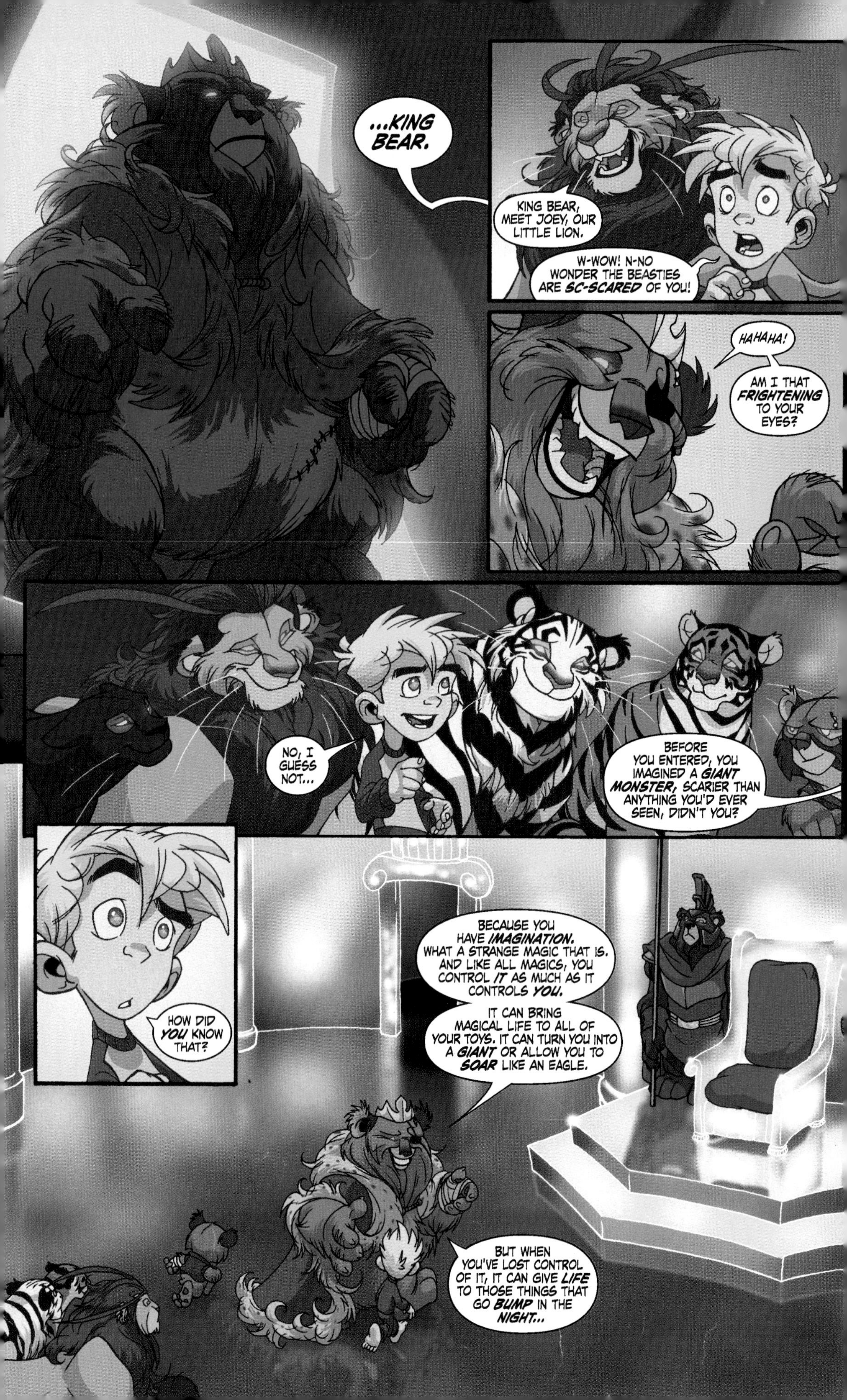
...KING BEAR.
KING BEAR, MEET JOEY, OUR LITTLE LION.
W-WOW! N-NO WONDER THE BEASTIES ARE SC-SCARED OF YOU!
HAHAHA!
AM I THAT FRIGHTENING TO YOUR EYES?
NO, I GUESS NOT...
BEFORE YOU ENTERED, YOU IMAGINED A GIANT MONSTER, SCARIER THAN ANYTHING YOU'D EVER SEEN, DIDN'T YOU?
HOW DID YOU KNOW THAT?
BECAUSE YOU HAVE IMAGINATION. WHAT A STRANGE MAGIC THAT IS. AND LIKE ALL MAGICS, YOU CONTROL IT AS MUCH AS IT CONTROLS YOU.
IT CAN BRING MAGICAL LIFE TO ALL OF YOUR TOYS. IT CAN TURN YOU INTO A GIANT OR ALLOW YOU TO SOAR LIKE AN EAGLE.
BUT WHEN YOU'VE LOST CONTROL OF IT, IT CAN GIVE LIFE TO THOSE THINGS THAT GO BUMP IN THE NIGHT...

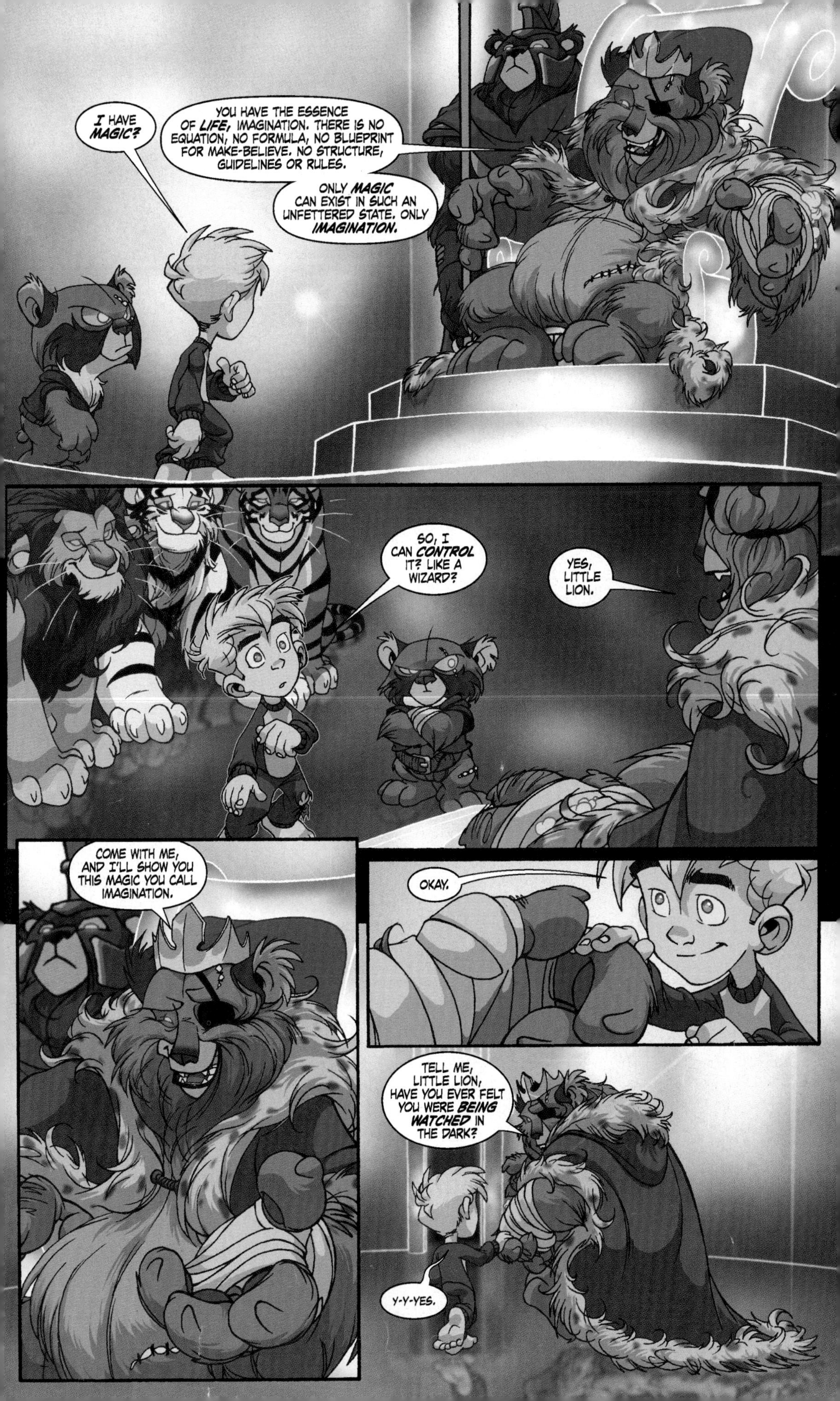

I HAVE MAGIC?
YOU HAVE THE ESSENCE OF LIFE, IMAGINATION. THERE IS NO EQUATION, NO FORMULA, NO BLUEPRINT FOR MAKE-BELIEVE. NO STRUCTURE, GUIDELINES OR RULES.
ONLY MAGIC CAN EXIST IN SUCH AN UNFETTERED STATE. ONLY IMAGINATION.
SO, I CAN CONTROL IT? LIKE A WIZARD?
YES, LITTLE LION.
COME WITH ME, AND I'LL SHOW YOU THIS MAGIC YOU CALL IMAGINATION.
OKAY.
TELL ME, LITTLE LION, HAVE YOU EVER FELT YOU WERE BEING WATCHED IN THE DARK?
Y-Y-YES.

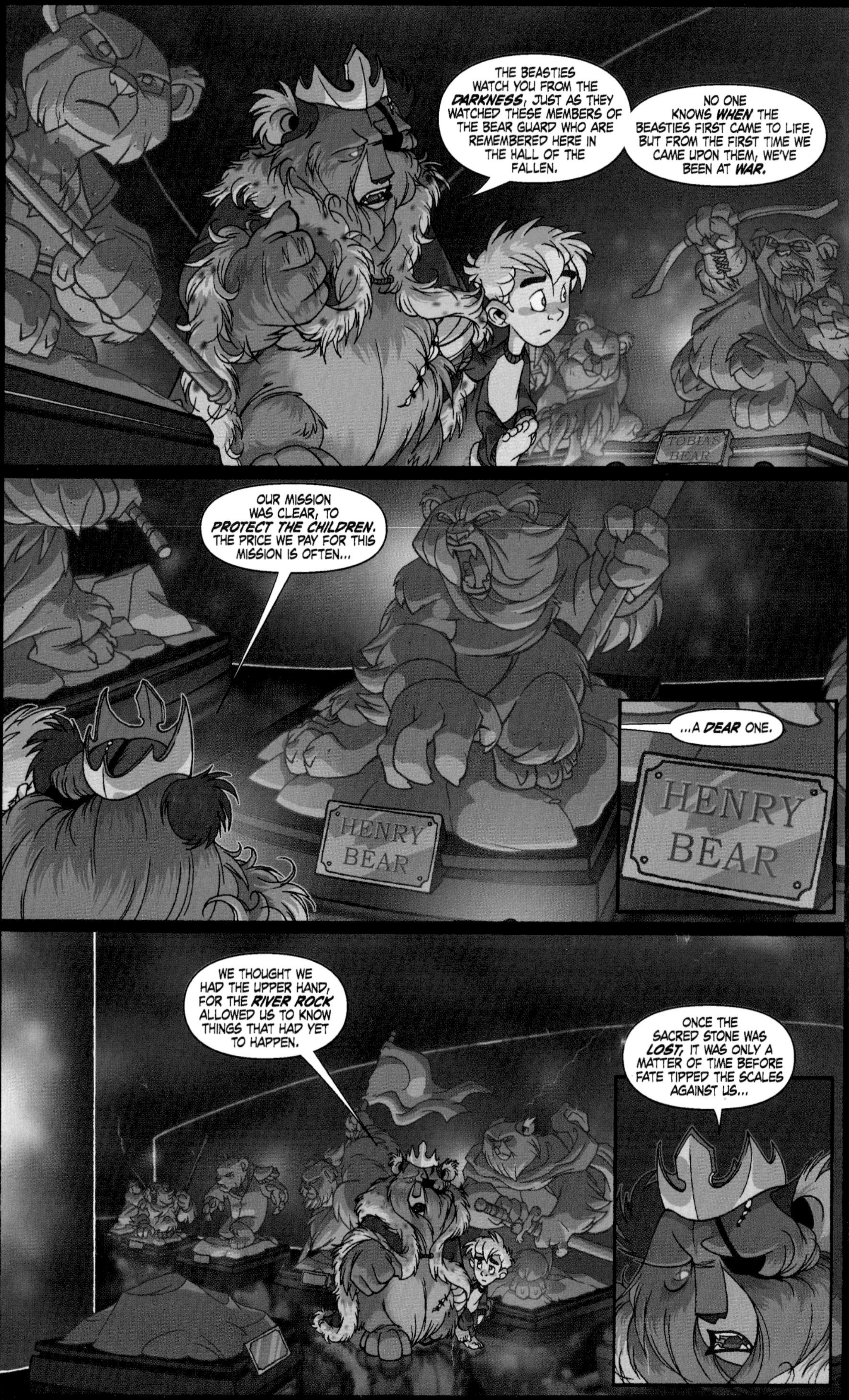

THE BEASTIES WATCH YOU FROM THE DARKNESS, JUST AS THEY WATCHED THESE MEMBERS OF THE BEAR GUARD WHO ARE REMEMBERED HERE IN THE HALL OF THE FALLEN.
NO ONE KNOWS WHEN THE BEASTIES FIRST CAME TO LIFE, BUT FROM THE FIRST TIME WE CAME UPON THEM, WE'VE BEEN AT WAR.
TOBIAS BEAR
OUR MISSION WAS CLEAR, TO PROTECT THE CHILDREN. THE PRICE WE PAY FOR THIS MISSION IS OFTEN...
HENRY BEAR
...A DEAR ONE.
HENRY BEAR
WE THOUGHT WE HAD THE UPPER HAND, FOR THE RIVER ROCK ALLOWED US TO KNOW THINGS THAT HAD YET TO HAPPEN.
ONCE THE SACRED STONE WAS LOST, IT WAS ONLY A MATTER OF TIME BEFORE FATE TIPPED THE SCALES AGAINST US...

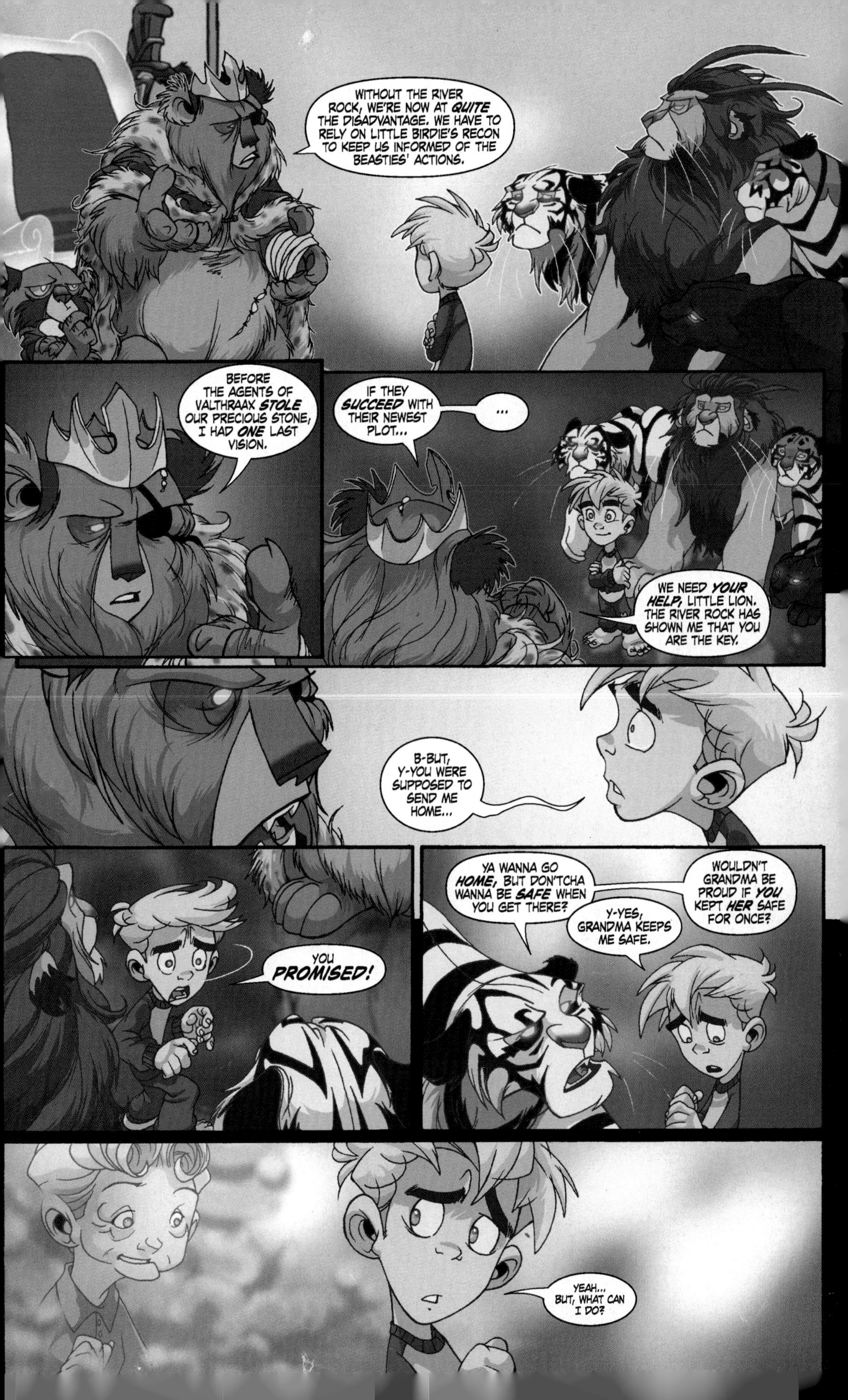
WITHOUT THE RIVER ROCK, WE'RE NOW AT QUITE THE DISADVANTAGE. WE HAVE TO RELY ON LITTLE BIRDIE'S RECON TO KEEP US INFORMED OF THE BEASTIES' ACTIONS.
BEFORE THE AGENTS OF VALTHRAAX STOLE OUR PRECIOUS STONE, I HAD ONE LAST VISION.
IF THEY SUCCEED WITH THEIR NEWEST PLOT...
...
WE NEED YOUR HELP, LITTLE LION. THE RIVER ROCK HAS SHOWN ME THAT YOU ARE THE KEY.
B-BUT, Y-YOU WERE SUPPOSED TO SEND ME HOME...
YOU PROMISED!
YA WANNA GO HOME, BUT DON'TCHA WANNA BE SAFE WHEN YOU GET THERE?
Y-YES, GRANDMA KEEPS ME SAFE.
WOULDN'T GRANDMA BE PROUD IF YOU KEPT HER SAFE FOR ONCE?
YEAH... BUT, WHAT CAN I DO?

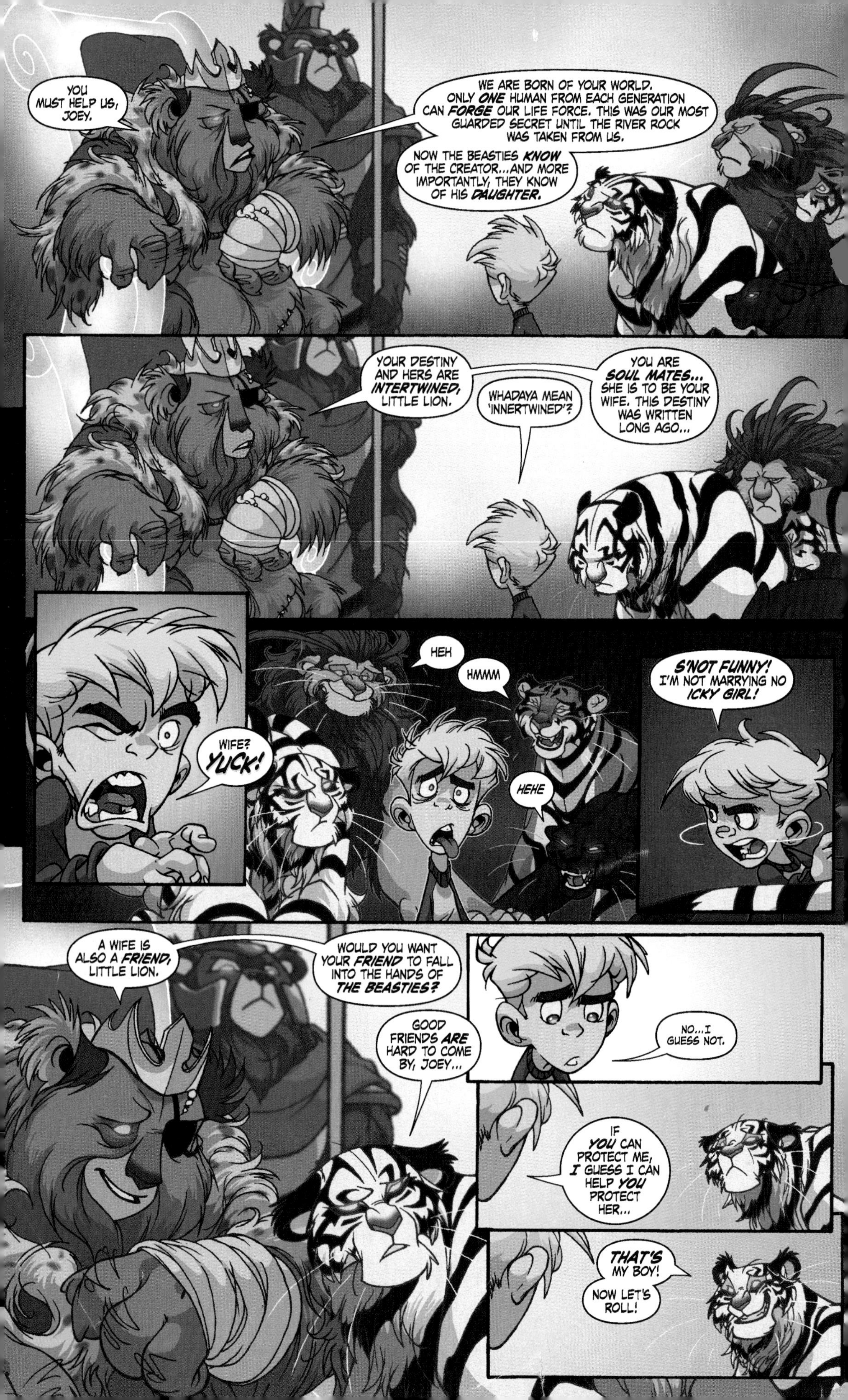
YOU MUST HELP US, JOEY.
WE ARE BORN OF YOUR WORLD. ONLY ONE HUMAN FROM EACH GENERATION CAN FORGE OUR LIFE FORCE. THIS WAS OUR MOST GUARDED SECRET UNTIL THE RIVER ROCK WAS TAKEN FROM US.
NOW THE BEASTIES KNOW OF THE CREATOR...AND MORE IMPORTANTLY, THEY KNOW OF HIS DAUGHTER.
YOUR DESTINY AND HERS ARE INTERTWINED, LITTLE LION.
WHADAYA MEAN 'INNERTWINED'?
YOU ARE SOUL MATES... SHE IS TO BE YOUR WIFE. THIS DESTINY WAS WRITTEN LONG AGO...
WIFE? YUCK!
HEH
HMMM
HEHE
S'NOT FUNNY! I'M NOT MARRYING NO ICKY GIRL!
A WIFE IS ALSO A FRIEND, LITTLE LION.
WOULD YOU WANT YOUR FRIEND TO FALL INTO THE HANDS OF THE BEASTIES?
GOOD FRIENDS ARE HARD TO COME BY, JOEY...
NO...I GUESS NOT.
IF YOU CAN PROTECT ME, I GUESS I CAN HELP YOU PROTECT HER...
THAT'S MY BOY!
NOW LET'S ROLL!

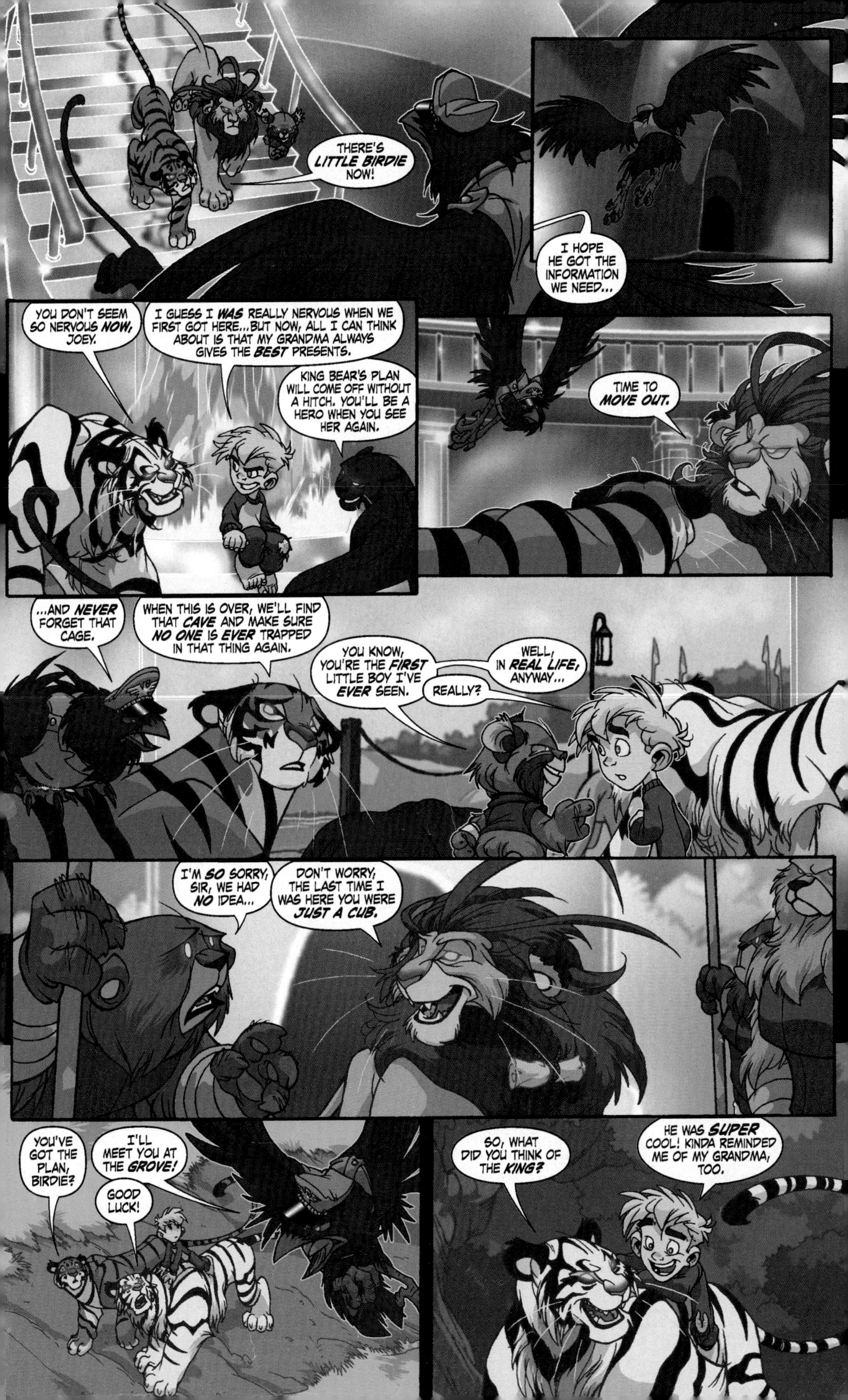
THERE'S LITTLE BIRDIE NOW!
I HOPE HE GOT THE INFORMATION WE NEED...
YOU DON'T SEEM SO NERVOUS NOW, JOEY.
I GUESS I WAS REALLY NERVOUS WHEN WE FIRST GOT HERE...BUT NOW, ALL I CAN THINK ABOUT IS THAT MY GRANDMA ALWAYS GIVES THE BEST PRESENTS.
KING BEAR'S PLAN WILL COME OFF WITHOUT A HITCH. YOU'LL BE A HERO WHEN YOU SEE HER AGAIN.
TIME TO MOVE OUT.
...AND NEVER FORGET THAT CAGE.
WHEN THIS IS OVER, WE'LL FIND THAT CAVE AND MAKE SURE NO ONE IS EVER TRAPPED IN THAT THING AGAIN.
YOU KNOW, YOU'RE THE FIRST LITTLE BOY I'VE EVER SEEN.
WELL, IN REAL LIFE, ANYWAY...
REALLY?
I'M SO SORRY, SIR, WE HAD NO IDEA...
DON'T WORRY; THE LAST TIME I WAS HERE YOU WERE JUST A CUB.
YOU'VE GOT THE PLAN, BIRDIE?
I'LL MEET YOU AT THE GROVE!
GOOD LUCK!
SO, WHAT DID YOU THINK OF THE KING?
HE WAS SUPER COOL! KINDA REMINDED ME OF MY GRANDMA, TOO.

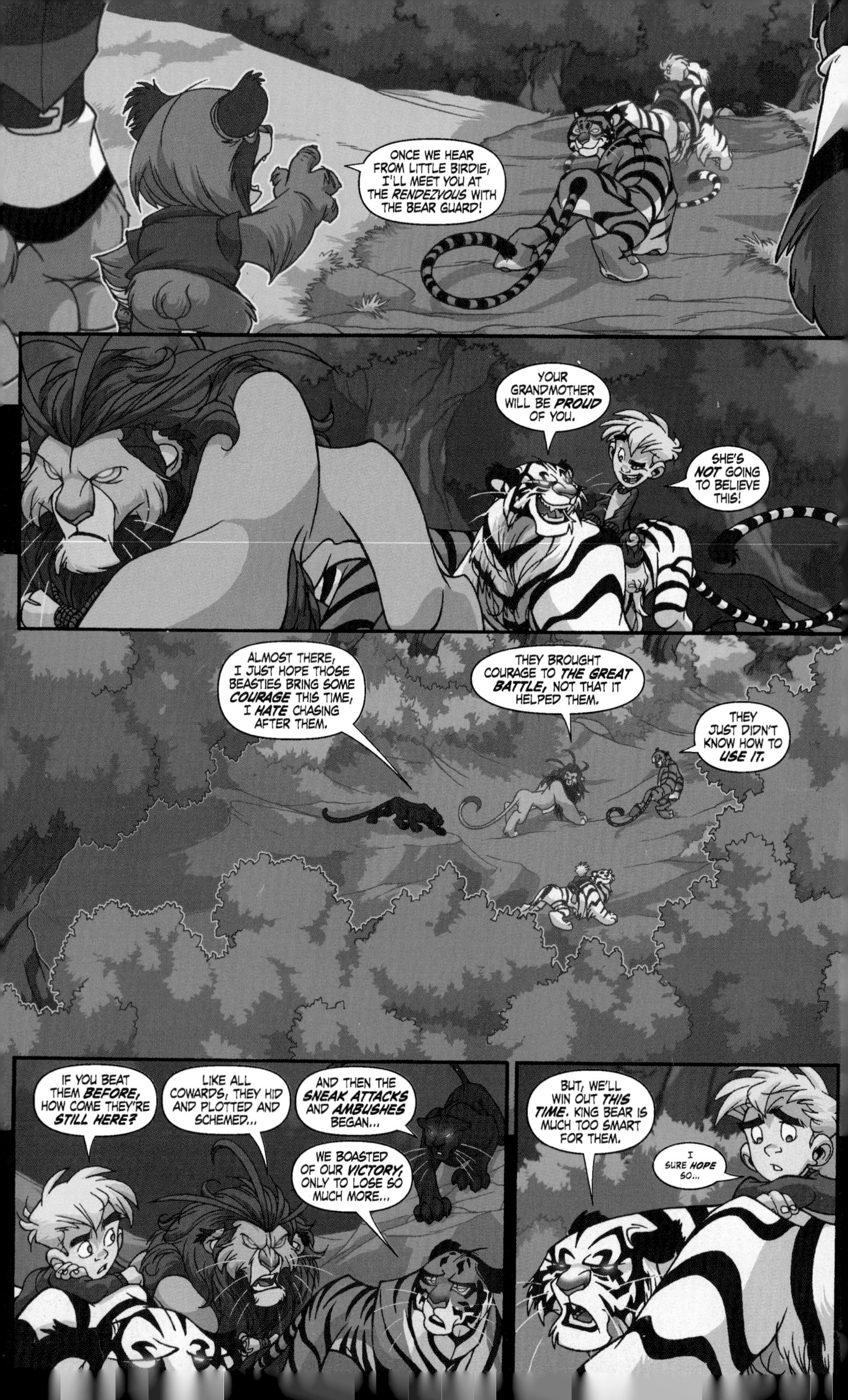
ONCE WE HEAR FROM LITTLE BIRDIE, I'LL MEET YOU AT THE RENDEZVOUS WITH THE BEAR GUARD!
YOUR GRANDMOTHER WILL BE PROUD OF YOU.
SHE'S NOT GOING TO BELIEVE THIS!
ALMOST THERE, I JUST HOPE THOSE BEASTIES BRING SOME COURAGE THIS TIME, I HATE CHASING AFTER THEM.
THEY BROUGHT COURAGE TO THE GREAT BATTLE, NOT THAT IT HELPED THEM.
THEY JUST DIDN'T KNOW HOW TO USE IT.
IF YOU BEAT THEM BEFORE, HOW COME THEY'RE STILL HERE?
LIKE ALL COWARDS, THEY HID AND PLOTTED AND SCHEMED...
AND THEN THE SNEAK ATTACKS AND AMBUSHES BEGAN...
WE BOASTED OF OUR VICTORY, ONLY TO LOSE SO MUCH MORE...
BUT, WE'LL WIN OUT THIS TIME. KING BEAR IS MUCH TOO SMART FOR THEM.
I SURE HOPE SO...

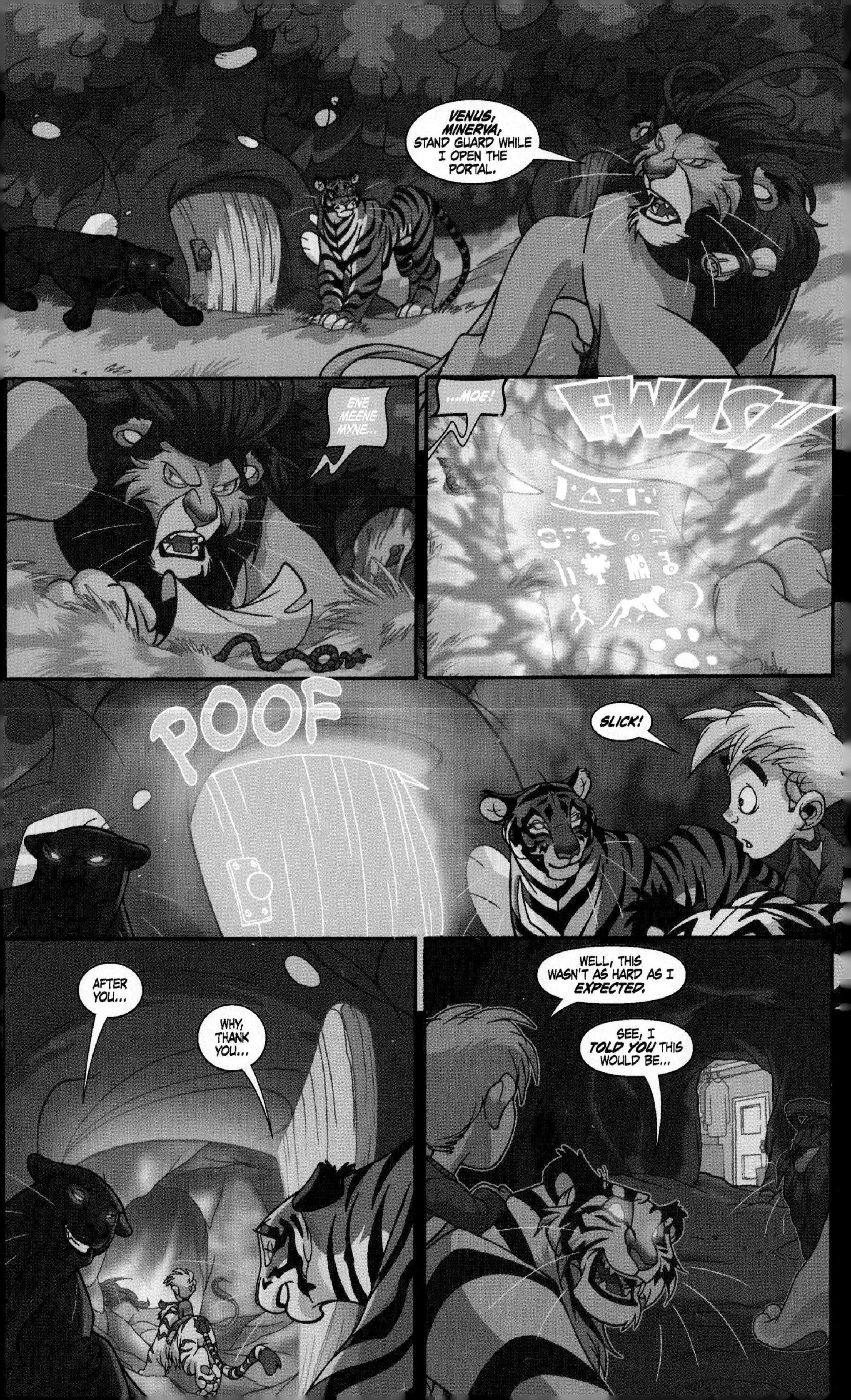
VENUS, MINERVA, STAND GUARD WHILE I OPEN THE PORTAL.
ENE MEENE MYNE...
...MOE!
FWASH
POOF
SLICK!
AFTER YOU...
WHY, THANK YOU...
WELL, THIS WASN'T AS HARD AS I EXPECTED.
SEE, I TOLD YOU THIS WOULD BE...

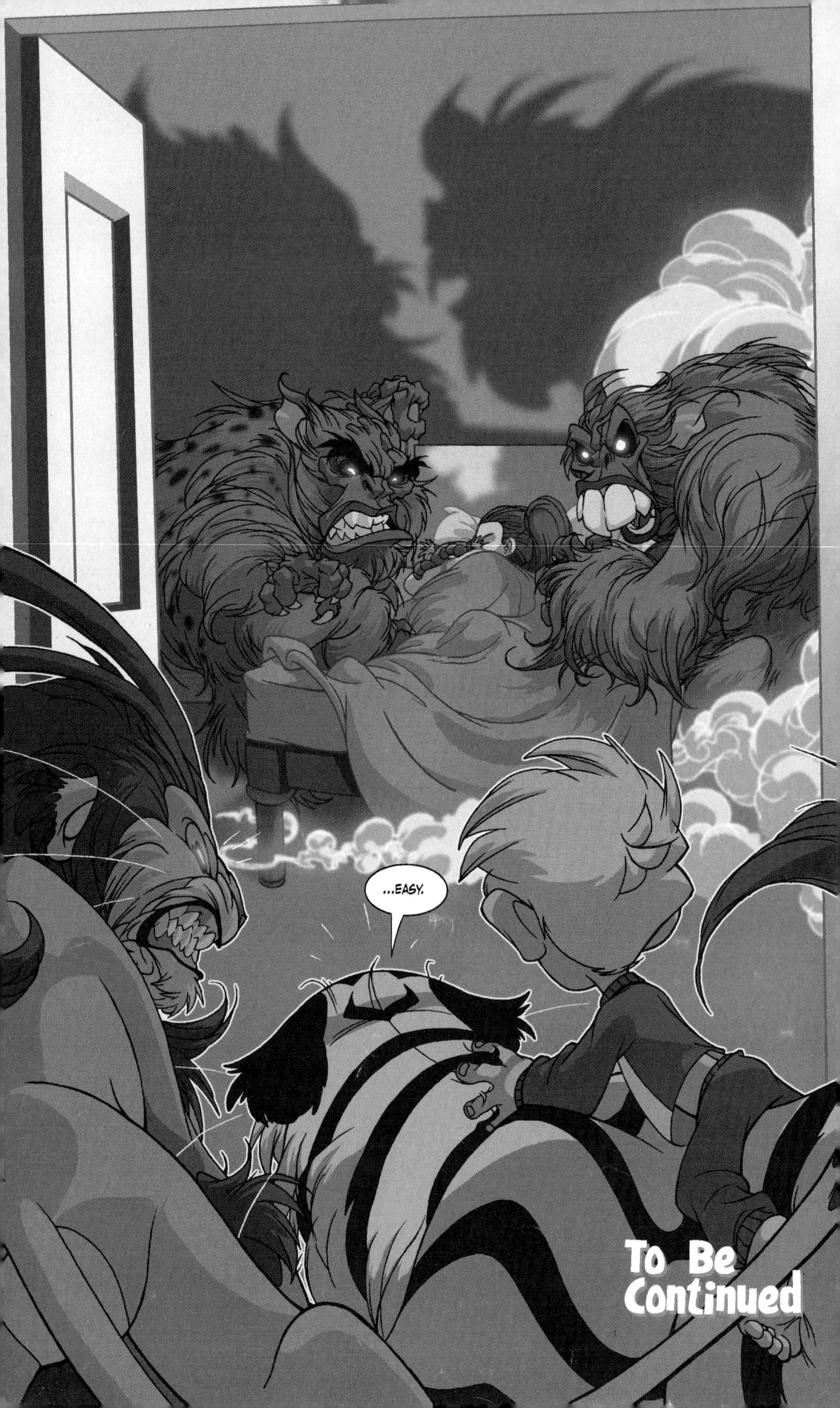

...EASY.
To Be Continued

Chapter three

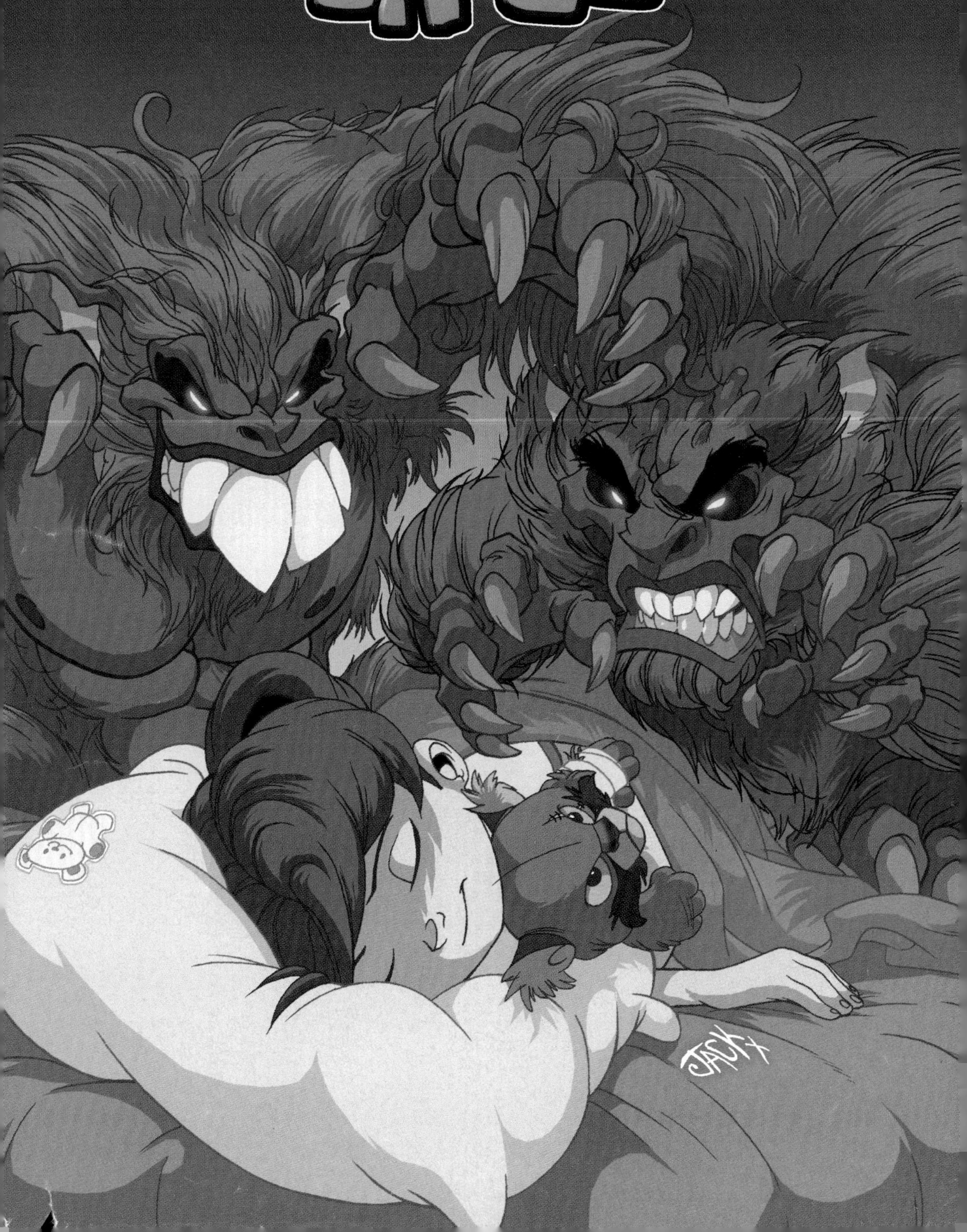
JACK

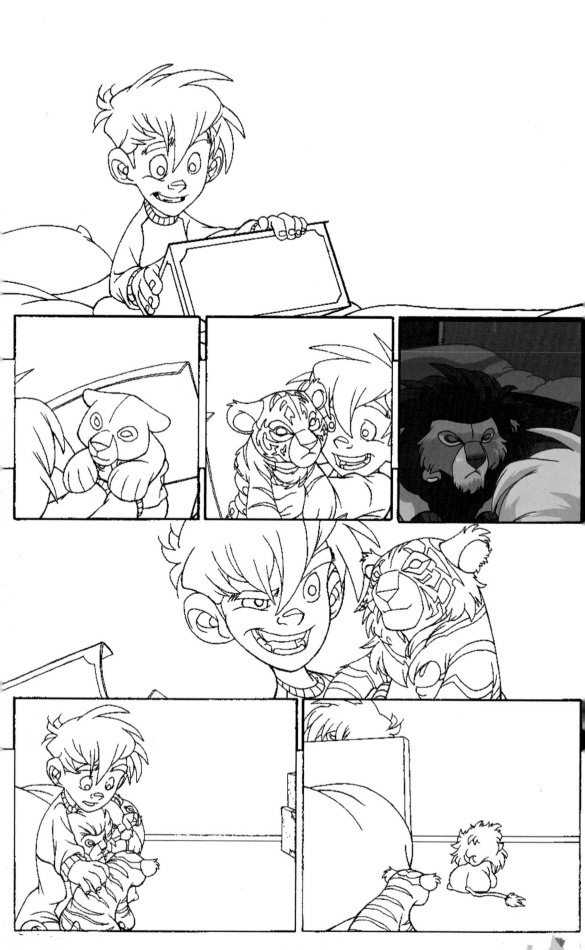

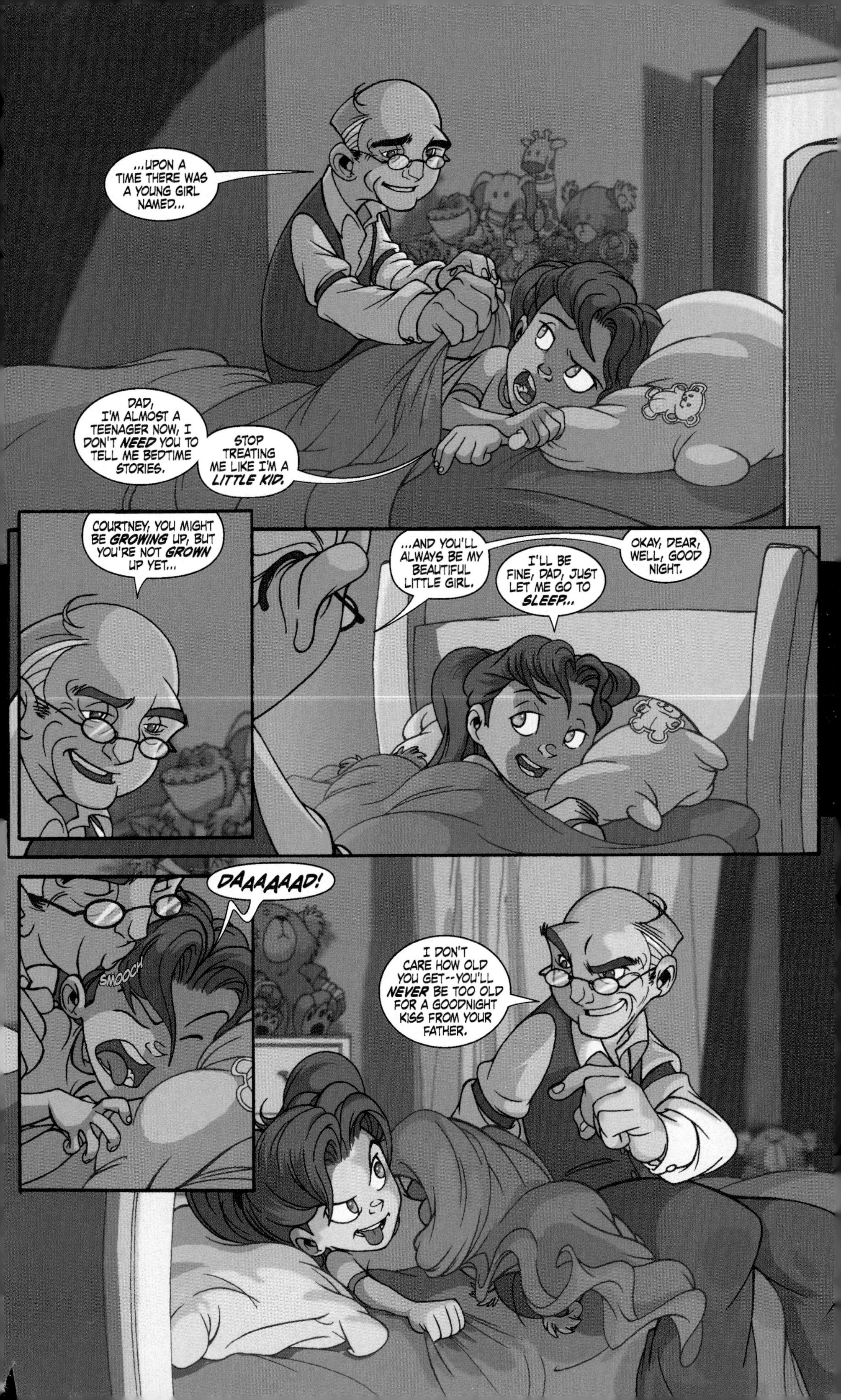
...UPON A TIME THERE WAS A YOUNG GIRL NAMED...
DAD, I'M ALMOST A TEENAGER NOW, I DON'T *NEED* YOU TO TELL ME BEDTIME STORIES.
STOP TREATING ME LIKE I'M A *LITTLE KID.*
COURTNEY, YOU MIGHT BE *GROWING* UP, BUT YOU'RE NOT *GROWN* UP YET...
...AND YOU'LL ALWAYS BE MY BEAUTIFUL LITTLE GIRL.
I'LL BE FINE, DAD, JUST LET ME GO TO *SLEEP...*
OKAY, DEAR, WELL, GOOD NIGHT.
SMOOCH
DAAAAAAD!
I DON'T CARE HOW OLD YOU GET--YOU'LL *NEVER* BE TOO OLD FOR A GOODNIGHT KISS FROM YOUR FATHER.

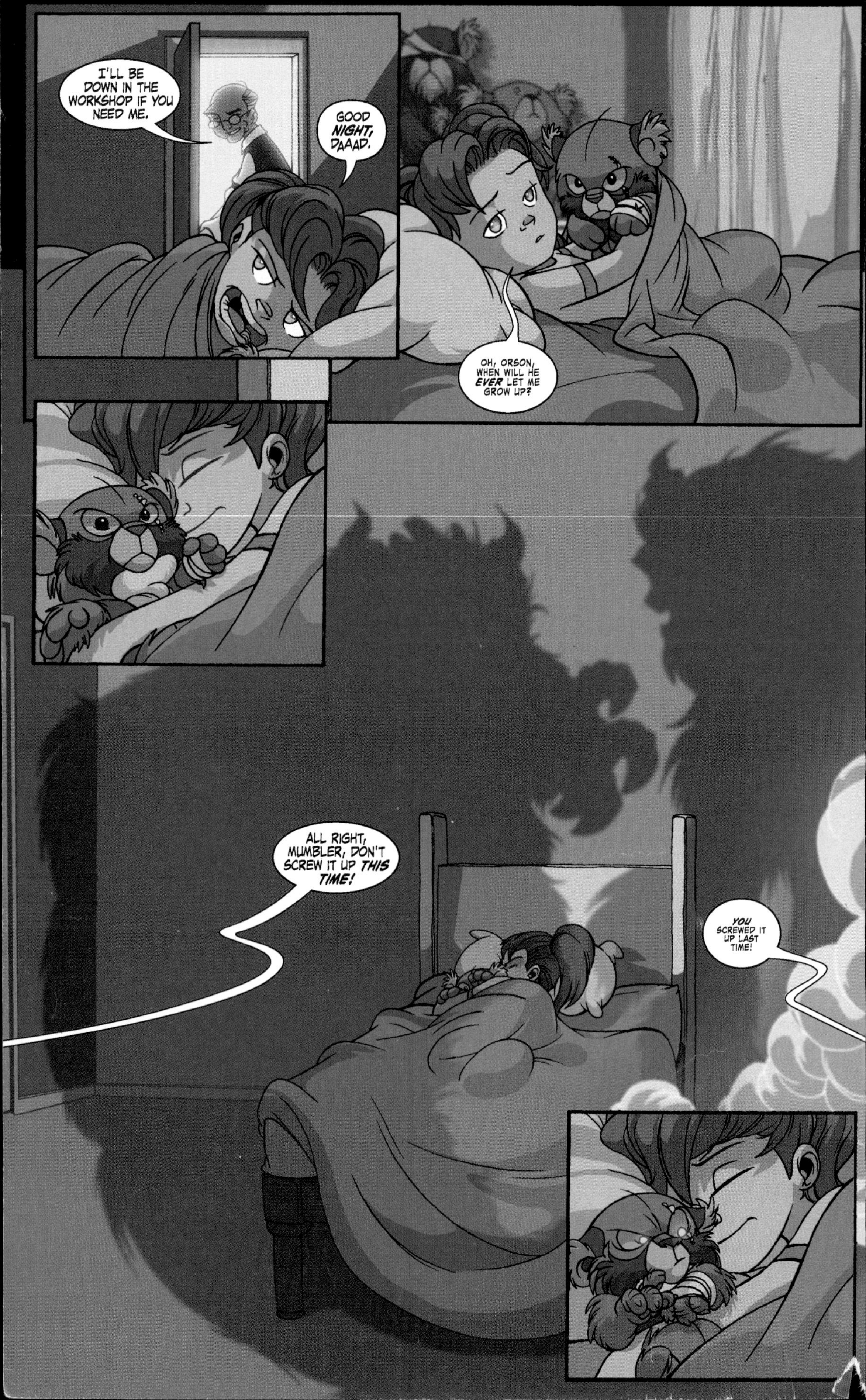

I'LL BE DOWN IN THE WORKSHOP IF YOU NEED ME.
GOOD NIGHT, DAAAD.
OH, ORSON, WHEN WILL HE EVER LET ME GROW UP?
ALL RIGHT, MUMBLER, DON'T SCREW IT UP THIS TIME!
YOU SCREWED IT UP LAST TIME!

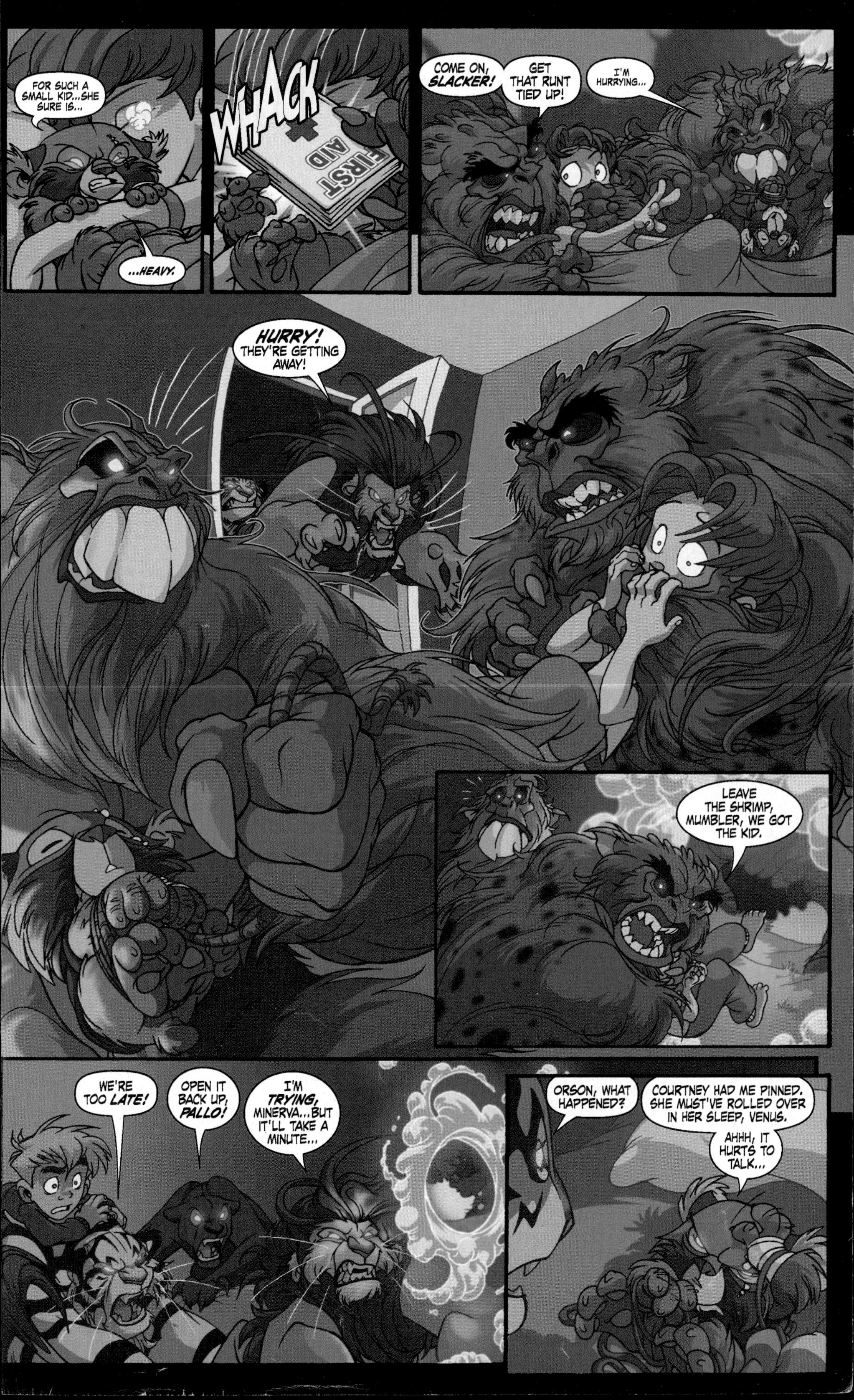
FOR SUCH A SMALL KID...SHE SURE IS...
...HEAVY.
WHACK
FIRST AID
COME ON, SLACKER!
GET THAT RUNT TIED UP!
I'M HURRYING...
HURRY! THEY'RE GETTING AWAY!
LEAVE THE SHRIMP, MUMBLER, WE GOT THE KID.
WE'RE TOO LATE!
OPEN IT BACK UP, PALLO!
I'M TRYING, MINERVA...BUT IT'LL TAKE A MINUTE...
ORSON, WHAT HAPPENED?
COURTNEY HAD ME PINNED. SHE MUST'VE ROLLED OVER IN HER SLEEP, VENUS.
AHHH, IT HURTS TO TALK...

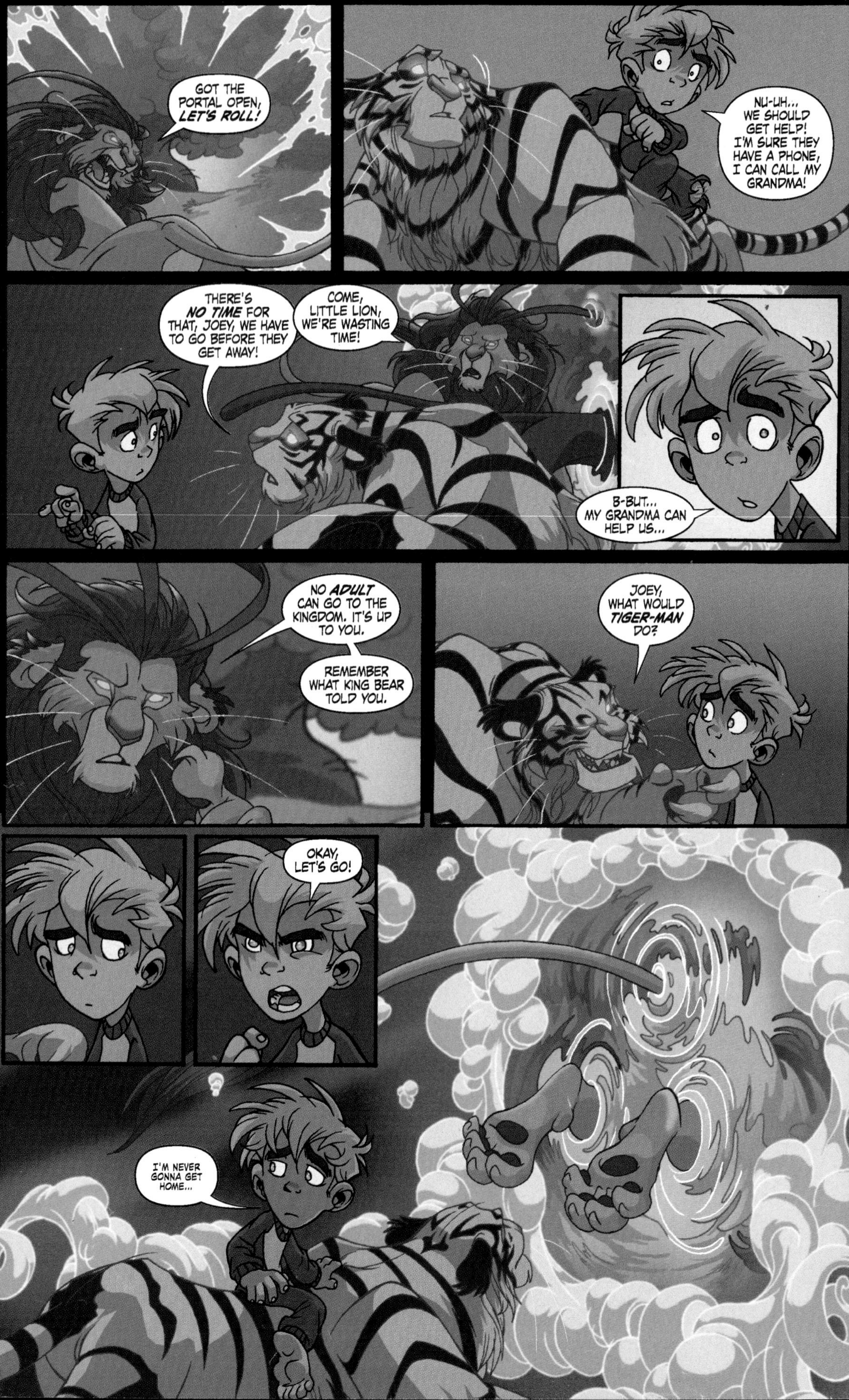
GOT THE PORTAL OPEN, LET'S ROLL!
NU-UH... WE SHOULD GET HELP! I'M SURE THEY HAVE A PHONE, I CAN CALL MY GRANDMA!
THERE'S NO TIME FOR THAT, JOEY, WE HAVE TO GO BEFORE THEY GET AWAY!
COME, LITTLE LION, WE'RE WASTING TIME!
B-BUT... MY GRANDMA CAN HELP US...
NO ADULT CAN GO TO THE KINGDOM. IT'S UP TO YOU.
REMEMBER WHAT KING BEAR TOLD YOU.
JOEY, WHAT WOULD TIGER-MAN DO?
OKAY, LET'S GO!
I'M NEVER GONNA GET HOME...

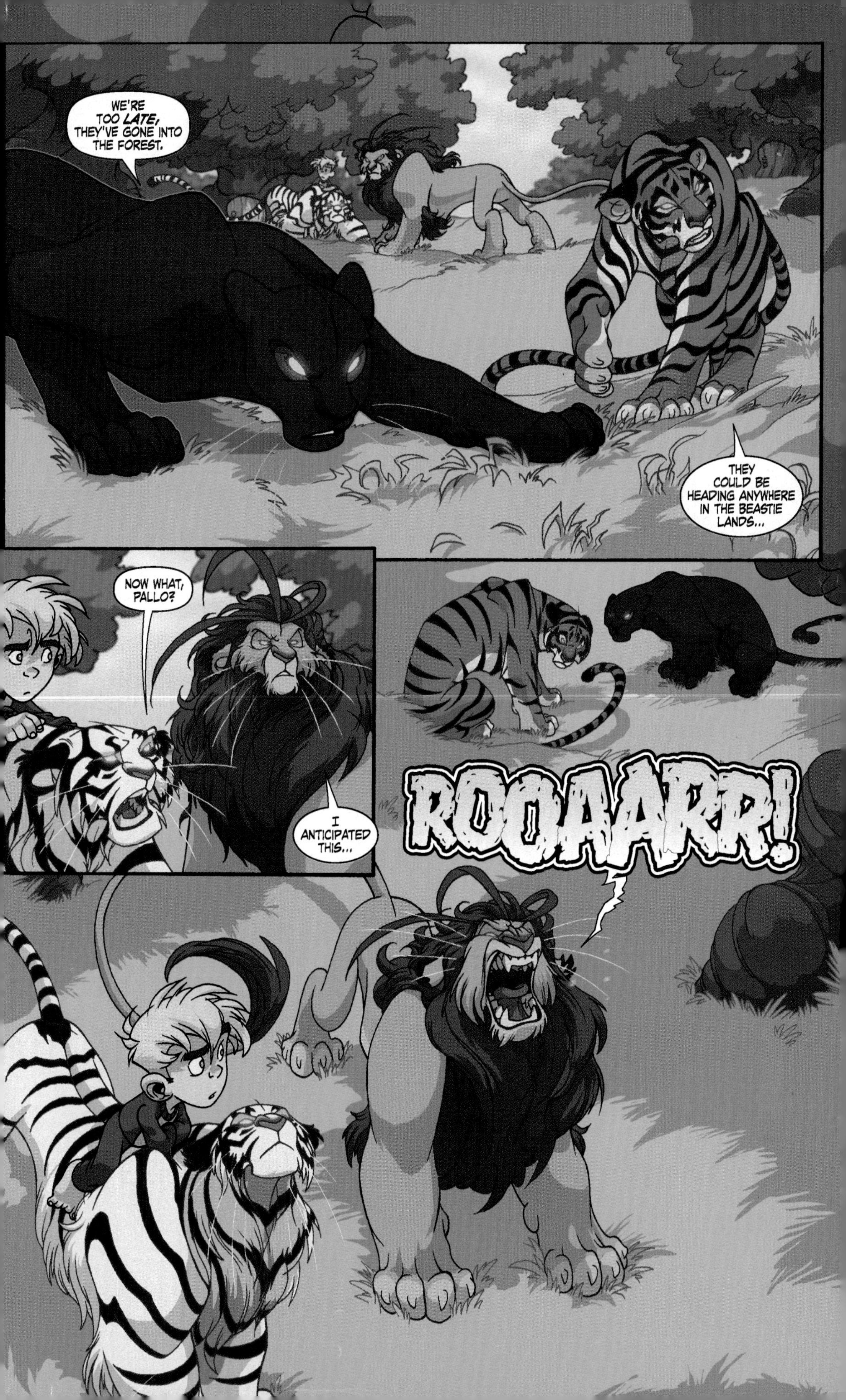
WE'RE TOO *LATE*, THEY'VE GONE INTO THE FOREST.
THEY COULD BE HEADING ANYWHERE IN THE BEASTIE LANDS...
NOW WHAT, PALLO?
I ANTICIPATED THIS...
ROOAARR!

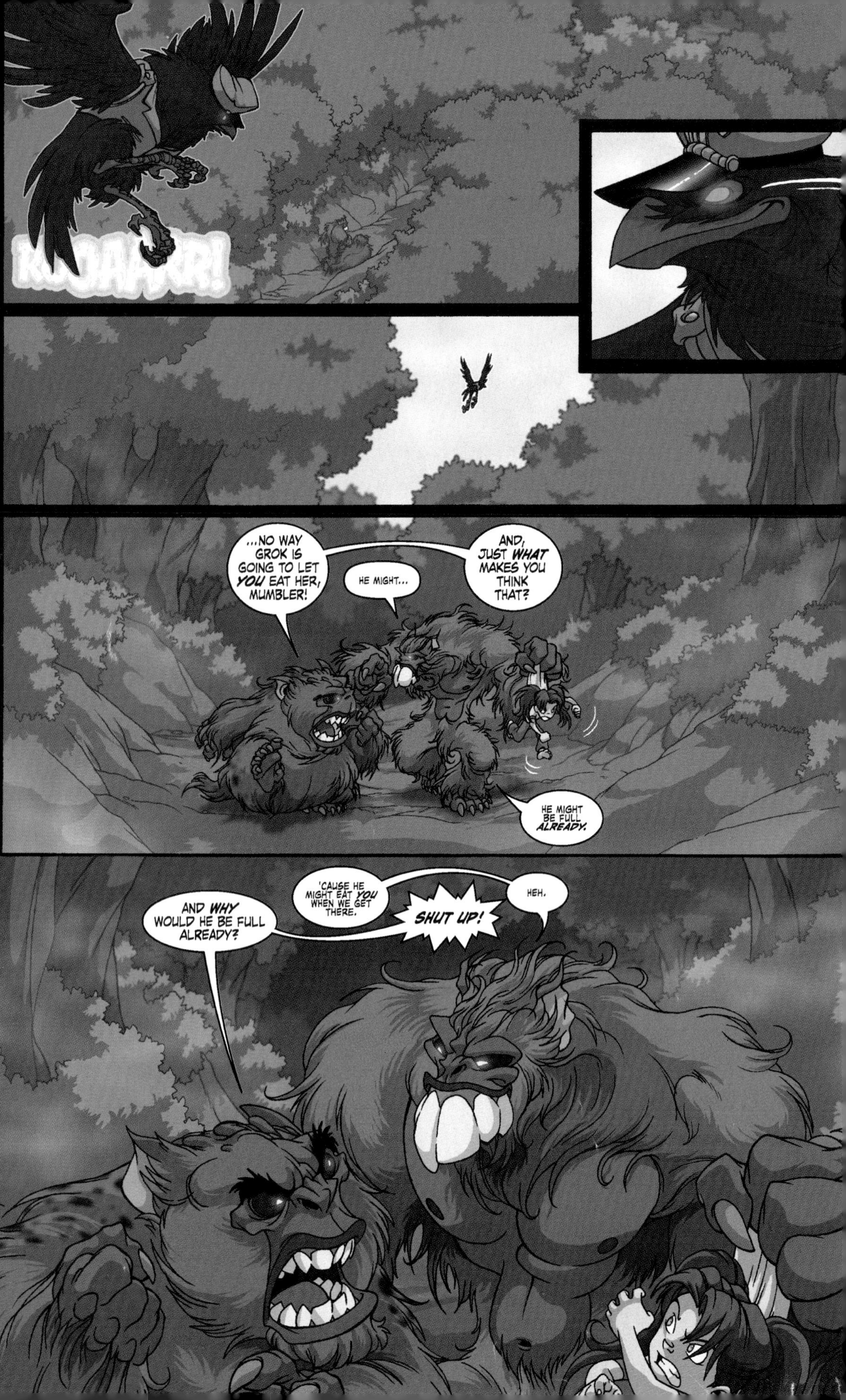

...NO WAY GROK IS GOING TO LET *YOU* EAT HER, MUMBLER!
HE MIGHT...
AND, JUST *WHAT* MAKES YOU THINK THAT?
HE MIGHT BE FULL *ALREADY.*
AND *WHY* WOULD HE BE FULL ALREADY?
'CAUSE HE MIGHT EAT *YOU* WHEN WE GET THERE.
SHUT UP!
HEH.

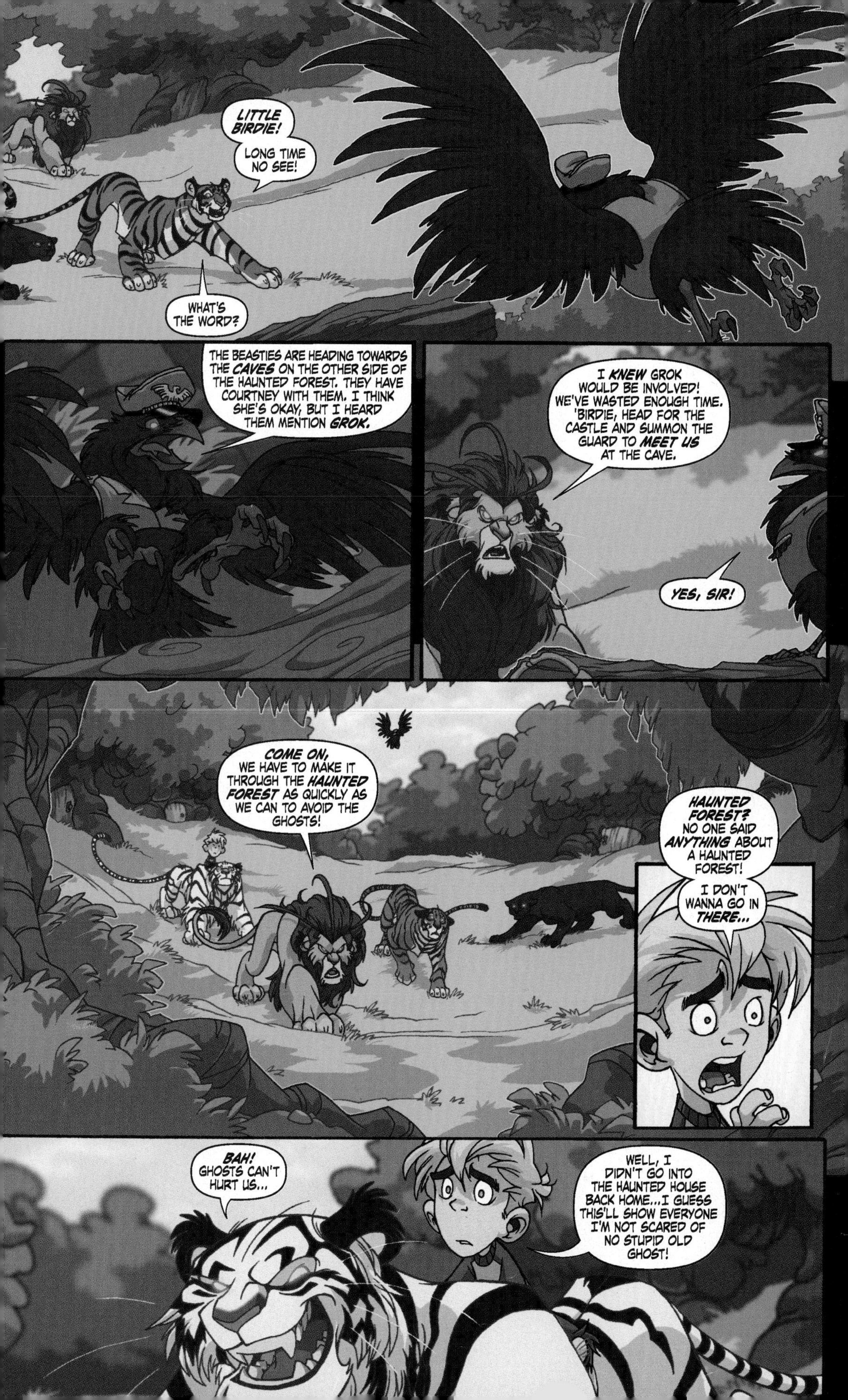
LITTLE BIRDIE!
LONG TIME NO SEE!
WHAT'S THE WORD?
THE BEASTIES ARE HEADING TOWARDS THE CAVES ON THE OTHER SIDE OF THE HAUNTED FOREST. THEY HAVE COURTNEY WITH THEM. I THINK SHE'S OKAY, BUT I HEARD THEM MENTION GROK.
I KNEW GROK WOULD BE INVOLVED! WE'VE WASTED ENOUGH TIME. 'BIRDIE, HEAD FOR THE CASTLE AND SUMMON THE GUARD TO MEET US AT THE CAVE.
YES, SIR!
COME ON, WE HAVE TO MAKE IT THROUGH THE HAUNTED FOREST AS QUICKLY AS WE CAN TO AVOID THE GHOSTS!
HAUNTED FOREST? NO ONE SAID ANYTHING ABOUT A HAUNTED FOREST!
I DON'T WANNA GO IN THERE...
BAH! GHOSTS CAN'T HURT US...
WELL, I DIDN'T GO INTO THE HAUNTED HOUSE BACK HOME...I GUESS THIS'LL SHOW EVERYONE I'M NOT SCARED OF NO STUPID OLD GHOST!

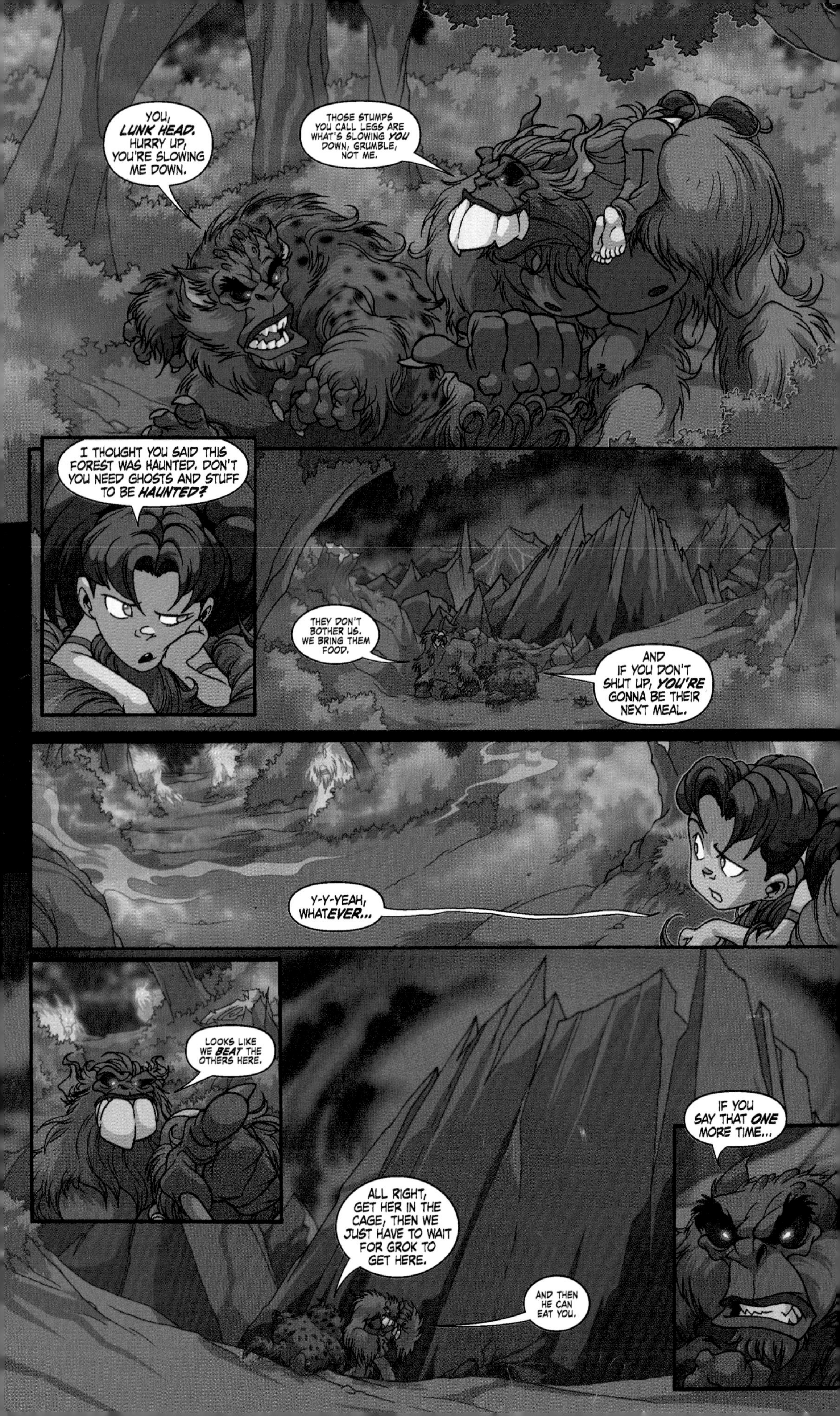
YOU, LUNK HEAD. HURRY UP, YOU'RE SLOWING ME DOWN.
THOSE STUMPS YOU CALL LEGS ARE WHAT'S SLOWING YOU DOWN, GRUMBLE, NOT ME.
I THOUGHT YOU SAID THIS FOREST WAS HAUNTED. DON'T YOU NEED GHOSTS AND STUFF TO BE HAUNTED?
THEY DON'T BOTHER US. WE BRING THEM FOOD.
AND IF YOU DON'T SHUT UP, YOU'RE GONNA BE THEIR NEXT MEAL.
Y-Y-YEAH, WHATEVER...
LOOKS LIKE WE BEAT THE OTHERS HERE.
IF YOU SAY THAT ONE MORE TIME...
ALL RIGHT, GET HER IN THE CAGE, THEN WE JUST HAVE TO WAIT FOR GROK TO GET HERE.
AND THEN HE CAN EAT YOU.

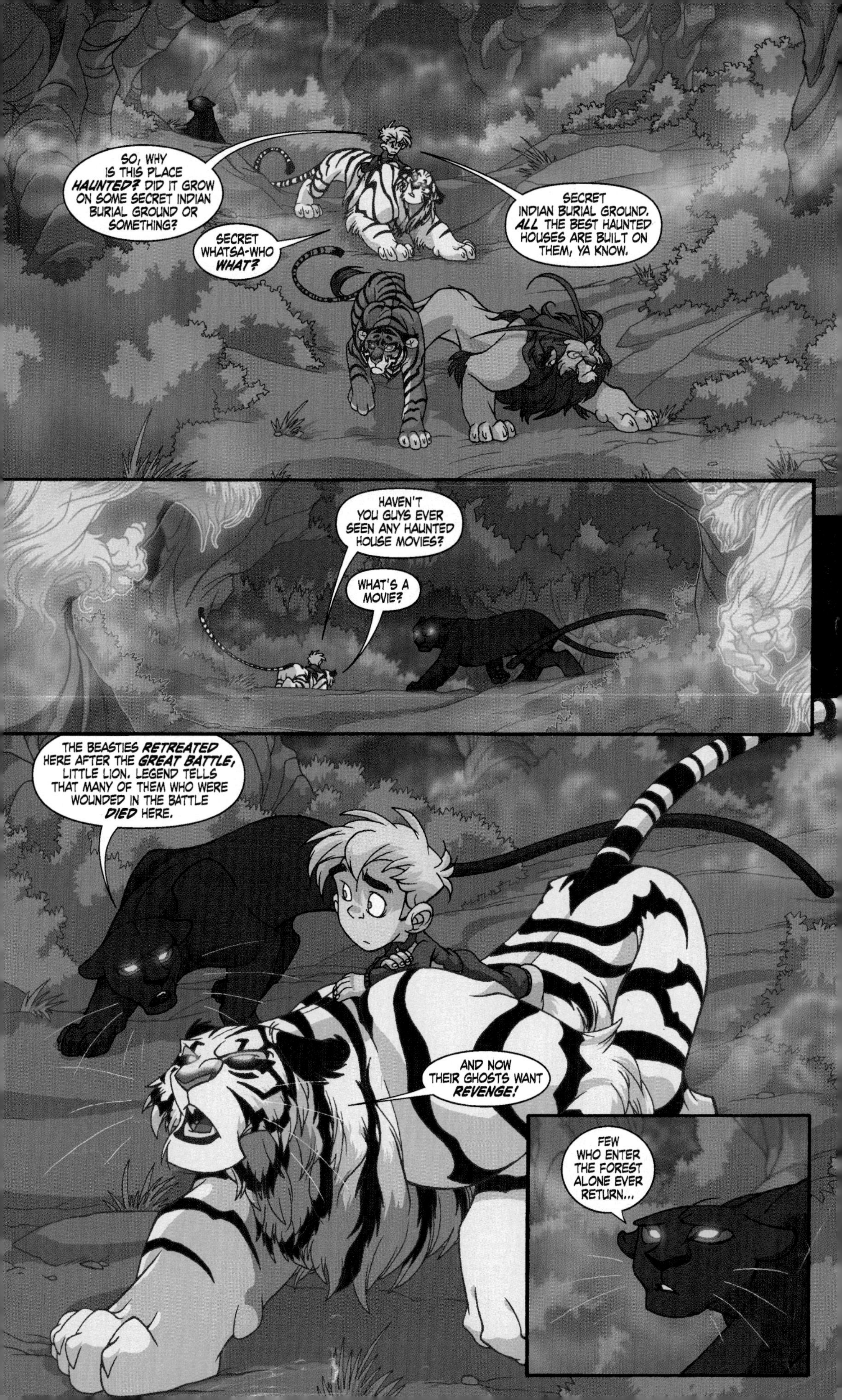
SO, WHY IS THIS PLACE HAUNTED? DID IT GROW ON SOME SECRET INDIAN BURIAL GROUND OR SOMETHING?
SECRET WHATSA-WHO WHAT?
SECRET INDIAN BURIAL GROUND. ALL THE BEST HAUNTED HOUSES ARE BUILT ON THEM, YA KNOW.
HAVEN'T YOU GUYS EVER SEEN ANY HAUNTED HOUSE MOVIES?
WHAT'S A MOVIE?
THE BEASTIES RETREATED HERE AFTER THE GREAT BATTLE, LITTLE LION. LEGEND TELLS THAT MANY OF THEM WHO WERE WOUNDED IN THE BATTLE DIED HERE.
AND NOW THEIR GHOSTS WANT REVENGE!
FEW WHO ENTER THE FOREST ALONE EVER RETURN...

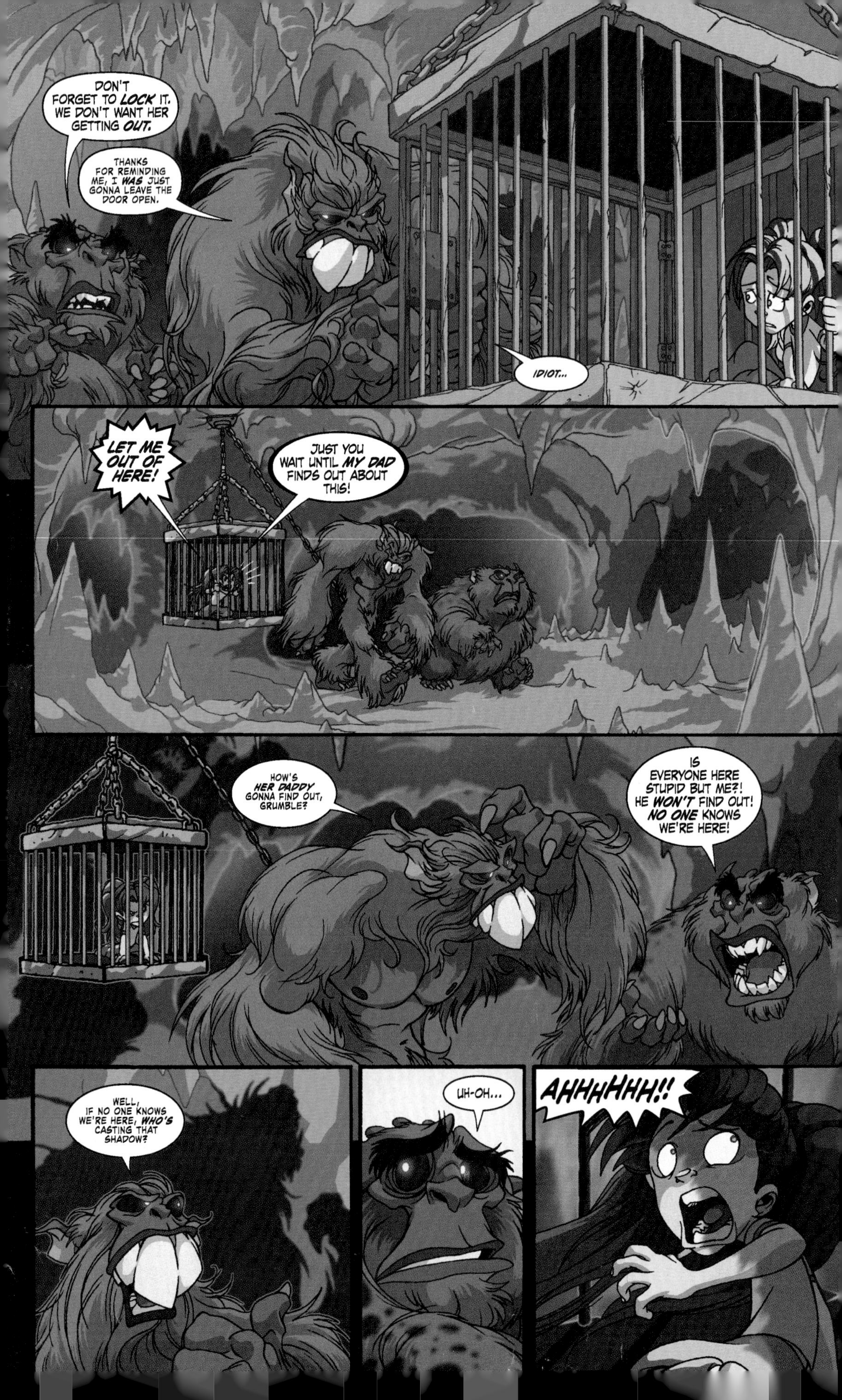
DON'T FORGET TO LOCK IT. WE DON'T WANT HER GETTING OUT.
THANKS FOR REMINDING ME, I WAS JUST GONNA LEAVE THE DOOR OPEN.
IDIOT...
LET ME OUT OF HERE!
JUST YOU WAIT UNTIL MY DAD FINDS OUT ABOUT THIS!
HOW'S HER DADDY GONNA FIND OUT, GRUMBLE?
IS EVERYONE HERE STUPID BUT ME?! HE WON'T FIND OUT! NO ONE KNOWS WE'RE HERE!
WELL, IF NO ONE KNOWS WE'RE HERE, WHO'S CASTING THAT SHADOW?
UH-OH...
AHHHHHH!!

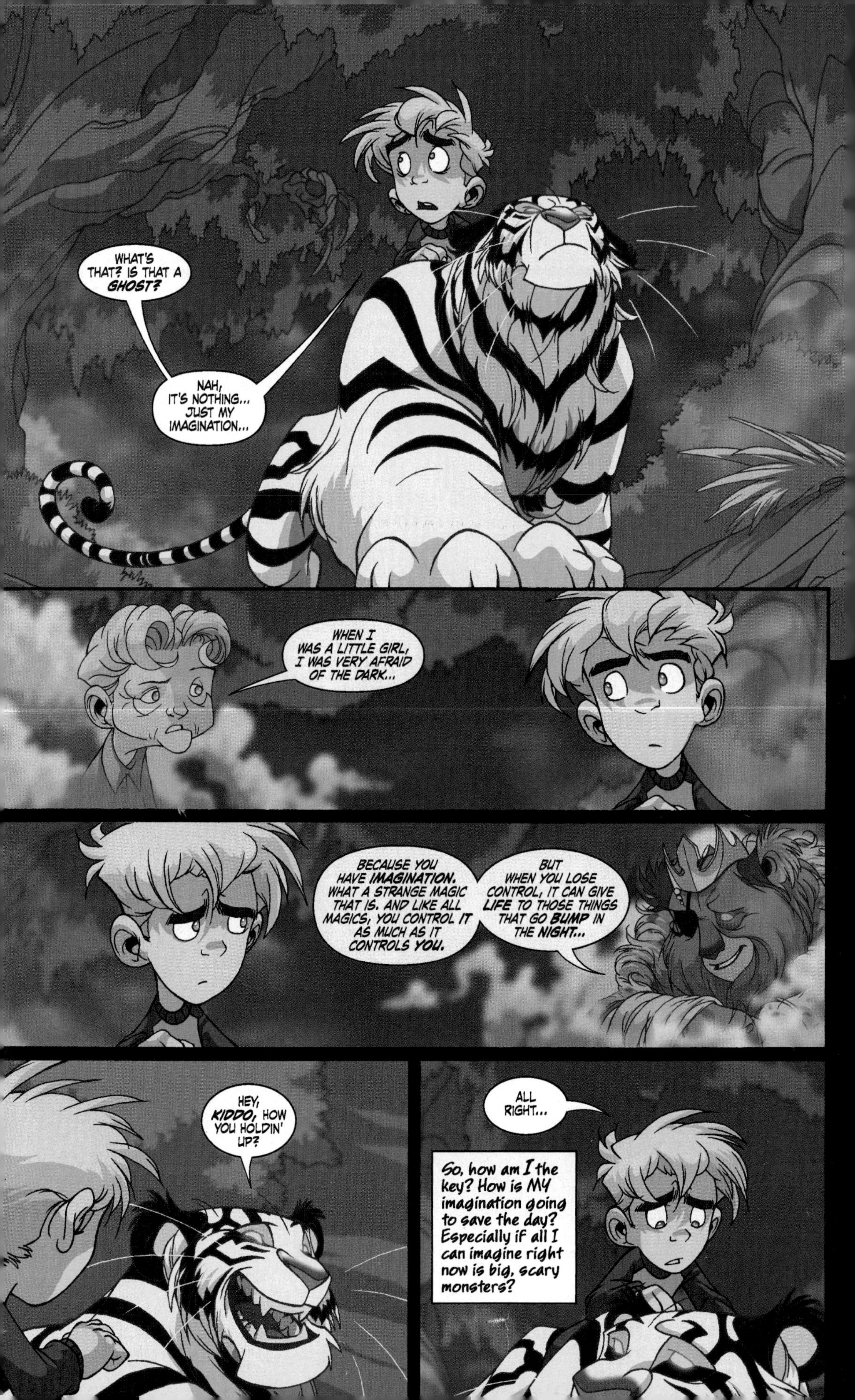
WHAT'S THAT? IS THAT A GHOST?
NAH, IT'S NOTHING... JUST MY IMAGINATION...
WHEN I WAS A LITTLE GIRL, I WAS VERY AFRAID OF THE DARK...
BECAUSE YOU HAVE IMAGINATION. WHAT A STRANGE MAGIC THAT IS. AND LIKE ALL MAGICS, YOU CONTROL IT AS MUCH AS IT CONTROLS YOU.
BUT WHEN YOU LOSE CONTROL, IT CAN GIVE LIFE TO THOSE THINGS THAT GO BUMP IN THE NIGHT...
HEY, KIDDO, HOW YOU HOLDIN' UP?
ALL RIGHT...
So, how am I the key? How is MY imagination going to save the day? Especially if all I can imagine right now is big, scary monsters?

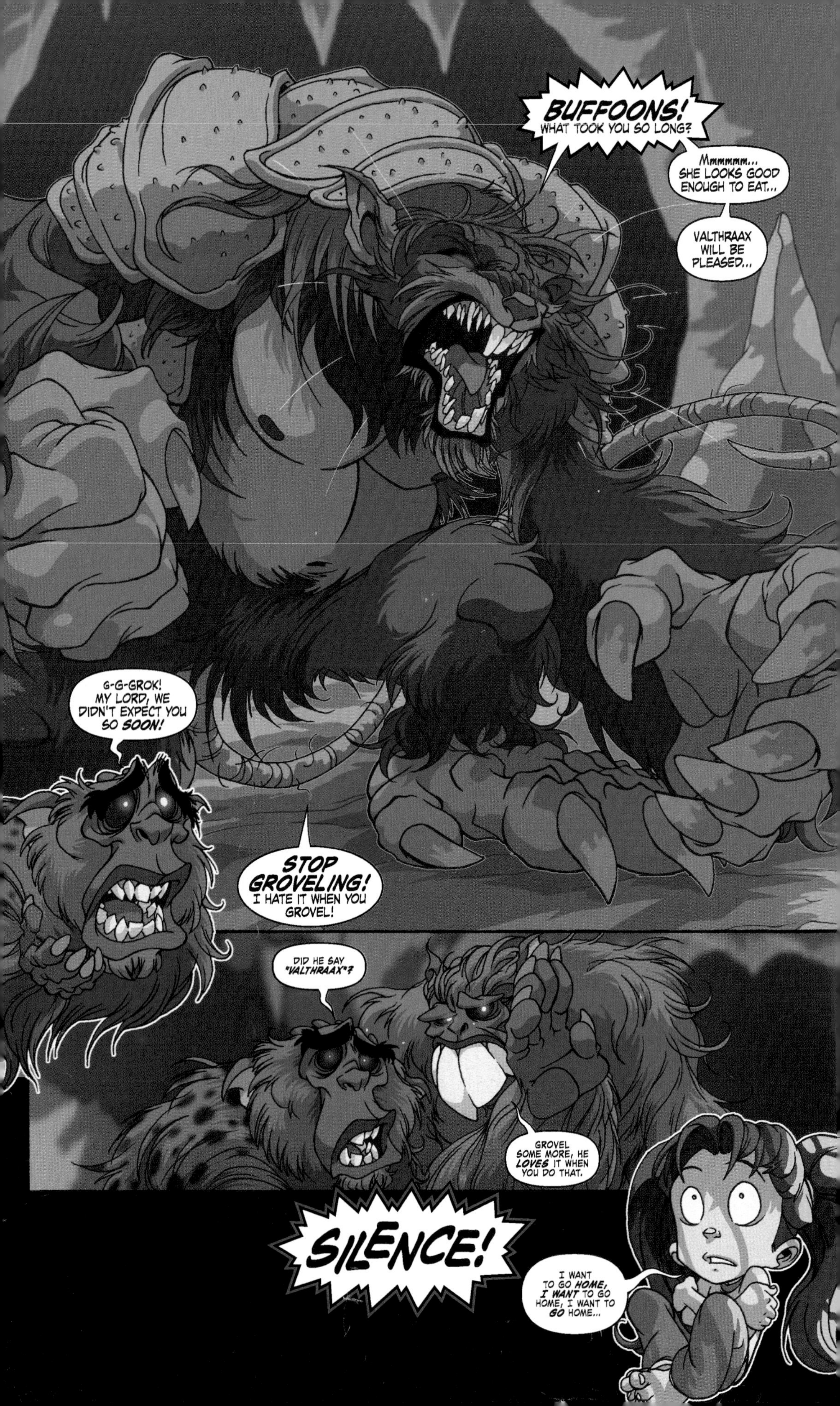
BUFFOONS! WHAT TOOK YOU SO LONG?
Mmmmmm... SHE LOOKS GOOD ENOUGH TO EAT...
VALTHRAAX WILL BE PLEASED...
G-G-GROK! MY LORD, WE DIDN'T EXPECT YOU SO SOON!
STOP GROVELING! I HATE IT WHEN YOU GROVEL!
DID HE SAY "VALTHRAAX"?
GROVEL SOME MORE, HE LOVES IT WHEN YOU DO THAT.
SILENCE!
I WANT TO GO HOME, I WANT TO GO HOME, I WANT TO GO HOME...

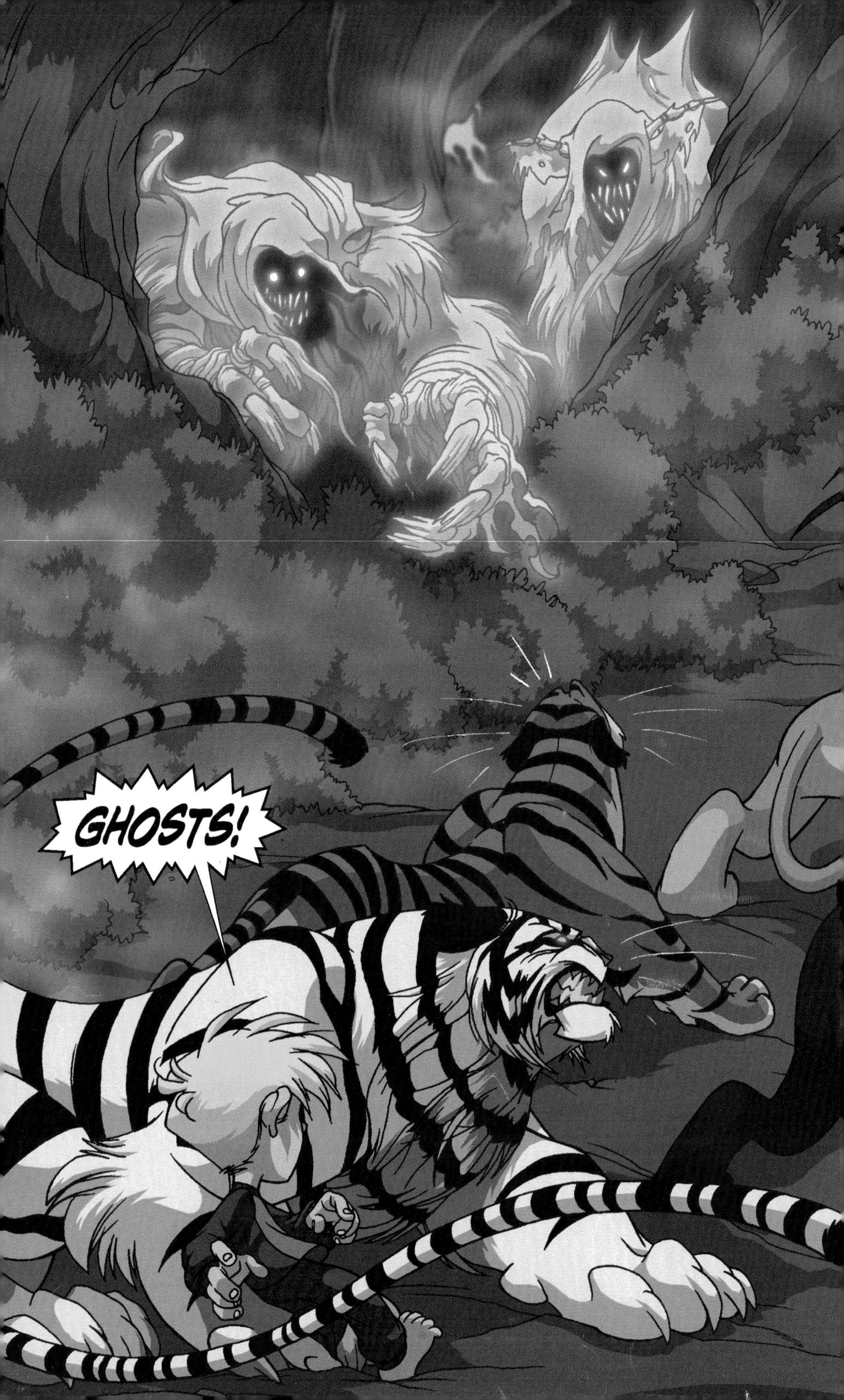
GHOSTS!

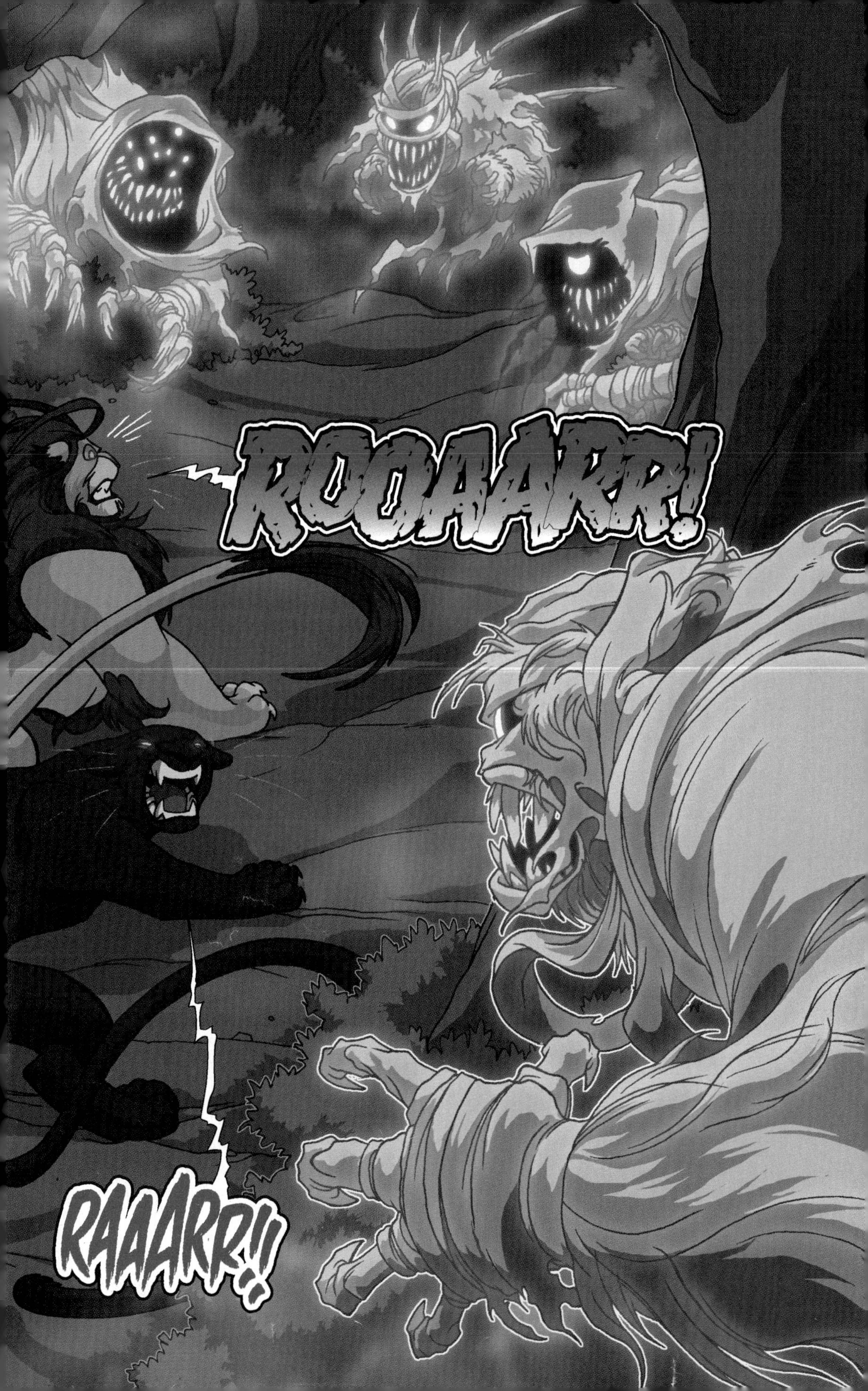
ROOAARR!
RAAARR!!

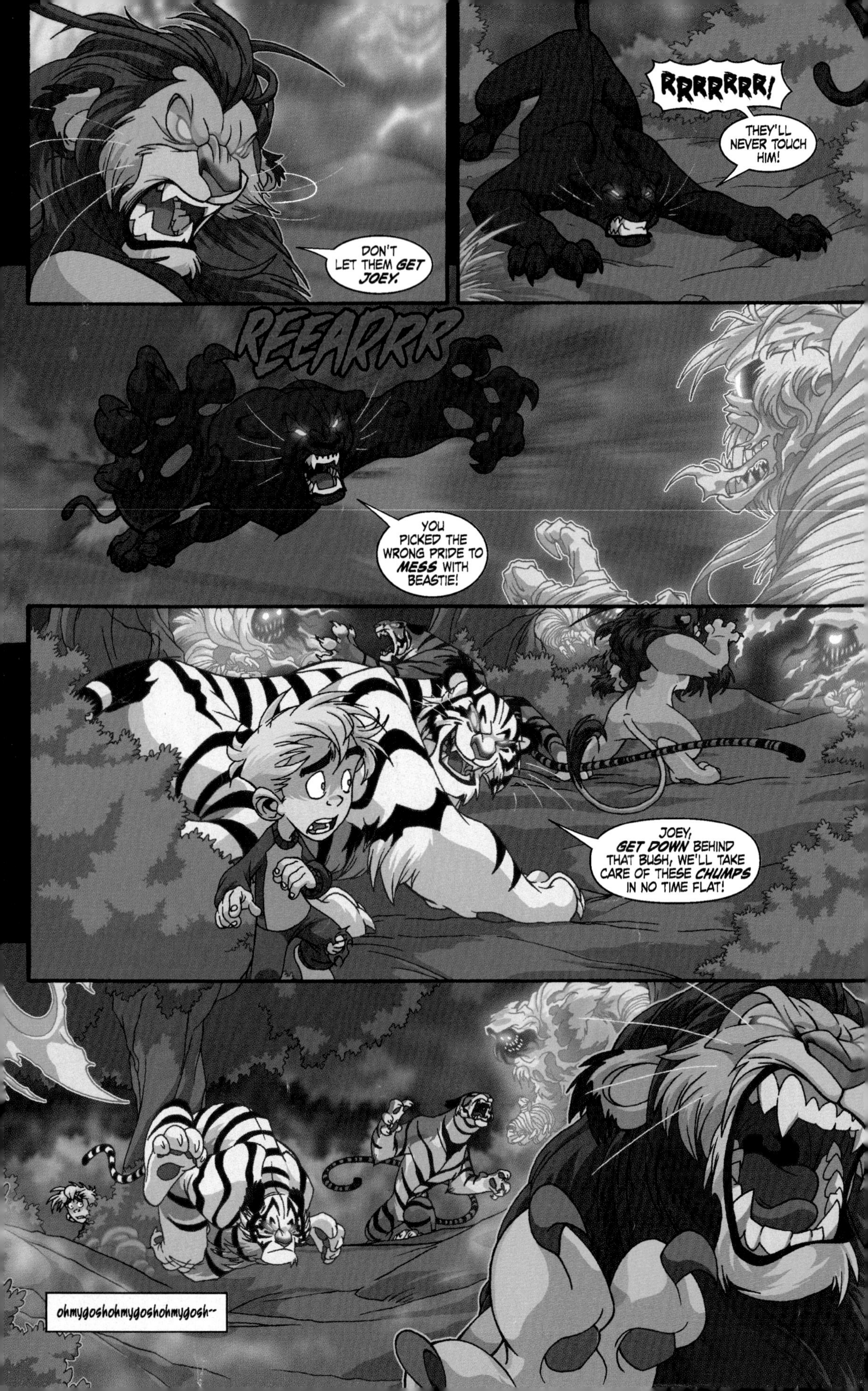
DON'T LET THEM GET JOEY.
RRRRRRR!
THEY'LL NEVER TOUCH HIM!
REEARRR
YOU PICKED THE WRONG PRIDE TO MESS WITH BEASTIE!
JOEY, GET DOWN BEHIND THAT BUSH, WE'LL TAKE CARE OF THESE CHUMPS IN NO TIME FLAT!
ohmygoshohmygoshohmygosh--

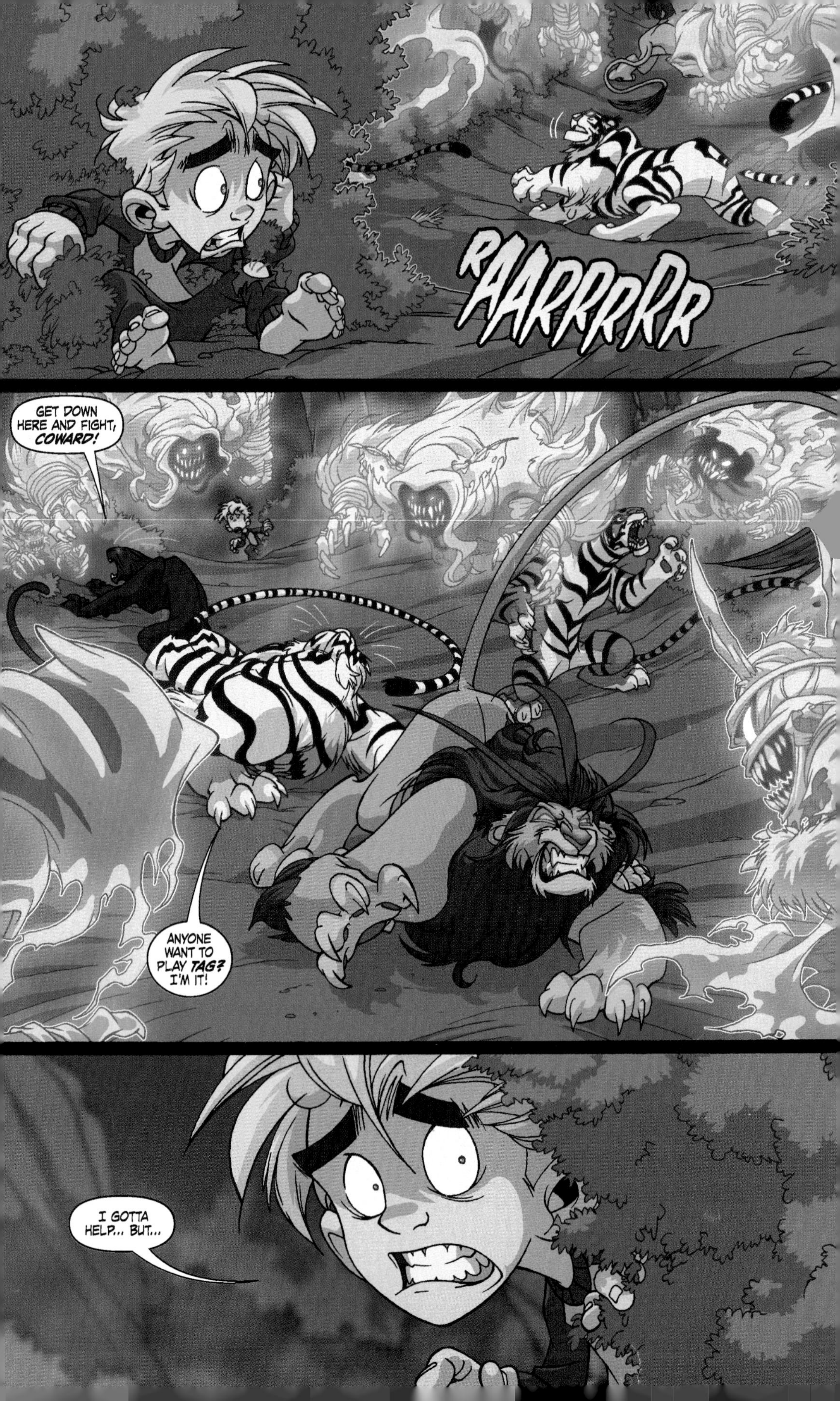
RAARRRRRR
GET DOWN HERE AND FIGHT, COWARD!
ANYONE WANT TO PLAY TAG? I'M IT!
I GOTTA HELP... BUT...

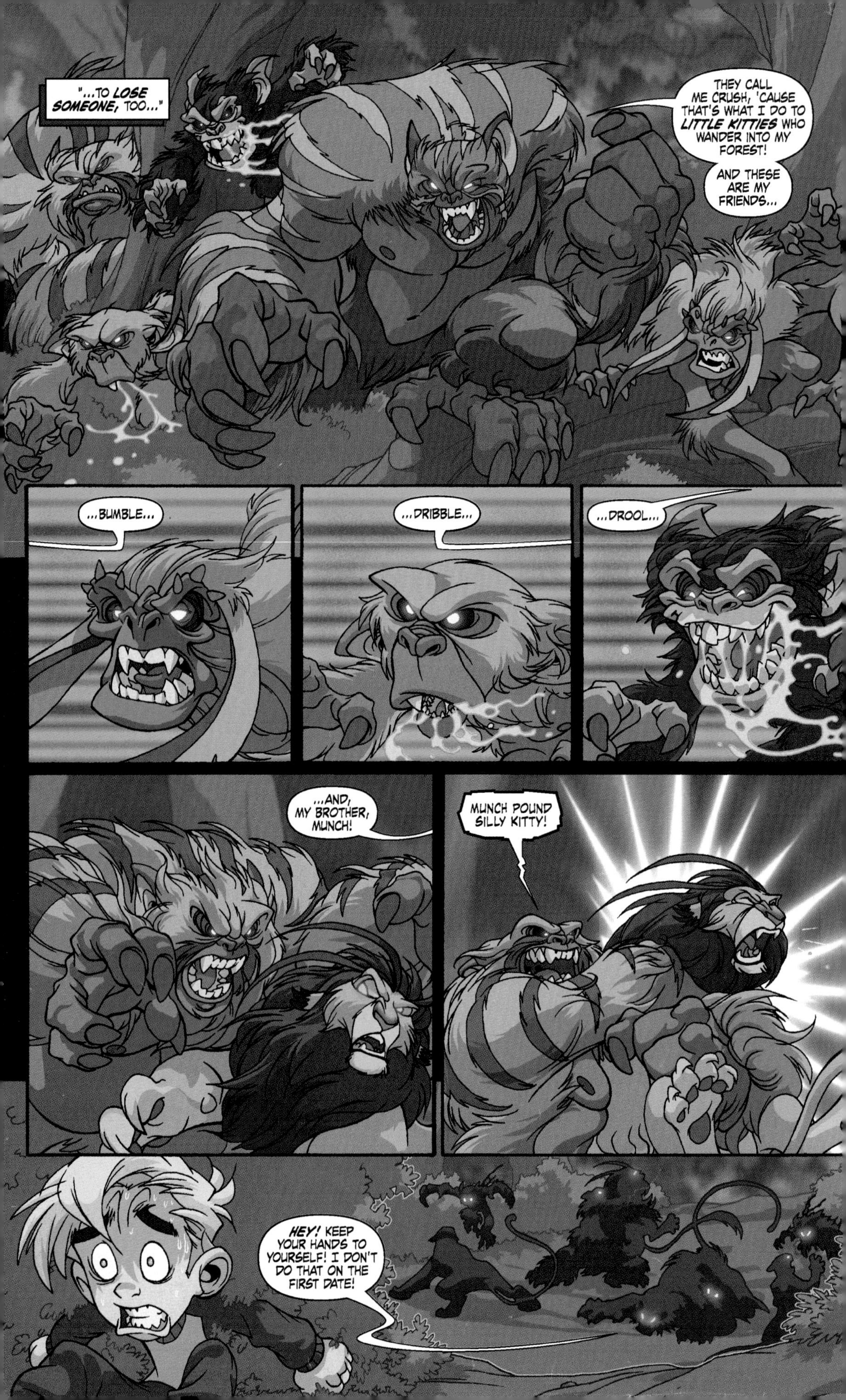
"...TO LOSE SOMEONE, TOO..."
THEY CALL ME CRUSH, 'CAUSE THAT'S WHAT I DO TO LITTLE KITTIES WHO WANDER INTO MY FOREST!
AND THESE ARE MY FRIENDS...
...BUMBLE...
...DRIBBLE...
...DROOL...
...AND, MY BROTHER, MUNCH!
MUNCH POUND SILLY KITTY!
HEY! KEEP YOUR HANDS TO YOURSELF! I DON'T DO THAT ON THE FIRST DATE!

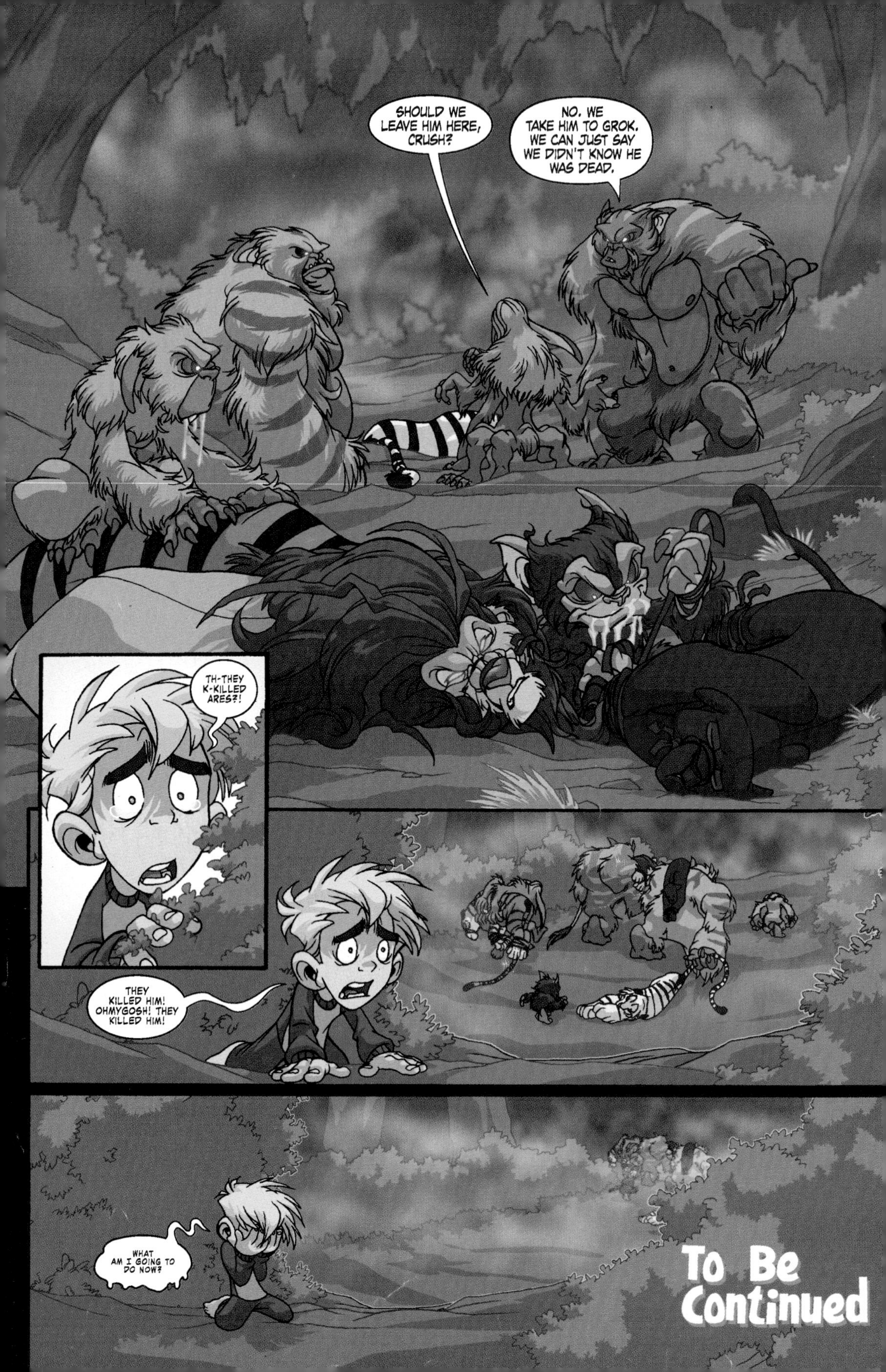

SHOULD WE LEAVE HIM HERE, CRUSH?
NO. WE TAKE HIM TO GROK. WE CAN JUST SAY WE DIDN'T KNOW HE WAS DEAD.
TH-THEY K-KILLED ARES?!
THEY KILLED HIM! OHMYGOSH! THEY KILLED HIM!
WHAT AM I GOING TO DO NOW?
To Be Continued

Chapter Four

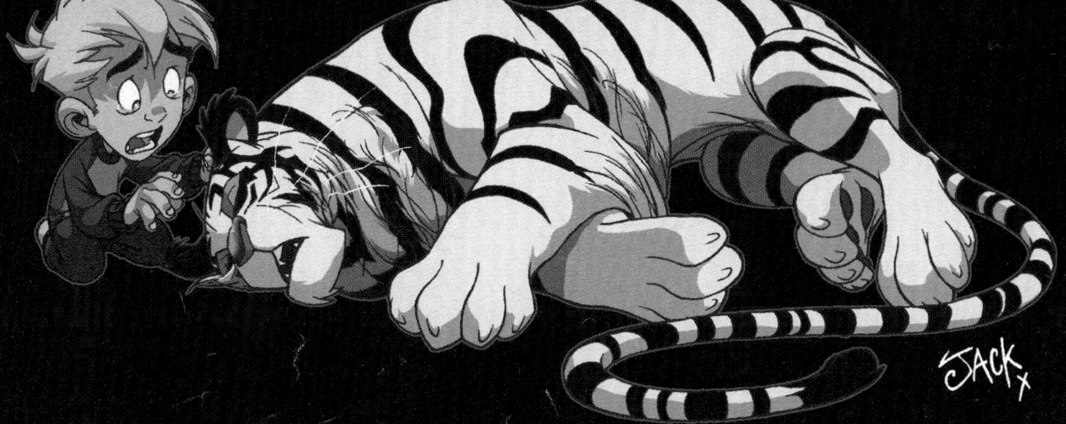
JACK X

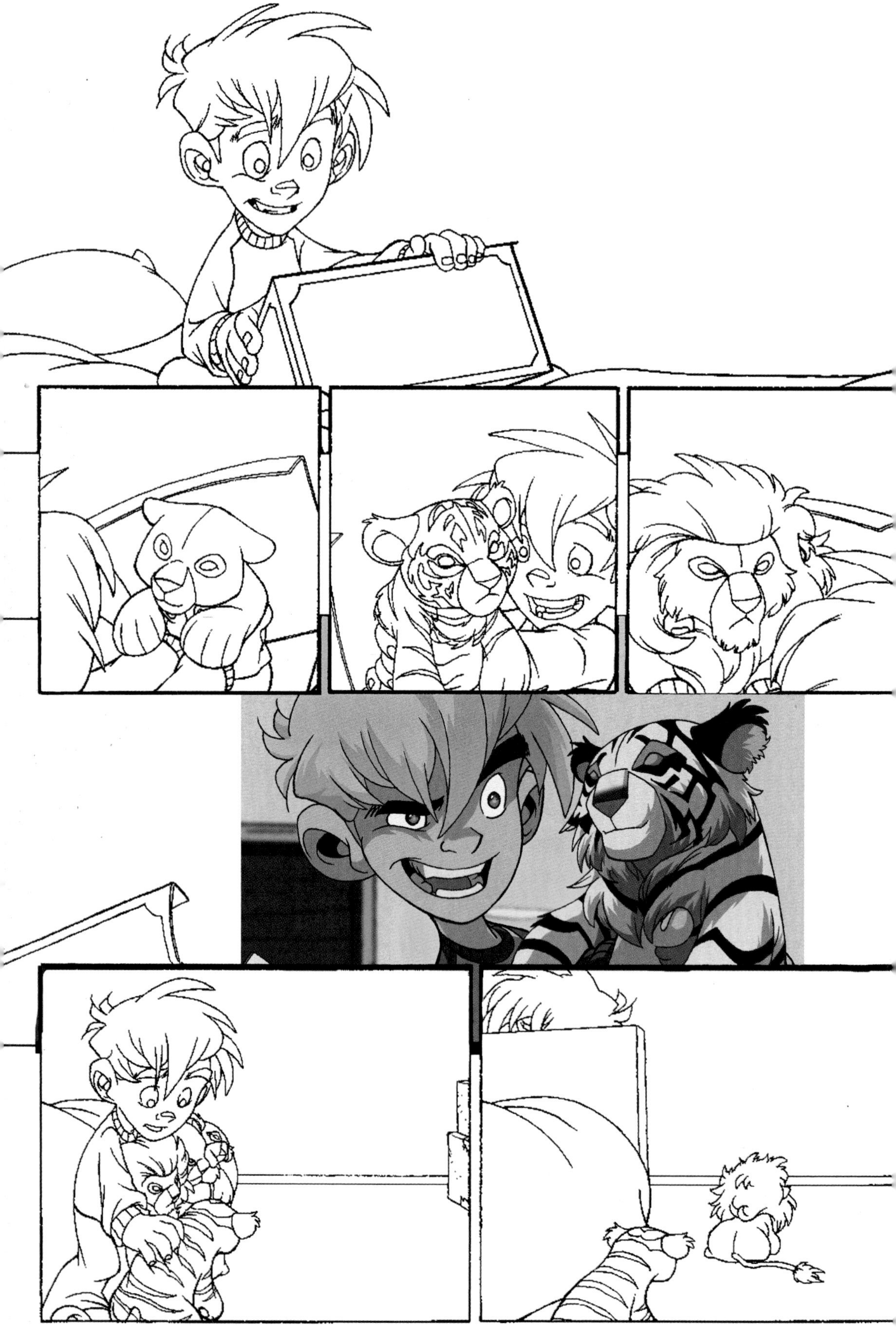

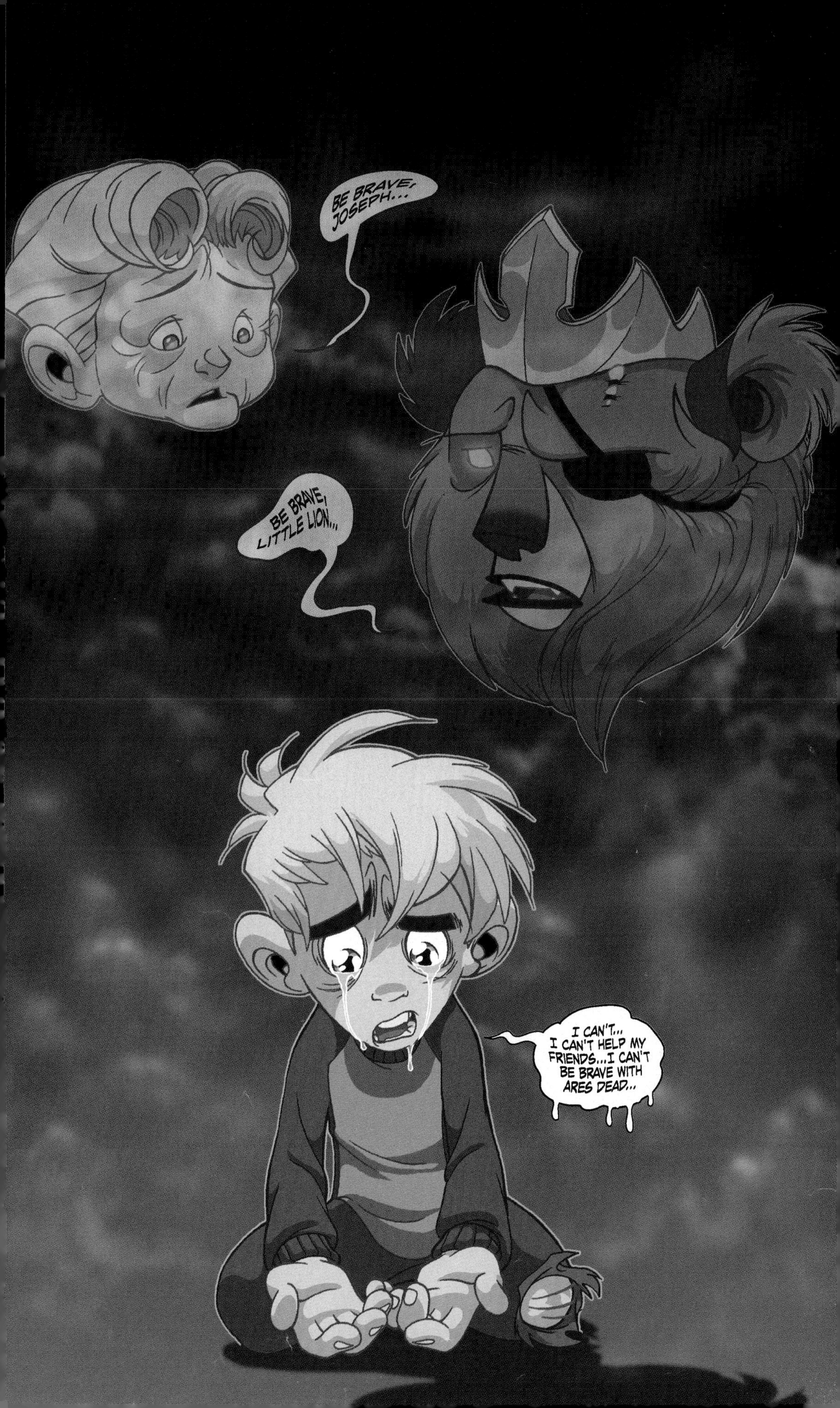
BE BRAVE, JOSEPH...
BE BRAVE, LITTLE LION...
I CAN'T... I CAN'T HELP MY FRIENDS... I CAN'T BE BRAVE WITH ARES DEAD...

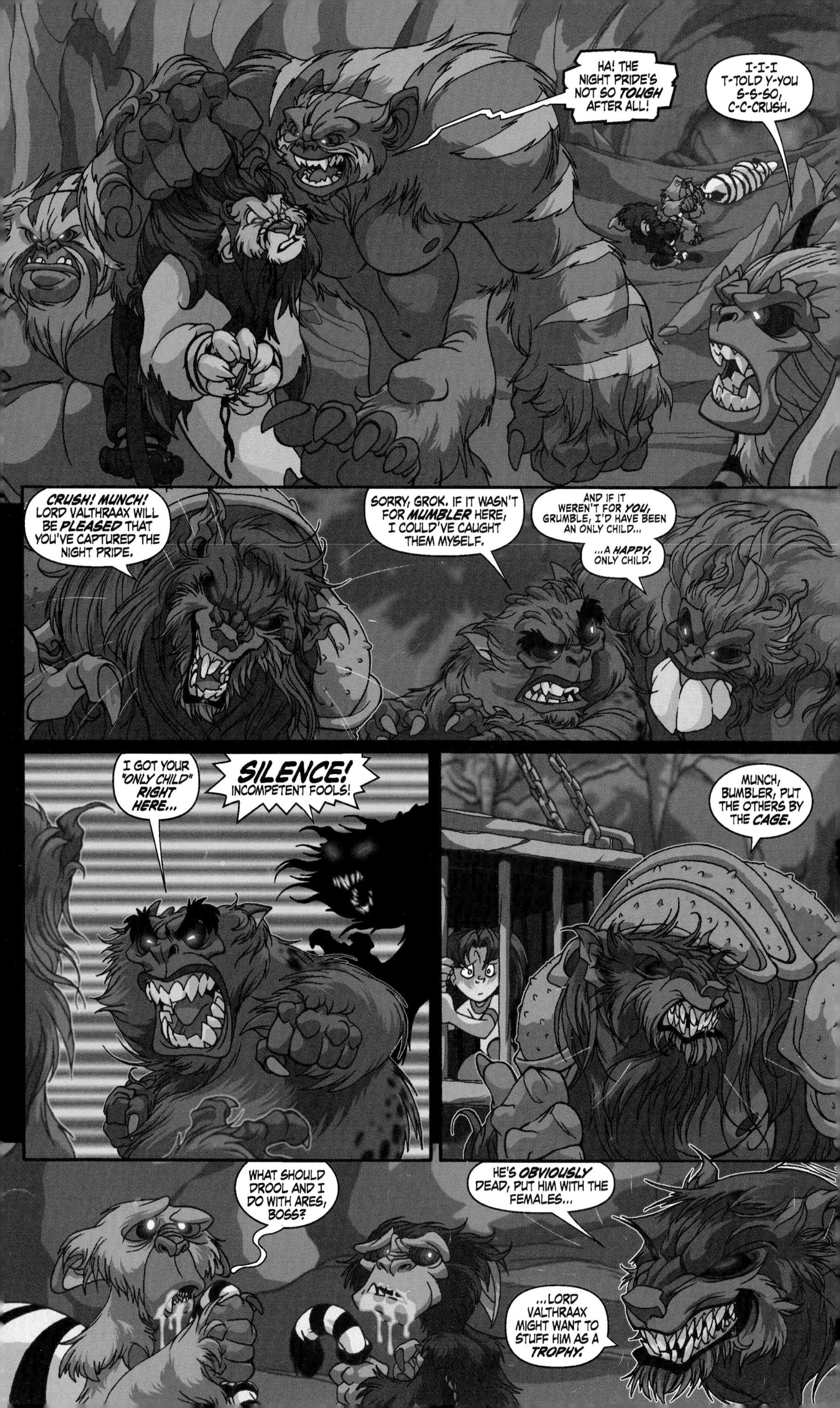
HA! THE NIGHT PRIDE'S NOT SO TOUGH AFTER ALL!
I-I-I T-TOLD Y-YOU S-S-SO, C-C-CRUSH.
CRUSH! MUNCH! LORD VALTHRAAX WILL BE PLEASED THAT YOU'VE CAPTURED THE NIGHT PRIDE.
SORRY, GROK. IF IT WASN'T FOR MUMBLER HERE, I COULD'VE CAUGHT THEM MYSELF.
AND IF IT WEREN'T FOR YOU, GRUMBLE, I'D HAVE BEEN AN ONLY CHILD...
...A HAPPY, ONLY CHILD.
I GOT YOUR "ONLY CHILD" RIGHT HERE...
SILENCE! INCOMPETENT FOOLS!
MUNCH, BUMBLER, PUT THE OTHERS BY THE CAGE.
WHAT SHOULD DROOL AND I DO WITH ARES, BOSS?
HE'S OBVIOUSLY DEAD, PUT HIM WITH THE FEMALES...
...LORD VALTHRAAX MIGHT WANT TO STUFF HIM AS A TROPHY.

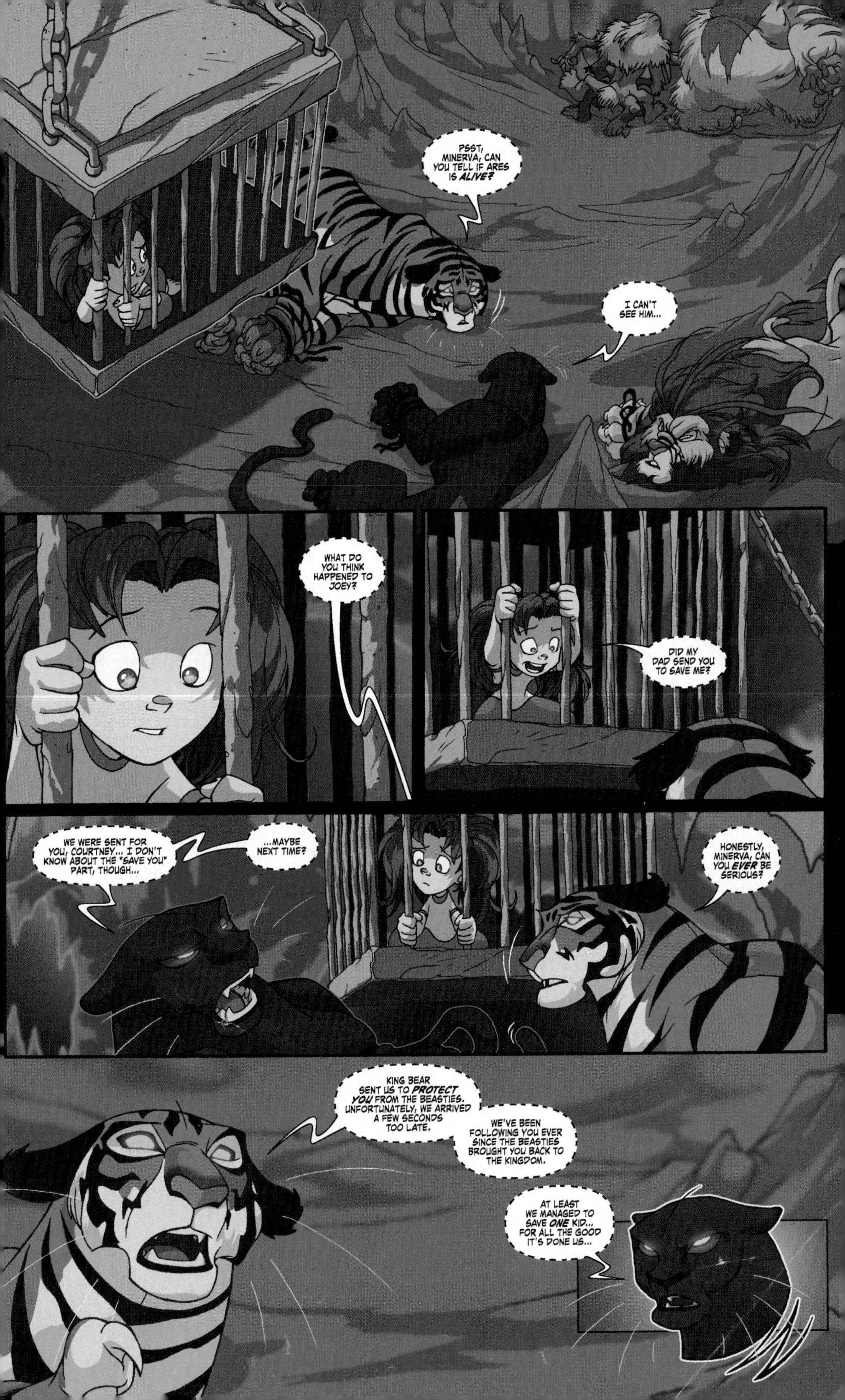
PSST, MINERVA, CAN YOU TELL IF ARES IS *ALIVE?*
I CAN'T SEE HIM...
WHAT DO YOU THINK HAPPENED TO JOEY?
DID MY DAD SEND YOU TO SAVE ME?
WE WERE SENT FOR YOU, COURTNEY... I DON'T KNOW ABOUT THE "SAVE YOU" PART, THOUGH...
...MAYBE NEXT TIME?
HONESTLY, MINERVA, CAN YOU *EVER* BE SERIOUS?
KING BEAR SENT US TO *PROTECT YOU* FROM THE BEASTIES. UNFORTUNATELY, WE ARRIVED A FEW SECONDS TOO LATE.
WE'VE BEEN FOLLOWING YOU EVER SINCE THE BEASTIES BROUGHT YOU BACK TO THE KINGDOM.
AT LEAST WE MANAGED TO SAVE *ONE* KID... FOR ALL THE GOOD IT'S DONE US...

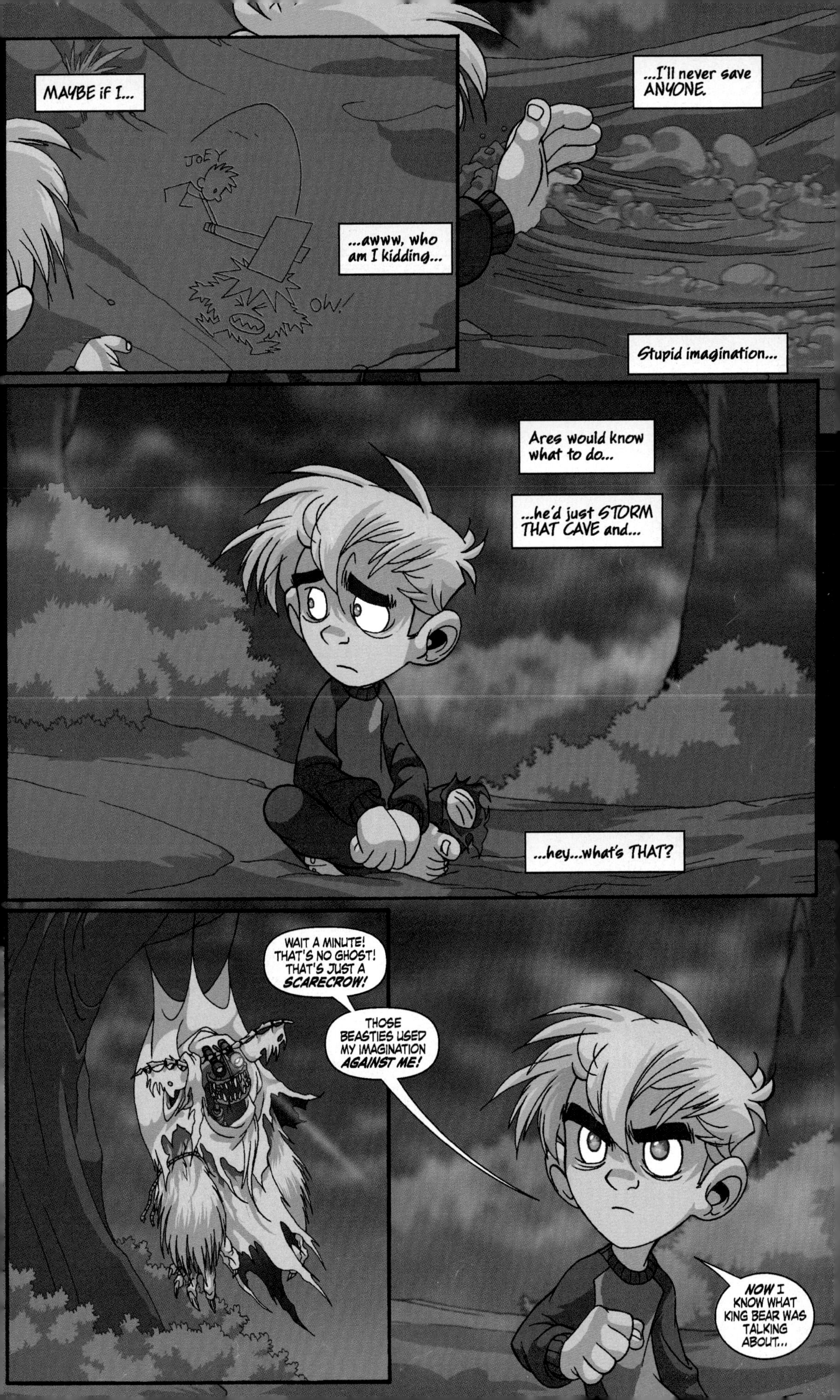
MAYBE if I...
JOEY
OW!
...awww, who am I kidding...
...I'll never save ANYONE.
Stupid imagination...
Ares would know what to do...
...he'd just STORM THAT CAVE and...
...hey...what's THAT?
WAIT A MINUTE! THAT'S NO GHOST! THAT'S JUST A SCARECROW!
THOSE BEASTIES USED MY IMAGINATION AGAINST ME!
NOW I KNOW WHAT KING BEAR WAS TALKING ABOUT...

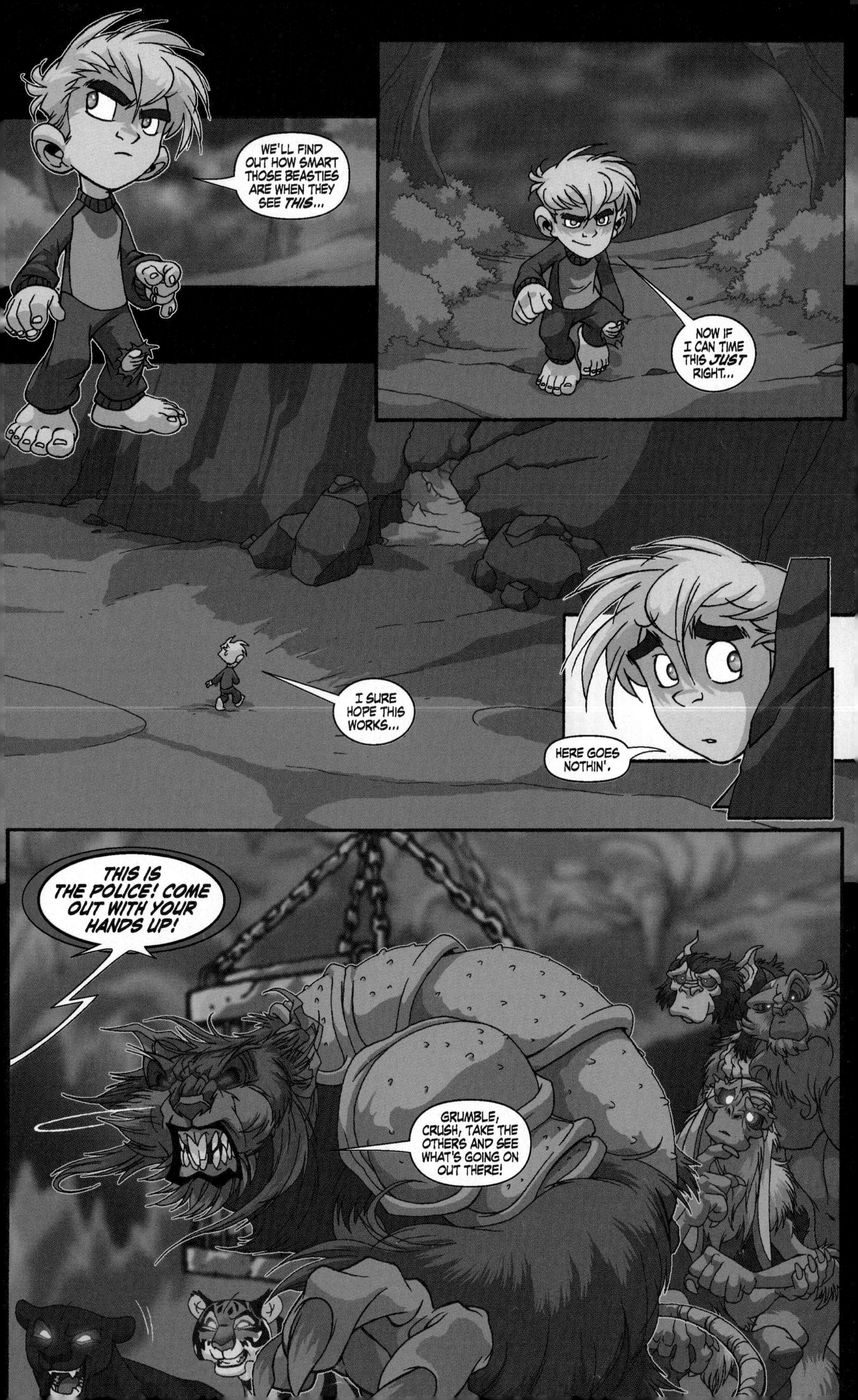
WE'LL FIND OUT HOW SMART THOSE BEASTIES ARE WHEN THEY SEE *THIS*...
NOW IF I CAN TIME THIS *JUST* RIGHT...
I SURE HOPE THIS WORKS...
HERE GOES NOTHIN'.
THIS IS THE POLICE! COME OUT WITH YOUR HANDS UP!
GRUMBLE, CRUSH, TAKE THE OTHERS AND SEE WHAT'S GOING ON OUT THERE!

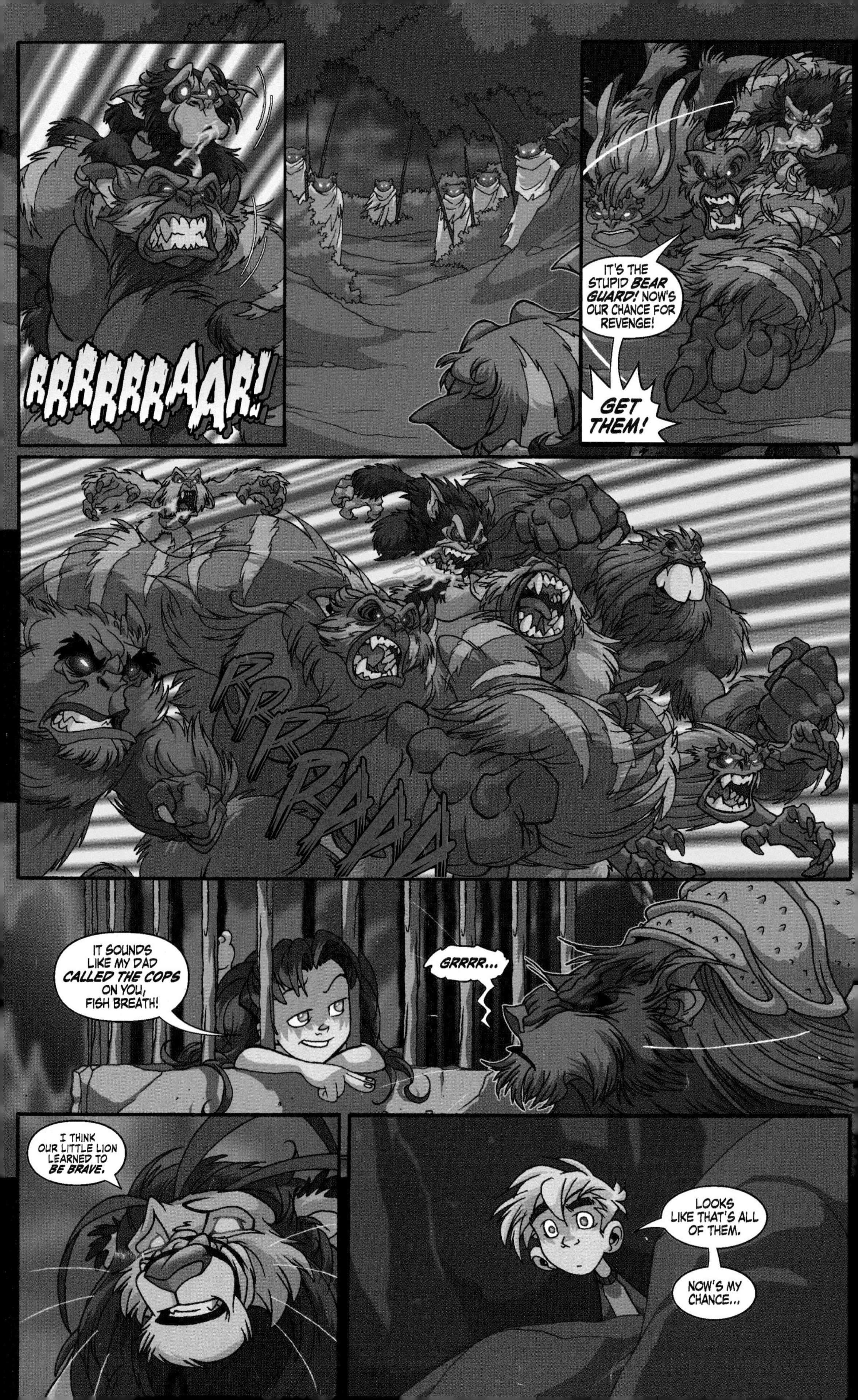

BRRRRRRAAR!
IT'S THE STUPID BEAR GUARD! NOW'S OUR CHANCE FOR REVENGE!
GET THEM!
RRRRAAA
IT SOUNDS LIKE MY DAD CALLED THE COPS ON YOU, FISH BREATH!
GRRRR...
I THINK OUR LITTLE LION LEARNED TO BE BRAVE.
LOOKS LIKE THAT'S ALL OF THEM.
NOW'S MY CHANCE...

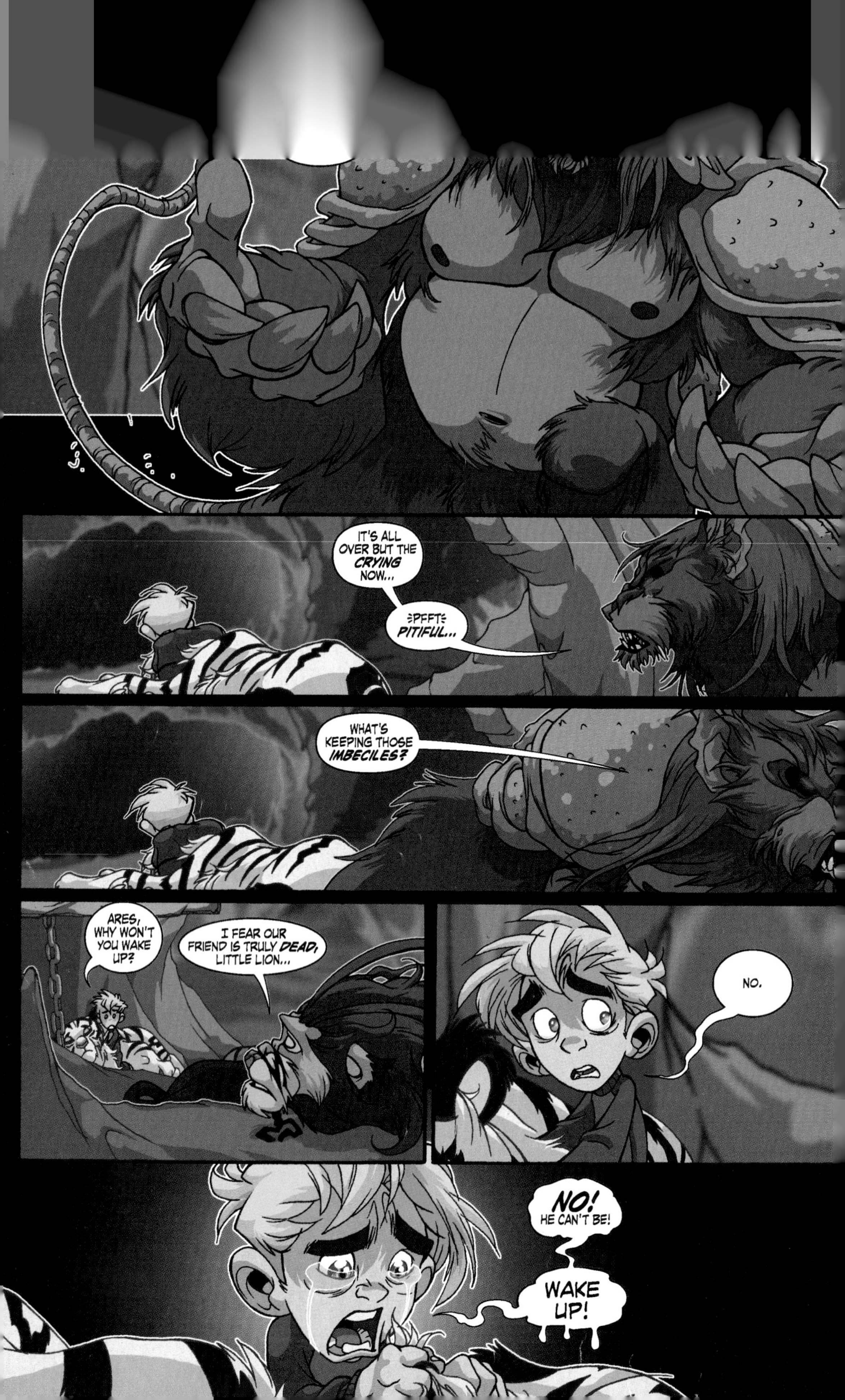
IT'S ALL OVER BUT THE CRYING NOW...
=PFFT= PITIFUL...
WHAT'S KEEPING THOSE IMBECILES?
ARES, WHY WON'T YOU WAKE UP?
I FEAR OUR FRIEND IS TRULY DEAD, LITTLE LION...
NO.
NO! HE CAN'T BE!
WAKE UP!

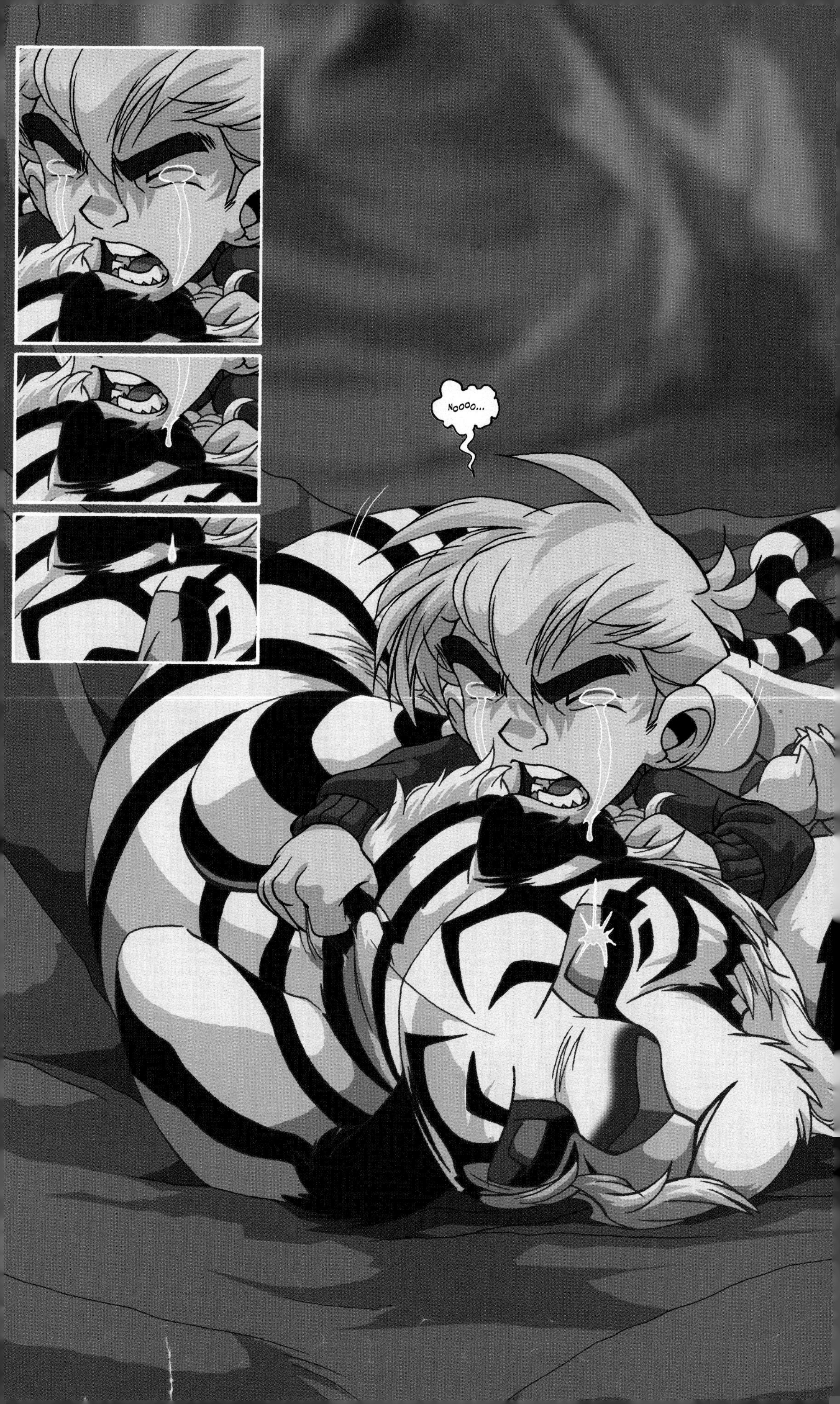
NOOOO...

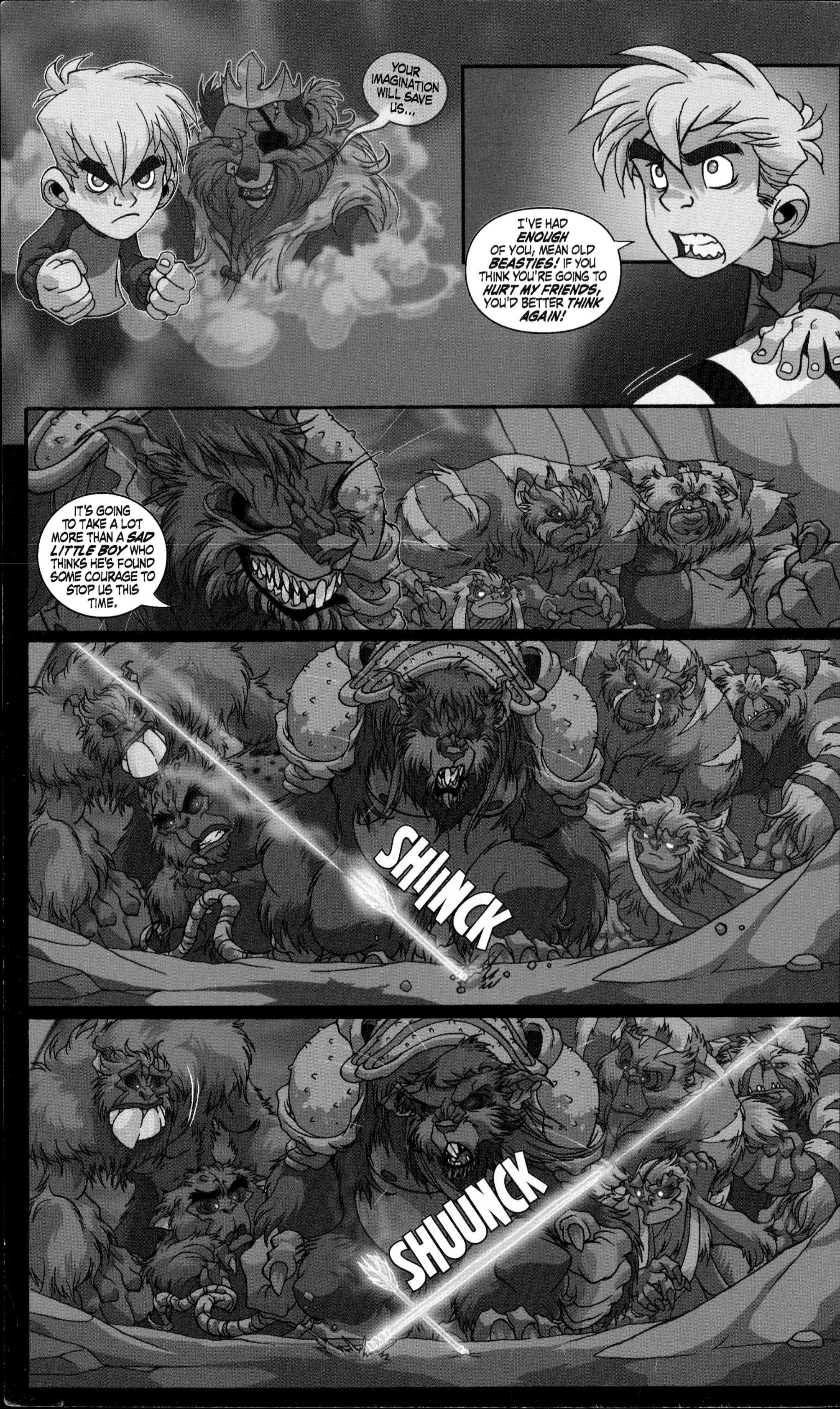
YOUR IMAGINATION WILL SAVE US...
I'VE HAD ENOUGH OF YOU, MEAN OLD BEASTIES! IF YOU THINK YOU'RE GOING TO HURT MY FRIENDS, YOU'D BETTER THINK AGAIN!
IT'S GOING TO TAKE A LOT MORE THAN A SAD LITTLE BOY WHO THINKS HE'S FOUND SOME COURAGE TO STOP US THIS TIME.
SHINCK
SHUUNCK

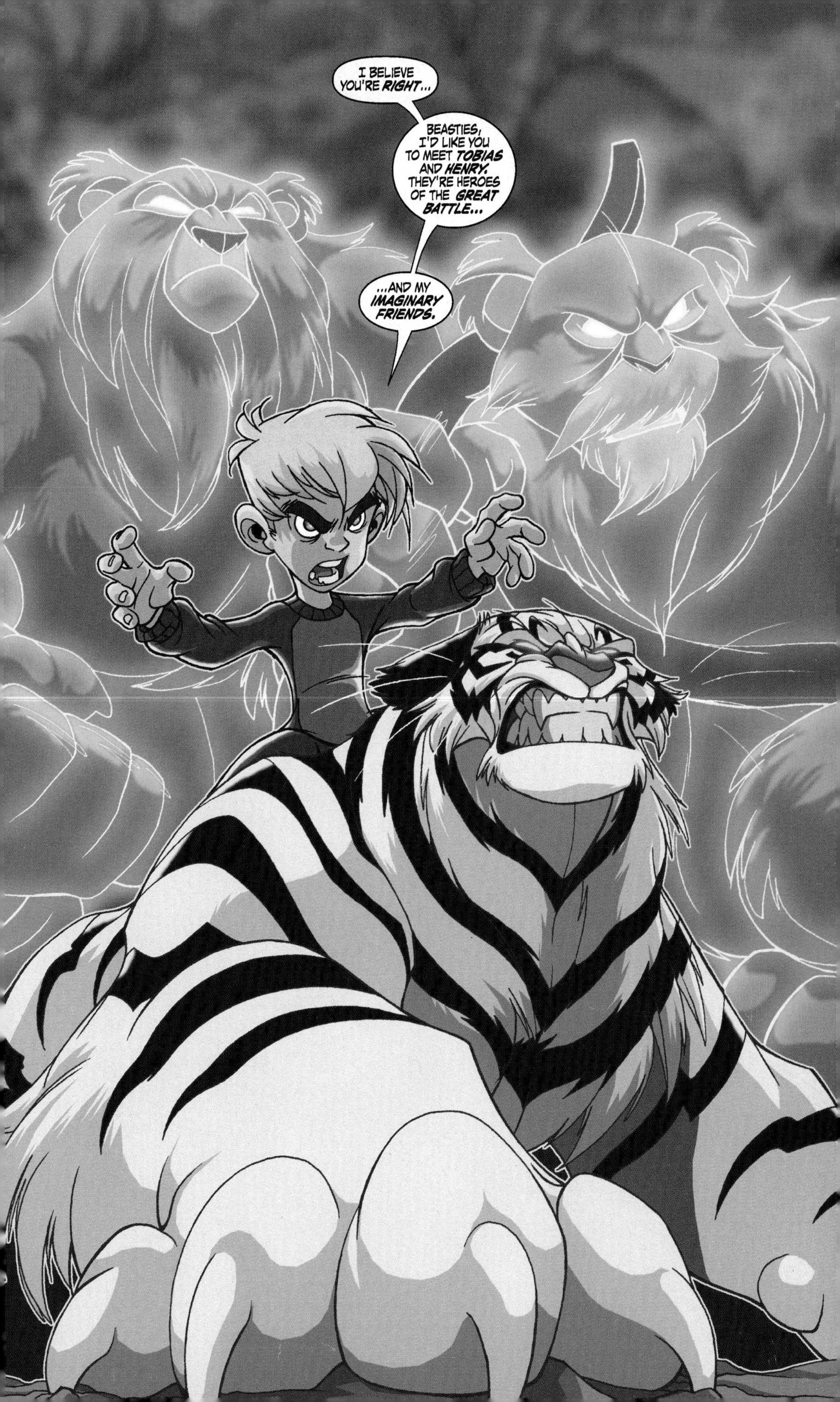
I BELIEVE YOU'RE *RIGHT*...
BEASTIES, I'D LIKE YOU TO MEET *TOBIAS* AND *HENRY.* THEY'RE HEROES OF THE *GREAT BATTLE*...
...AND MY *IMAGINARY FRIENDS.*

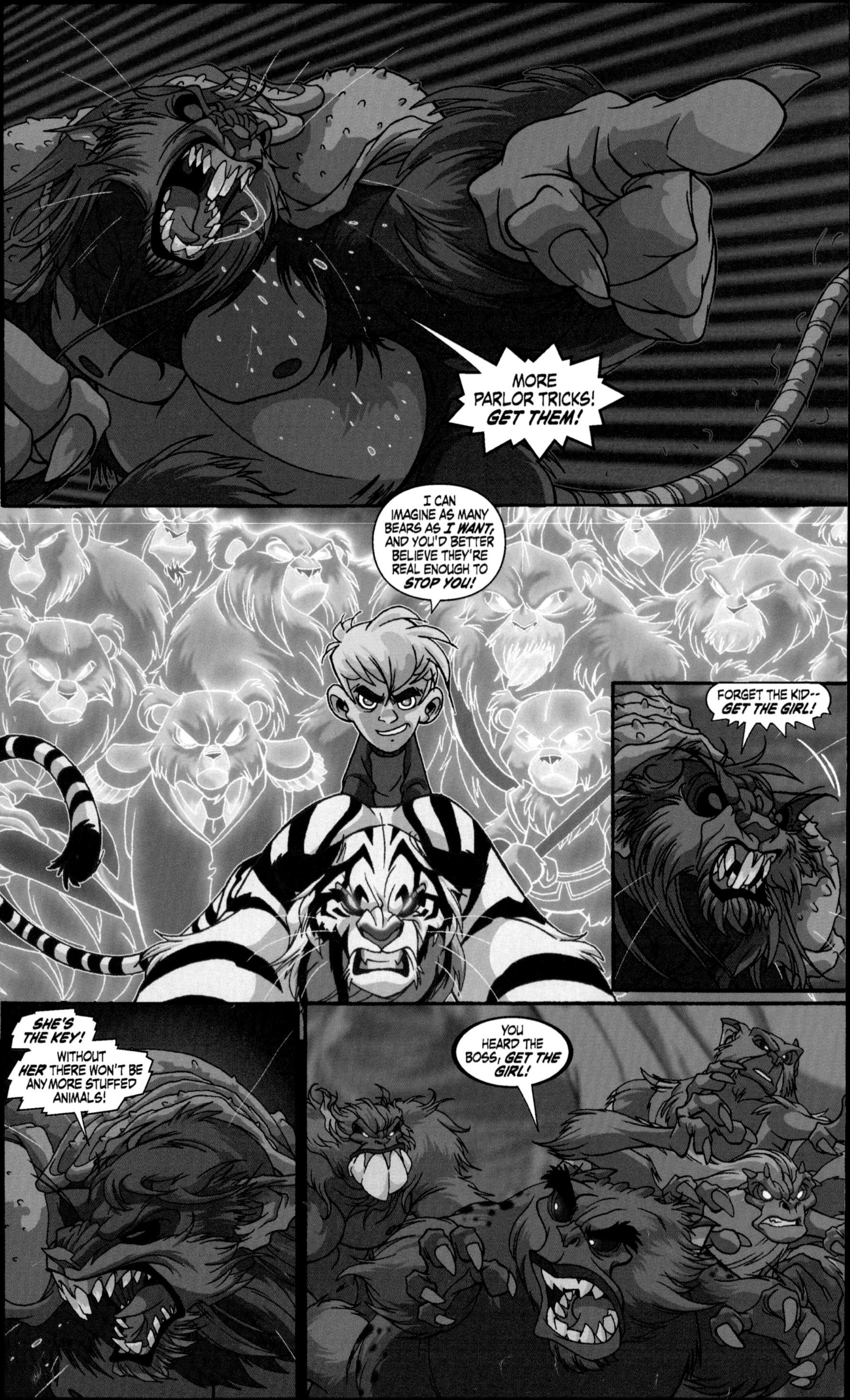
MORE PARLOR TRICKS! GET THEM!
I CAN IMAGINE AS MANY BEARS AS I WANT, AND YOU'D BETTER BELIEVE THEY'RE REAL ENOUGH TO STOP YOU!
FORGET THE KID-- GET THE GIRL!
SHE'S THE KEY! WITHOUT HER THERE WON'T BE ANYMORE STUFFED ANIMALS!
YOU HEARD THE BOSS, GET THE GIRL!

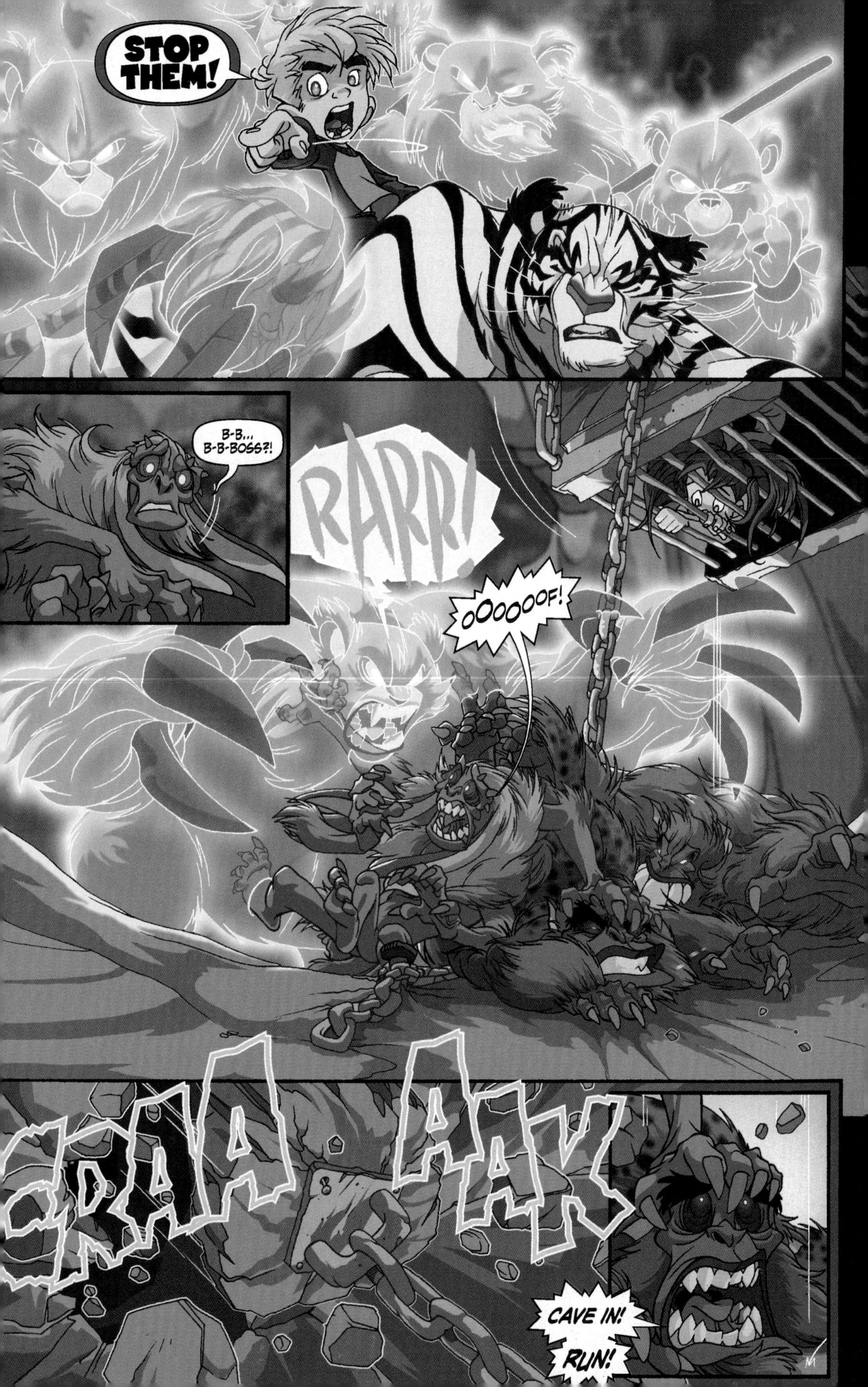
STOP THEM!
B-B... B-B-BOSS?!
RARR!
OOOOOOF!
CRAAAAK
CAVE IN!
RUN!

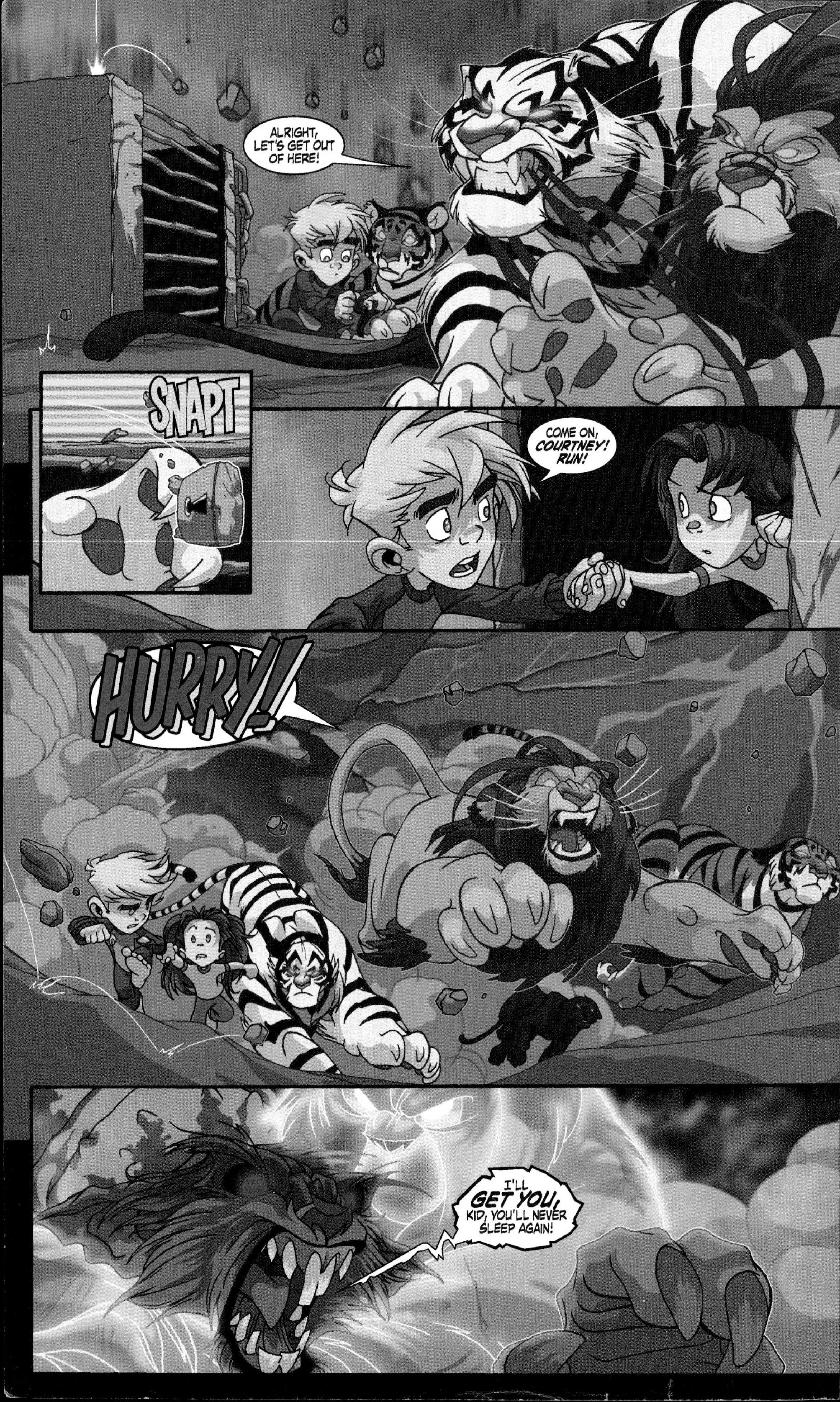
ALRIGHT, LET'S GET OUT OF HERE!
SNAPT
COME ON, COURTNEY! RUN!
HURRY!!
I'LL GET YOU, KID, YOU'LL NEVER SLEEP AGAIN!

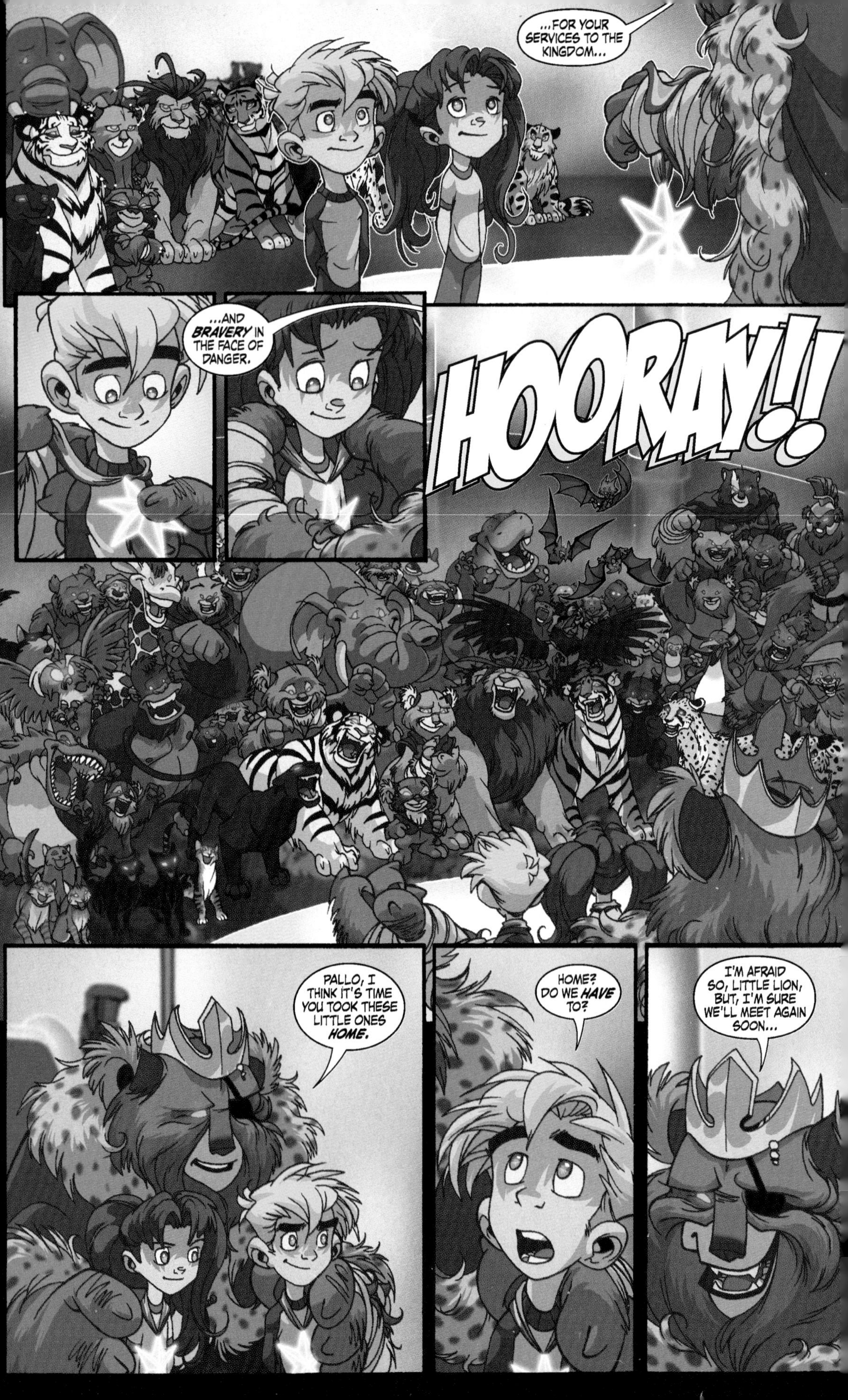
...FOR YOUR SERVICES TO THE KINGDOM...
...AND BRAVERY IN THE FACE OF DANGER.
HOORAY!!
PALLO, I THINK IT'S TIME YOU TOOK THESE LITTLE ONES HOME.
HOME? DO WE HAVE TO?
I'M AFRAID SO, LITTLE LION, BUT, I'M SURE WE'LL MEET AGAIN SOON...

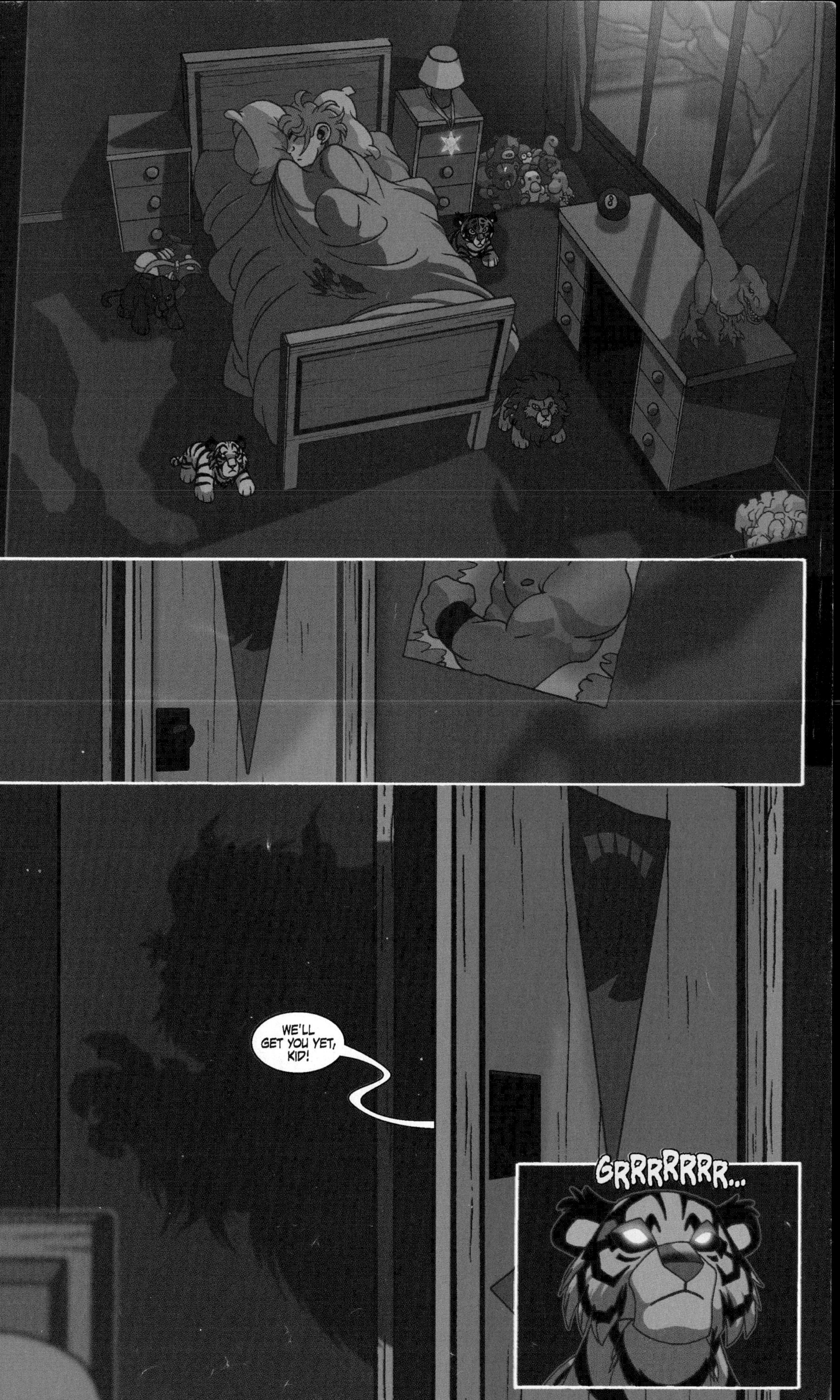
WE'LL GET YOU YET, KID!
GRRRRRRR...

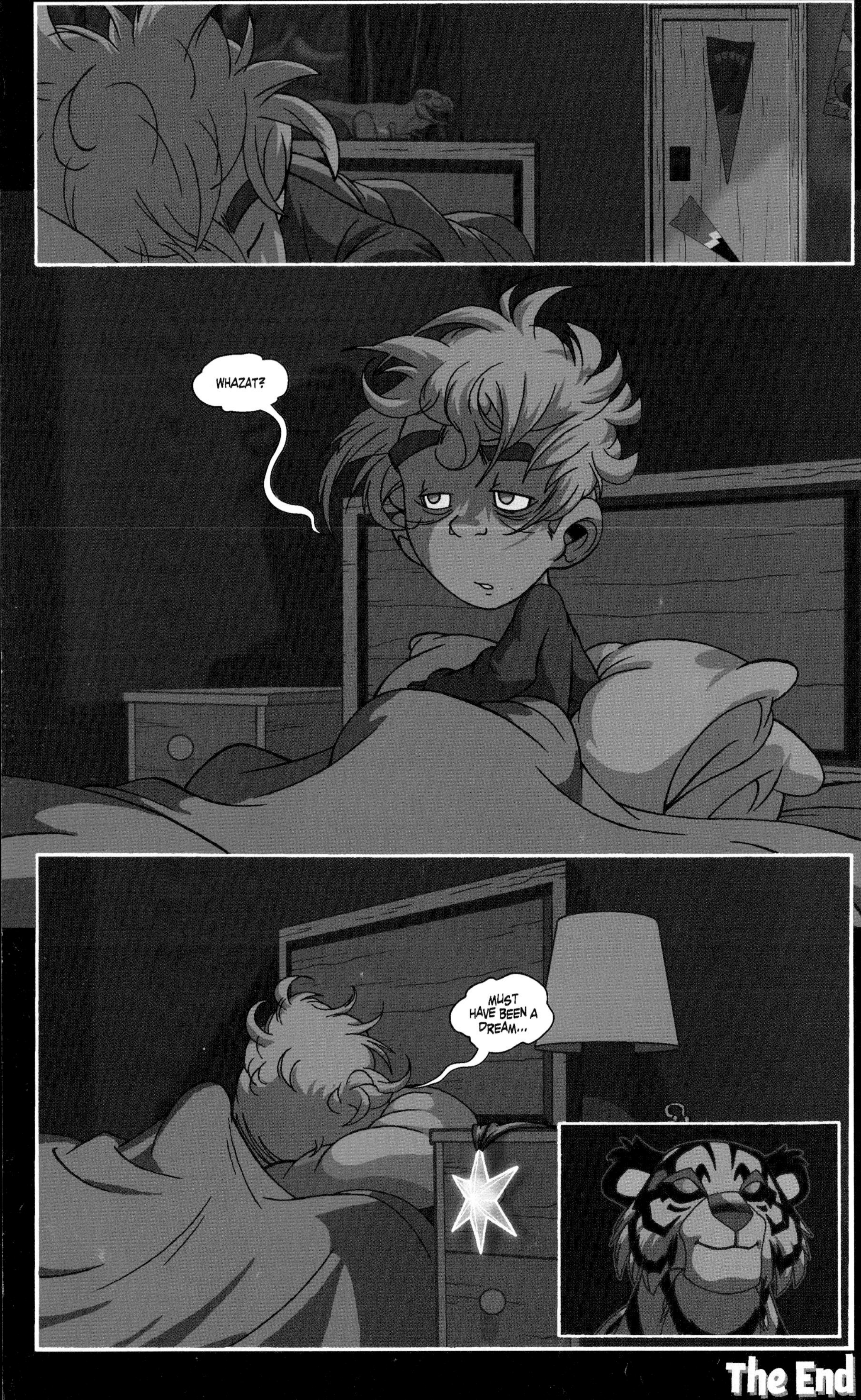
WHAZAT?
MUST HAVE BEEN A DREAM...
The End

In the spring of 2005, not long after *Lions, Tigers and Bears* #1 came out, my friend Mike Banks contacted me and told me he had some great news for me.

For those who don't know, Mike Banks is the owner of Samurai Comics, a two-store comic shop chain in Phoenix, Arizona. Well, not only is Mike a smart businessman, one of the "new breed" of comic shop owners popping up all over the land, but Mike's rapidly becoming a pillar of the Phoenix community. You see, Mike, his wife Moryha, and the rest of the staff of Samurai Comics are continually involved in literacy programs at local schools and libraries, toy and food drives for local children and families, reading programs at local schools and various other charity endeavors. Samurai has been an immeasurable help to Runemaster Studios in setting up our "Comic Book Exchange Programs" in local schools and libraries.

On top of that, the Samurai stores are always open to local kids (of all ages) for gaming, anime festivals and as a place where folks can hang out in a fun and exciting atmosphere.

Well, given all that, when Mike calls and says he has some great news, I knew he wasn't exaggerating. I spent about five milliseconds in my mind guessing (wrongly) what it was before I asked him to fill me in...

As it was, Mike had spent the last several years working with the Arizona Republic, (the major newspaper here in Phoenix), the Arizona Diamondbacks, (our Major League Baseball team) and the Maricopa County Library System on a Children's Literacy Program to get kids reading during the summer months when they weren't in school.

As Mike filled in the details, I began wondering who the story-teller was in this conversation, as he did a pretty good job introducing the major characters, presenting the goal and laying out some challenges which had me hooked long before he lead me to the climactic finish.

It seems the Arizona Republic was dedicating the entire back page of the Sunday Comics section each week for ten weeks to the Children's Literacy Program and they wanted a local person to provide a story for the kids. When Mike heard this, he immediately sent them a copy of *Lions, Tigers and Bears* v1 #1 and told them this would be perfect.

Thankfully, the Republic, Diamondbacks and the librarians all agreed with Mike's assessment and they wanted to reprint *LTB* in the paper.

However, instead of trying to rehash something Jack and I had already done in the pages of the comic book, we decided it would be best to create an all-new story.

So, for those of you who were unable to get a copy of the Sunday Edition of the Arizona Republic in the Summer of '05, turn the page for your chance to read the story.

If you're interested in continuity, this tale takes place a short time after volume I and not long before volume II.

After that, you'll find a six page Tiger-Man yarn Jack Lawrence and I created for the Ronin Studios' Tsunami Relief Fund Comic.

I hope you enjoy reading these as much as we enjoyed creating them!

-Mike Bullock

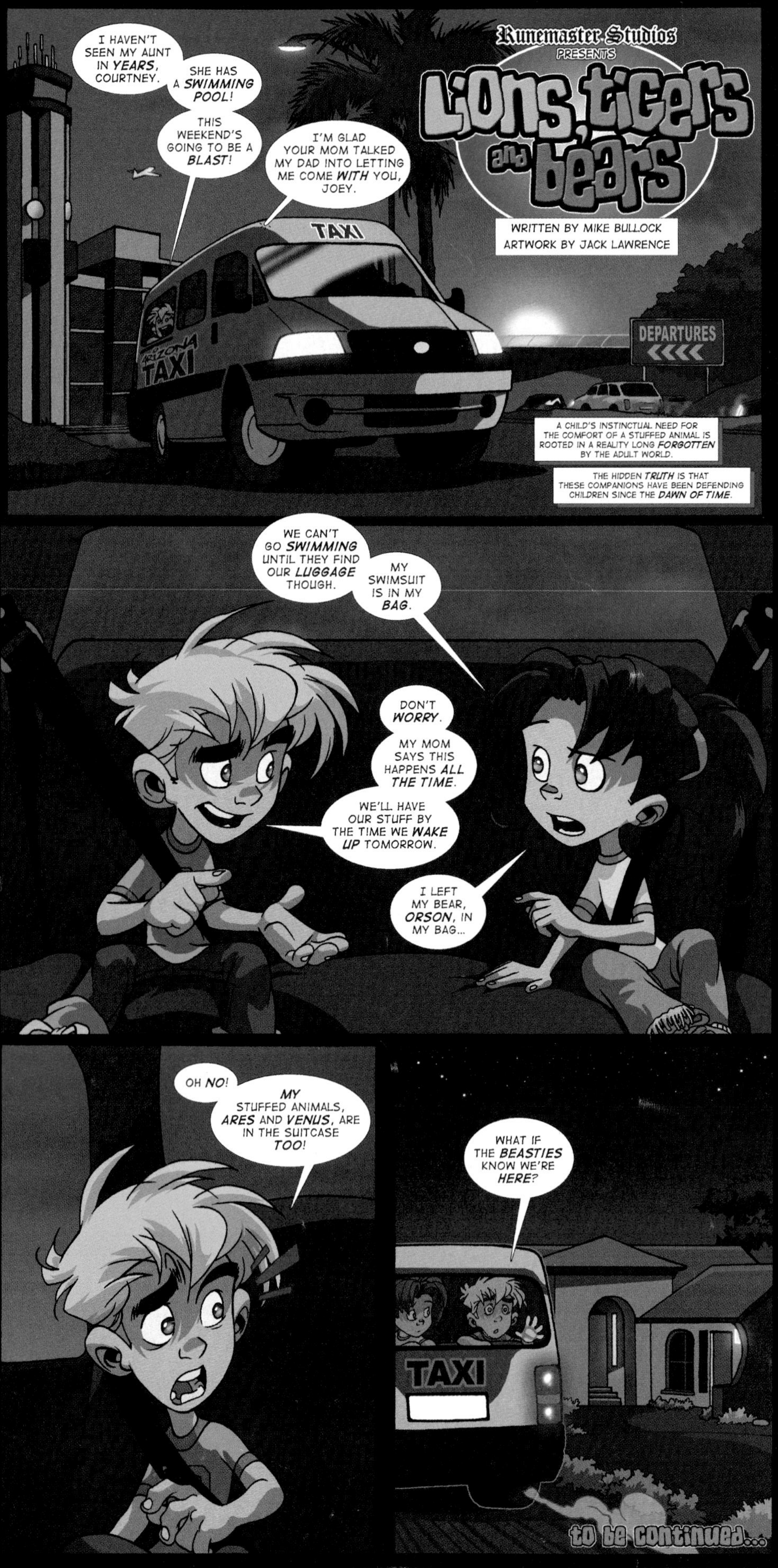
Runemaster Studios
PRESENTS
Lions, tigers and bears
I HAVEN'T SEEN MY AUNT IN *YEARS*, COURTNEY.
SHE HAS A *SWIMMING POOL*!
THIS WEEKEND'S GOING TO BE A *BLAST*!
I'M GLAD YOUR MOM TALKED MY DAD INTO LETTING ME COME *WITH* YOU, JOEY.
WRITTEN BY MIKE BULLOCK
ARTWORK BY JACK LAWRENCE
TAXI
ARIZONA TAXI
DEPARTURES
A CHILD'S INSTINCTUAL NEED FOR THE COMFORT OF A STUFFED ANIMAL IS ROOTED IN A REALITY LONG *FORGOTTEN* BY THE ADULT WORLD.
THE HIDDEN *TRUTH* IS THAT THESE COMPANIONS HAVE BEEN DEFENDING CHILDREN SINCE THE *DAWN OF TIME*.
WE CAN'T GO *SWIMMING* UNTIL THEY FIND OUR *LUGGAGE* THOUGH.
MY SWIMSUIT IS IN MY *BAG*.
DON'T *WORRY*.
MY MOM SAYS THIS HAPPENS *ALL THE TIME*.
WE'LL HAVE OUR STUFF BY THE TIME WE *WAKE UP* TOMORROW.
I LEFT MY BEAR, *ORSON*, IN MY BAG...
OH *NO*!
MY STUFFED ANIMALS, *ARES* AND *VENUS*, ARE IN THE SUITCASE *TOO*!
WHAT IF THE *BEASTIES* KNOW WE'RE *HERE*?
TAXI
to be continued...

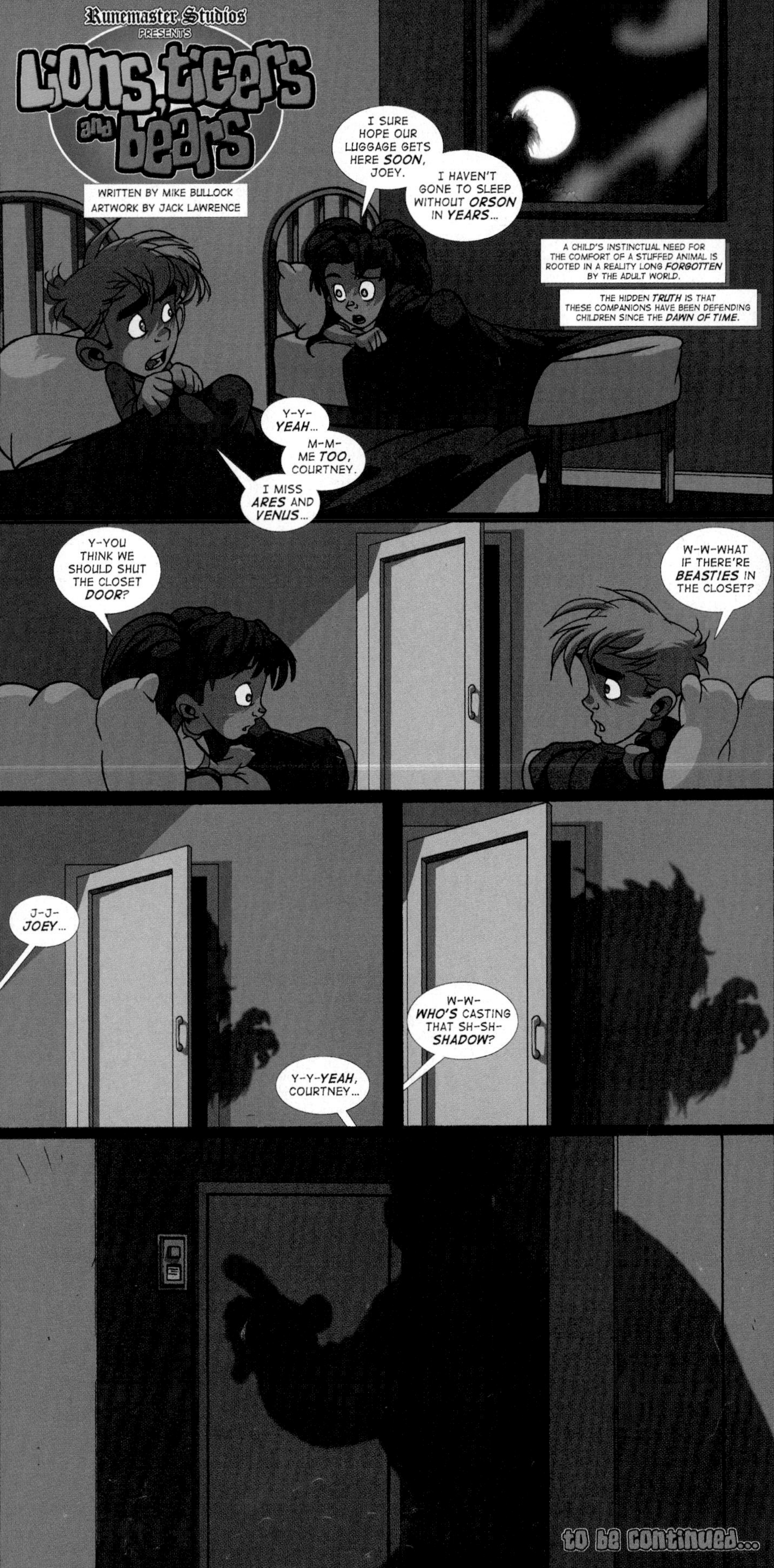
Runemaster Studios
PRESENTS
Lions, tigers and bears
WRITTEN BY MIKE BULLOCK
ARTWORK BY JACK LAWRENCE
I SURE HOPE OUR LUGGAGE GETS HERE SOON, JOEY.
I HAVEN'T GONE TO SLEEP WITHOUT ORSON IN YEARS...
A CHILD'S INSTINCTUAL NEED FOR THE COMFORT OF A STUFFED ANIMAL IS ROOTED IN A REALITY LONG FORGOTTEN BY THE ADULT WORLD.
THE HIDDEN TRUTH IS THAT THESE COMPANIONS HAVE BEEN DEFENDING CHILDREN SINCE THE DAWN OF TIME.
Y-Y-YEAH...
M-M-ME TOO, COURTNEY.
I MISS ARES AND VENUS...
Y-YOU THINK WE SHOULD SHUT THE CLOSET DOOR?
W-W-WHAT IF THERE'RE BEASTIES IN THE CLOSET?
J-J-JOEY...
Y-Y-YEAH, COURTNEY...
W-W-WHO'S CASTING THAT SH-SH-SHADOW?
to be continued...

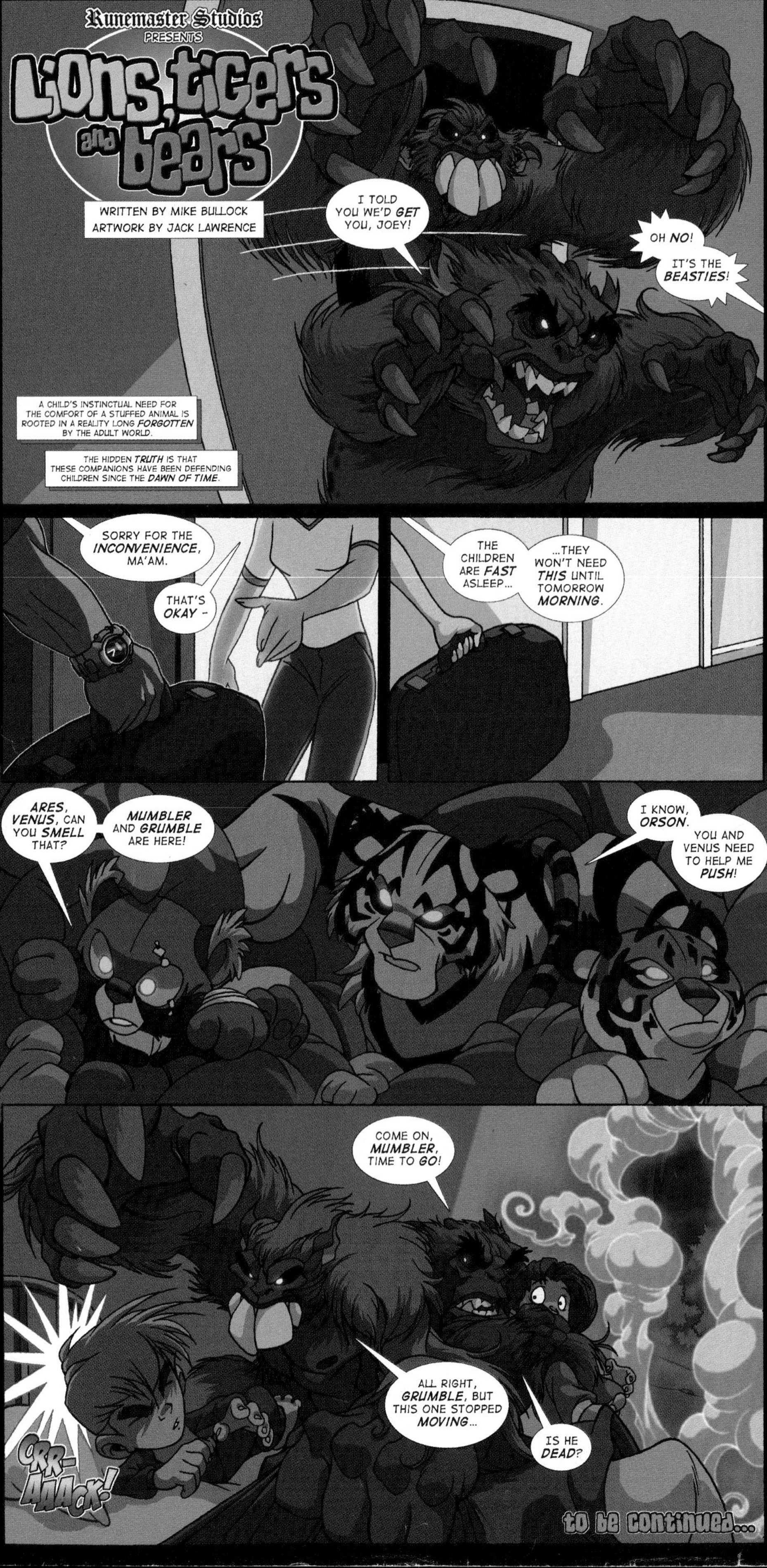
Runemaster Studios
PRESENTS
Lions, tigers and bears
WRITTEN BY MIKE BULLOCK
ARTWORK BY JACK LAWRENCE
I TOLD YOU WE'D GET YOU, JOEY!
OH NO! IT'S THE BEASTIES!
A CHILD'S INSTINCTUAL NEED FOR THE COMFORT OF A STUFFED ANIMAL IS ROOTED IN A REALITY LONG FORGOTTEN BY THE ADULT WORLD.
THE HIDDEN TRUTH IS THAT THESE COMPANIONS HAVE BEEN DEFENDING CHILDREN SINCE THE DAWN OF TIME.
SORRY FOR THE INCONVENIENCE, MA'AM.
THAT'S OKAY -
THE CHILDREN ARE FAST ASLEEP...
...THEY WON'T NEED THIS UNTIL TOMORROW MORNING.
ARES, VENUS, CAN YOU SMELL THAT?
MUMBLER AND GRUMBLE ARE HERE!
I KNOW, ORSON.
YOU AND VENUS NEED TO HELP ME PUSH!
COME ON, MUMBLER, TIME TO GO!
ALL RIGHT, GRUMBLE, BUT THIS ONE STOPPED MOVING...
IS HE DEAD?
CRR-AAACK!
to be continued...

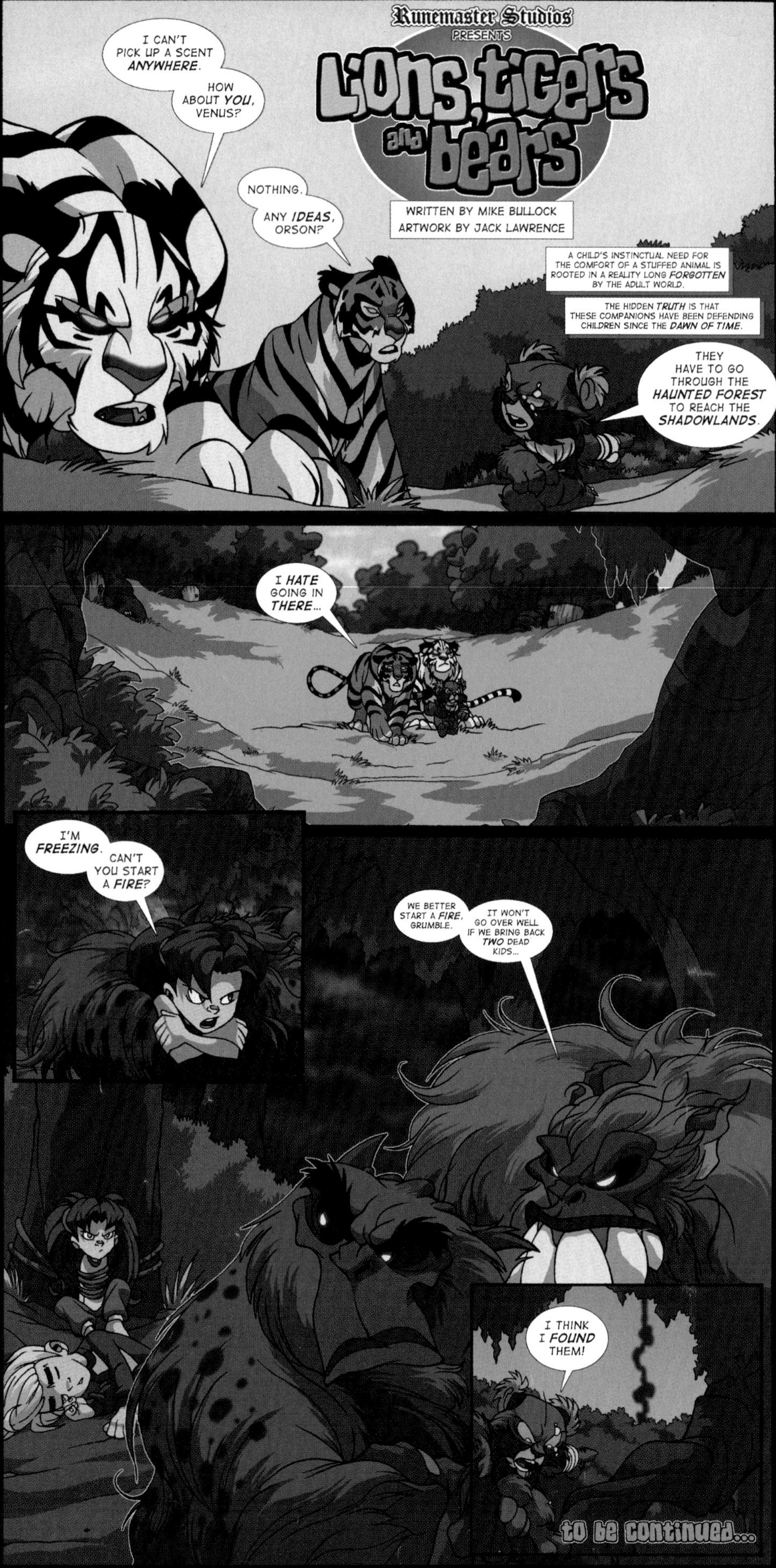
Runemaster Studios
PRESENTS
Lions, tigers and bears
I CAN'T PICK UP A SCENT ANYWHERE.
HOW ABOUT YOU, VENUS?
NOTHING.
ANY IDEAS, ORSON?
WRITTEN BY MIKE BULLOCK
ARTWORK BY JACK LAWRENCE
A CHILD'S INSTINCTUAL NEED FOR THE COMFORT OF A STUFFED ANIMAL IS ROOTED IN A REALITY LONG FORGOTTEN BY THE ADULT WORLD.
THE HIDDEN TRUTH IS THAT THESE COMPANIONS HAVE BEEN DEFENDING CHILDREN SINCE THE DAWN OF TIME.
THEY HAVE TO GO THROUGH THE HAUNTED FOREST TO REACH THE SHADOWLANDS.
I HATE GOING IN THERE...
I'M FREEZING.
CAN'T YOU START A FIRE?
WE BETTER START A FIRE, GRUMBLE.
IT WON'T GO OVER WELL IF WE BRING BACK TWO DEAD KIDS...
I THINK I FOUND THEM!
to be continued...

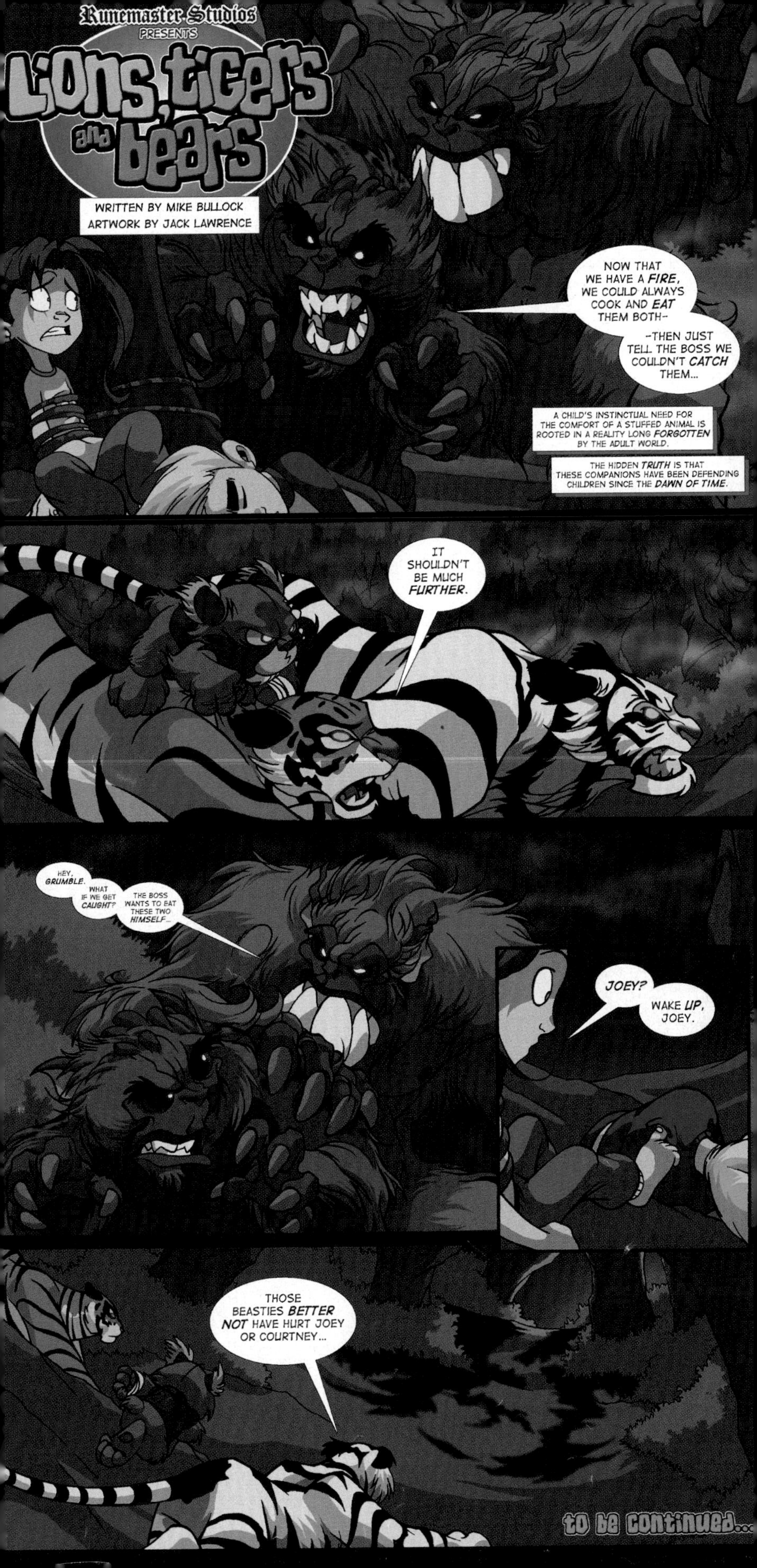

Runemaster Studios
PRESENTS
Lions, Tigers and Bears
WRITTEN BY MIKE BULLOCK
ARTWORK BY JACK LAWRENCE
NOW THAT WE HAVE A FIRE, WE COULD ALWAYS COOK AND EAT THEM BOTH–
–THEN JUST TELL THE BOSS WE COULDN'T CATCH THEM...
A CHILD'S INSTINCTUAL NEED FOR THE COMFORT OF A STUFFED ANIMAL IS ROOTED IN A REALITY LONG FORGOTTEN BY THE ADULT WORLD.
THE HIDDEN TRUTH IS THAT THESE COMPANIONS HAVE BEEN DEFENDING CHILDREN SINCE THE DAWN OF TIME.
IT SHOULDN'T BE MUCH FURTHER.
HEY, GRUMBLE.
WHAT IF WE GET CAUGHT?
THE BOSS WANTS TO EAT THESE TWO HIMSELF...
JOEY?
WAKE UP, JOEY.
THOSE BEASTIES BETTER NOT HAVE HURT JOEY OR COURTNEY...
to be continued...

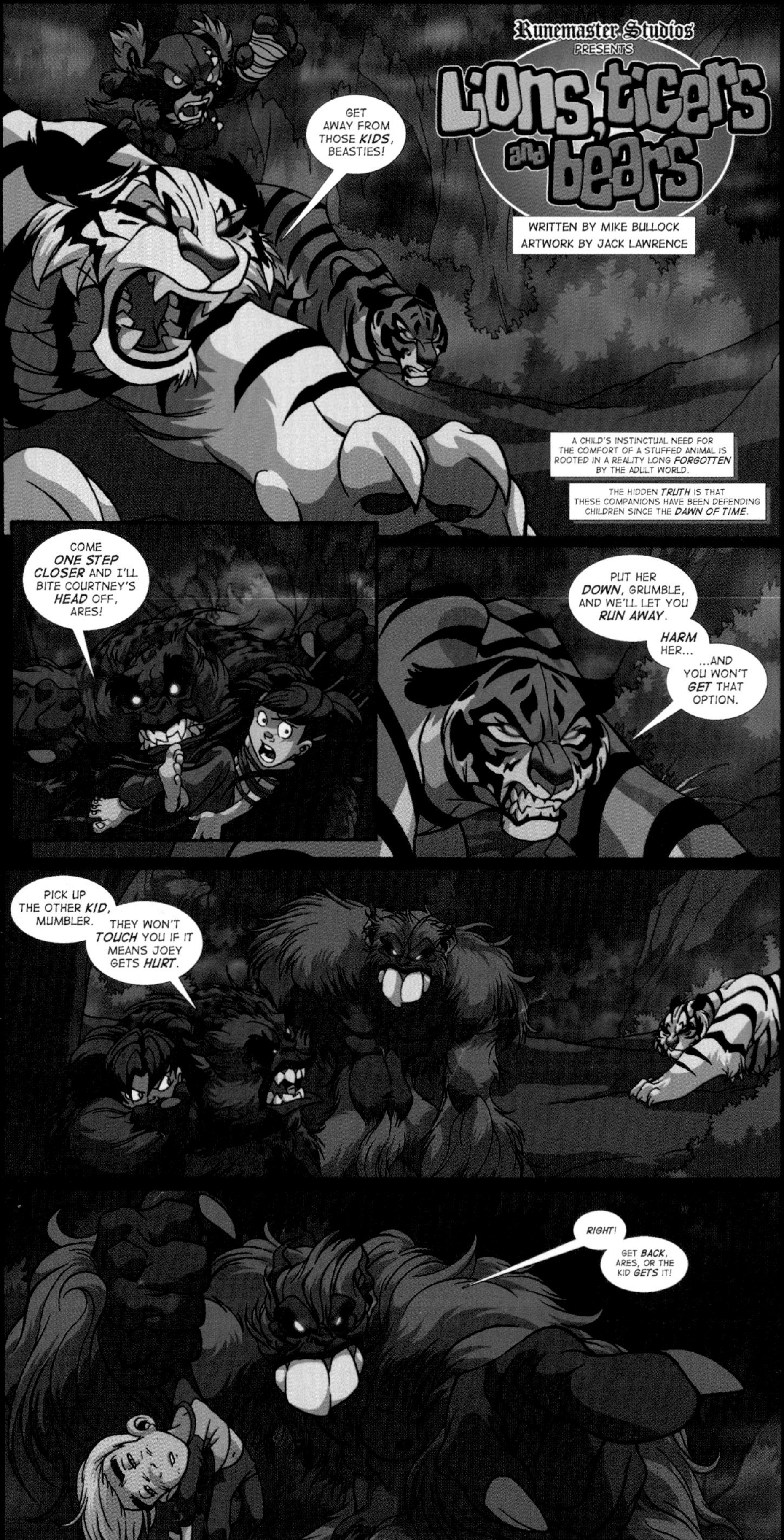

Runemaster Studios
PRESENTS
Lions, tigers and bears
WRITTEN BY MIKE BULLOCK
ARTWORK BY JACK LAWRENCE
GET AWAY FROM THOSE KIDS, BEASTIES!
A CHILD'S INSTINCTUAL NEED FOR THE COMFORT OF A STUFFED ANIMAL IS ROOTED IN A REALITY LONG FORGOTTEN BY THE ADULT WORLD.
THE HIDDEN TRUTH IS THAT THESE COMPANIONS HAVE BEEN DEFENDING CHILDREN SINCE THE DAWN OF TIME.
COME ONE STEP CLOSER AND I'LL BITE COURTNEY'S HEAD OFF, ARES!
PUT HER DOWN, GRUMBLE, AND WE'LL LET YOU RUN AWAY.
HARM HER...
...AND YOU WON'T GET THAT OPTION.
PICK UP THE OTHER KID, MUMBLER.
THEY WON'T TOUCH YOU IF IT MEANS JOEY GETS HURT.
RIGHT!
GET BACK, ARES, OR THE KID GETS IT!
to be continued...

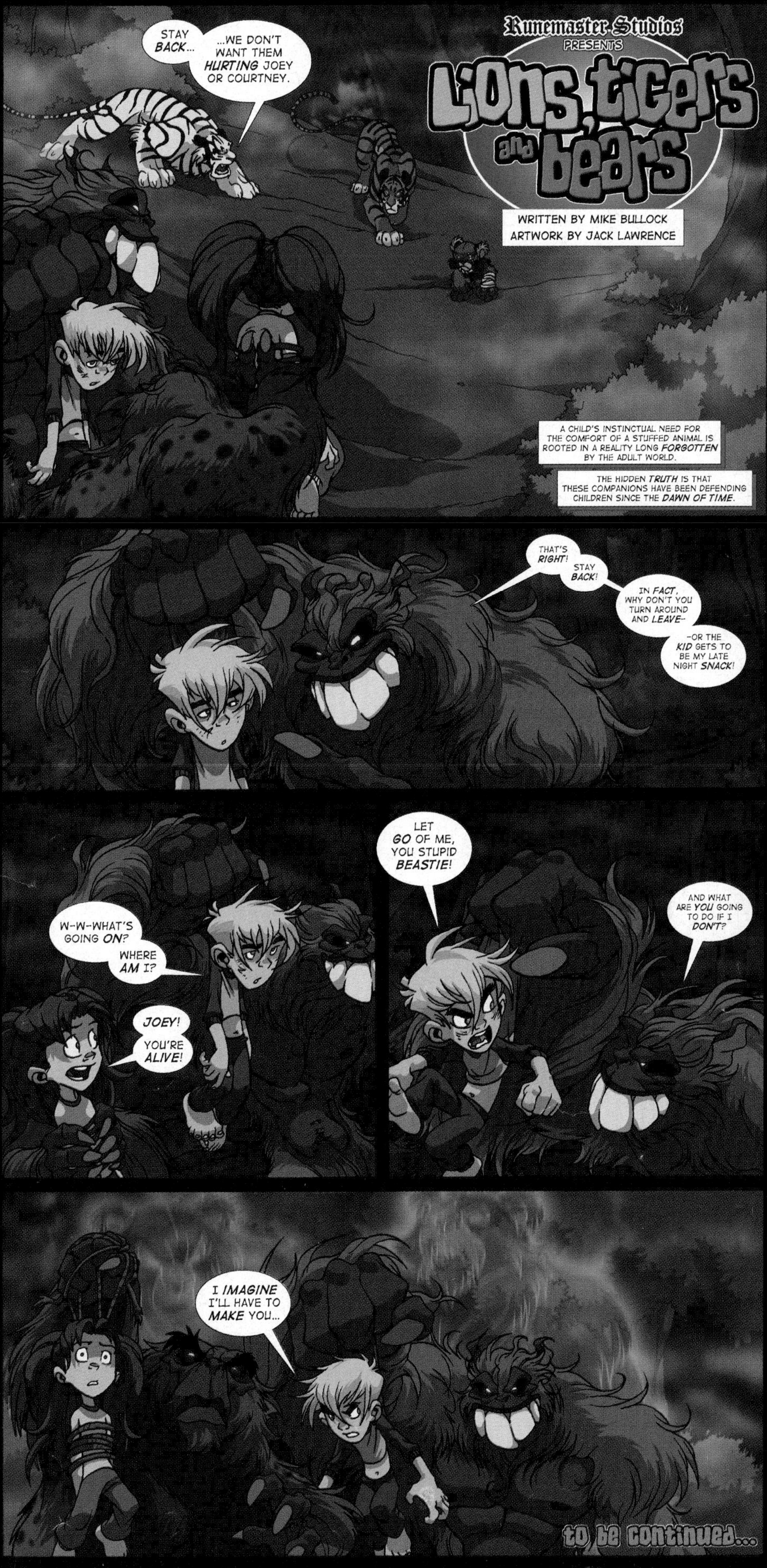

STAY BACK...
...WE DON'T WANT THEM HURTING JOEY OR COURTNEY.
Runemaster Studios PRESENTS
Lions, tigers and bears
WRITTEN BY MIKE BULLOCK
ARTWORK BY JACK LAWRENCE
A CHILD'S INSTINCTUAL NEED FOR THE COMFORT OF A STUFFED ANIMAL IS ROOTED IN A REALITY LONG FORGOTTEN BY THE ADULT WORLD.
THE HIDDEN TRUTH IS THAT THESE COMPANIONS HAVE BEEN DEFENDING CHILDREN SINCE THE DAWN OF TIME.
THAT'S RIGHT!
STAY BACK!
IN FACT, WHY DON'T YOU TURN AROUND AND LEAVE--
--OR THE KID GETS TO BE MY LATE NIGHT SNACK!
W-W-WHAT'S GOING ON?
WHERE AM I?
JOEY!
YOU'RE ALIVE!
LET GO OF ME, YOU STUPID BEASTIE!
AND WHAT ARE YOU GOING TO DO IF I DON'T?
I IMAGINE I'LL HAVE TO MAKE YOU...
to be continued...

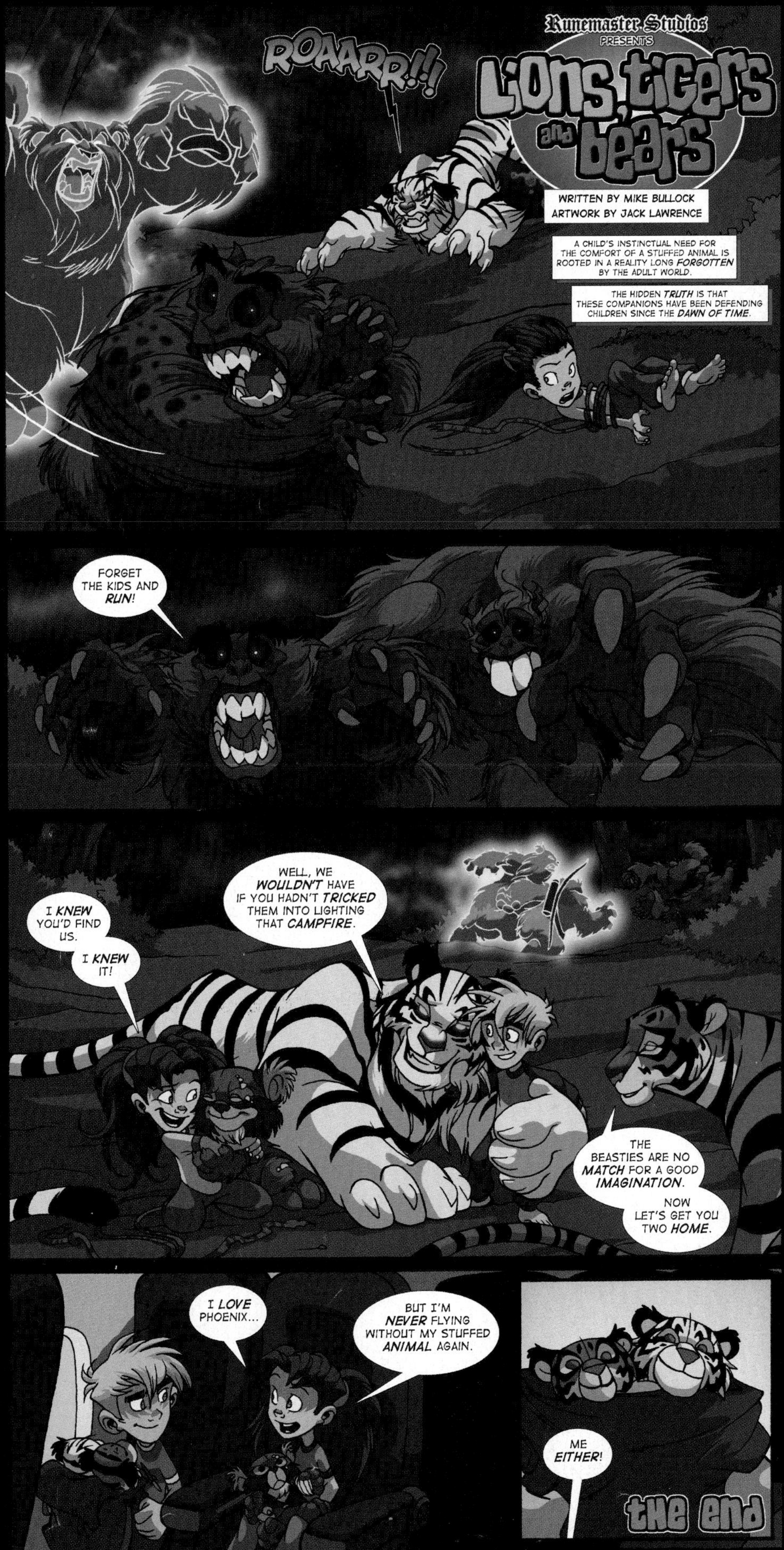
Runemaster Studios
PRESENTS
Lions, tigers and bears
ROAARR!!!
WRITTEN BY MIKE BULLOCK
ARTWORK BY JACK LAWRENCE
A CHILD'S INSTINCTUAL NEED FOR THE COMFORT OF A STUFFED ANIMAL IS ROOTED IN A REALITY LONG *FORGOTTEN* BY THE ADULT WORLD.
THE HIDDEN *TRUTH* IS THAT THESE COMPANIONS HAVE BEEN DEFENDING CHILDREN SINCE THE *DAWN OF TIME*.
FORGET THE KIDS AND *RUN*!
I *KNEW* YOU'D FIND US.
I *KNEW* IT!
WELL, WE *WOULDN'T* HAVE IF YOU HADN'T *TRICKED* THEM INTO LIGHTING THAT *CAMPFIRE*.
THE BEASTIES ARE NO *MATCH* FOR A GOOD *IMAGINATION*.
NOW LET'S GET YOU TWO *HOME*.
I *LOVE* PHOENIX...
BUT I'M *NEVER* FLYING WITHOUT MY STUFFED *ANIMAL* AGAIN.
ME *EITHER*!
THE END

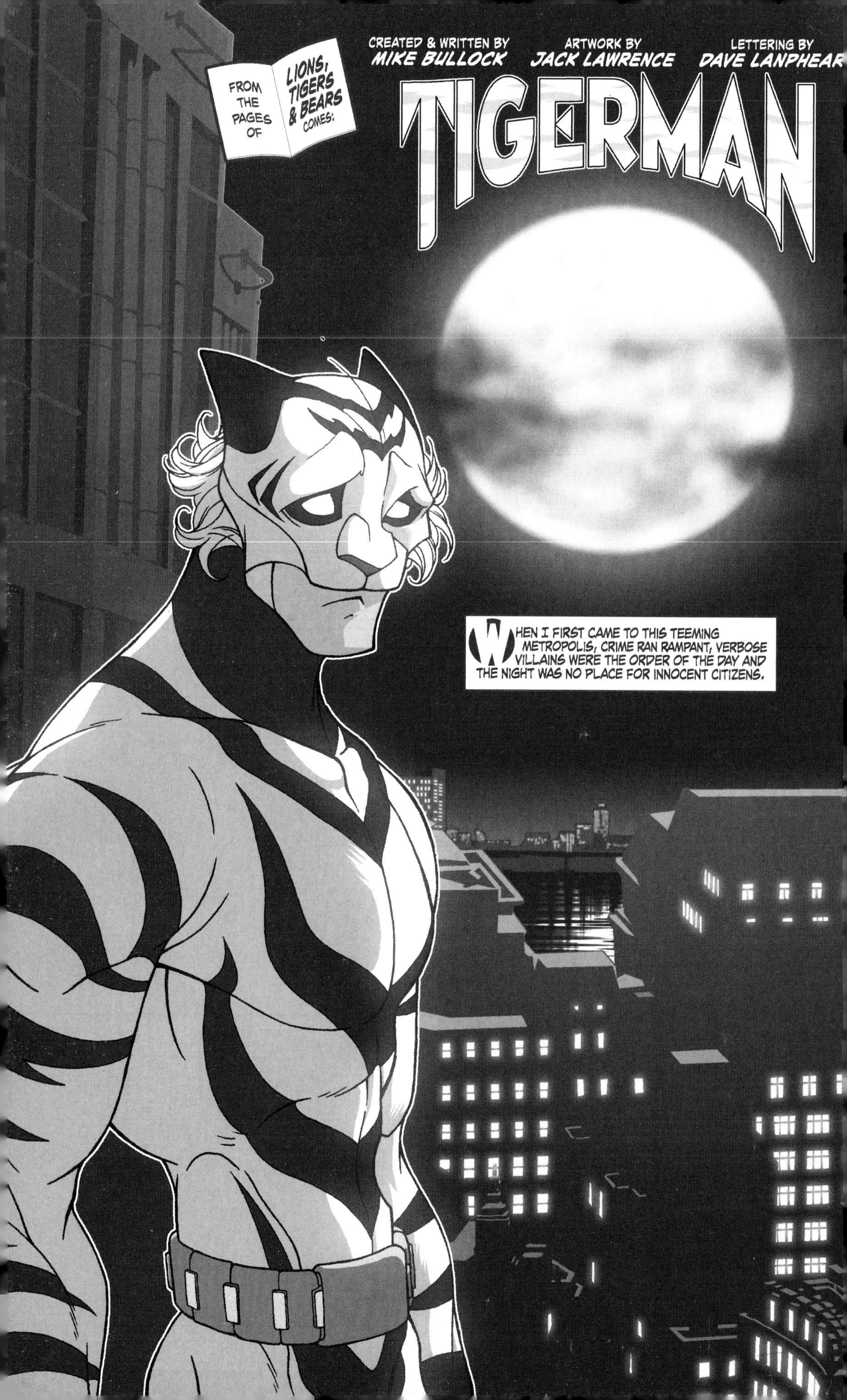
CREATED & WRITTEN BY
MIKE BULLOCK
ARTWORK BY
JACK LAWRENCE
LETTERING BY
DAVE LANPHEAR
FROM THE PAGES OF
LIONS, TIGERS & BEARS
COMES:
TIGERMAN
WHEN I FIRST CAME TO THIS TEEMING METROPOLIS, CRIME RAN RAMPANT, VERBOSE VILLAINS WERE THE ORDER OF THE DAY AND THE NIGHT WAS NO PLACE FOR INNOCENT CITIZENS.

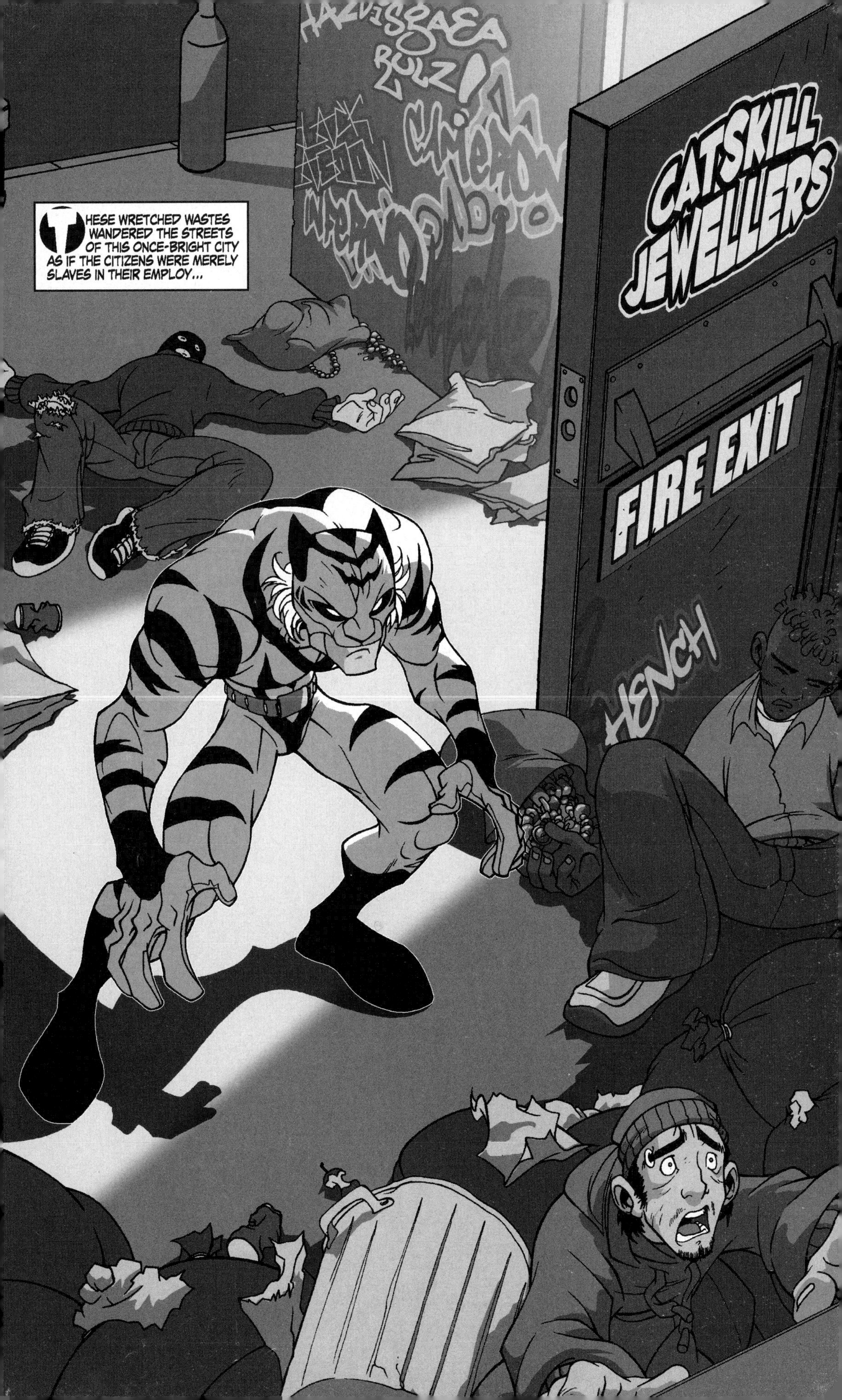
THESE WRETCHED WASTES WANDERED THE STREETS OF THIS ONCE-BRIGHT CITY AS IF THE CITIZENS WERE MERELY SLAVES IN THEIR EMPLOY...
CATSKILL JEWELLERS
FIRE EXIT
HENCH

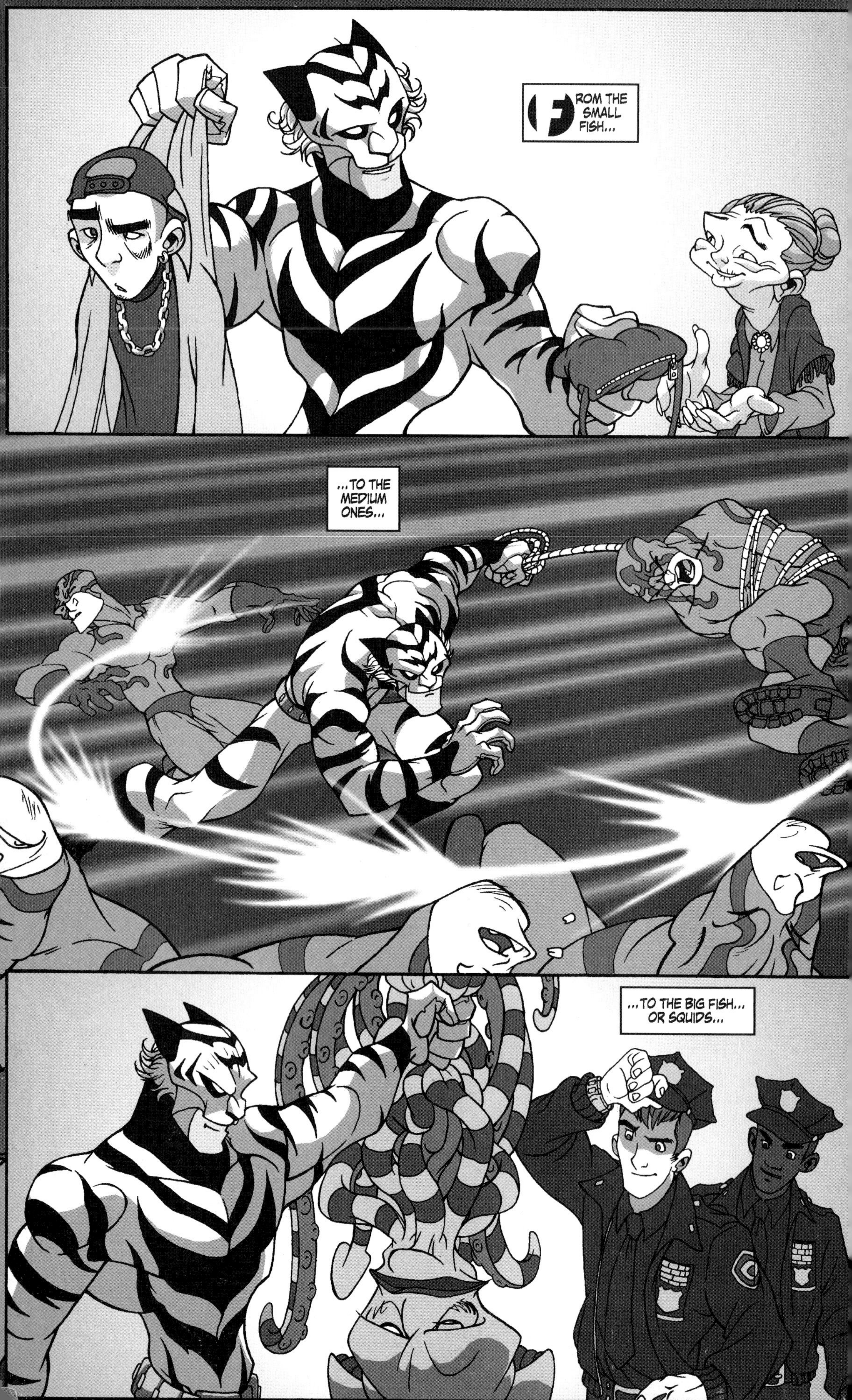
FROM THE SMALL FISH...
...TO THE MEDIUM ONES...
...TO THE BIG FISH... OR SQUIDS...

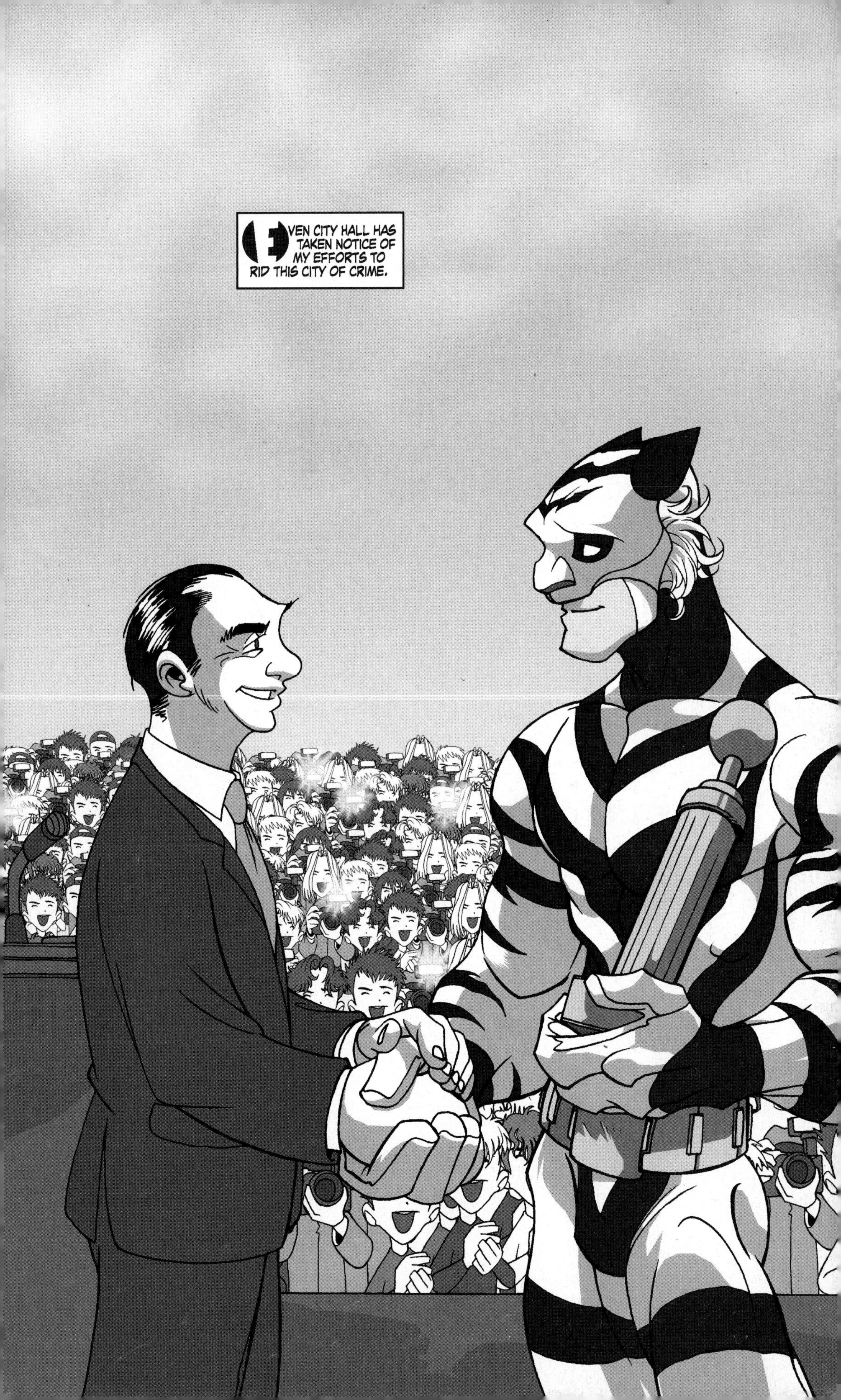
EVEN CITY HALL HAS TAKEN NOTICE OF MY EFFORTS TO RID THIS CITY OF CRIME.

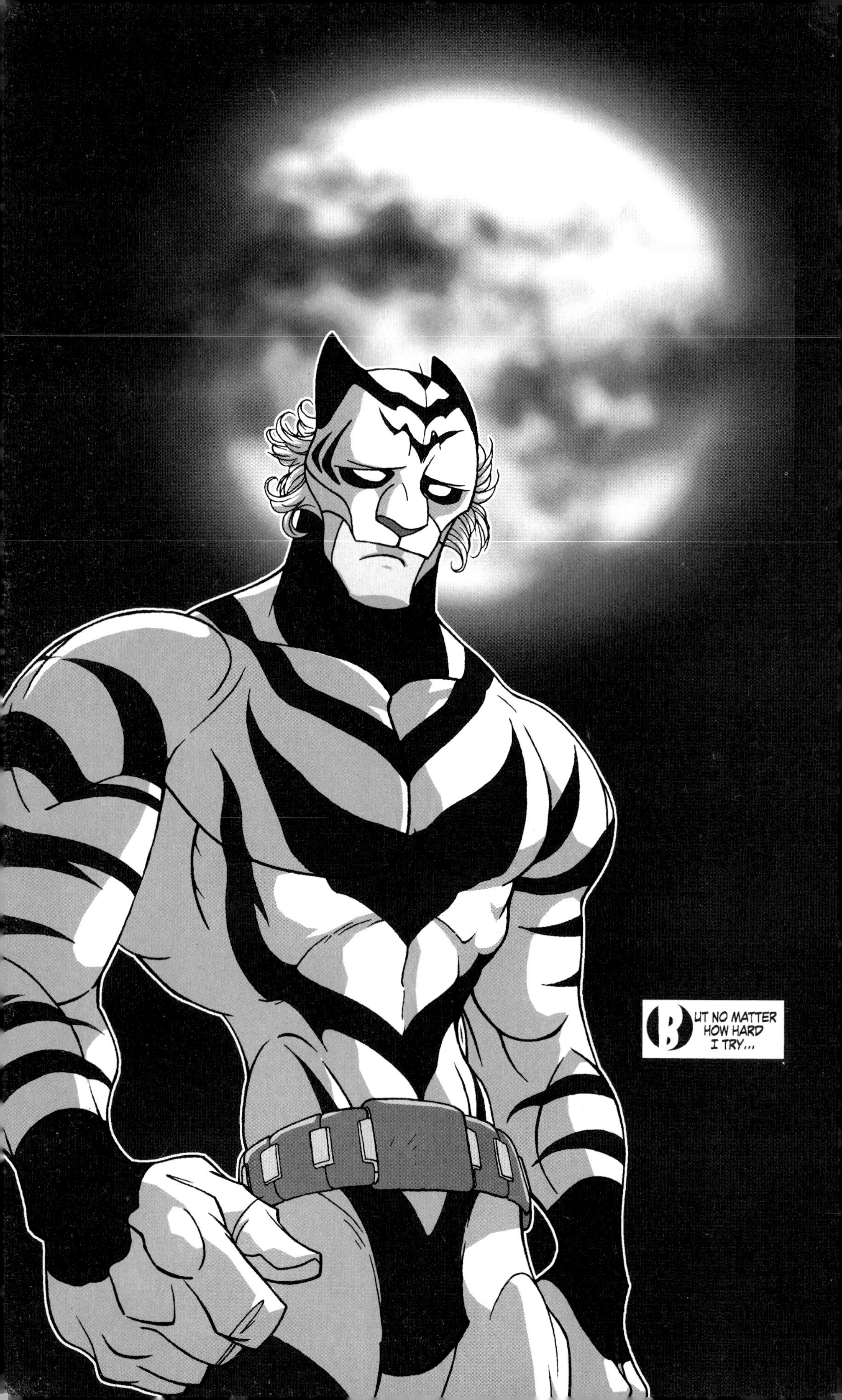
BUT NO MATTER HOW HARD I TRY...

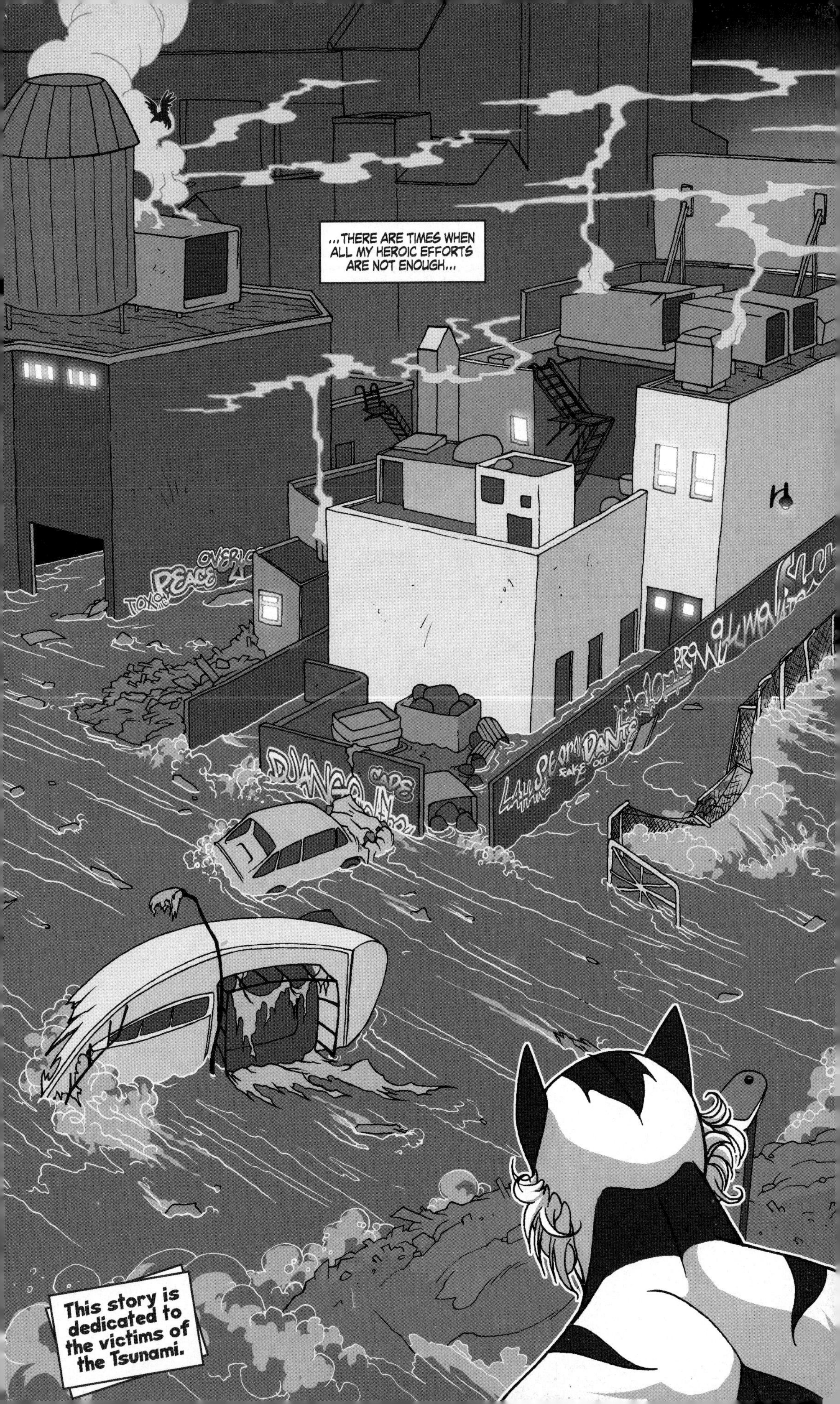
...THERE ARE TIMES WHEN ALL MY HEROIC EFFORTS ARE NOT ENOUGH...
This story is dedicated to the victims of the Tsunami.

Pin Up Gallery

Andy Runton
Alter Egos

Jack Lawrence
Cornered

Luke Ross ⚡ Jason Keith
The Mission

Todd Nauck & Jack Lawrence
My Hero

Derrick Fish
Joey and Company

Theo Bain
Quiet Time

Fabio Laguna
Saturday Morning

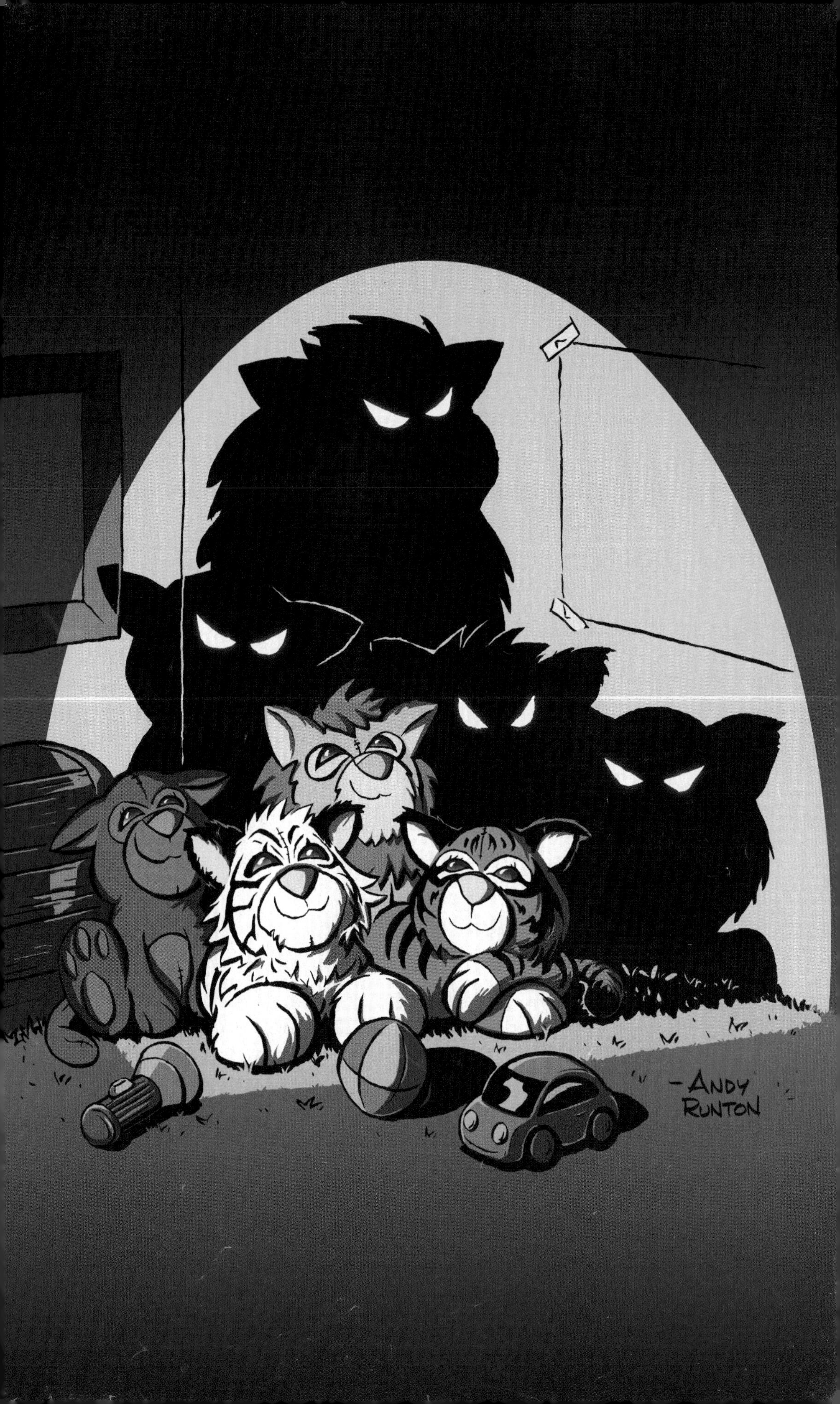
-ANDY
RUNTON

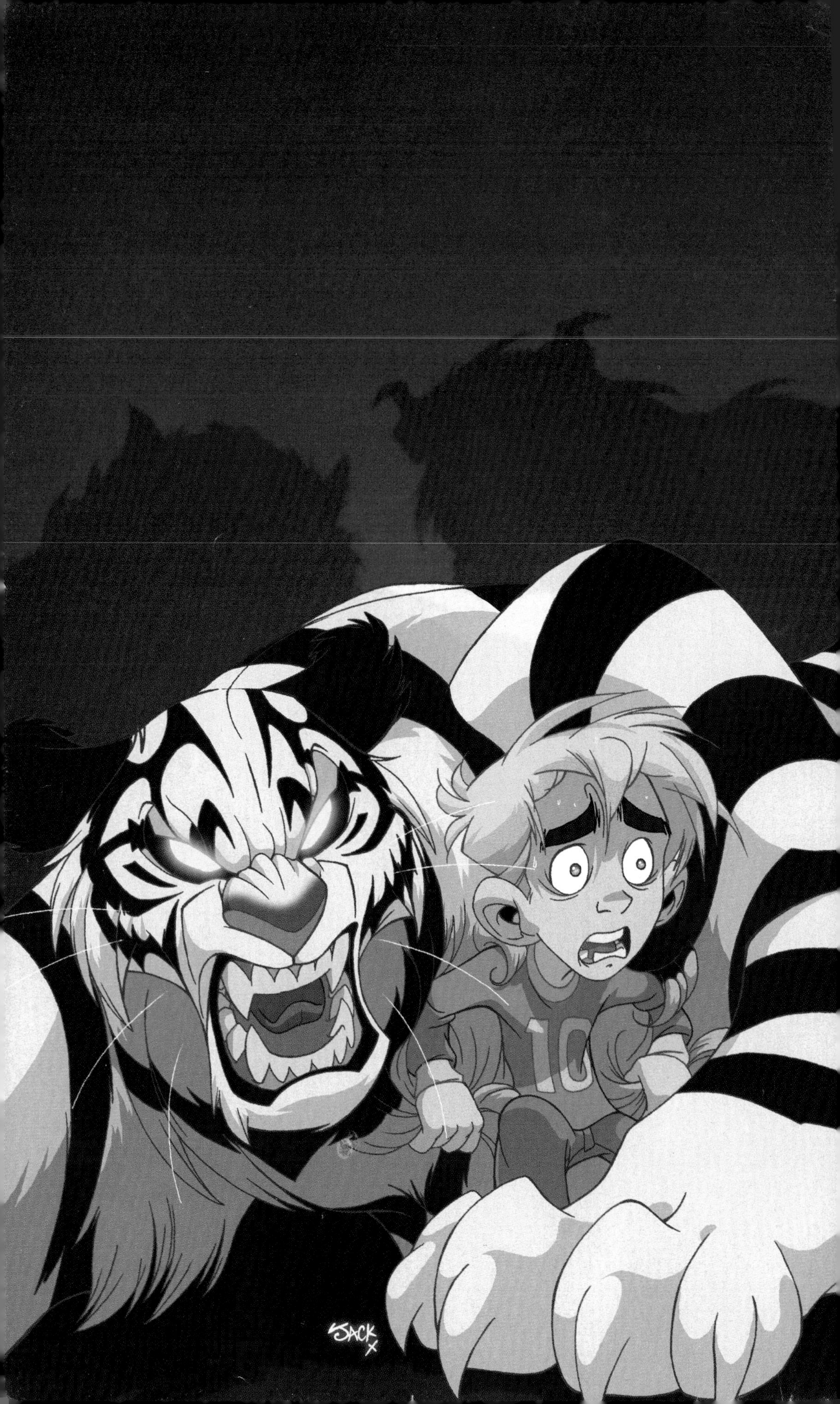
10
JACK

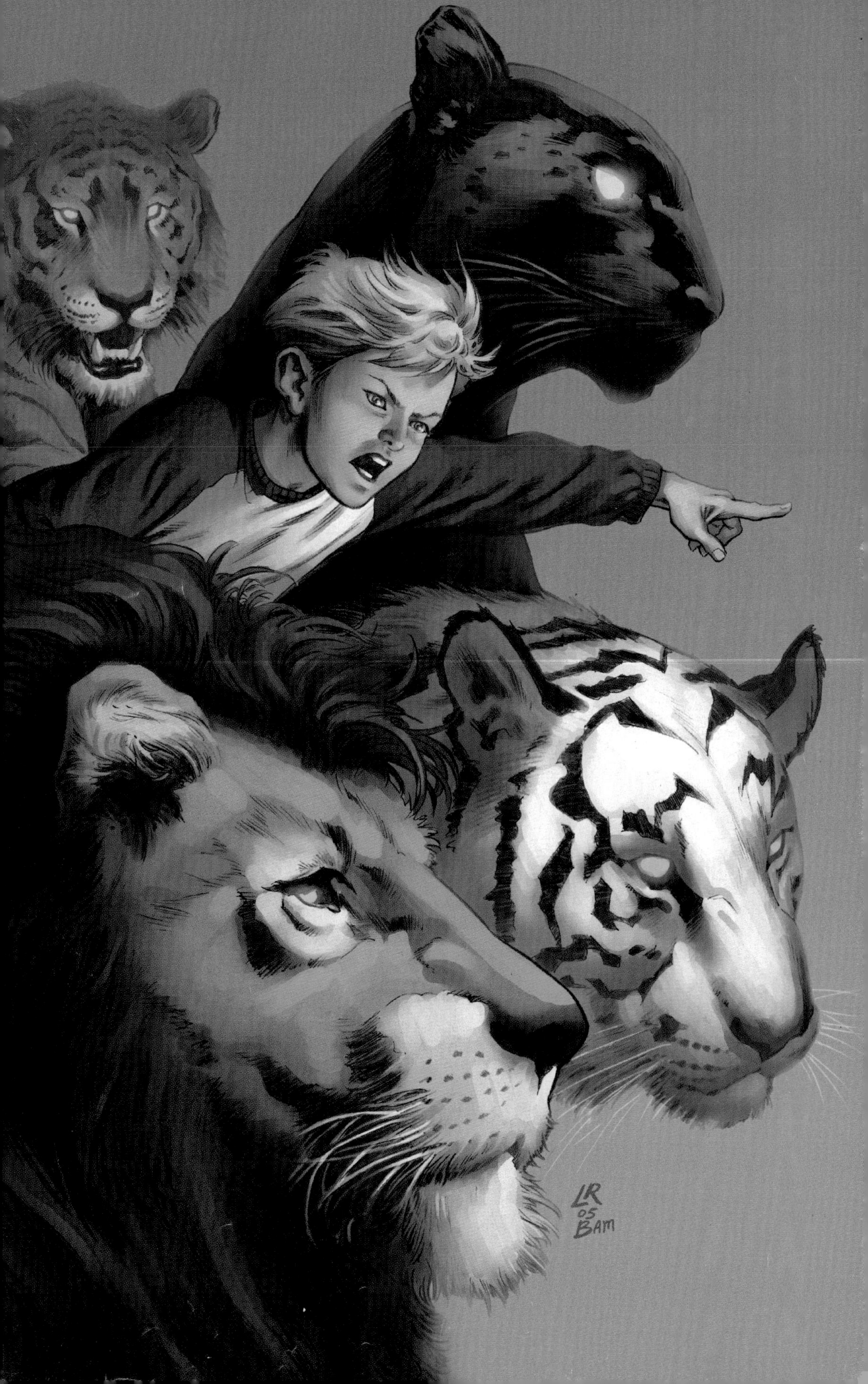
LR
05
BAM

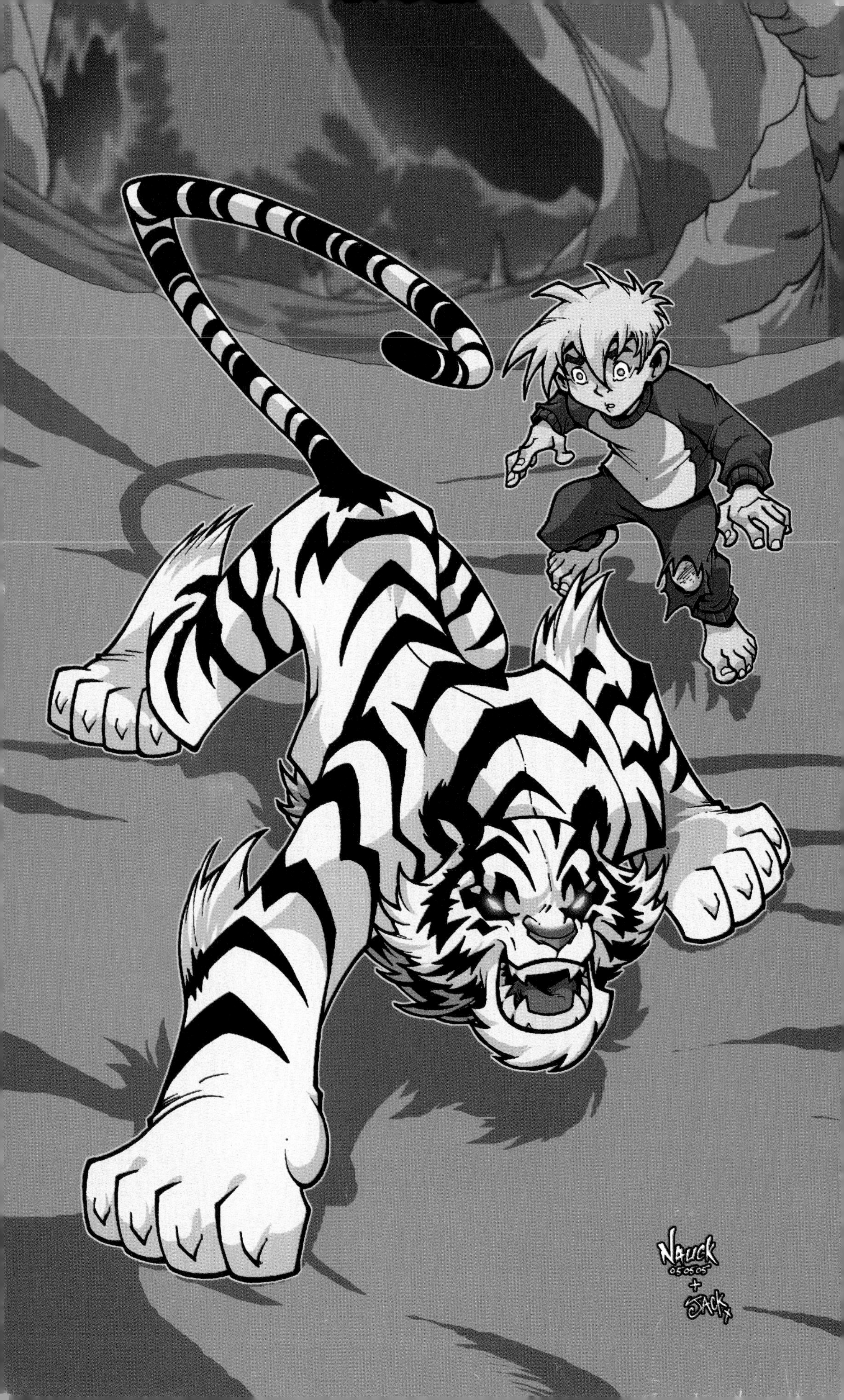
NAUCK
05 05 05
+
JACK

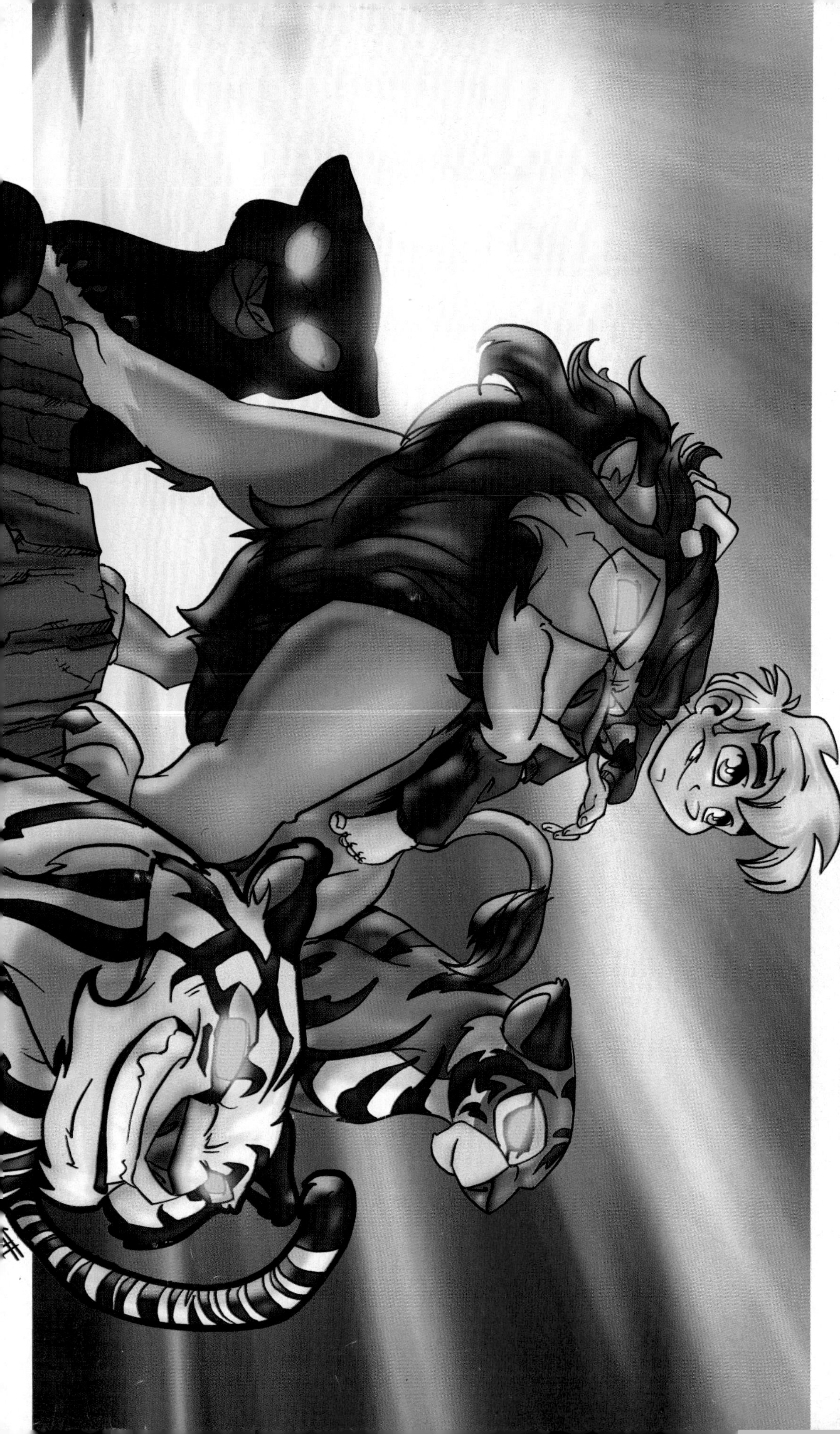

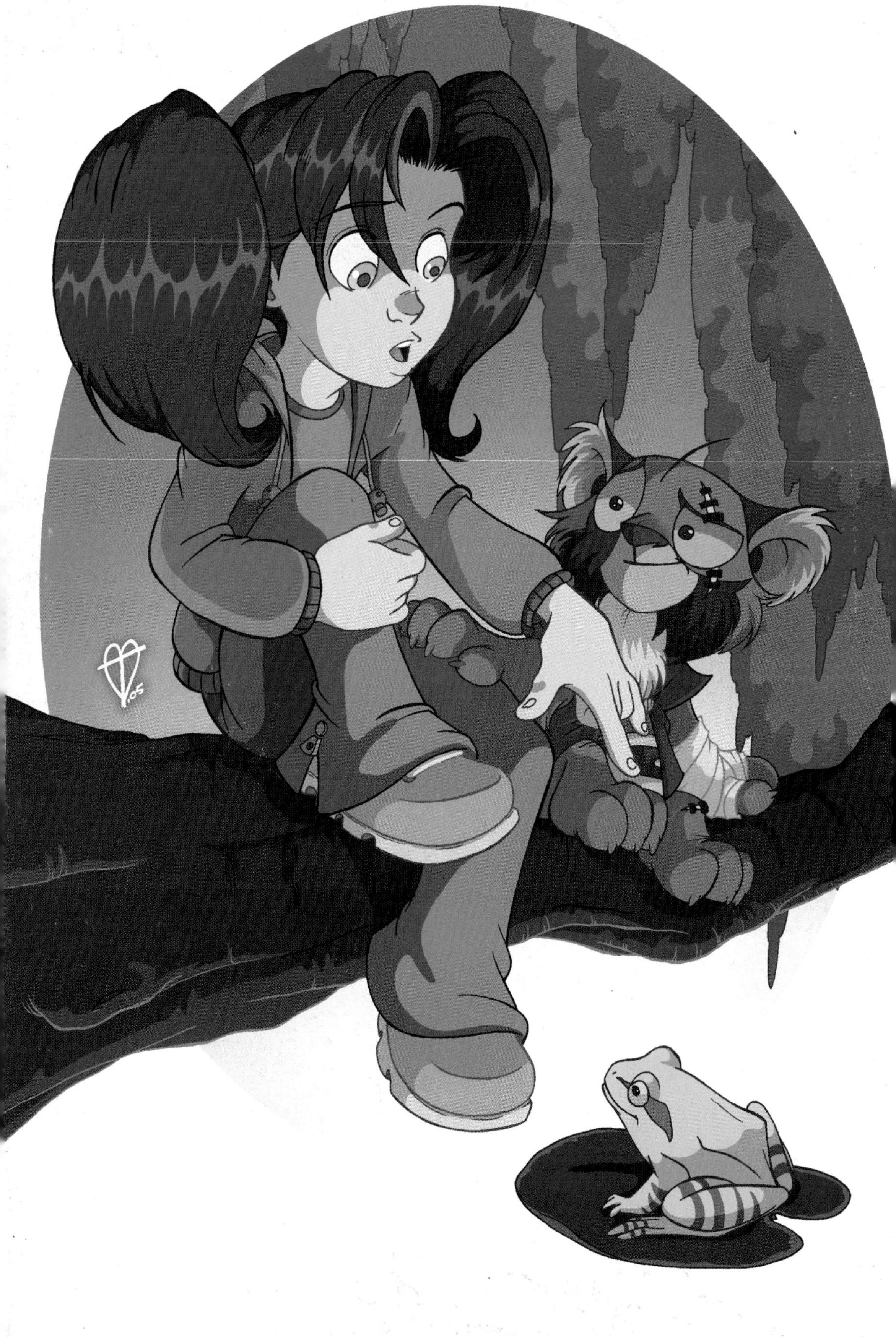

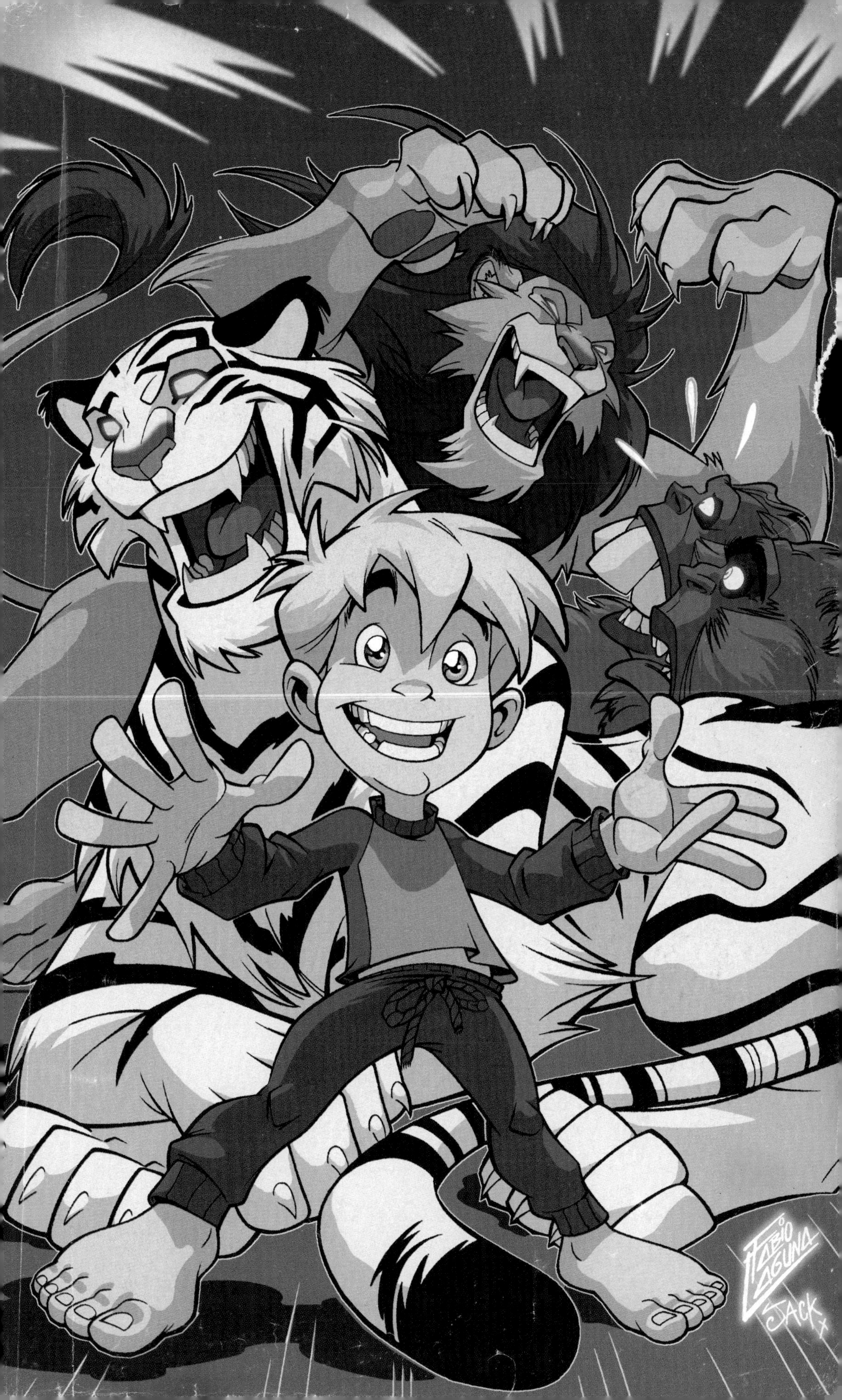
FABIO LAGUNA
JACK

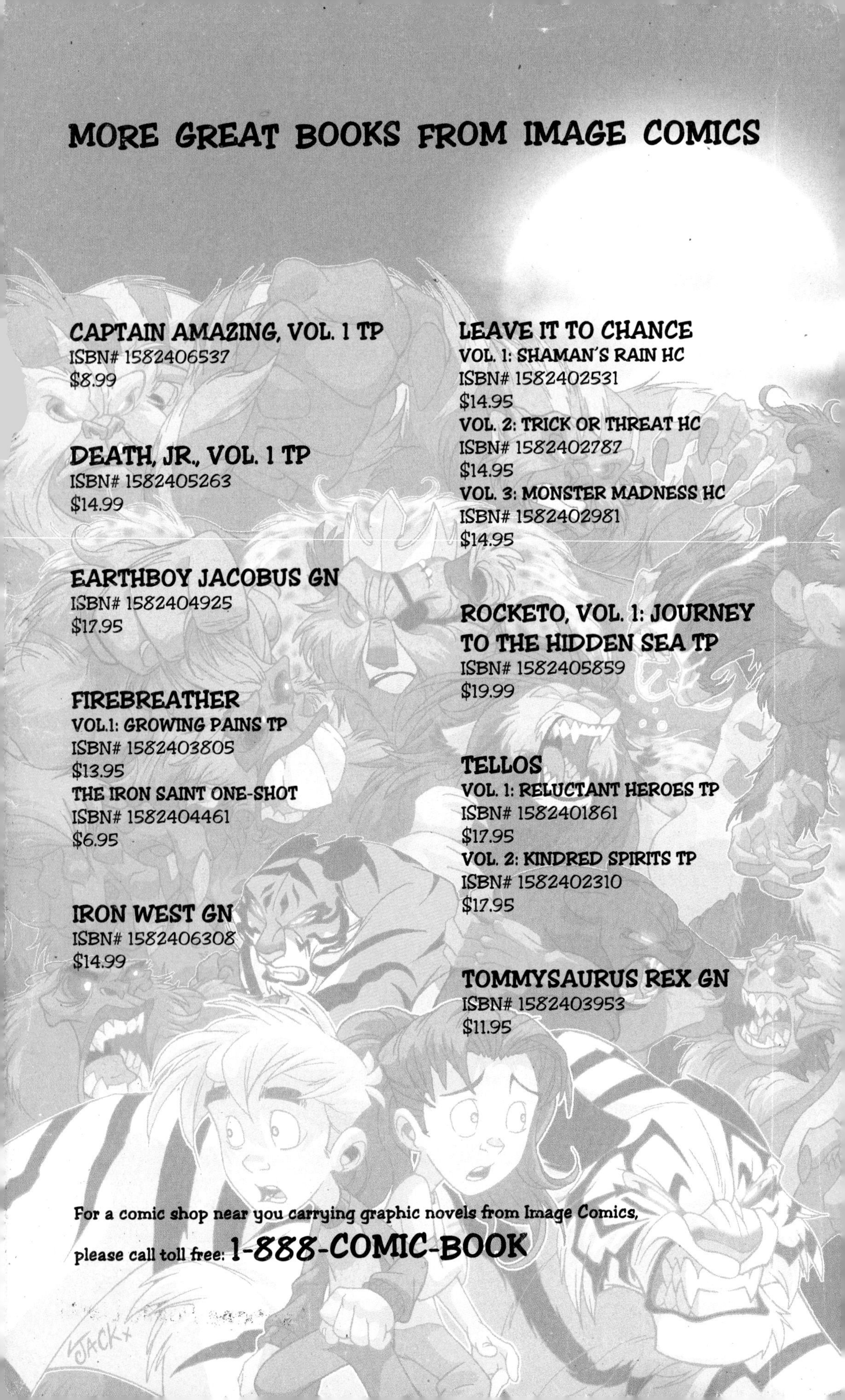
MORE GREAT BOOKS FROM IMAGE COMICS
CAPTAIN AMAZING, VOL. 1 TP
ISBN# 1582406537
$8.99
DEATH, JR., VOL. 1 TP
ISBN# 1582405263
$14.99
EARTHBOY JACOBUS GN
ISBN# 1582404925
$17.95
FIREBREATHER
VOL.1: GROWING PAINS TP
ISBN# 1582403805
$13.95
THE IRON SAINT ONE-SHOT
ISBN# 1582404461
$6.95
IRON WEST GN
ISBN# 1582406308
$14.99
LEAVE IT TO CHANCE
VOL. 1: SHAMAN'S RAIN HC
ISBN# 1582402531
$14.95
VOL. 2: TRICK OR THREAT HC
ISBN# 1582402787
$14.95
VOL. 3: MONSTER MADNESS HC
ISBN# 1582402981
$14.95
ROCKETO, VOL. 1: JOURNEY TO THE HIDDEN SEA TP
ISBN# 1582405859
$19.99
TELLOS
VOL. 1: RELUCTANT HEROES TP
ISBN# 1582401861
$17.95
VOL. 2: KINDRED SPIRITS TP
ISBN# 1582402310
$17.95
TOMMYSAURUS REX GN
ISBN# 1582403953
$11.95
For a comic shop near you carrying graphic novels from Image Comics,
please call toll free: 1-888-COMIC-BOOK
JACK+